The Reckoning

Also by Sam Kates

Pond Life and Other Stories

The Village of Lost Souls

That Elusive Something

The Cleansing (Earth Haven: Book One)

The Beacon (Earth Haven: Book Two)

Strange Shores and Other Stories

Ghosts of Christmas Past & Other Dark Festive Tales

The Elevator: Book One

Jack's Tale (The Elevator: Book 2)

The Lord of the Dance (The Elevator: Book 3)

The Elevator Omnibus: The Complete Trilogy

The Reckoning

Earth Haven: Book 3

Sam Kates

First edition published December 2015
by Smithcraft Press
Second edition, May 2018
This paperback edition, June 2018

ISBN 978-1-912718-08-5

www.samkates.co.uk

*To Katie and Samantha,
for making me as proud
as any dad has ever been.*

Acknowledgements

During the two years or so I've been working on this trilogy, many people have freely given advice, suggestions and plain encouragement, the importance of which should never be underestimated. A big thank you to:

- my first readers – Linda Crowhurst, Kerry Byrne, Paul Adams, Delyth Rabone and Sebastian Pentecost;

- all the Js – wife Joanne, parents John and Jocelyn, and brother Julian;

- the good folk at Smithcraft Press, from whom I have parted company but still think of fondly – Adam, Craig and Jeannette;

- supportive family, friends and colleagues;

- last, but by no means least, every reader who has given up their hard-earned cash and valuable time to read one or more of the *Earth Haven* books. You make all the hard work worthwhile.

Contents

Part 1: Ar Hyd y Nos
(All Through the Night)

Chapter One

The salty tang of the English Channel hung in the fine mist rising from the sea. It stung the woman's throat, raw from bouts of copious vomiting. The heavy swells, which had tossed the boat about like a rodeo novice all through the night, calmed with the coming of dawn; the ominous creaking of the boat's timbers ceased. Aletta could tell from the translucent lightness of the vapour that the sun had risen. Soon the mist would be burned away, but she dreaded what she would then see. That it would be the Thames estuary, for which they had been aiming, she seriously doubted.

A pack of bottled water had been flung under one of the benches which ran around the inside of the boat. Aletta stooped and tore open the plastic wrapping to extract a bottle. She sipped cautiously, wary about keeping the water down. Her stomach muscles felt torn from the amount of retching she had performed throughout the endless night.

They had put out from Ostend the previous morning into the southern reaches of the North Sea. The Pole—she could not recall his name—had appeared confident that, provided they maintained a heading of west-north-west, they would strike the Thames at its mouth. Once there, he reckoned they could navigate the river into the heart of London. It was why he had insisted on choosing this small boat, which had smelled worse than Stockholm Fish Market when they set out, but was now hellish with the sour odour of vomit.

Aletta and the other woman had wanted to take a luxury cruiser, or large trawler, but the men had overruled them on the basis the draughts might be too low. At least, that is what she thought was the objection. Difficult to be sure when none of them spoke English as their first language.

A swell smacked the prow with sufficient force to send up a plume of spray. Her stomach lurched. She feared she would cough up the few sips of water she had managed to swallow and turned her head to face over the side. The sea slid past like a gently rolling meadow. The occasional ripple or clump of weed were all that marred the smooth surface. Her stomach calmed and she turned back.

The Pole was curled into a ball beneath the prow. The spray did not appear to have disturbed him, but the other men were stirring. The second woman was out of sight in the wheelhouse at the stern; it was too small to hold more than one person. As far as they could tell—the woman had the least English of them all—she was from a village in the Italian Alps. Short and stocky, a face like weathered bark, the woman would let out streams of Italian, apparently not caring she spoke too fast for anyone else, with only a smattering of the language between them, to keep up. She had been the last of the five to arrive in Ostend. It was evident she hadn't understood the words of the message which had led them there, but their import had nevertheless made themselves known, had grown into a compulsion, until the woman could not resist any longer.

Like Aletta. The message had come to her in the dark hours before dawn, while she lay sleeping in a luxury hotel on the shore of the Baltic Sea. Her English was better than the Italian woman's, but she had not been able to fully translate the words—they had been delivered too quickly. Maybe because it had arrived while she slept, the message had imprinted itself on her subconscious and the occasional word or phrase kept popping to the forefront of her mind. *United Kingdom* she understood: *Förenade Kungariket* or *Storbritannien* in her native Swedish. She had never been there, but a feeling had started to develop that a visit was overdue. *Reckoning* also nagged at her. At first, she had not known what it meant, but gradually a sense of the word came to her: *räkenskapens dag.* Day of reckoning.

Aletta's stomach gave a low grumble as the boat began to bob in a heavier swell. The two men lying near the Pole sat up, blinking in the daylight. The younger, dark-haired and dark-eyed, was from

Croatia. She could not remember his name, either. The older, in his mid-thirties, was from Hungary. His name was Levente.

He had been the first of her companions Aletta had met on arriving in Ostend. Once their initial suspicion of each other had been overcome, they discovered the only language they had in common was English, and they each knew enough to make themselves understood. So it was that, falteringly, they told each other a similar tale. How they had fallen ill when many of their loved ones had already perished; had awoken to find they might be the only person still living in the entire world; had received a message—the first message—they had not fully understood, but had gleaned more meaning from the compulsion which came over them not to wander and to dispose of decomposing bodies.

Slowly but surely, the compulsion had worn off and they began to search for other survivors. Aletta set out from her home town of Uppsala, north of Stockholm, travelling the coast south towards Malmo. She was glad to leave. Wolves, normally so wary of man, had become emboldened by his absence and were starting to roam outside the central forests. Aletta had passed beyond the dark period of survivor's guilt and had no wish to provide a fresh meal for creatures whose howling she could hear approaching nearer with every passing night.

Before she reached Malmo, the second message came while she slept. It came also to the Hungarian. A new urge had taken them over: to travel to the United Kingdom to witness some sort of face-off. Between whom or why, neither of them had any idea.

The new compulsion grew stronger and they made for the western coastline, both struck by the same idea: Ostend was a ferry port, easier to reach for them than Calais, yet close enough to England to make the voyage manageable. Or so they'd thought.

Levente nodded at Aletta and she offered a forced smile in return. She pointed towards the plastic bottles in their packaging, where she had left them beneath the bench.

"Water," she said.

The Hungarian rose unsteadily and stepped to the bench. He

tossed a bottle to the Croatian, who caught it deftly.

Levente sipped warily from his bottle. Not one of the five on board was a sailor. Each had suffered during the long night. Aletta's stomach grumbled again; the bobbing motion was increasing.

The man gestured at the mist with the bottle.

"Where we?"

Aletta shook her head and glanced down at the compass dangling from her neck.

"West. We are going west."

The Hungarian raised his bushy eyebrows. "Good. *Igen?*"

Aletta shrugged.

The voyage from Ostend had begun well. The sun warmed their heads while they manoeuvred the vessel out of the marina and into a calm sea. Although it became blustery within the hour and a strong cross current wanted to carry them south-west towards the English Channel, the boat's engine worked manfully to keep them on a west-north-west course. Until, with a bang and puff of blue smoke, it stopped.

While the Pole and Levente fiddled with the engine and the air became filled with frustrated curses in Polish and Hungarian, the boat drifted. It had still been drifting, at the mercy of the currents and with no sight of land, when darkness fell and the breeze stiffened.

Aletta blinked when sunlight struck her eyes. The mist was lifting. At the same time, she realised she could hear a sound: the hiss of breaking waves, growing louder.

She stared over the prow, waiting for the last of the mist to burn away in the strengthening sunlight, and gasped.

"Land," she muttered. Louder. "Land!"

Immediately ahead rose white cliffs of chalk, gleaming like freshly-washed sheets. Waves broke onto a narrow strand of dark shingle at their base. The boat rode the waves, dipping and bucking as it had during the night. Aletta clutched the gunwale tightly and let out a sour belch, but relief at seeing land quelled any further sickness.

Levente shouted something in Hungarian. The Croatian joined him on the bench and Levente thumped him joyfully on the back.

Aletta looked behind her when she heard an exclamation. The Italian had emerged from the wheelhouse. Looking pale and wretched, she pointed at the cliffs and let out a stream of gibberish. Aletta ignored her.

In the prow, the Pole rose to his knees. He glanced back and grinned.

"Dover," he said.

Milandra closed her eyes and, with practised ease, allowed her psyche to slip free. She did not send it reaching out, but inwards, delving the fathoms of the collective memory she held within her like some unimaginably vast library.

She had found a promising section, an area that would, if it were truly a physical library, be a hard-to-find corner thickly layered in dust and cobwebs, where her footsteps would not echo in the deep gloom because the air seemed dead from inactivity.

The tightly-bound 'books' of memories and experiences appeared nondescript and uninteresting. Their very blandness made them attractive to Milandra; she was beginning to suspect what she sought had been deliberately disguised to discourage any Keeper (for only a Keeper could directly access the memory banks) from glancing inside.

Milandra found the section and randomly picked a memory. She opened it and her mind's eye widened when a ship filled her vision…

Blacker than jet, smoother than glass, vaster than a mountain range, it moved through space like an obsidian meteor. A large sun growled and flared like a blacksmith's furnace at the blast of the bellows. The ship had already passed the fourth and final planet of the solar system, was accelerating into the furthest reaches of the system's gravitational field, when the smaller craft appeared.

Eight vessels, little more than a scouting party, but still capable of inflicting severe damage with their antimatter-seeking missiles.

The black ship was built for speed, not battle.

Trying to evade the smaller craft by vertical or horizontal thrusts would merely expend huge reserves of energy in an exercise in futility that would also slow its rate of acceleration. The smaller vessels were capable of changing direction within moments through deployment of on-board gyroscopes and would be able to train their missiles on the larger ship regardless of what manoeuvres it attempted.

Its best chance—likely its *only* chance—of escaping ruin lay in speed.

The black ship did not deviate from its full-ahead course. It continued towards the small craft, ever accelerating while the gravitational clutch grew weaker.

Flares of light indicated missiles had been loosed and were streaking towards the antimatter-coated hull of the black ship.

More light flared when the missiles changed direction in an effort to match the increase in velocity of their target.

Too late, their own speed hampered by increasing gravitational pull as they advanced, the scout vessels adjusted course to try to intercept the black ship when it passed high above, or beneath, or to the side of them, depending on their relative orientation.

One vessel dropped back. Light flashed when it let loose another missile, which streaked away at a steep angle which appeared to stand little chance of intercepting the fast-approaching target. A series of flashes was followed by a steady flicker while the projectile drained its energy cells in first achieving and then maintaining a trajectory which, upon reassessment, seemed it might be well-judged.

The missile was not designed to detonate—an explosion in space is of limited effect—but to penetrate. It clipped an edge of the ship's black hull, shearing off a slither of panelling that would have little impact on the ship's ability to move through deep space. More significantly, the missile's brief passage through the rim of the hull also damaged beyond repair the high-gravity thrusters concealed beneath the panelling, thrusters that would be essential for manoeuvring safely when the ship arrived at its destination five or six months hence.

Unhindered, for now, the ship broke clear of the final tug of the solar system's gravity and entered deep space. Accelerating to close to light speed, the dark matter coating its hull found and clung like a limpet to the unseen current of dark energy that drives the universe's expansion. The ship winked out of sight.

The pursuing missiles attempted to follow the ship until their energy cells became depleted, then drifted into the void.

Milandra opened her eyes.

"Interesting," she murmured.

The Celtic Manor Resort stands in acres of grass and woodland alongside the M4 motorway near Newport in South Wales. Before the Millennium Bug put paid to such events, the Resort had played host to a Ryder Cup and a NATO summit. But never before had it been the venue for a funeral.

On top of a rise near the main hotel entrance, a clutch of people stood around a hole dug in the fifteenth green of the Roman Road golf course. The spring had so far been mild and the grass on the hitherto immaculate green had taken on a feathery, shaggy appearance. By summer's end, the greens and fairways would be indistinguishable from the rough.

The hole was deep, but not particularly wide. Child-sized. A mound of earth stood next to it, a brown stain on all the greenery. Next to the mound stood two men. Between them they held a short length of rope from which dangled a bundle wrapped in a cotton sheet. Not a large bundle, for the body it contained was only ten years old and emaciated.

A teenage girl, her forehead wrapped liberally in white bandage, looked on. She gazed at the couple standing across from her. The man was in his mid-twenties, hair greying prematurely. By his side, glancing up at the man from time to time as if to say, 'I don't mind doing nothing, but when are we going to do *something*?'

sat a black dog. Mouth set in a thin line, the man stared at the hole with an expression of helplessness.

No thought the girl. *Not helplessness. Horror. Tom looks totally horrified. Like… like this reminds him of something dreadful from his past.*

Next to Tom stood a woman, perhaps ten years his senior, fighting to remain composed. She noticed the girl's gaze and attempted a smile. Not very successfully. Her face crumpled when tears breached her fragile defences.

Poor Ceri thought the girl. *The Bug took her son and now she's watching another child being buried.*

Near Tom and Ceri stood the Irish girl with the ready smile and whiskey-fumed breath: Colleen. No sign of the smile now. Next to her stood the doctor, Howard. He gazed into the distance, his face grim.

The girl with the bandaged head—her name was Brianne Penrose, but everyone called her Bri, like the cheese but without the e—owed Howard her life. She pushed the thought away; the moment was sombre enough already. Instead, she thought of Will. These memories she could not so readily dismiss.

That loving, infuriating boy had shoved her out of the way at Stonehenge and taken the bullet intended for her high in his left shoulder. Bri had thought he was dead there and then. When Tom had come staggering to the Range Rover, bearing Will in his arms, she had assumed it was so they could afford him a proper burial. When Tom ordered everyone out of the car and laid Will on the back seat, she complied numbly, her mind a jumble of sorrow and bewilderment. It was only when Tom began whispering frantically to the doctor, who rushed forward to start working on the boy, that realisation hit home.

"He's still alive?"

Tom nodded brusquely. "Come with me," he said. "You too, Ceri. Oh, and you'd better come as well, Joe."

Bri hadn't even noticed the new person who accompanied Tom. A boy not much older than her. She barely gave him a second glance.

The next few hours passed in a blur. A faltering walk through the bitter cold of a January dawn to the nearby village where Tom and Ceri had left their car. A mad dash behind the Range Rover to a hospital in Salisbury. Stumbling about in the dark of an echoing basement trying to find the emergency generators, when she didn't even know what they looked like. Helping Peter lug plastic containers of petrol to the basement.

By then she resembled a punch-drunk boxer, almost out on her feet. Over the previous twenty-four hours, she had cycled in excess of one hundred and fifty miles, tramped across freezing fields, and had a gap in her memory unexpectedly restored only to find she would have preferred it to remain buried; she had been shot at and witnessed her best friend take the bullet intended for her. All on a couple of hours' snatched sleep on a concrete floor.

Tom had insisted she lie down in a corner and close her eyes. Her last memory of that morning was the *chug-chug-chug* of the generator spluttering to life.

She'd awoken lying on a hospital bed, a drip protruding from her arm. Pale winter sunlight struggled to dispel the sense of mustiness about the room. Ceri was propped into a chair by the side of the bed, snoring softly. Bri tried to turn towards her and the needle tugged at her arm.

"Oww!"

Ceri's eyes opened. "Wait, Bri! Let me fetch Diane."

She returned moments later, followed closely by a mousy-blonde woman. Diane Heidler looked pale and drawn, but managed to summon a shadow of a smile.

Bri was in no mood to return it. "Is Will all right?"

Diane glanced away and busied herself removing the needle from Bri's arm.

"It's saline," she said in her American drawl. "To hydrate you while you slept. Despite the lack of refrigeration, it hadn't spoiled."

Bri hissed at the stinging sensation when the needle withdrew. She stared at Ceri, who suddenly seemed to find the pattern of the tiled floor fascinating.

"Ceri?" Bri spoke softly, though she wanted to scream at the top of her voice. "Will. Tell me. Is… is he… dead?"

Bri's thoughts were pulled back to the present and the fifteenth green when a man stepped forward. She couldn't remember his name. Jacques or Jean or something beginning with J. Something French.

He nodded at the two men holding the sheet bundle and they lowered it into the hole. It swayed while it descended and Bri could make out a shape poking through the cloth. A bony elbow or knee. She swallowed, wanting to turn away, but unable to. When the bundle had disappeared into the hole and come to rest, the men dropped the ends of the ropes in after it and stepped back.

Bri took a deep gulp. She felt a hand tug at hers and clutched it gratefully. Now she could tear her horrified gaze away and glance at the boy standing beside her.

Will looked painfully pale and thin, all anaemia and angles. His left shoulder was heavily bandaged, arm strapped across his chest in a tight sling allowing no movement.

Bri bent towards him and whispered, "That could have been you they're chucking mud onto. Never save my life again. My heart couldn't stand it." She bent further and planted a kiss on his temple. When she straightened, her own temple twinged beneath the bandage, but it faded as quickly as it started, no comparison to the headaches that had plagued her a couple of months ago.

Will gave her a strained smile, then turned to listen to Jean or Jacques, who mumbled something in French before raising his voice. His English wasn't quite fluent, and was strongly accented; nevertheless, each word was heard clearly by the small congregation.

"Her name is Vanessa. She is ten. I found her in Calais. Living among corpses. Living…" he cleared his throat "…off corpses. She was sick when I found her. Already dying. I did not bring her with me so she could be made well. Rather, that she would not die alone. If we have nothing else to offer then we can offer this:

companionship during our last hours. I fear to expect anything more. I fear hope has abandoned us."

He bowed his head. The two men who had lowered the body into the hole stepped forward and began to shovel in earth. Another voice spoke.

"As long as we still breathe we have hope." It was Joe, the boy who had joined them on the night the Beacon had been activated. Nearly all trace of the effects of the electrical treatment to which he had been subjected had gone. Now and then he would pause and his face go blank while he searched for an elusive word, or he would frown in consternation while he tried to remember something from his past, but such incidents were growing rarer. "More and more people are coming every day. Within the last hour another group has come from Ireland. People have been arriving from America. Some of them have brought guns. We can fight. There is our hope."

"Not now, Joe," said Tom. "Save it for the meeting. That will be the time to discuss such matters. Not here."

Joe opened his mouth, then closed it again. He turned and walked back down the hill to the hotel. Others in the small gathering followed him.

Bri watched the two men fill the grave. They patted down the mound with the shovels and stepped back. The remaining people glanced at each other and, wordlessly, began to drift away.

In December, of the seven billion people inhabiting Earth Haven sent into a coma by the Millennium Bug, a mere 1.42 million of them awoke. By late January, when a message went out to Western Europe and the east coast of North America, around 550,000 of these survivors had already perished. Some through malnutrition or diseases caught from rotting corpses, others through fatal encounters with local fauna. Many more succumbed to guilt that they had survived when everyone else they knew and loved hadn't; they welcomed the black pit yawning to greet them when the rope tightened, the water rose over their heads or lifeblood gouted from sliced veins.

The message sent by Milandra, assisted by Jason Grant, Peter Ronstadt and Diane Heidler, on the morning the Beacon had been activated was not in truth economical. It *could* have reached most of Europe, almost as far as Asia, and maybe half of Africa if they had ignored North America, but the energy required to cross the Atlantic and still retain sufficient strength to deliver a persuasive message meant they could not reach as many closer countries as otherwise would have been possible.

"We could have covered far more land," Diane remarked to Peter a few days after the message had been sent, while they waited at Salisbury Hospital to see whether Will would pull through.

"True. But Tom and Ceri—Ceri in particular—were keen on reaching the United States." He shrugged. "Due to the common language, I suppose."

"More people should have been reached. More help could have come."

"That is not our concern. Humanity must make its own case for survival and strength of numbers will not help. As it is, I fear too many of them will want to fight our people. Like Tom did when we went in search of guns."

"Hmm. I think his experiences at the Beacon have cured him of that notion."

"Maybe. But many others will think aggression is their best hope." Peter shook his head. "Only certain ruin lies down that path."

Around seven percent of the remaining survivors received the message. A small number of those were indifferent, too caught up in their own worries to care about wider concerns, and they ignored it. Some were too ill or weak or debilitated to even attempt to journey to the U.K. Others were willing, but lacked the means of travelling across water, or the wherewithal to improvise, or the knowledge to utilise the means at their disposal.

Its island status had served Britain well in times gone by, had kept Hitler and other would-be invaders at bay, but with navigational systems that relied on electricity defunct, and knowledge of how to use more antiquated methods of navigation, like sextants, which had been dying out anyway in the technological age, now all-but extinct, the seas surrounding the U.K. presented an almost impenetrable barrier.

Nevertheless, many made the attempt. Hundreds died as a result of encounters with wildlife that, without man's subduing influence, had grown aggressive; or as a result of attempting to traverse inhospitable terrain without suitable equipment and support. Thousands perished in February gales and March squalls that whipped the seas into heaving, tumultuous terrorscapes.

The few aeroplane pilots who still lived and attempted the journey by air failed when their engines let them down or they discovered too late that their limited flying experience did not give them the ability to pilot a craft through storm-ridden skies across the Atlantic Ocean. One Lear jet, piloted by a former U.S. naval pilot from Petersburg, Virginia, took off from the States with sufficient fuel to reach the U.K., provided there were no strong headwinds to contend with. The plane, with its pilot and eight passengers, almost made it. Arriving within sight of the U.K. after dark, thick cloud masking the streetlights now illuminating parts of West London, the pilot circled a few times, desperately trying to get a handle on his location, before the engines spluttered to a halt and the plane came down in the Irish Sea.

Still, men and women can demonstrate extraordinary determination and invention when they need to. By the time March turned to April, almost six thousand people had gained the shores of the British Isles. The majority had travelled the shorter distances from mainland Europe, most traversing the English Channel, while some intrepid travellers hiked the length of the Channel Tunnel, battling past pockets of bad air. A boatload of six people arrived from Iceland, the most northerly point the message had reached. But perhaps almost a thousand all told, showing the greatest determination and invention, arrived from

Canada and the United States.

Among them were a man named Zach and a woman named Amy.

Chapter Two

Zacharias Abraham Trent did not consider himself to be a lucky man. Yes, he had survived three tours of Vietnam, but they had cost him his only friends along with a large chunk of sanity. True, he had unexpectedly come into a vast sum of money that allowed him to avoid the early grave he was fast drinking himself into, but he had become an orphan in the process. And he had awoken from the Millennium Bug, but it had left him hearing incorporeal voices and wondering whether forty years of solitude had really healed the hurts inflicted in Asian jungles.

The first voice had been forceful, instructing him not to wander far. It had been compelling enough that Zach had obeyed it without question and had taken weeks for its effects to wear off.

The second voice was nowhere near as persuasive as the first, suggestive rather than imperative. It nevertheless possessed an attractive quality that made him want to do as it said. The main difference this time was that Zach was not alone. His companion also heard the voice, tempering (though not removing entirely) Zach's suspicion that he might be crazy.

When Zach informed Amy he was heading for a harbour or marina where he might find a vessel capable of transporting him across the Atlantic Ocean, she grinned. As usual, it shaved years off her appearance and made Zach half-regret turning down her offer to be his bed mate.

"I'm coming, too," she said. "You didn't leave me behind in Portland and you ain't leaving me behind now."

Zach regarded her steadily. "This won't be no jaunt down the coast to Connecticut. This'll be a couple of thousand miles of ocean with storms and currents and icebergs, most prob'ly."

"Icebergs? Like sunk *The Titanic*?" Amy chewed her top lip, then stuck out her chin. "I'm still coming."

Zach hesitated, unsure whether to say it, but decided to jump in. "Good. I've kind of got used to having you around."

Amy's grin turned wider. Since hooking up with Zach, she had shed a few pounds and her skin had become clearer, more in keeping with her youth. She bathed regularly in the ocean, despite the sometimes freezing temperatures, and changed clothes frequently. There was a ready supply of new clothes in every town through which they passed. Her diligence at keeping herself clean prompted Zach to bathe and change his own clothes a little more often than he might have otherwise.

Zach found himself experiencing an unusual sensation: pleasure, brought on by making another smile. He quite liked it. Maybe he was getting better at this social intercourse.

The second voice had come to them while they slept in a seafront town in Connecticut. The town contained a small marina, mainly for skiffs and fishing boats designed for coastal waters. One or two larger yachts might have been capable of crossing the ocean, Zach thought, but he dismissed any notion of attempting such a voyage under sail. Even had he possessed the necessary knowledge and experience, which he didn't, he would need more than Amy to help crew the vessel. Moreover, Zach had read that sailing the Atlantic from the U.S. to Britain was a lot tougher, due to trade winds and currents, than coming the other way. And there were certain times of year when conditions were more favourable to attempt a crossing, but he had no recollection of when they might be.

Zach believed the two of them might stand a chance in a motorised cruiser designed to handle the rigours of an ocean, although he would still need to rely on Amy to maintain course and keep a look out for trouble of the storm or berg kind while he slept or took care of the engines. Much as he was growing used to and had—dare he admit to himself—started to enjoy her company, Zach had no confidence she would prove to be anything more than a passenger on a transatlantic crossing.

In the days immediately after hearing the second voice, Zach took them south, following coastal roads. He drove with his window down despite the chilly air, his ears alert for the sound of engines and his eyes turned seawards as often as he dared.

The sky darkened when they entered the state of New York and snowflakes like lace doilies began to float serenely from the sky. The wind picked up and that was that for serenity. They holed up in a house in Larchmont and waited out the blizzard. Three weeks later, when the thaw had begun, they left. Snow still lay thick on the ground, but the sky had shed its load. Zach had plenty of experience with snow; he knew when the clouds had no more to give. His pick-up managed what snow remained without problem, although the going was slow.

He headed inland to bypass New York City, figuring there was a high probability the roads onto or off the islands were impassable because of stalled vehicles. He had no intention of abandoning his pick-up just yet.

They made their way through northern New Jersey. Without traffic and industry, and despite the thaw continuing, the snow had hung around and hindered their progress for longer than it would have in the days before the Millennium Bug. But now, when Route 35 almost touched the shore and they could see Staten Island lying to the north, the last of the snow thinned and Zach drove once more on asphalt.

"Easier going from here on," he remarked.

"I guess."

The listlessness in Amy's tone made Zach glance to his right. She was staring out of the window, chewing at a strand of hair. Forty years of solitude had not imbued Zach with tact or social graces.

"You sick or something?"

"Nope." She sighed. "Used to come to Jersey with Momma every August. Her sister lived here."

Zach supposed she might be upset, reminded by their location of her mother and aunt, and that maybe he should say something comforting. Damned if he knew anything comforting. Instead, he asked, "New Jersey has marinas?"

"Yep. Aplenty. Momma used to drag me to them. She liked

looking at boats."

"Big ones? Ocean-going?"

"Don't know nothing 'bout boats."

"Well, reckon I'll get off the highway. It's bending inland a little. We need to hug the shore."

"Whatever."

Zach left the highway at the next ramp and followed lesser roads, keeping the ocean in sight to his left as much as he could. When they stopped at marinas, Amy got out to stretch her legs, but showed not a scrap of interest in the yachts and pleasure cruisers moored alongside pontoons or bobbing at anchor. Zach regarded them with a critical eye.

He was no expert on boats, but had expanded his knowledge greatly thanks to the public library in Bridgeport. The most recent and, he supposed, doomed-to-be last ever edition of *Voyaging Under Power* had joined his meagre list of possessions. He read it by flash- or candlelight each evening before falling asleep. In essence, their needs boiled down to this: a cruiser thirty-six feet in length or longer, with a seaworthy displacement hull, a slow-turning diesel engine cruising at around eight knots and a large fuel capacity.

Nothing fitted the bill at the marinas they visited. Even had a suitable vessel been available, it did not solve the other problem, that of having a crew to help manage a transatlantic passage. If a solution did not present itself, Zach had already resolved to make the attempt with only himself and Amy, though he did not relish the prospect.

That is when Lady Luck smiled upon him.

They had stopped for a picnic lunch on a beach near a wide creek running into the ocean. To their right, beyond the creek, extended a headland. It was from around the headland the noise came.

Zach paused in mid-chew.

"Can you hear that?"

It wasn't necessary that Amy replied. She had already turned and was staring out towards the headland, her chestnut hair whipping in the breeze. The noise grew louder and its source came into sight.

Cutting through the waves as if they didn't exist came a sleek, white motor cruiser.

With a grinding *scrunch* that made the deck shudder, they ran aground. If Aletta hadn't been clutching the side of the boat, she might have fallen off her perch on the bench. She rose unsteadily to her feet. The Pole had already vaulted the prow and was splashing to shore. The Croatian was following him.

Levente looked back.

"Come!" His eyes glittered in the spring sunlight.

He swung his legs over the gunwale and dropped from view.

Aletta hurried forward. When she reached the prow, the Hungarian came back into sight, standing thigh-deep in the surf, holding out a hand to help her. The two other men had already reached the narrow strip of shingle lying between the waves and the foot of the white cliffs.

"Come!" Levente repeated. He smiled encouragingly.

Aletta reached out and allowed her hand to be engulfed in his. Using him as an anchor for her weight, she swung her legs over the side. Pushing off with her free hand, she dropped into the sea. It only came up to the top of her thighs, but she gasped.

Levente laughed and released her hand.

"Cold, *igen?*"

"Yes." Despite the shock at how icy the water felt—her legs were already turning numb—Aletta was so relieved to be out of the boat she returned the man's grin.

He glanced back up and she followed his gaze. A lined face looked down at them. Levente held up his hand. Before the Italian could grasp it, Aletta had a thought.

"One moment." She called to the other woman. "Water! Get water! Er... *acqua!*"

The woman frowned, then nodded.

She disappeared, to reappear within moments holding the plastic packaging containing the remaining three bottles of water. She leaned forward and handed the bottles to Aletta, who took them in her left hand and held out her right to help the woman down.

Leaning precariously over the side of the boat, the Italian grabbed both Aletta's and Levente's proffered hands, but instead of lifting her legs over, she continued to slide forward so that she exited the boat head first.

A large wave hit Aletta, splashing up her stomach, and she took an involuntary step back on soft, shifting shingle. The Italian woman kept coming, gaining momentum as her legs slipped over the gunwale.

"*Szar!*" exclaimed Levente, struggling to keep his feet.

The next moment, Aletta found herself on her back in icy water, a rather plump Italian woman on top of her. Another wave broke, this time over Aletta's head. Her world turned green, filled with the muffled, bubbling sounds of rushing water.

The weight lifted from her and she struggled to her feet, receiving another faceful in the process. She spluttered and spat, grimacing at the briny taste in her mouth.

The sound of hearty laughter made her glance at Levente, who clearly found the sight of her greatly amusing. The Italian woman stood next to him. She was short and the sea came up to her waist, yet her chest and shoulders looked to be dry. Using Aletta as a landing mat had apparently saved her from a ducking.

"*Mi dispiace,*" said the woman and bowed her head gravely.

"It's okay," said Aletta and found she meant it. Despite being soaked to the skin, it felt so good to be out of the wretched boat nothing could dampen her spirits. "But let us go. I'm cold."

She turned and started wading to shore. The waves tried to knock her to her knees, but she swayed with them and was able to avoid going back under. After stepping beyond the last wave, she stooped and picked up the bottles of water, still in their packaging, which had ridden the waves ashore. She could hear the Hungarian chortling and the Italian woman splashing behind her.

The Pole and the Croatian had walked along the narrow strip of shingle to the left, but were returning, shaking their heads.

"No good," said the Pole. He pointed behind him. "Dover that way, but no good. Cliffs too high. Sea too fast."

Aletta shivered. The sun felt warm on her head, but it would take hours to dry her sodden clothes. She needed fresh ones.

She looked to the right. A high, rocky promontory blocked the view so she could not tell what was immediately beyond it. Farther away, a white line suggested that the cliffs continued to provide a distant barrier to them reaching dry land.

"We need to get past that," she said, pointing to the promontory, "and hope there are no cliffs the other side. We must be quick."

The waves were already breaking at the foot of the outcrop. The thin stretch of shingle that led to it was growing thinner by the minute.

"Come, then," said the Pole.

He strode in that direction, the Croatian close on his heels. The Italian woman let loose a stream of what sounded from the tone like invective, but fell into step behind Aletta. Levente brought up the rear.

The sea was lapping at their feet by the time they reached the base of the promontory. When it shifted under the weight of inrushing water, the shingle crackled like breakfast cereal. The waves striking the foot of the outcrop boomed when they hit with increasing force.

The Pole stopped. Spray soaked him while he regarded the foaming rocks.

"Water too strong," he said solemnly. He nodded out to sea. "We must go there. Make a… a rope, with our hands."

"A rope?" said Aletta. "Ah. A chain."

He nodded. "Yes. A chain." He held out his left hand to Aletta. She took it in her right. "You next," he said, looking at the Croatian. "Then you." He nodded at the Italian woman, who muttered something under her breath. He turned to Levente. "You last."

The Hungarian shrugged, but took hold of the Italian woman's left hand with his right. Despite her struggle with English, she seemed to understand the plan and did not object when her other hand was grasped by the Croatian. He also took hold of Aletta's left hand.

The Pole led them back into the water. Although Aletta's clothing was already soaked through, she gasped again at the cold. Waves were coming in at a lick and dashed against her legs. If she hadn't such a tight grip on the men's hands, she would have been knocked over.

When the water was to his waist, the Pole turned to face the shore and began to crab sideways. Aletta followed, presenting her back to the force of the waves. Once or twice, they lifted her off her feet, but she rode the swell and maintained her death-like grip on the hands, helping her to keep her balance. In this way, the five people moved steadily past the promontory.

The shoreline immediately the other side came into view. Aletta could see white cliffs rising sharply away far to the right, but in front of them the outcrop shrank inland to tree-lined slopes. Only a hundred yards or so away, sunlight glinted off the windows of a building standing a short walk beyond a sandy stretch of beach. Aletta breathed a sigh of relief.

The force of the waves subsided when they had cleared the outcrop and the going became easier. The Pole stopped moving sideways and headed for the shore. When the water came up only to his knees, he let go of Aletta's hand. Aletta did the same with the Croatian's hand and stumbled ashore unaided. She waited until she was clear of the reach of waves before sinking to her knees in the sand.

A sleepless night punctuated by bouts of sickness, two icy soakings and struggling through a racing tide had left her feeling exhausted. She wasn't the only one. The Italian woman collapsed to the sand next to her with a long sigh.

"Ah, dry land good, *igen?*" Levente smiled down at her.

Aletta nodded. Despite the warmth of the sun on her head and the sand beneath her, her teeth chattered uncontrollably.

"Come," said Levente. He pointed up the beach where the Pole and the Croatian were making for the building. He strode away after them.

Aletta dragged herself to her feet. The Italian woman made no move to follow. She knelt in the sand, head bowed to her chest, uttering low moans. Her woollen skirt hung sodden and heavy in the sand about her.

"Let's go," said Aletta, holding out a hand. The Italian continued to look down and moan. Aletta pushed her gently on the shoulder. "Come on. We need to find dry clothes. And food. Er, *cibo?*"

The woman glanced up. "*Cibo? Sì!*" She grasped Aletta's hand.

With the last of her strength, Aletta hauled the older woman to her feet. Still clutching hands, they stumbled across the sand in the men's wake.

The building, a two-storey construction with a flat roof, turned out to be a tavern. *The Coastguard* had been abandoned by its owners and securely locked. The men picked up a wooden bench. With a roar of encouragement from Levente, they used it to ram through a ground floor window that gave into a bar. The interior was blessedly free of the stink of stale corruption. Aletta barely noticed the musty smell of non-habitation.

In the living quarters they found a motley collection of clothes, about which it could be said they were dry if not well-fitting. They abandoned their sopping clothes; the new ones would do until they reached Dover.

Wrapping herself in dry garments helped Aletta begin to warm up. A few tots of brandy from the well-stocked bar completed the job. They also found enough unspoiled food in the pub kitchen to fill their stomachs, no easy task given their stomachs were so empty.

The question of transport was easily and unexpectedly solved.

In a car park next to *The Coastguard* they found four cars with their keys still in the ignition. Scattered around the cars, or blown into nearby trees by the wind, were various items of clothing. Of the clothing's or vehicles' former owners there was no sign.

"They took a last walk," said Levente, nodding out to sea.

Aletta swallowed. She scanned the shoreline—the tide was completely in now—and could see no hump in the sand that might be a washed-up corpse, but his words rang true. On her journey south along the Baltic coast, she had spied a number of pathetic bundles of clothing left at the water's edge. The first one had a note on top wrapped in a plastic bag and weighted down with a stone. She picked it up and read it. Later, when she had stopped shaking, she replaced it and hadn't the stomach to approach any other bundles she came across.

The cars' batteries were dead, but the group possessed enough manpower to get two of them rolling and bump start them.

Within three hours of the boat beaching, they were driving into a silent and deserted Dover on a sunny spring lunchtime. There they paused, leaving the car engines idling, to change into new, well-fitting outfits.

Before climbing back into the car, the Pole pointed towards the sea. "There is the port," he said. He pointed inland. "That way is London."

"That is where we are going?" asked Aletta.

"Of course," he answered. "Where else?"

Had they driven to the port, they might have noticed a hand-printed poster affixed to the port entrance. Despite being protected by a plastic wallet, damp had found its way onto the paper, causing the ink to run. Nevertheless, the printing remained legible. It read:

To anyone arriving from the continent: avoid London! Follow the M4 motorway west. AVOID LONDON!

Milandra stepped outside for the first time in weeks. A fresh breeze whipping off the Atlantic made her gasp. Spring sunlight warmed her head. She could sense her cells greedily lap it up like weaning kittens. It had been more than five months since she had felt the Florida sun on her shoulders; the Cornish sun wasn't as warm, nor as energising, but welcome nonetheless.

She turned her face towards it and sighed.

Weeks she had spent shut away indoors, trawling the mammoth vault of her people's memories, only emerging long enough to eat. Day upon day of fruitless hunting had not daunted her. She knew with a certainty she could not explain that what she was seeking was there to be found. Hidden away, disguised, not meant to be discovered, although she did not know why.

She could do with a few hours in sunlight to recharge her batteries. A walk to exercise her underused muscles would also do her good.

Milandra strolled down the hill towards the sea. Jason Grant found her a few hours later, sitting on a stone bench watching the grey waves roll in, listening to the gulls wheel and cry. The sun had gone behind scudding clouds, but she could still feel its heat; her cells had opened up like spring buds, maximising their exposure to the invigorating rays.

Grant was capable of stepping lightly, but he made no effort to mask his approach. She turned her head and smiled up at him.

"Here you are," he said. "I saw the door to the cottage was open. When I couldn't find you inside, I guessed I'd find you watching the ocean. Been enjoying the sunlight?"

"Mm. It's warmed up around here since I locked myself away."

"You've been in there for near a month. And, yep, the weather's improved, though still not exactly Florida. Now, if only the darned rain would stay away…"

They lapsed into a few moments' silence. Milandra turned her head to watch the waves. The sun came back out, performing the alchemist's trick of turning leaden sea to molten gold.

Milandra could sense the curiosity in her right-hand man. Hardly surprising. She had shut herself away with orders not to be disturbed and had given Grant only the tersest hint why.

"Come, Jason, sit by me." Milandra patted the bench next to her and waited until he had settled himself. "Where are the other Deputies?"

"They've gone on ahead as planned. They've taken the drones to clear the hotel of any, er, undesirable materials."

"Were they curious about what I was up to?"

"Simone in particular was suspicious. She thought I was in on it, but I let her probe—only a little—and she could see I was as clueless as them."

"You let her probe you? Risky."

"Not really. I know how to lock away memories so that no one, not even the Chosen, will see." He grunted. "Lavinia didn't say much, as usual. Wallace bellyached as he does, though not as much as I was expecting him to. He's been in a strange mood since we activated the Beacon."

"Is Simone still calling him Raccoon?"

"Yep. So is Lavinia. His black eyes had healed by the time you placed yourself in isolation, but the nickname seems to have stuck. Again, strangely, it doesn't seem to irritate him as much as you'd expect."

Milandra was silent for a moment. Then she said quietly, "The boy survived."

"He did?"

"I contacted Ronstadt a couple of weeks ago. The bullet from George's gun entered high to the left of his chest and exited below his shoulder blade. Extensive soft tissue damage, but no major organs nicked. He'll probably never regain full use of his arm, but he's a lucky kid. As it was, he nearly died through shock and blood loss."

"The doctor you found saved him?"

"With Diane Heidler's help. She has experience as a nurse in field hospitals in the last world war."

"Lucky kid indeed. Wallace would be relieved to know he pulled through, although we can hardly tell him."

"Not without revealing where our sympathies lie." Milandra

chuckled. "Seems George isn't the stony-hearted bastard he'd have us believe."

"What about the girl?"

"Heidler, again. Under her direction, the doctor removed a blood clot from behind her skull. It apparently took a lot of persuasion to get him to attempt the procedure."

"And the girl's abilities?"

"They seem to remain intact. She helped heal the drone I saw escape at Stonehenge."

"The one who gave Wallace one of his black eyes?"

"Yes. The damage caused by the electrical treatment had begun to reverse itself. He's still young and not fully developed physically. She helped the process along and the drone—should probably stop calling him that—is near to normal."

Grant gave a low whistle.

"What about Rod?" asked Milandra. "Has he taken them to the hotel in the bus?"

"Yup. And his fishing poles. He's found a new love in his life. Says he's going to go somewhere warm when all this is over and live off freshly-caught fish to the end of his days."

They lapsed into further silence. The sun rode high in the sky. Milandra sighed with pleasure. She glanced at Grant.

"I suppose you're curious what I've been doing shut away on my own for weeks."

He shrugged. "Figured you'd tell me when you're good and ready."

"Do you remember that book you suggested I read about a house whose inner dimensions were greater than its outer? Can't remember what it was called. *House of* something."

"*House of Leaves.*"

"That's the one. It freaked me out a little."

"Me, too. If I recall correctly, I recommended *Imajica* as well. I wanted you to read them as good examples of how astonishing human imagination can be." Grant turned his head to look at her, eyebrows raised. "What does it have to do with anything?"

"In *House of Leaves*, they find a stairwell they follow down and it seems to have no end. I think there were corridors leading off at each landing."

Grant nodded.

"Well," continued Milandra, "that's what our group memory is like. An endless stairwell with an endless number of corridors leading off. Each corridor is jammed full of memories and experiences that have accumulated for over sixty million years. That's what I've been doing for the last month. Searching those endless corridors."

"Searching. For what?"

"This will sound a little kooky, but I'm not sure what I'm looking for, other than I'll know when I find it. And I'm close. I've found the memory of the ancients leaving Earth Home. Their ship was attacked by eight smaller craft. A missile sheared off a propulsion unit that would have been used to slow descent when it arrived at its destination."

"And without that the ship crashed." Grant breathed out deeply. "Whose memory was it?"

"Huh!" Milandra gave a start. "D'you know, I hadn't thought of that. Hmm. There are other memories hidden away where I found that one. Maybe when I view them I'll discover through whose eyes I am seeing."

She reached out and patted Grant's knee.

"Thank you, Jason. As always, your fresh way of looking at things has taught me there are other perspectives I need to consider. We'll talk some more in a few days."

Grant nodded. Again Milandra was struck by how unselfish he could be. If he had further questions churning around in his mind—and he did; she knew him too well—he kept them to himself.

She stood and stretched. "My goodness, the sun has done these old bones a heap of good. Would you do me one last favour and help me take more food to the cottage? There's not much left and I've a feeling I'll need plenty of hearty meals to help me complete my search."

"Sure." Grant stood. He towered a good six inches or more above Milandra. "The neighbouring cottage has been stockpiled so we won't need to haul it far. When next you're ready to come out, return here. I won't be far away and I'll come."

Milandra smiled up at him. "And with luck I'll have some answers, though I'm as yet uncertain of the questions."

They turned their backs to the afternoon sun and walked side by side up the hill.

Chapter Three

Carrying a bottle of red wine and two glasses, Tom Evans stepped from behind the bar. He was about to take a seat at a table looking out into the hotel foyer when Ceri Lewis, approaching from the stairwell leading to the guest rooms, shook her head curtly.

"Nope," she said, walking past him. "We just buried a child and it's April. I'm not in the mood to stare at a Christmas tree."

Tom glanced at the tree. A shower of pine needles carpeted the floor around its base. The branches, brown and forlorn, sagged beneath their load of baubles. With a shrug, Tom followed Ceri into the bar's large seating area to two leather sofas facing each other across a low table.

He eased himself into the sofa opposite Ceri and held out the bottle.

"Chilean Merlot," he said. "Will this do you?"

"It contains alcohol, doesn't it?" She didn't smile.

Tom unscrewed the bottle top and glugged wine into the glasses. He sat back and sipped at the inky liquid, allowing his gaze to wander through the bar's plate glass windows.

A patio area gave way to a tree-cloaked hill. Among the trees, a rope assault course wound its way between the trunks and boughs. Tom knew the ropes were there, but could no longer see them. Unlike the dead Christmas tree in the foyer, the trees outside were bursting with vitality. Fresh shades of green rippled and swayed in the spring breeze. Sap-laden leaves hid the ropes and tyres from view. Sunlight lent the scene a simple beauty that made Tom want to rub his eyes.

From behind him he became aware of the clink of glasses, bustle of movement and muted conversation while people filled the bar. The need to be amongst company had been anticipated: the hotel's extensive cellars had been raided to fully restock the bar with wines, spirits and bottled beer.

Tom strained to catch snatches of conversation from the huddled groups nearest him. He could make out French; from another group a language that sounded strange and harsh to his untrained ears—a Scandinavian language, maybe.

Europe was supposed to be one large community, he mused. A common people separated by an uncommon number of differing languages and dialects.

No American accents; not here. All hotel rooms had long been taken by the time of the first arrivals from the States, so newcomers had been directed to nearby towns and villages where Europeans were clearing properties for occupation. There had been no reports of animosity from any one group towards another. Spaniards, Italians, Norwegians, Germans, Portuguese and Dutch would need to get along with each other and the Americans. Reviving old enmities would be the ultimate exercise in pointlessness, even with man's record of futile struggles. Maybe the Cleansing had perversely achieved something good: the reconciliation of man with his basest nature. Now, at the end of all things.

Tom shifted in his seat when he became aware of Ceri staring at him. She had lit a cigarette and tendrils of smoke curled from her nostrils.

"What?"

"We're running out of time." Her voice had lost its earlier edge. She sounded tired. Defeated.

"I know." He leaned forward and refilled their glasses. "I feel we should be doing something, but after Stonehenge…"

Ceri took a slurp of wine and a deep drag on her cigarette. "I've overheard some of the newbies talking. Those I can understand, anyway. They don't know what's happening, why they've been called here, but some of them are spoiling for a fight. They remind me of you *before* we went to Stonehenge."

"And much use I was when it came down to it." He thought for a moment. "Maybe if they want to fight, they should."

"We can hardly stop them, but I think it would be a mistake."

She favoured Tom with a keen look. "You felt them, too."

"Who? What?"

"When we followed Bri into the stone circle. That group of people, or whatever they are. All they did was stare at me and I couldn't move. I could feel them scratching around inside my head like cockroaches." Ceri shuddered.

Tom took a mouthful of wine and savoured the tingling sensation in the back of his throat. Ceri was still regarding him expectantly.

"I felt them." He didn't say it, but the invasion of his mind had been frighteningly rapid and almost complete.

"Surely now you have to accept they're not performing some accomplished mind trick. They possess power. Real power."

Tom nodded. "When I loosed both barrels of the shotgun, I was only moments away from being frozen solid like you."

"And don't forget we had some protection from Peter and Diane. Yet four or five of them acting together were able to get past that protection, no bother. Imagine what five thousand of them together can do. And when the rest of them arrive? Seventy thousand added to those already here. They'll make us turn on each other. Or walk into the sea."

"But they can do that whether we fight or not. Maybe people have the right to choose how they die."

Ceri sighed. She drained her glass. While Tom refilled it, she lit another cigarette.

Tom leaned back, his glass also full. The bottle was empty.

"I've never told you," he said, "but you were awesome that morning at Stonehenge. Awesome and scary. I was very glad to be on your side."

Ceri snorted, but her expression turned serious almost immediately. "That's another thing, Tom. Forget about their psychic powers for one moment. They also know how to handle guns." She glanced around at the knots of people in the bar. Tom didn't need to follow her gaze to know they consisted of people of both sexes and all ages, from young teens to pensioners.

"Unless most of the newbies are masking their military know-how behind veneers of girls and old men, we possess neither the physical prowess nor gun knowledge to stand the slightest chance in a war."

Tom considered for a moment. "Might be some with military experience, though they'll be in the minority. But, seriously, will it make much difference? Take Joe. He's itching to fight after what they did to him, yet he's never fired a gun in his life. Everyone here will have lost loved ones to the Millennium Bug. They'll want to make a gesture of defiance, no matter how futile." An image passed across his mind: forcing his mother's knees to bend so her body would fit into the impromptu grave. He blinked the image away. "Can't say I blame them."

Ceri gave a resigned sigh. "Well, we ought to make them aware at the meeting what they're up against. If they still decide to fight, at least it will be an informed decision." She regarded the last few drops of wine left in her glass. "Let's open another bottle."

Amy reacted slower than Zach. He had stood, removed his jacket and was waving it at the boat like a black flag by the time she rose to her feet. She felt mildly foolish, but joined in by waving her arms half-heartedly. Her clothes, however, remained firmly in place; it was too darned cold to remove them.

At first, there was no indication the boat's occupants had spotted them. Then the rumble of its engine changed pitch and the front end turned towards shore. Amy dropped her arms to her side; they were starting to ache.

"No good," muttered Zach.

"Huh?"

He pointed impatiently with one arm while he used the other to shrug his jacket back on. "Too shallow and rocky. They won't be able to get close enough to do more than holler."

Amy looked to where the narrow waves lapped at the land. The gently-sloping foreshore was a mix of sand, mud and rocks, the latter predominating and continuing into the water. They poked above the surface like the barnacled back fins of a leviathan.

Zach gestured to the boat, waving his hands in front of his chest and shaking his head in an exaggerated manner.

The people on the boat must have understood what he meant, or had already reached the same conclusion themselves, for the boat turned parallel to shore and slowed. A man appeared near the top deck—he was too far away for Amy to make him out clearly, though she thought he looked quite old.

The man pointed towards the headland from behind which the boat had appeared. He moved his right hand repeatedly in a chopping motion. Amy glanced at her companion, unsure what the man was trying to tell them. Zach seemed to understand. He nodded his head vigorously and gave the thumbs up.

The man raised both his hands in the same signal and disappeared back into the boat. The engine grumbled deeper and the boat began to turn back the way it had come.

Zach frowned. "That engine sounds a little rough."

"It does?" It sounded to Amy like the noise any engine would make.

"Come on," said Zach. "Back to the pick-up."

Amy started towards the remains of their lunch, meaning to clear up.

"Leave it for the gulls," growled Zach. "We need to get to the other side of the headland, and quick. Don't want them to think we're not keen. Could be our passage across the ocean. We ain't flush with choices."

This was quite a speech by his standards. Amy was about to comment, but he was striding towards his truck.

With a shrug, she followed.

Zach gunned the engine and set off towards the headland.

"Try not to lose sight of her," he muttered.

The white boat was already hidden from view by a row of worn and weathered fishermen's shacks. By the time the sea came back into sight, the boat had disappeared.

"It's gone," Amy said. "They must've already drove round that corner."

Zach glanced to his left. "Yep. They've *sailed* or *cruised*—not 'drove'—past the headland."

"Whatever."

Amy didn't much care about the correct terminology. She hadn't been lying when she'd told Zach she had no interest in boats. The thought of being on one, crossing an entire ocean, did not fill her with glee. Yet the idea of stepping onto another country gave her a sensation that had largely been missing from her life: anticipation. She had already travelled as far as she had ever been from home. If they were able to hitch a ride on the white boat, soon she would be walking in a new land, one that of course she had heard about, but never dreamed she would actually visit. And there was something else, something that made her stomach flutter in a not unpleasant way.

"How many... um." She cleared her throat. "How many people d'you reckon are on that thing?"

"It's a beaut. Prob'ly has berths for eight passengers plus crew. Course, the passengers *are* the crew. Why?"

"Just wondering."

She stared straight ahead, but glimpsed from the corner of her eye Zach glance her way.

"Could be men on there," he said. "Young men."

Amy felt her colour rise, but also a spark of defiance. Why the heck shouldn't she want there to be young men on that tub?

"I hope so," she said. "No offence."

Zach grunted.

"There's something I don't get," said Amy. "How d'you know they're fixin' on going to England?"

"Same reason we want to go there."

"That voice?"

"I reckon."

"But where did it come from? Whose was it?"

Zach shrugged. "It'll take someone a good deal smarter than me to answer that."

Amy shivered. She didn't like to think much about the voices. The first time she heard one inside her head, she'd assumed she must be crazy. The second time, her taciturn companion had also heard it. Maybe they were both crazy.

"Let's say they are going, how will we get them to take us?"

"Ask 'em, I guess," said Zach. "But I ain't got no airs or social graces."

"Me, neither." *It's why you agreed to me coming with you.* She didn't voice the thought; some things were understood without being spoken.

"Been on my own a long time. Through choice."

"So?"

"These last few weeks. Picking up with you. Wanting to join up with a bunch of strangers. S'pose you'd say it's out of character."

"And, so?"

Zach stared straight ahead. They were approaching the far side of the headland. The ocean, wilder and whiter here, could be seen in the distance.

"I guess," he continued, "my gut instinct is still to be on my ownsome. But something—that voice—is tamping it down."

"Right. We need to get on this boat and get, er, *cruising*, before your instincts drown out the voice."

"Something like that."

They drew closer to the ocean. Froth-crested waves rode in from hundreds of yards out, breaking on shingle and sucking back with a *shloop* sound Amy could hear above the pick-up's engine. Away to their left, out beyond the point where the waves began their steady rise, the white boat hove into view.

"There it is," said Amy, her stomach fluttering as though ten anxious moths had been released. "Let's follow 'em to find out where they park—"

"Dock."

"Okay. *Dock.* Then we make friends, I guess."

Zach chuckled, without humour. "Yep. It's what me and you are good at, ain't we?"

Amy didn't bother replying.

Howard Newton glanced down at his patients.

Will lay on his right side, breathing deeply. It would be quite some time before he would be able to lie on his left side or sleep comfortably without painkillers.

Next to him on the wide bed, Bri lay on her back, snoring softly. The wound had stopped weeping a week ago and had nearly closed. Maybe in a few more days, the bandages could be removed to speed up the final stages of the healing process.

Howard breathed a soft sigh. The procedure to remove the blood clot still gave him cause to sit up in the middle of the night, body slick with sweat and heart pounding.

The boy had been bad enough, but Howard hadn't had time to worry about that. He had simply been presented with an unconscious, heavily-bleeding child and reacted by instinct.

It was Diane who had stepped up when Howard's instinct and G.P. training had not been sufficient. It was she who showed him how to clamp torn blood vessels and how to pack the wound with sterilised gauze. She it was who, when the generators had been restarted and illuminated the echoing corridors of Salisbury Hospital in a flickering, yellow light, knew where to find the blood, the coagulating and plasma-enhancing drugs, the antibiotics, the drainage tubes and suture kits.

"He's one lucky kid," Diane said, once they were satisfied they had done all they could for Will. He lay unconscious, attached to drips and tubes, left shoulder heavily bandaged. "The angle of trajectory—slightly downwards, left to right—meant the slug missed the vital organs, all major blood vessels and the nerve junctions contained within the shoulder. Luckier still, the slug passed through the muscle and soft tissue to the side of the rib cage and emerged beneath the extreme edge of the clavicle. No bone slivers to contend with."

"Thank heavens for that," said Howard with some feeling.

"The slug must have been full metal jacket since there was no fragmentation inside the body cavity. Judging from the relatively small exit wound, .308 calibre so less internal damage than a higher calibre round would have caused.

"Still, we're likely to lose him from blood loss or infection. We *might* have been in time getting the blood and plasma and antibiotics into him. They *might* still be viable. Although the power has been off for weeks and the hospital's emergency gennies would only have run for a few days at most, the temperature has been near enough freezing most of the time they don't appear to have spoiled." She shrugged. "Even if blood loss or infection don't kill him, shock probably will. His only hope is he's young and strong. Whether strong enough, only time will tell."

Will's slight frame had indeed proved hardy enough to withstand the trauma of being shot. After nearly forty-eight hours of deep, coma-like sleep, he awoke and, in a croaky voice, asked for a drink. Bri, who had not left the boy's side since she herself had awoken from a coma-like sleep, burst into tears.

Now the soft sound of someone clearing their throat brought Howard out of his reverie. He glanced across to where Colleen O'Mahoney sat watching him, a gentle smile on her lips.

"You should be proud," she said, low enough not to wake the sleepers.

Howard joined her on the settee beneath the picture window looking over the South Wales countryside. The green fields and woods were broken by a curving ribbon of grey that had once teemed with continuous activity, like lines of beavering ants, but which now lay still: the M4 motorway, which stretched eastwards all the way to London. In the distance could be seen the stanchions and cables of the Severn Crossing, the suspension bridge between Wales and England.

"They were extremely fortunate," said Howard. "By rights, they should both be lying six feet under the golf course with that poor French girl."

"They were extremely fortunate they had you." Colleen's accent was soft and unmistakably Irish. She lifted her glass and drained the last of the amber liquid it held.

"I wouldn't have been able to save them on my own," said Howard. "I'm a G.P., not a surgeon. I remember practising incisions on cadavers during my hospital rotation, but nothing had prepared me to treat a gunshot wound and operate on a subdural haematoma. Nope. Diane was the one who really saved them. Without her directing me, I'd have messed it up. As it was, it was more luck than judgment." He uttered a short, humourless laugh.

Colleen gestured towards her empty glass. "Sounds like you could do with one of these."

"Not yet." He nodded towards the bed. "I'm confident they're both past the worst of it, but I don't want to take the chance on one of them suffering some sort of relapse and me being too sozzled to react."

"Okay. Fortunately for me, I don't feel bound by such constraints." She reached for the bottle of Jameson's.

Milandra closed the door to the cottage behind her, preoccupied with what Grant had told her about his update from Tess Granville in London.

Small sections of the city had been reconnected to the Grid. More would be illuminated each week. By the time the Great Coming took place, Tess reported that around a third of the city should be powered up.

She also informed Grant that humans had been pouring into the capital from mainland Europe. A trickle that became a stream that had grown into a raging torrent.

Tess had been surprised by the first arrivals, but she was quick on the uptake. Grant acknowledged she had been the ideal person to take charge while he relaxed in Cornwall. As soon as Tess realised there was a steady influx of people, she organised squads to roam the city capturing any humans they encountered. The captives were sent to Hillingdon Hospital, where the electrical treatment centre had once more become operational. Humans walked in; drones shambled out. They were put to work alongside

British drones, clearing and salvaging and switching off electrical appliances.

If Tess wondered why the humans were arriving in such numbers, she didn't speculate to Grant. And Grant had not, of course, been able to express anything but surprise at the turn of events without raising suspicions he'd had something to do with it.

Milandra shook her head; she had more pressing concerns. She crossed to the bed and sank into it, closing her eyes. She *reached* inwards.

Having visited once, she could easily find her way through the labyrinthine passageways to the dusty corner where she had discovered the memory of the ancients' ship leaving Earth Home. Many other memories crowded the virtual shelves. Some slim—if they were books, they would be little more than pamphlets—some novel-sized. Milandra chose a thick one at random and delved inside…

A landscape. Thickly-wooded slopes reared over lush vegetation. Rain fell in gentle showers; when it stopped, puffs of steam rose from the trees under the benevolent gleam of a huge, red orb dominating the sky. Great winged creatures skimmed the jungle, soaring on hot draughts, alighting on tangled nests built in rocky crevices of the highest peaks.

Glass domes glinted above the canopy like rubies in firelight. Burnished ziggurats and pagodas poked through the treetops like gigantic totem poles. The polished tops of pyramids glowed blood-red.

Whoever's eyes she was looking through was moving over the jungle. She glimpsed padded seats, thickly-paned windows, robed and cloaked travelling companions.

Milandra delved deeper, allowed herself to become fully immersed so that she experienced sounds and smells and sensations. The deep *thrum* of a powerful engine; a crackling air of tension, mirrored by the taut expressions on her companions' faces; a sinking feeling in her stomach when the craft swooped down to a clearing near an imposing, domed structure.

The scene changed to a fragranced interior. Cool marble floors and columns glowed in sunlight magnified by the glass dome overhead. Trailing plants climbed towards the light; multi-hued flowers exuded scents of summer and spice. It should have been a soothing, relaxing space.

Two groups of people faced each other across a vast expanse of tabletop. Milandra remembered the wood from which it was made: *isuz*. As easily fashioned as pine, tougher than teak. The people had been seated on long stone benches running the length of the table, but had risen to their feet, faces flushed deeper than could be accounted for by the ruddy glow of sunlight. A babble of raised voices, speaking in a language Milandra had never before heard, yet recognised. It was the ancient forerunner of the tongue which she and her fellow star travellers had brought with them to Earth Haven.

Amidst the tumult, Milandra could not follow precisely what was being shouted, although some words she could pick out. *Mamui*: loyalty. *Palduranki*: betrayal. *Tuhazu*: fight.

The man in the centre of the group across the table looked directly at the person through whose memory Milandra was observing and fell silent. Lips set into a grim line, he raised a slender black rod. It was marked with intricate designs down its entire length; the air around it seemed to shimmer and grow dimmer.

The din of voices died while all eyes turned to watch the man. The balmy air tingled with hushed expectancy.

Without lowering his gaze, the man brought up his other hand. A grimace, a grunt, and the rod snapped in two. The pieces dropped to the table with a dull clatter. A collective shudder ran around the chamber.

Before she and her stony-faced companions turned and swept from the building, the person whose body Milandra occupied uttered one phrase into the charged silence.

"*Ki'am lu ama.*"

So shall it be.

The memory flickered, faded and Milandra opened her eyes.

Judging from the failing light, most of the afternoon had passed while she'd been immersed in the memory. She needed food and to discuss what she'd seen with Jason Grant. It might help her to make more sense of it.

But first, there was another memory that had attracted her attention; a slim one that shouldn't take long to view.

When Milandra opened her eyes inside the memory, she was looking once more through the gaze of another. This time, she could see who it was.

Chapter Four

Zach drove slowly to stay abreast of the cruiser. The road hugged the coast with no buildings erected seaward, and it was easy to keep the boat in sight. When it turned towards the shore, Zach grunted.

"They're aiming for that inlet."

Ahead, the road bent sharply to the right to follow the course of a narrow gap which channelled the sea inland. Zach brought the pick-up to a stop at the head of the inlet. A sign by the side of the road read, 'Marina 200 yards'.

He watched the cruiser approach. It rode the waves with an easy grace bordering on contempt.

The passage smoothed as the cruiser entered the mouth of the inlet. Its engine barely above idling, it motored past them. From the windows of the cabin on the top deck, two faces peered at them: a pretty white female and a youthful black male. Zach felt Amy stiffen. Her bottom lip tucked between her teeth and she chewed on it like it was beef jerky.

"Something wrong?" he asked mildly.

Amy shook her head, but continued to chew on her lip.

"Look, missy," Zach said, keeping his voice level, "my buddy in 'Nam was black as ink. Ray Walker Junior from Louisiana. Best friend a man could ask for. Saved my life. I couldn't return the favour."

"It's my momma. She said…" Amy let out a great sigh.

Zach regarded her solemnly. Her glance fluttered towards him, but she couldn't meet his gaze. "Whatever poison your momma has filled your head with, let it go. If you can't do that, lock it away."

She nodded, continuing to chew her lip before turning towards him. This time, she didn't drop her gaze.

"Okay," she said and nodded again. "It's okay."

"Good. Let's keep it that way."

Zach got the pick-up rolling and headed after the cruiser, which was disappearing around a bend.

The marina wasn't large, but exclusive.

"Wow-wee," said Zach, parking as close to the landing stages as he could. "Must be millions and millions of dollars' worth of boats here."

There were at least three other moored cruisers which appeared they might withstand an Atlantic crossing, but Zach agreed with the choice the other people had made. The white cruiser coming in to dock was the biggest, the most modern and looked robust enough to cross a hundred oceans.

Zach killed the engine and opened the door to get out.

He stopped when he felt Amy's hand on his arm.

"What about guns?" she asked. "We don't know anything about these folks."

Zach patted his jacket. "Got my Beretta. Don't want to frighten them by carrying openly. Best way to start a gunfight—carry guns."

He got out and closed the truck door. He walked to the front and leaned against the hood. Amy got out and started forward.

"Wait," said Zach. "Let them tie up. Don't want to make 'em jittery."

Amy shrugged and stepped to his side.

Three people appeared on the lower deck of the cruiser: two women and a man. The man—the youthful black male who had peered at them earlier—leapt lightly to the landing stage. He held a rope that he wound around a cleat attached to the dock, before walking smartly along the stage to help the younger of the two women down. She, too, clutched a rope that she wrapped around a cleat. With a reverse engine thrust and a churn of water, the cruiser settled against the mooring, bumping gently on the floats dangling from its sides. The young couple pulled the ropes tight and tied them off.

"Neatly done," murmured Zach.

The second woman remained on deck. She gazed at Zach and

Amy, her face expressionless. Grey-haired, bespectacled, maybe in her sixties. Cradled beneath one arm, she held a rifle. The boat's engines were cut and an older man joined the woman on deck; the same man who had gestured to them when they first noticed the cruiser. He, too, carried a rifle.

The older couple watched Zach and Amy while the younger couple began to walk towards them.

"Smart," muttered Zach. "Clear line of sight. The youngsters will likely stop short so we can't jump 'em."

Sure enough, the couple stopped walking ten yards away from the pick-up. The man took two further paces forward.

In his early twenties, well turned out, hair closely cropped. He must be keeping it trimmed despite all that had happened. He had a certain bearing, one that Zach recognised.

"Howdy, son," said Zach. "I'm Zach Trent. This here is Amy Kerrigan."

The young man nodded. "Sir, ma'am. Before we go any further, please tell me if you are carrying any weapons."

"Amy's clean." Zach pointed to the breast of his zipped-up jacket. "I have a pistol in my inside pocket. I ain't reckoning on having any reason to take it out." He patted the hood of the truck. "Got some military hardware inside. A few M16 assault rifles and a couple of pump-action shotguns. And my hunting rifle."

Zach didn't miss the slight widening of the man's eyes at the mention of the assault rifles.

"You military, son?"

"Yes, sir. I was in my third year at West Point when everyone started dying."

"Gonna tell us your name?"

"Franklin Jones, though Frank will do." He pointed over his shoulder with a thumb. "That's Sarah."

"Pleased to make your acquaintance, Frank." Zach nodded at the young woman. "Sarah."

"Pleased to meet you," said Amy and stepped forward, her right hand outstretched.

Frank's eyes widened. On the boat, the older woman brought the rifle up and pointed it in their direction.

"Ma'am, please step back," said Frank, holding his hands out in a warding-off gesture.

Zach remained slouched against the hood of the pick-up. "Come back to me, Amy," he said softly.

Amy returned to Zach's side, a perplexed frown creasing her brow. "Sorry," she mumbled. "Only trying to be friendly."

"No, ma'am," said Frank. "I'm the one who should apologise." He glanced back at the cruiser and moved his hands up and down. The grey-haired women slowly lowered the rifle. "These are strange times. Not many of us left and we're suspicious as heck of each other."

"Nothing wrong with being careful," said Zach. "We intend you no harm."

"What *do* you want?" asked the woman, Sarah. She had been watching them with narrow eyes.

"If you'll pardon the expression," said Zach, "I'll shoot from the hip. We'd like to hitch a ride with you folks. To Britain."

"What makes you think that's where we're headed?" asked Frank.

"I'm guessing you heard the same voice we did."

Sarah gasped. "*You* heard the voice too?"

"Look," said Zach, spreading his hands, "why don't we all sit down and get to know each other a little? Like people used to do."

"Sir," said Frank, "I'd feel easier about taking you to meet Elliott and Nan if you weren't carrying that pistol."

Zach looked at the young man for a long moment. Frank returned the gaze steadily. If there was deception in his mind, he hid it well.

"Okay," said Zach.

"Wait!" Amy laid a hand on his arm. She reduced her voice to a rough whisper. "We gonna walk down there unarmed with them toting rifles?"

"If they're fixin' on shooting us, they could have done it by now."

Amy's bottom lip tucked itself between her teeth. She sucked on it, staring at him with wide eyes, then glanced back to the waiting couples and the cruiser.

"Okay." She let go of Zach's arm.

He turned and walked to the driver's door. Unzipping his jacket, he removed the Beretta and opened the door. Making sure his movements were deliberate and could be seen by Frank, he dropped the weapon onto the bench seat. He closed the door and locked it. Stepping around the vehicle, he locked the passenger door.

"Okay, son, now I'm clean as a whistle. Amy, too."

"What about knives?" asked Sarah.

Zach shook his head, keeping his gaze fixed on Frank. "My hunting knife's in the pick-up. You can frisk me if you want. I'll allow it. Once."

The young man hadn't taken his eyes off Zach the whole time. He shook his head. "Don't think that'll be necessary, sir. Er, Zach, was it?"

"Yep."

"Then, please, Zach, will you and Amy accompany us to the cruiser?"

"Be glad to."

Sarah turned and walked back the way she had come. Frank waited for Zach and Amy to approach. He held out his hand to Amy.

"Pleased to meet you, Amy."

Zach felt a moment's disquiet, but Amy didn't hesitate. She took his hand and shook it.

"Pleased to meet you, Frank."

"Zach." The young man held out his hand. Zach took it. The grip was firm and strong.

They followed Frank along the landing stage.

Simone Furlong strolled on sands beneath jagged cliffs. Further along, where the beach narrowed to a thin strip, perched on top of cliffs overlooking the Atlantic, stood the hotel where they would await the Great Coming.

The drones remaining from the twenty they had brought with them from Amesbury had cleared nearly all the corpses from the hotel. Soon, despite their ranks having diminished somewhat, the drones would complete their task.

They had lost one drone back in the village, where Milandra and Jason Grant remained. Simone had come across the drone, a young male, being torn apart by three starving dogs. It had been too late to save it—its throat had already been torn out—so she stayed to watch. The dogs did not approach her; even in their deranged condition, they retained instincts of self-preservation. She let them eat their fill before probing their frenzied minds and showing them in no uncertain terms what would happen if they continued to make a nuisance of themselves. With bowed heads, tails tucked between legs, the dogs backed away, whining. They had not been bothered by those dogs again.

There had been many corpses in the hotel, almost every room opening to the buzz of flies and odour of stale putrefaction. The hotel's function room, rather pretentiously labelled by the ornate sign attached to the door as 'The Grand Ballroom', had been littered with used glasses, empty champagne bottles and streamers, as though the residents had held an end-of-the-world bash before retiring to the guest rooms to expire in a drunken haze. Simone often wondered what getting drunk was like. She had tried alcohol, but it made her sweat and shake and want to throw up. She really couldn't see the attraction.

Rats had taken up residence in the hotel, grown fat on rotten meat in the kitchens and rotting meat in the bedrooms. Simone rounded them up one by one, marched them down the steps to the beach and watched in fascination while she made them leap into the bonfire. The fatter the rat, the louder the *pop* and, my, how those rats had popped.

Cats had also moved in, grown fat on fat rats. They hissed and spat at any drone that came near. When Simone or Wallace or Lavinia approached, the cats fell silent. Ears pressed flat to skulls, belly fur brushing the ground, they slunk away to shadowed corners from where they peered with wide, dark eyes. Days later, when Simone had finished dealing with the rats and thought to extend the sport to the fat felines, there was not one to be found.

And now she was bored.

Lavinia Cram and George Wallace were up in the hotel, directing the drones in their clearance work. The bus driver, Rodney something-or-other, was off somewhere fishing. Fishing! That was a drone pastime, not worthy of higher beings. Not that it stopped her tucking with gusto into the catch he fried up each evening.

She poked at a pebble with the toe of her sneaker, stooped and picked it up. Hefting it in her right hand, she judged its weight and ballistic qualities.

Two drones worked near the foot of the steps, banking damp seaweed onto a smoking pyre built on dry sand above the high tide line. As the seaweed dried it would burn, but slowly, keeping the fire alive for they still had use for it. Although most of the corpses had been disposed of—they burned easily, little more than skin bags of bone held together by clothes—the drones were also destroying the stinking mattresses and bedding on which the bodies had lain. With windows and doors thrown wide to the elements, it would not be long before all trace of its former occupants would be scoured from the hotel.

The male drone forking seaweed onto the pyre was middle-aged. In the wind whipping off the ocean, wisps of greying hair flapped like ribbons on a desk fan. From her distance of thirty or so yards, Simone could not see the line of spittle running down its chin, but the damp patch on its chest was visible. *Disgusting creature*, she thought. The female was older, moving stiffly on arthritis-ravaged knees, struggling to lift clumps of seaweed from the barrow.

Simone drew back her arm, took careful aim and let fly. The

pebble sailed through the air and struck the female on the back of the head. It dropped to its knees, head slumping forward.

"Whoop!" Simone yelled, jumping with glee. "Strrr-ike, and you're out!" She clapped her hands and laughed.

The male drone continued to stack seaweed on the bonfire, oblivious to what had happened. The female drone hadn't moved from its kneeling position in the sand. Blood ran in rivulets from its bowed head, turning the white hair scarlet. A dark stain was forming on the filthy blouse it wore,

"Hey!" Simone shouted. "No slacking. On your feet."

In the thirty seconds it took her to close the distance over the loose sand, the stain on the back of the drone's blouse had spread considerably.

"Oops," said Simone. "That might have been too good a shot." She probed.

The drone's mind, such as it was, was fading fast. Simone went deeper, curious as to what remained of the individual the drone once had been. Fragments only. A man, resplendent in fresh-faced vitality and morning suit, turning before an altar; the same man, a little older, smiling and holding out a tiny, swaddled form; a young boy lifting up his hands to be hugged, tears running down grubby cheeks. The boy's face began to melt and run like heated wax. The memories were dispersing like wind-tossed smoke as the drone died.

Simone pulled back a level. She needed to work fast if she wanted to tidy up this little mess. There was no problem implanting the impulse. The drone had nothing remaining with which to resist; little enough with which to obey.

Withdrawing completely, she watched the drone jerk to its feet. Blood dripped from the flapping wound on its head. With what must have been the last of its will, the drone tottered forward and began to clamber the embankment of smoking seaweed. Its strength ran out before it could reach the summit. It slumped face-down and lay still.

Simone let out a deep sigh. Entertainment was hard to come

by and all too fleeting these days.

Her thoughts turned to Milandra, and why she and Grant had remained behind in the village. It was obvious the Keeper was up to something, but she had no idea what it could be. Hmm, yes, Milandra was the Keeper, but for how much longer?

It irked Simone that she had never laid eyes on Earth Home. Yet, if she had, she would not now be the Chosen. That title had come to her fortuitously: she happened to be the next female to be born after the Keeper who preceded Milandra had died in some stupid war between the Babylonians and the Kingdom of Judah. (The Keeper before that, the one who had travelled to Earth Haven as one of the original ten thousand, had died even more unnecessarily a millennium earlier after becoming involved in a land dispute on the banks of the Nile; Simone did not know the full story—others' stupidity did not interest her greatly—but understood it to have involved a crocodile.) When she succeeded Milandra, she had no intention of allowing herself to be drawn into any situation which placed her at personal risk of harm. All that knowledge, all that *power*, at their fingertips and they had let it slip away like so much dry sand.

Simone started when the voice barked in her mind: *Simone! Will you quit killing the drones!*

She glanced up in the direction of the hotel. Wallace stood at the cliff's edge, gazing down at her.

Screw you, Raccoon! she sent back. *Why don't you quit your whining? That's the third one this week. We'll have none left at—*

Simone blocked him out. George Wallace had always been odious; since the Beacon had been activated, he had become tedious. It wasn't even fun to josh him about the two black eyes he'd suffered. They had healed completely in less than two days, but the old Wallace would have been good for yuks for months when he rose to the bait every time it was offered. The new Wallace had become withdrawn and introspective. Boring.

The Chosen sighed again and turned back to the pyre. The male drone had partially covered the smouldering corpse of the female with strands of seaweed. It continued to work, paying her not the slightest attention, but its movements were growing laboured as it tired. It surely was too old, too decrepit, to justify its continued existence.

Simone's eyes narrowed.

The roads into England's capital city were largely clear. The two cars made good progress, only slowing to weave around the occasional abandoned vehicle or small knot of wreckage. Some vehicles still contained the remains of their occupants: forlorn, ragged remnants, creamy skulls grinning between leathery scraps of flesh.

Only once did they find their way completely barred. A line of military jeeps and lorries stretched across the road. Broken bodies of civilians and soldiers dotted the tarmac either side of the blockade. Whether it had been set up to keep people in or out of London, it was difficult to tell.

Levente pulled on the handbrake and stepped out of the car. The Pole and Croatian appeared from the leading car. Aletta and the Italian woman stayed put.

The Pole disappeared inside one of the army lorries, while Levente and the Croatian moved from soldier to soldier, picking up rifles, examining them, before letting them fall back to the road. The weapons had been lying there for months, completely open to the elements. Maybe they had started to corrode.

Aletta's father had owned a hunting rifle, which he had shown her how to use during her teen years. During her adult years, she had barely used a gun, but could see some wisdom in acquiring one now.

The Pole reappeared, clutching a rifle. He called to the others. They, too, clambered into the lorry. Soon Levente returned to the car, carrying two rifles and grinning. The rifles looked nothing like Aletta's father's hunting rifle. These were shorter, more compact, meaner-looking, with magazines. The Hungarian also carried a canvas bag. He shook it before placing it on the back seat with the rifles and Aletta heard a clunk of metal on metal.

"Bullets," he said. He pointed an index finger beneath a raised thumb. "Bang!" His grin grew wider.

Aletta returned it, a little half-heartedly. *Boys will be boys.*

They took a detour around the blockade via a series of side streets. Soon they were nearing the city centre and Aletta was catching sight of buildings and landmarks she recognised from movies, although her knowledge of London was not so great as to be able to name them.

Apart from animals and birds, which darted and flapped away at their approach, the streets remained deserted. The first stirrings of disquiet tingled in Aletta's stomach.

"Where are the people?" she wondered aloud.

Levente snorted. "Dead, of course. All dead."

"No. I mean the people like us. Survivors. There must be some."

The Hungarian shrugged.

They drove deeper into the heart of the city and still there was no sign of human life. Aletta's unease intensified.

"This is wrong," she muttered.

Levente glanced at her. He seemed unconcerned, but the sense of things being out of kilter, even in this upside-down world, kept growing inside Aletta. Became a certainty.

The car containing the Pole, Croatian and Italian had pulled a little ahead. It turned a sharp bend to the left and Aletta caught the red flash of its brake lights coming on before it drove out of sight.

"Slow down!" she hissed. She thumped the dashboard with her fist. "Slow down!"

Again Levente glanced at her, this time wearing a puzzled frown. He did not appear to share Aletta's rising sense of panic, but stepped on the brake nonetheless, muttering under his breath in Hungarian. They approached the bend at a crawl and edged forward until the road into which the lead car had disappeared came fully into view.

"Stop!"

She could have saved her breath. Levente had already brought their vehicle to a halt and was peering past her down the street, eyes wide.

The other car, too, had stopped, maybe thirty metres away. A loosely-clustered group of around ten people stood in the road ten metres or so farther on. Behind them, two black four-by-fours or SUVs were parked nose to tail across the road, blocking it.

The new people all bore arms, mainly snub-nosed submachine guns, slung at their sides from shoulder straps. Each of them stared intently at the first car.

Both front doors of the car—it had only two doors—stood open. The Pole climbed out from behind the steering wheel. The Croatian stepped out of the passenger side, holding one of the assault rifles from the blockade a few miles back. But something was wrong. Both men moved unnaturally, jerkily. They stumbled a couple of steps before coming to a swaying stop in front of the car, their backs towards Aletta and Levente. The rifle fell from the Croatian's hand to the road. He made no move to pick it up.

A woman at the front of the group, slim and maybe of Japanese descent, stepped forward. It was difficult to tell from Aletta's vantage point, but she thought the woman was looking past the men into the car.

There was movement at the open passenger door. The Italian woman emerged, holding another of the assault rifles. As she cleared the door and straightened, she brought the barrel of the rifle around towards the group of people.

The Japanese woman raised her submachine gun to chest height and fired a short burst. The Italian dropped the rifle and took half a step back before her knees gave way. She crumpled to the road, twitched once and lay still.

Through a haze of shock, Aletta became aware of two things. Levente had started an unintelligible stream of harsh-sounding monologue; the Japanese woman had noticed their car and was motioning forward others in the group.

"*Paska!*" exclaimed Aletta, forgetting in her panic to speak

English.

The Pole and Croatian remained standing in an unnaturally stiff pose at the front of their car. Aletta's view was partially obstructed by a group of four people, led by the Japanese woman, striding down the road towards them. The group passed the motionless Italian, then the rear of the other car. One of the SUVs was moving, swinging around to face them.

Aletta turned to Levente. Still muttering, he was staring at the prostrate form of the Italian woman.

"Let's go!" she hissed.

Aletta felt something tickle her head. She raised her hand to brush whatever it was away, but realised something odd: the tickling sensation was coming from *inside* her head. Levente must have felt something, too. He flapped at his head as if shooing away a bothersome fly.

"Get us out of here!" Aletta yelled.

The sensation increased. It felt as if a cluster of bristle-legged spiders had found its way inside her skull and scratched to be let out.

No, not spiders. Something worse, something clutching and grasping, sapping her will, threatening to steal her very being. With the last of her mental strength, Aletta screamed.

"Move!"

The Hungarian seemed to snap out of a trance. He shoved the gear stick into reverse and gunned the throttle. The car shot backwards.

An overwhelming compulsion came over Aletta to put the car into neutral and apply the handbrake. She reached out with her right hand and clutched the gearstick. Before she could shift it, her hand was engulfed in a larger hand that held hers tight, preventing it from moving.

"S'okay," hissed Levente. He was concentrating on the view in the rear mirror. "The feeling will pass."

Aletta nodded. The compulsion had already lessened. Her will was returning.

"I'm all right," she said. "Turn us around. We need to get out of here."

Levente released her hand and she removed it from the gearstick. The sensation of something taking over her mind was not one she ever wanted to experience again.

The Hungarian craned around to look behind them and swung the steering wheel hard over. The car bumped the kerb and came to a jerky stop. He moved the gearstick into first and edged forward, turning the wheel hard to the right to complete the turn.

Aletta gave a low moan.

"Hurry! They are coming."

From the street down which their companions had turned appeared one of the black SUVs. The windscreen and side windows were tinted so Aletta couldn't see in, but she would have bet its passengers included a slim, Japanese woman clutching a submachine gun.

Levente straightened the car and pressed the accelerator. The car shot forward in the direction from which they had come.

The scratching sensation began anew inside Aletta's skull. She glanced behind. The black vehicle had a more powerful engine and was gaining.

She moaned again.

Levente must have felt it, too. He floored the throttle, making the engine scream in protest.

The compulsion to disengage the car's gears and yank on the handbrake was trying once more to take over Aletta's will. Terror lent her strength to resist, but she would not be able to do so for long. Despite Levente's best efforts, the SUV was still gaining and the compulsion grew ever stronger.

"There," gasped Aletta.

She pointed ahead to their right. They were approaching a narrow side street, the one from which they had emerged when detouring past the roadblock.

"Too fast," muttered Levente. "But can't slow down."

The closer the chasing vehicle approached, the stronger the

takeover of Aletta's mind became. If they reduced speed to negotiate the right turn, the black car would be on them and she would have to give in. She suspected this time Levente would not try to prevent her; would probably stop the car himself when his will, too, was lost to whatever arcane power was at work.

A plan—half-baked, reeking of desperation—came to her, occupying the last scraps of her mind remaining within her control.

"Slow down when we near the turning," said Aletta.

"What? No!"

"There's no time. You'll have to trust me."

Levente's jaw clenched tightly. He nodded.

"Slow down a little," said Aletta. "Keep off the throttle and press the clutch."

They were on the junction. Levente stepped off the accelerator and touched the brake. He dipped the clutch and the engine shrieked as it over-revved.

"Now!" shouted Aletta. "Turn hard to the right."

Levente obeyed and the car veered towards the side street. But it was travelling too quickly to make the turn. They were on course to slam into the wall of the building that stood on the corner.

Gritting her teeth, Aletta grabbed the handbrake lever and yanked it up, keeping the release button firmly depressed. The back end of the car stopped in mid-spin when the rear wheels clung to the road, rubber burned and some distant part of Aletta prayed the tyres would take this manoeuvre without blowing.

"Straighten!" she gasped. "Throttle!" She released the handbrake.

The car shot forward, Levente manfully struggling to correct its course. It rocked dangerously when he over-corrected and headed straight for the parked vehicles lining one side of the street. He yanked the wheel back the other way. With a squeal of grinding metal, the front wing glanced off a parked Toyota.

"Not too much!" yelled Aletta. "And keep accelerating."

Levente's knuckles grew white while he battled the steering

wheel. With another sickening lurch, the car began to head towards the cars parked on the other side. But the Hungarian was getting its measure and this time corrected without hitting anything.

Aletta jerked her head around in time to see the black car pass the junction. It hadn't slowed.

"Yes!" She thumped her thigh. "They don't know the road is blocked."

With a start, Aletta realised her mind was once more completely her own.

Levente now had the car fully under control. He kept them moving quickly, but not so fast that negotiating these narrow back streets became hazardous.

He favoured Aletta with a huge grin.

"To turn like that. Crazy lady! How you know?"

Aletta grinned back. "When I was young and, yes, perhaps a little crazy, I drove a rally car in the forests of Finland. Not in competition, you understand. For fun."

Levente's grin grew even wider. "For fun! Ha! You should drive, not me."

"You're doing fine." Aletta sobered as an image crowded her mind. "They killed the Italian."

The Hungarian's grin faded. "Yes. The Pole, the Croatian…" He shook his head.

"Who are they?"

"Bad people. Very bad people. We keep away."

Aletta pushed away the vision of the old woman's crumpling body. It was replaced by one not much better: a powerful black car smashing through a roadblock, shoving rusting army lorries aside as it rushed to intercept them. When Levente pulled the car up to the junction down which they'd turned when leaving the main road, her heart felt like it was trying to escape up her throat. She glanced fearfully to her left when the main road came into view and let out her breath in a hot rush. The road was clear.

Levente turned right onto it and picked up speed. The

blockade was a good half-mile behind them.

"Where we go?" he asked.

"Away from London. It is wrong here. Once we have left the city, hmm… We came from the east. Let's go west."

Chapter Five

Joe Lowden felt nearly as good as new. Nearly.

After remembering his own name while lying in an office in Amesbury, much of his memory had remained shrouded in a haze. He suspected much of it still would if it wasn't for that girl, Brianne.

During the long days in Salisbury, waiting to see if the boy would pull through and before Bri underwent her own life-threatening procedure, she had sat down and looked at Joe so intently it reminded him a little of *them*.

"What…" He cleared his throat. When he tried again, his voice sounded less tremulous. "What are you doing?"

"Up there." Bri pointed towards her forehead. The cut in her hairline had dried to a black scab, but the skin around it remained raised and bruised. "They did things to you."

It wasn't a question. Joe waited.

"There's stuff you don't remember," she continued. "You know your name, right? And where you come from?"

"Grimsby."

"Right. What were your parents' names?"

"Er…" Joe wrinkled his nose with the effort of trying to remember. He could see their images—him grimy and dark-eyed, her lip-painted and pie-eyed—but their names remained elusive. He shook his head.

Bri pointed to her forehead again. "They damaged you in there. Zapped you. Like they did to Will. I made him better." She shrugged. "Dunno if I can make you better, but I'd like to try."

"How?"

"Don't resist me."

Before Joe could comprehend what she meant, he felt it. A sensation inside his mind. Not like when *they* had taken control of him in Hillingdon—that had been a sense of violation, a sort of mental rape, which he had been powerless to resist. This was gentler, less invasive, more a feathery tickle than a full-frontal assault, and he understood he could block the intrusion if he wished.

Don't resist me.

Joe stared into the girl's eyes. They had taken on a slightly glazed appearance, like those of a mannequin. When they swam out of focus, his attention shifted to what was happening inside his mind. To what was returning.

As morning mist on the Humber scatters in the rays of summer dawn, the fog overlaying his memories dispersed.

He barely noticed the girl grimace and wipe at the dribble of dark blood that had appeared on her top lip, rise unsteadily to her feet and turn to lurch away.

"Bri," he called, before she reached the door.

She half-turned. Ashen. Blood ran freely from her nose; she clutched at it with smeared fingers.

"Michael and Brenda," said Joe.

"Huh?"

"Michael and Brenda. My parents' names."

Bri smiled. It left her lips almost as soon as it had appeared, but it reignited the youth in her eyes. In that moment, Joe felt more warmth for her, a girl he barely knew, than he had ever felt towards anyone.

Whatever Bri had done to him had not driven the fog away entirely. Tiny pockets remained, small gaps, the odd word he had to reach for if he could recall it at all, or the occasional friend or distant relative whose name he could not conjure from the depths. But all in all his mind was pretty much whole. Healed.

The wide void remaining within himself was not one of absence of memory. More an absence of longing, or *fulfilled* longing. He recognised it for what it was: an insatiable appetite he had fed for many of his teenage years. There were words for what he had been on his way to becoming: crack head, e-tard, psychonaut, speed freak. He did not know how much time had elapsed since he had unwillingly stepped into the curtained cubicle in Hillingdon Hospital, for how long he had been clean, but the *need* for chemical stimulation had not returned with his memories. Yet the void remained and he realised, with a reformed addict's cold certainty, he'd better fill it or sink back into it. And once he was back down, there would be no second reprieve.

He did not have to look far for a substitute. The desire for vengeance might seem to some as irrational as the need to pop pills or snort powder, and with Bri's help Joe had made almost a full recovery from the harm dealt to him by *them*—indeed, a strong case could be made for them having done him a favour in a roundabout way by curing him of his drug habit—but rationality rarely has a part to perform in the sordid cycles of addiction and abstinence. Joe hated *them*, from the sandy-haired Aussie in her tight jumper, who had 'directed' him at the point of a gun to the casualty department of the hospital, to the black-eyed man he'd knocked down at Stonehenge, and every dominating, indifferent bastard he'd encountered in between. He hated them with a passion that equalled or surpassed the old longing. Thus the void was filled.

During the longer days after Bri had been operated on, while both she and the boy recuperated, Joe planned. He spent many daylight hours in a place that would have held little attraction to the old version of him—Salisbury Library. There he learned that everything he would need he was likely to find within a thirty-mile radius of Newport in South Wales where they were next headed. If not, then a fifty- or sixty-mile radius.

When they arrived at the Celtic Manor, he went quietly about recruiting his team. In the nearby once-Roman town of Caerleon, he befriended two recently arrived and gung-ho Americans, and one Albanian with mechanical skills, who spoke excellent English and who didn't seem to care about Joe's tale of mind-controlling aliens so long as he would get to fight someone.

Suitable transport was easily located in the town and restored to working order by the Albanian.

Joe waited until he knew the proposed day of the meeting—he

wanted to be back in time for that—and for the funeral of the young French girl to take place. He guessed people's minds would then be too preoccupied with their own sense of mortality to notice he had gone.

If anyone did remark on his absence, or that of the Americans or Albanian, during the few days leading up to the meeting, Joe never learned of it. Not that it would have mattered. The meeting itself was to overshadow all else that took place in those first weeks of April.

Amy followed Zach along the landing stage to the white boat. She hung back a little, tired of feeling afraid, unsure how to feel anything else.

The young woman, Sarah, reached the boat and climbed lithely up the plastic ladder which had been lowered over the side. Sarah was young and slim and sexy. Just looking at her snug jeans reminded Amy how overweight and frumpy she was.

And prejudiced. Her momma had told her things about the blacks who lived in the apartment above theirs in Portland. Things that Amy had believed without question and that skewed her views of all people with skin darker than hers. Savage; subhuman; as likely to ravage Amy as look at her; liable to take her purse along with her purity.

Momma had spewed her bile into the impressionable mind of a naïve girl who already believed, due to the actions of one man, that all men were violent and perverted. 'Selfish, slap-happy dimwits with brains in their dicks,' was a typical Ann-Marie Kerrigan description of the male species.

The black man, Frank, also climbed the ladder, Zach not far behind. Amy took a deep breath. Laboriously, ungainly, making the plastic creak ominously, she climbed up after Zach. At the top, she perched precariously while she tried to swing her leg over the rail.

It wasn't Zach who turned back to help her. Amy felt her upper arm taken in a firm grasp. Her leading leg completed its forward swing and her other followed in a rush. She stumbled against her helper and felt two strong arms wrap her in an embrace that prevented her falling headlong onto her face.

"Thank you," she muttered and stared into the clear eyes of Frank.

He loosened the tight embrace. When she had steadied herself, he let her go.

"You're welcome."

Amy felt the blush rise from her neck. When she realised that Zach and Sarah had turned to watch her impromptu display of ineptitude, the warmth spreading into her cheeks became a blaze. Zach wore an expression of mild amusement. Sarah's lips pursed into a look of disapproval. Amy understood, with a flash of feminine intuition, that Sarah was sweet on Frank.

Surely, she thought while she dropped her gaze in confusion, this sexy girl would not view Amy as competition. And how could she, Amy, even consider the notion, what with her poisoned upbringing? Not for the first time since waking to find her dead, Amy questioned her mother's philosophies, something she would not have dared to do when her mother was alive. Momma had been possessed of a way of peering into her daughter's soul, to the dark secret thoughts, and seeing them for the filth they were. Or, at least, the filth Ann-Marie Kerrigan made them appear with her lashing tongue and tainted passions.

When she felt her high colour had faded enough not to dazzle, Amy lifted her head. Towards the back of the boat, the deck widened into a seating area. Zach was sitting on a comfortable-looking chair alongside the older couple. The rifles were no longer in evidence. Frank sat to one side; Sarah stood a little behind him, leaning against the deck rail.

Amy stepped hesitantly forward. The grey-haired woman looked up at her approach and smiled. It was a pleasant smile, the first Amy had seen in months, and she found herself returning it.

"Hello," said the woman. "My name is Nancy. But call me Nan. Everyone does. Please, won't you take a seat?"

Resisting the urge to curtsey, Amy sat in the empty chair next to Zach.

The older man also smiled at her. What hair remained on the sides of his head was white and fuzzy, like unteased wool, and his face was as lined as crumpled paper. But his eyes were sharp behind spectacle lenses.

"Hi," he said. "I'm Elliott."

Amy nodded. She felt tongue-tied, overawed by this new company. Even had her mother not kept her closeted from other folk, to the point of insisting Amy spent work breaks by her side, the sort of people she might have been allowed to interact with would not have been like these. Nan and Elliott, Frank and Sarah, in their confident, diffident manners, their speech and their bearing, looked cultured and assured, a social world away from her and Zach.

Her momma had kept Amy from other folk, so she said, to protect her innocence. Since spending time in Zach's company, she had already concluded her mother's views on men were jaundiced, corrupted by the wastrel who had been Amy's father. Amy's own faint recollection of him confirmed that, in this at least, Momma had been correct. But that did not mean all men were like him. She suspected Zach was far from a perfect sample of modern-day manhood, but even he gave lie to her mother's generalisations.

As for black people, Amy had begun to guess at the truth before the Millennium Bug put paid to black, white and every colour in between. Once or twice, when Momma allowed her to descend alone the six flights of stairs from their apartment to put out the trash, Amy had passed the young black man who lived above them. Far from leering at her or trying to grab her butt or wristwatch, the youth stepped aside to allow her to pass and had even offered to help. Amy glanced away and shook her head while she hurried past, but doubt had set in.

Now Frank was extending that doubt; changing it to certainty. Amy stole glances at him when she thought Sarah wasn't looking. Everything about him added weight to the mounting case against Ann-Marie Kerrigan being a domineering, lying bigot. If slow to outright merriment—but who wasn't in this drab new world?—Frank was quick to smile. He was often quiet and thoughtful, listening to others speak, not rushing to interrupt, yet expressing himself eloquently and efficiently when moved to join in.

Amy paid scant attention to the conversation, happy to let Zach do the talking for them both. When she had first sat down, she sensed a degree of tension. Zach seemed wary—after all, these people had been pointing guns at them only minutes before—but every time she broke off her surreptitious observation of Frank, the talk appeared to be less stilted, more relaxed.

"You don't say much."

Amy looked up. Sarah had stepped around Frank to stand in front of her. The others continued their conversation; Zach was saying something about how he had taught himself basic mechanics.

"Um, I guess not," Amy said.

Sarah nodded towards Zach and lowered her voice. "You with him?"

"We been travelling together since Portland."

Sarah rolled her eyes. "Are you *with* him?"

"You mean, like *sleeping* with him?" Amy shook her head. "Uh-huh."

"Well, see him?" Sarah put out her hand and rested it on Frank's shoulder. "I am *with* him." She brought back her hand and rubbed at her stomach, bringing into relief the bump previously concealed by her sweater. "I'm carrying his child." She dropped her voice to little more than a whisper. "So, missy, keep those cow eyes off him." She held Amy's gaze for a moment, before turning away.

Amy looked down at her feet, cheeks burning once more. It was only the movement of people standing that made her glance up.

Zach, Frank and the older man were on their feet.

"The engine room's this way," said Elliott. Amy would not forget that name; *E.T.* was one of her favourite movies. "Sarah, you're the closest thing we have to a mechanic. You'd better come, too."

"Sure," said Sarah and followed the men through a door into the body of the cruiser.

The grey-haired lady—Nan—looked at Amy and patted the seat vacated by Zach.

"Come, my dear," she said. "Sit by me and let's get to know each other."

Amy moved seats, feeling like the country bumpkin smelling of cow manure who's stumbled into the mayor's ball. To hide her unease, she said the first thing that came into her head.

"Sarah's a mechanic?"

"Not really. Her father was an auto mechanic and she picked up a lot of useful knowledge. But only of car engines. She hasn't been able to identify what's wrong with *The Lady*'s engine."

"*The Lady*?"

"You are sitting on the deck of *The Lady Jane*. She's a fine launch. Whoever owned her must have been extremely wealthy."

Amy shrugged. "Don't know nothing 'bout boats."

Nan gave a light laugh. "Nor me. But I do know a little about the cost of quality. My Larry was a self-made millionaire, but we could never have afforded anything like this. Not even if we'd sold the Ranch."

Amy gasped. "You had a ranch?"

"Not really a ranch. Leastways, not a working one. A few miles out of Pittsburgh. Far enough away to be in the country, but near enough to take advantage of city life if ever Larry or I felt the call. 'The Call of the Riled' was how he referred to it, on account of city folk always coming across as being worked up over something." The woman's eyes grew misty. "I was a housewife, or that's what it would have said on my resume, if I'd ever needed one. Don't let that job title fool you. I can bake apple pie that will make angels sing on your tongue, but the rifle I had pointed at you earlier… Larry and I used to hunt together. It never bothered him that I bagged more deer. I could have shot you through either eye or taken off your nose if you'd turned sideways."

"Um…"

Nan leaned forward and patted the back of Amy's hand companionably. "Don't look so worried, dear. You were in no real danger so long as you didn't act threateningly. There was a moment when you stepped toward Frank I almost…" She chuckled. "Elliott said to me, 'She only wants to shake hands, Nan. Don't shoot her.' So I didn't. And I'm glad I didn't. I think we're going to be good friends."

Amy wasn't sure what to say. She had never had a friend before, not unless she counted Zach, the crusty old coot. She wasn't entirely certain she wanted her first friend to look like a kindly grandmother who talked about shooting people with a strange glint behind her old lady spectacles.

"Er, do you think we can join you?" she asked.

"Well, we sure need another two people to share the driving, though I think they call it piloting, and to keep a watch on the instruments. Radar, that sort of thing, so we don't go ploughing into a whale or iceberg. Elliott reckons the navigational and warning equipment will still work out at sea. Most probably. And we sure as heck need someone who knows a thing or two about engines. We've been chugging up and down the shore, not only to get us all used to steering *The Lady*, but to attract attention of anyone in the vicinity. Now if your companion can smoothe out the clink in the engine, I'd say your passage is secure. We daren't set off to cross an entire ocean with doubt about the engine. It's a long way to England."

"Ain't never been further than Jersey before."

"Where you from, Amy? I'm judging New England from your accent."

"Portland in Maine. Lived there with Momma. She's dead."

"So's my Larry." The old woman's eyes misted again. "We had three children. Every Christmas they'd come home to the Ranch, no matter how far away they'd moved. Having children of their own didn't stop the tradition. Five grandchildren, from a toddler still in diapers to a twelve-year-old tomboy, who'd have grown up to be belle of the ball. They brought the virus with them." A single tear rolled down her cheek. "Two of them were coughing and sniffling, complaining about how bright the light was. Within thirty-six hours, we had all retired to our beds with the drapes tightly closed. I came round from the fever in a house filled with wrapped presents and festive food waiting to be cooked. I thought from the smell the food had started to spoil. The power went within a day or two, but it was still on when I woke up." She grew very still. "It wasn't the food that had started to rot. It was my family." The tear reached her jowls and hung suspended for a moment like a chip of pure ice.

Amy watched it fall, more unsure than ever what to say. She was saved from further discomfort by the vibration of the boat's engine, sounding exactly like it had earlier to her ears.

"Oh," said Nan. She had removed her spectacles to wipe at her eyes. Now she replaced them and peered at Amy. "Maybe Zach could fix the problem."

Moments later he appeared, wiping his hands on an oily rag, followed closely by a smiling Elliott.

Zach looked at Amy.

"We're going to Britain," he said.

"Great," she replied, and found she meant it.

The main hotel building overlooked the motorway. Ceri and Bri raided the hotel's shops for nail varnish and lipstick. Together they painted a huge multi-hued arrow on a bedsheet. Colleen helped them attach the sheet to a motorway sign; anyone approaching by vehicle could not miss it.

Ceri lay in bed thinking about the last six weeks or so since they had left Salisbury and driven here. It was she who suggested they try the Celtic Manor. If she had to die, she wanted to be at home in South Wales when it happened.

In the other bed occupying the room, Tom snored softly. Dusty, curled up at his feet, raised his head and looked at her. His tail wagged once before he laid his head back down and closed his eyes. Ever since the hotel outside Wick, where they had discovered the Watson family rotting in their beds, Ceri had shared a bedroom with Tom and Dusty. Not being alone in the dark hours helped keep the fear at bay and she generally slept soundly these days, despite the approaching menace. During the two weeks that Tom and Dusty had gone off with Peter on what Ceri privately considered to be a fools' errand, she had slept alone and awoken every night, bathed in sweat, throat dry and hoarse as if she had screamed herself awake.

She would have liked Bri and Will to sleep in an adjoining room—she didn't want them sneaking away in the middle of the night again—but it made more sense for Howard to be nearest them. Not that the youngsters were still in mortal danger from their injuries, but it didn't hurt to be careful. Will and Bri slept in a double bed in the main bedroom of a family suite, Howard and Colleen in twin beds in the room leading off it.

When they broke into the hotel, they were met by staleness and mustiness, but no smell of decaying bodies. Beds were made up, minibars and tea-making facilities fully stocked, clean towels hung on handrails. Not a corpse to be seen. The spa pool had been drained, and beer pumps and coolers disconnected, but otherwise the hotel looked ready to resume business.

Fresh and frozen produce in the kitchens had, of course, spoiled, but a hotel this size stocks a great deal of canned, jarred and dried products. They had eaten like kings at first, when the only guests were nine people and one dog. When newcomers began to arrive and their stocks began to dwindle, Peter organised what he called 'foraging parties' to supermarkets and town centres to bring back more supplies. There was enough food lying about to last them well into the following year, even with their swelling numbers. Dying before summer of starvation was not a danger they faced. Living beyond the summer seemed a little more problematic.

Before people started to arrive from the continent, Peter and

Tom had gone off in the Range Rover, Dusty in the back seat, and travelled the coastline, calling at every major port to put up handmade warnings to steer clear of London. Two weeks it had taken them of hard driving.

"Travelling the coast of Britain was always something I'd planned to do," said Tom on their return. "Lisa—she was my girlfriend—liked the idea. We reckoned we could have done it in a leisurely six weeks over a school summer holiday." He grimaced. "Never imagined I'd do it in a fortnight, not once stopping to take in the scenery. And being extra cautious in the south-east not to attract attention from alien invaders." He snorted. "It's impossible to say that without it sounding ridiculous."

"It would have taken us longer, but we decided not to do Devon and Cornwall," added Peter. "We placed notices prominently on all the major roads leading from those counties." He glanced at Tom. "Not to be argumentative, but technically you humans are as much 'alien invaders' as we are."

Tom opened his mouth to retort, but Ceri was in no mood for a fight. She laughed and grabbed Tom's arm.

"He's right and you know it. I'm glad the three of you are back. Let's have a drink to celebrate."

Ceri had spent the two weeks of their absence getting to know the new members of the party. She liked them all.

Howard possessed a gentle disposition, and had earned her eternal gratitude by saving the lives of both Bri and Will. He had been helped in no small part by Diane Heidler, which softened Ceri's heart towards her. Ceri couldn't claim in all honesty to have begun liking the woman, whom she still found to be aloof and distant, but she now accepted her as a valued member of their small group.

The Irish girl, Colleen, had a certain sweetness about her; an attractive sweetness, not the cloying kind. She also possessed a degree of frailty, which she hid behind a haze of alcohol. Once or twice, when Colleen thought no eyes watched her, Ceri had seen a haunted expression pass over her features, the look of a young girl, lost and alone.

'The eternal night' is how Colleen referred to their existence these past few months. Ceri had spent an evening in the bar with her, matching Colleen vodka for whiskey until they had both become barely capable of ascending the stairs to bed.

"That's what it's felt like to me," said the Irish girl, not yet slurring her words. "The eternal night. Ever since I woke up to find Sinead rotting in bed beside me, I feel as if I've been living through one endless period of darkness."

"*Ar Hyd y Nos,*" murmured Ceri.

"Sorry?"

"It's a Welsh hymn my dad's choir used to sing. It means 'All Through the Night'."

"All through the night. I like it. All through the night, the endless, eternal night. Would you sing the hymn for me?"

Softly, falteringly, with tears running down her cheeks, Ceri did.

Then there was Joe, with his northern accent and reticence about his past. Apart from telling them he was from Grimsby, a single child who lost both parents to the Millennium Bug, he spoke very little about what he had done before the world went crazy. He talked freely about what had happened to him upon arriving at Hillingdon Hospital. Ceri nodded while he related the part when he tried to run and was stopped in his tracks by nothing more than an intense stare from a group of people.

"The same thing happened to me in Stonehenge," she said. "They took control of my body. My mind was still my own, but I couldn't move."

"They made me move," said Joe. "Like a puppet." His eyes, grey and grim, held no humour. "They marched me behind a curtain and made me lie down on a piss-covered bed. They attached things to my forehead… er, what d'you call them?"

"Electrodes?"

"Aye. That's when I screamed like a six-year-old girl. Probably pissed myself, too. Don't remember much after that. Until the town outside Stonehenge."

Joe spoke about his senses returning a little at a time, about being bussed to the ancient monument and the feeling something bad was about to happen.

"I hung back," he said. "I didn't know what they were going to do to us, but no way did I want to be near the front of the queue." He sighed. "Just as well for me. They slit the poor bastards' throats then set them on fire."

While he talked, Joe fiddled with his hands, clasping and unclasping his fingers, cracking his knuckles, making intricate finger shapes. Occasionally, he would stand and pace to and fro as though he couldn't bear to sit still for long. He reminded Ceri of herself the last time she had tried to give up smoking.

"When *they*—" he almost spat the word "—began to come out of the stone circle, they made the few of us who remained return to the buses. I slipped away when no one was looking. At least, I thought no one was looking, but I'm not too sure. The woman in charge, a fat, black woman—Sandra… no, that's not right. Milandra! I think she saw me, but she didn't tell anyone." He frowned. "That's odd. Wonder why she let me escape."

"It seems Milandra has some sympathy for humans," said Ceri. "She helped Peter and Diane send out a message to Europe and America. Hopefully, people will start arriving from there soon. And someone else helped; one of her Deputies, I think Peter calls them."

"Pardon me for not feeling grateful. I don't trust them further than I can throw them."

"What did you do after you'd slipped away?"

"Nothing much. Hung about in the dark listening to the shooting. I was dying to get my hands on a gun. I'd show the fuckers. A dog ran past me; turned out it was Dusty. Not long after, a woman came out of the circle, crawling backwards on her arse. One of *them*. I stepped forward, but she had already stumbled away towards the buses. A good-looking lass, that one."

Ceri had not, at the time, paid the woman he was talking about much attention. Her focus had been elsewhere. "She was with a man," she said. "He's the one who shot Will."

"I saw him," said Joe. "He came out not long after the woman. His cheek was swelling and bruised."

"Tom whacked him with the butt of his shotgun."

"Good for Tom. I gave him a bruise the other side. He fell down. I wanted him to fight back. I wanted to hit him again and again. But he scrambled away, not even looking at me. It wasn't long before Peter appeared. Another one of *them*, but he said he was on our side. I was going to thump him anyway, but he ran into the circle. Then another one came from the darkness—Diane. I thought about thumping her, but I was still not quite right in the head and she's a woman. If I learned anything when I was a kid, it's not to hit women. I didn't want to end up like *him*, bitter and twisted and stinking of fish."

Ceri did not know to whom Joe was referring, but didn't want to interrupt.

"Mind," he continued, "Diane's not exactly a woman, is she? Still, I'm glad I didn't hit her. She helped save the young 'uns."

Ceri did not point out that Joe was himself only a year or two older than Bri and probably also qualified as a 'young 'un'.

"Diane led me into the circle and, well, the rest you know." Joe shrugged. "So what happens now? We can't sit around here waiting to die."

"We wait for others to arrive from Europe and, with luck, America. Then we decide."

"What's to decide? There's only one thing I want to do. Go after *them*. Take the fuckers down."

Ceri could see the fervour in Joe's eyes. There would be no dissuading this one. Nonetheless, she made the effort. "We have to make them see we are worthy of not being completely eliminated as a species. That we have a lot to offer and are capable of living alongside them in peace and harmony. Going to war against them might not be the best way to demonstrate that."

Joe's eyes opened wide. "You have got to be shitting me. Live alongside them? Peace and fucking harmony after what they've done? Bollocks to that! I don't think we should stop until every last one of them is dead."

"Or we are," Ceri said quietly.

"From what I hear, that's going to happen anyway."

"Maybe. Maybe not. When you said 'every last one of them', I hope you weren't including Peter and Diane?"

Joe looked at her long and hard, but didn't reply.

Dusty raised his head again and uttered a soft whine, interrupting Ceri's memories.

"It's okay," she whispered. "Go back to sleep."

She turned towards the window. Daylight peeked around the edge of the curtains. She might as well get up.

A tension pervaded the hotel. Ceri had sensed it all about her in the bar the previous afternoon. The more people that poured into South Wales, the greater the tension grew, like a vast beast feeding on their fears. They had no way of keeping accurate records, but Tom reckoned more than three thousand people had so far made it to the Celtic Manor. Most of them now occupied the neighbouring towns and villages.

He had agreed with her there was no point in further delaying the meeting. Without something to aim for, the tension would cause someone to snap. A couple of scuffles had already broken out. People needed to be told what had happened and why they had been called to Britain.

Today they would hand-print some simple notices and pin them to lamp-posts and shop doorways in those nearby settlements. The meeting was scheduled for the day after tomorrow.

It was time for the remnants of humanity to make a call.

Chapter Six

Spring sunshine bathed Will when he stepped out of the shade of the portico outside the hotel entrance and turned up a steep hill. His strength was gradually returning, but he was panting with exertion by the time he made it to the top.

To his right lay the fifteenth green, beneath which they had buried the poor French girl. It was during the funeral that Will had glanced in this direction and caught a glimpse of something that piqued his interest. He was fed up of sitting around the hotel or lying in bed trying to get comfortable. While eating breakfast of muesli soaked in apple juice—Ceri insisted he eat the vile stuff to help rebuild his strength—he'd determined that this morning he would do a little exploring.

His objective lay before him: a fenced-off area with miniature bridges, windmills and other structures guaranteed to attract the attention of a ten-year-old. He stood for a moment to catch his breath.

When Will was five, a baby tooth became infected, making his cheek swell like a hamster's and throb like a banged thumb. The ache in his shoulder was worse than that abscess. With the aid of an extraction and a course of antibiotics, the abscess had disappeared in a few days. The shoulder pain had been present, in varying degrees of intensity, for weeks. The pain was bad enough; the itching was worse. Will longed to tear off the bandages and gouge beneath the skin where, in the torn flesh between chest and shoulderblade, the itching was at its most unbearable.

He had left the breakfast table before Howard and Colleen appeared with his morning dose of painkillers. To try to forget the urge to scratch, he reminded himself why he had the pain and what he would be missing if it didn't exist. More accurately, *who* he would be missing.

If he hadn't shoved Bri out of the way, she would have been shot. He understood he had been lucky on many levels. The bullet could have hit him in the heart or in the lungs or in a nartery (Will didn't know what a nartery was, but it sounded nasty). It could have been the type of bullet that broke up inside him. It could have been a bullet that lodged in his shoulder, not passed conveniently through. He could have lost too much blood or gone into shock.

He understood he might have died; that he had already endured a whole heap—a shitload, his mum would have said—of pain and that he had a lot more to look forward to; that he would probably never regain full use of his left arm. Yet he would not, if offered, relieve himself of any of these burdens if it meant Bri would have to bear them in his place. She had saved him from the dogs. She had lifted the fog from his mind that made him forget who he was. She had saved him from the nasty spacemen when they tried to make him obey their will. She had protected him from the rats while they made their way around London.

Will would be eleven in August. He also understood from all he'd overheard from the grown-ups it was unlikely he'd make it to his birthday. Neither would Bri or Tom or Ceri; he was less certain about Peter and Diane, but he didn't think Dusty was under threat. More spacemen were on the way, their destination marked out by the bacon-thingy they'd activated in the ring of stones. Will could still close his eyes and see blood-stained stones, slumped bodies and the flicker of flames licking over them; he could still smell the stomach-churning sweetness of the smoke filling the circle. But if he'd experienced nightmares about what had taken place at Stonehenge, he experienced them no longer; they were lost in the drug-swirled delirium into which he'd sunk while his body teetered on the verge of giving up. If he ever worried about what might happen when the rest of the spacemen arrived, how they would kill him and his friends, it was only in some abstract, shadowy way upon which he found it impossible and unnecessary to focus.

Such are the minds of ten-year-olds. Will was far more excited at seeing a spaceship than the prospect of what its arrival might herald.

Now that curiosity returned to the fore. His breath regained, he went to see what lay behind the fence.

For the next twenty minutes, he forgot the nagging pain in his shoulder while he followed the path around the crazy golf course. How he yearned to be able to take hold of a golf club and hit a ball up the ramp to clear the stream. His gaze strayed to the wooden hut, which would contain the putters and balls, but with a stab of adult clarity he knew that to swipe at a ball using only his right hand would lead to the temptation to wriggle his left arm free of the sling which kept it tucked tightly to his chest, and that in so doing he could set back his shoulder's recovery by months. Instead, he contented himself with tracing the course with his feet, picturing hitting shots over the stone bridge or into the dark mouth of the tunnel.

So loud was the imaginary crowd of onlookers, which cheered wildly his every masterful stroke as if he played for the deciding point of the Ryder Cup itself, he did not notice the other's approach. The first Will became aware of the spectator was when he passed through a man-shaped shadow that hadn't been there earlier.

Will raised his head sharply, drawing a deep, hissing breath when the action jarred his wound.

A large man in a dark leather jacket stood leaning against the fence. From Will's perspective, he looked a giant. Will wasn't concerned now his initial fright had dissipated. New people had been arriving at the Celtic Manor for weeks.

"Sorry if I gave you a scare," said the man. His voice was soft, not deep like a giant's should be, and he had a strange accent. He stood with his back to the sun, his features masked in shadow. "Which player were you pretending to be?"

Will named his favourite player, an Irishman.

"Ah. One of the finest players ever to come out of the north. I caddied for him once. Before he became famous, you know."

"Oh, wow," breathed Will. "Are you from Ireland?"

"Born and bred. Not spent much time there in the last ten

years, mind. Too busy travelling the world. With my work, you understand."

"What did you do?"

"Ah, if I told you I'd have to kill you." The man gave a soft laugh. A light chill touched Will's neck, though the air remained still and warm. "Top secret work, you see. Government business." The man raised a hand to his face. Will couldn't make it out clearly due to the back-glare of the sun, but he thought the man was tapping the side of his nose.

Before Will could ask the hundred and one questions about spies and James Bond that sprang to mind, the man stiffened when a voice, with a similar accent to his own, called from the direction of the hotel.

"Will? *Will?* Where are you? It's time for your meds."

"I'm up here, Colleen."

The man remained leaning against the fence. Perhaps Will only imagined he crouched a little as though trying to make himself look smaller.

Colleen appeared over the brow of the hill and came to a stop when she saw Will wasn't alone.

"Will? Who's that you're with?"

Will shrugged. The man hadn't told him his name.

The giant straightened and slowly turned towards Colleen. She gasped and her eyes widened. Her hand came up to clutch at the neck of her blouse as if she had suddenly grown cold. Will looked from one to the other, bemused by the charged atmosphere. Then the man spoke.

"Hello, my beaut."

The sun had risen, tinting the sea the shades of an old photograph. Jason Grant was waiting for Milandra on the stone bench overlooking the ocean.

She sat next to him and wrapped her arms about herself against the fresh morning breeze.

"That was quick," said Grant.

"I've found the stash of memories I was seeking. I wanted to share the most recent with you so you can mull them over."

"While you return…?"

Milandra nodded. "There are maybe another five or six in this hidden-away section to view. I think I'll get the full lowdown once I'm done. Maybe another few days."

"I'll bring more food to the staging point next door."

"Thank you. I'll need it." She sighed. "Though once again this sunlight is doing more good than all the best cuisine in the land could do, let alone canned meat and fruit."

Grant chuckled. "Canned cuisine ain't quite the same."

"Especially canned strawberries. Why would anyone want to can a strawberry?" She pulled a face of disgust. Then grew serious. "About those memories. I know whose they are."

Grant turned to look sharply at her, all signs of laughter gone. "You do?"

"Yep. I'll come to that in a minute. In the first memory, I was in some sort of flying craft. Not exactly an airplane, or a helicopter, yet not a million miles away from either. Perhaps some sort of combination. Doesn't really matter. What's more important is where we were. And when."

Grant's expression changed to frank curiosity.

"It was Earth Home, but not like we've ever seen it. I believe the memory was of an event that took place within a century or two of the ancients departing and we making the planet our home. When we lived on the surface, not burrowing beneath it like moles. It was covered in dense vegetation. Such vibrant colours, Jason. Trees as tall as the Empire State Building. Flowers the size of cars. And the fragrances…

"There were flying creatures. Huge, like Lear jets, with golden feathers of an eagle, the red crest of a rooster and beaks like the bucket of a digger. They soared above the jungle, scooping insects and smaller birds out of the air. I think they were *essurgal*."

"*Essurgal*," Grant murmured. "I thought they were the stuff of legend."

"They existed. Large as life and twice as ugly. The person whose memory I was reliving wasn't alone. Ten, maybe twelve, travelling companions. Grim-faced, on serious business. The flying craft came in to land in a clearing near a domed building. We went in, all on one side of a vast table. Other people lined the opposite side. I think they were on the opposite side in more than one sense, judging from what each side said to the other and how they said it."

"What language was it?"

"I'm fairly sure they were speaking Old Tongue."

"Huh. You mean like we spoke on Earth Home?"

"We spoke a modern version. Theirs was archaic. It's the first time I've heard it, but I could understand the sense of it even when I couldn't grasp the detail."

"Wouldn't you be able to understand the language if it's spoken by the person whose memory it was?"

Milandra shook her head. "I don't *become* her. It's different from when we probe a living subject. Then, if we go deep enough, we can share the subject's emotions and draw on their knowledge. With stored memories, it's more like viewing a movie track. I get a sense of what they were feeling and can smell what they smelled, but I don't get to share their deeper knowledge."

"Ah, okay. Wondered if it might be different for the Keeper." He shrugged. "What were they talking about?"

"It was heated and grew nasty. Accusations were being thrown by both sides. I think the population of Earth Home had separated into two distinct camps. I was part of a delegation from the visiting camp."

"Like a trade delegation?"

"More like a negotiating party."

"What were they negotiating?"

"War."

Grant's eyes filled with unspoken questions.

"That's about all I know so far, Jason. There is more to learn and I shall learn it during the course of the next few days."

"You said you know whose memories you've been viewing?"

Milandra nodded. "She was dressing in front of a full-length mirror. An imposing woman. Tall, slim, but with an air of easy grace. Long, dark hair. Oval eyes, brown as chestnuts, but filled with sorrow. She looked like an Indian princess. A warrior princess. She clad herself in armour the colour of burnished copper. Every movement dripped with sadness and reluctance, as if she was resigned to going through with something she regretted to the depth of her being."

"And you know who she was?"

"I have an inkling."

He waited.

Milandra hesitated. It was more than an inkling. A conviction.

"It's Sivatra."

Grant gasped. "Sivatra? The first Keeper?" He let out his breath in a low whistle.

"I'm almost certain of it."

"But…" Grant frowned. "What does it mean? And why did she hide these memories away like she never wanted them to be seen?"

Milandra slowly shook her head. "Of that I am less certain. But I'll continue to look. Something tells me…"

"What?"

It was Milandra's turn to frown. "Not sure. But I think that it's important I find what I'm seeking quickly. Before the rest of our people arrive." She stood and brushed herself down. "I still don't know what it is, Jason. All I'm really sure of is I'll know it when I find it."

They passed out of the spreading suburbs of Greater London to the south. Although they encountered no one, they did not feel safe to turn to the west until the city was far behind them and they could once more smell the sea.

Levente drove across the rolling South Downs, sticking to minor roads whenever possible. They did not know where they were going; there seemed no need to hurry, except to put distance between themselves and whatever had happened back there.

The roads were empty, except where they had to squeeze past a tangled wreckage of blackened cars. The vehicles had welded together, making it difficult to tell where one wreck began and another ended. The surface of the road had bubbled and melted around the accident site, lending it the look of a petrified tar pit.

Animals were a more prevalent hazard. Cows often lay on the tarmac, enjoying the sun-warmed surface. They raised their heads to lazily watch the car pass, but made no effort to move out of the way. Sheep ambled across the roads, moving to fresh pastures, which lay in abundance in the meadows and moorland all around. Foxes, squirrels, rabbits, a weasel or two, and the occasional dog and cat darted away or watched them pass with a considering glance. Dormice and hedgehogs scurried along the verges, lately awoken to a markedly different world to that in which they had retired to their long winter sleep.

When the petrol gauge dipped towards red, Levente turned onto a main road and drove along it until they came to a filling station. He rummaged in the boot of the car and extracted a tyre iron, which he used to smash the glass in the entry door, allowing them to squeeze into the shop. While the Hungarian rooted around behind the cash desk, muttering to himself, Aletta looted the shelves of foodstuffs: packets of biscuits, bags of crisps and bars of chocolate. She considered the rows of wine bottles and beer cans. Shrugging, she added a few bottles and a couple of four-packs to her stash.

Uttering an exclamation of triumph, Levente emerged from behind the cash desk clutching a bunch of keys. He unlocked the door to make it easier for Aletta to transfer her goodies to the car, then proceeded to the forecourt where he used one of the keys to unlock a metal cover.

"*Benzin*," he said in response to Aletta's enquiring glance. "Er, gasoline?"

"Ah. I believe the British call it petrol."

"Yes. Petrol. *Jó.*"

In the shop they found several plastic fuel containers, each capable of holding five litres. Levente grabbed a flashlight—a torch the British called them, thought Aletta—and fiddled with batteries. He grinned when the torch lit up. Grunting with effort, for he wasn't a small man, Levente climbed down the metal staples set into the brick wall of the narrow shaft revealed beneath the metal cover. Aletta passed a container down to him and listened to his muffled curses. Just when she thought his endeavours must end in failure, the curses were replaced by the rhythmic sound of a hand pump.

The Hungarian's smiling face reappeared in the opening and he handed to her a heavier, sloshing container. "Petrol good. It has not, er…" He held up a clenched fist and spread his fingers out in a rapid motion. "Poof! Gone. How you say?"

"Evaporated."

Aletta returned the man's grin and passed him another empty container. While he disappeared to fill it, she emptied the first one into the car's petrol tank. She didn't have to wait long by the shaft entrance for Levente to reappear with another full container.

In this way, they refilled the car and placed eight full containers in the boot.

They drove until sunset and stopped overnight in a small village west of Southampton. They didn't know it, but they were less than twenty miles from Stonehenge from where the voice that called them to the U.K. had originated.

Neither of them felt much like talking. They shared a bottle of wine and spoke haltingly about the earlier events in London, but could make no sense of them. They agreed they had not imagined their minds being invaded by some external intelligence, which had nearly succeeded in taking over their wills, but could agree on little else and fell into a brooding silence.

Aletta drifted to sleep with the image of the Italian woman's knees folding and body crumpling playing across her mind.

After a restless night, they took to the road again under a brisk spring sky.

Still uneasy, afraid of running into people like those they had encountered in London, if 'people' is what they were, they kept to minor roads. The green and yellow shoots of weeds poked through potholed surfaces as nature began the slow but inexorable task of reclaiming its territory.

While the morning wore on and they had seen no sign of human, or quasi-human, life, they began to relax a little. When they passed a blue sign bearing a white symbol and 'M5', Aletta said, "Let's go on there. It's a motorway."

"Motorway?"

"A wide, fast road. Maybe we will find clues to what has happened here."

The signs indicated they had a choice: the road ran to the south or to the north.

"I think north," said Aletta, after consulting a roadmap she had picked up in the filling station. "To the south there is Devon and Cornwall. Nothing else."

"Where we now?"

"Er, in Somerset, I think. To the north are many cities."

Levente glanced at her. His expression made the hair on her arms rise and the skin pimple. The man, so big and strong, looked terrified.

"Cities bad."

"London was bad. We don't know about the others."

He shook his head. "No cities."

"Okay. But we'll go north. If there are answers, maybe that's where we'll find them."

Levente did not look convinced, but took the slip road signposted M5N. As they drove onto the motorway, Aletta began to giggle. The Hungarian glanced at her in concern.

"Sorry," she spluttered. "We've come onto the north side, but we could have gone onto the south side and still gone north." She waved her arm at the three lanes stretching away into the distance. "The road is empty." To their right, on the other side of a narrow strip of rough ground and a crash barrier, the three southbound lanes were also deserted.

Levente snorted and some of the tension seemed to drain from him.

"North," he said. "Correct side of road. Like good people. Even though is really wrong side." He shook his head. "Crazy British to drive on left."

Aletta relaxed back into her seat. Lulled by the steady *thrum* of the engine, her eyes drooped closed and she began to sink into slumber, only to be jerked forward against her seat belt when Levente brought the car to a screeching halt.

"What—" she began, but was thrust against the belt again when he slammed the vehicle into reverse and began to career backwards.

Aletta glanced wildly around, convinced with an abrupt and irrational certainty the people who had chased them in London were now bearing down on them. But the road ahead, behind and to either side was empty.

She was thrown back into her seat when Levente once more brought the car to a sudden stop. He unbuckled his seat belt and thrust open the door.

"Levente! What's happening?"

He seemed to become aware for the first time of how frightened she was.

"Excuse. Come."

He didn't wait, but was out of the car and striding to the side of the road, where a huge sign indicated the northbound lanes led in the direction of strange-sounding places with names like Bridgwater and Weston-super-Mare.

Aletta fumbled at the catch of her seat belt.

"Mare?" she muttered. "Like a horse?"

The Hungarian stood in front of the gigantic sign. In the bottom right hand corner, at eye level, a clear plastic wallet had been attached with tape. Inside the wallet, written on paper in thick black ink was the message:

Go west—M4. KEEP AWAY FROM LONDON!

Levente raised a bushy eyebrow. "M4? Another—how you call them—motorway?"

Aletta nodded and read the message again.

"Keep away from London," she murmured. "A little late for that. Well. Shall we find this M4?"

The Hungarian pursed his lips. "If trap, why say 'keep away from London'? Or maybe that why is trap. Trick us two times."

"Double-bluff."

He looked at Aletta. "What you think?"

"Let's find the M4 and follow it west. But slow. Careful." She thought of the two military rifles Levente had acquired in London, which lay on the back seat of the car. "First, though, I want to be sure I can use those guns."

Late the following morning, another blustery spring day, Levente brought the car to a halt on the empty westbound lanes of the M4 on the outskirts of Newport. In silence, they regarded the spreading, modern hulk of a building sitting on a hill, dominating the landscape. A sheet attached to a road sign billowed in the breeze. A multi-hued arrow scrawled on the sheet pointed towards the building.

Aletta was the first to speak.

"I guess that is where we will find out what is going on."

"Or we find our end."

Aletta shrugged. "*Que sera, sera.*"

The Hungarian gave a thin smile. He put the car into gear and drove towards the motorway exit.

The surface of the Atlantic Ocean resembled a gigantic, grey carpet being relentlessly shaken. *The Lady Jane* rode the swell with ease, maintaining the steady nine knots at which they had kept her since putting out from New Jersey almost two weeks before. Their stock of food and water was holding up well, the supply of diesel even more so. The cruiser had been built to cross oceans; her fuel capacity had not yet been depleted by half and they should sight land within a few days.

By Zach's reckoning, they were now well into March. They should land on mainland Britain with spring having taken a firm grip on the island. He still longed to feel warmth on his back. From what he had heard about Britain's climate, he was more likely to feel rain than sunlight, but even that would be an improvement from the snow and ice of the White Mountains in Maine.

Zach entered the pilot's cabin carrying two steaming mugs. He handed one to Elliott, who sat at the controls maintaining the east-north-east heading that should take them into the English Channel.

"My grandfather was from Portsmouth," Elliott had informed them a few days into the voyage. "He came over to the States in the 1920s. Unless anyone has any objection, that's where I'd like to make land. If I get chance, I'm going to pay a visit to the village where my grandfather was born." No one had objected.

"Thanks," said Elliott, accepting the mug from Zach. He took a sip. "Ah! Hits the spot. Strong enough to dissolve iron—just as I like it. How's Amy?"

"Not throwing up for once. That girl is surely no sailor." Zach grunted. "Sarah *is* throwing up."

"Morning sickness in the afternoon, eh? You know, I've been wondering about her pregnancy."

"Like whether the foetus will die of the Millennium Bug?"

Elliott glanced sharply at him. "You've wondered about it, too. So, what do you reckon?"

Zach shrugged. "I was a grunt and an alcoholic and a recluse."

"And I was a high school English teacher from Philly due to retire next year. I intended writing the next Great American Novel. Maybe I'll write about the end of the human race instead. Hmm, yes, when we reach Britain I'll start keeping a journal in case someone, somehow comes after us. Because if that babe Sarah's carrying *does* perish from the Millennium Bug, whether because the virus is still active—I don't think that's likely, but then I'm no microbiologist—or because the mother's a carrier of the disease, then the human race is doomed." He uttered a short laugh. "I've a feeling the baby could be born healthy and we'd still be doomed."

"I guess we'll find out in six or seven months. If we have that long."

Both men regarded each other for a moment. Elliott spoke first.

"You and I have been thinking along similar lines. Please don't take this the wrong way, but you're a lot smarter than you appear. I think the gruff mountain-man exterior hides a keen intellect."

Zach took a long sip of coffee. "Don't know 'bout that. What I *do* know is the voice I heard mentioned something 'bout some reckoning. That don't sound like we're heading to anything good."

"'A final reckoning for mankind.' Those were the words I heard."

Zach nodded.

"I agree with you," continued Elliott, "that whatever we're headed toward is not likely to be good. Yet instead of altering course and making for the Mediterranean, go and hide out on a Greek island or in an Egyptian pyramid, we're continuing on to what we're both agreed is most likely danger."

"There was something in the voice that makes me want to go anyway."

"Again, we are in accord. Whatever this danger may be, I feel it is my duty to face it. Maybe there is something I can do to help." Elliott took a final slug of coffee to drain his mug. He smacked his lips. "That's better. I have been thinking about what the message might mean and have come to no firm conclusions. You?"

Zach drained his own mug before answering. "I've got no friends. No family. Kept myself away from most everyone for forty years. But now mankind is greatly diminished, I find I'm ready to be part of it again."

"Well, there's certainly a lot more room now to stretch and not touch anyone."

"I don't mean that I'm glad most folk died. I'd prefer they lived and I could stay in my cabin in the woods. But—" he shrugged "—it's happened."

"Do you have any theories how it happened? A mutated strain of swine or bird flu, perhaps?"

An image popped into Zach's head, as clear as if he was still standing beside his pick-up in front of the hardware store that cold December morning. "I saw something," he said slowly. "Around the time of the outbreak. A woman. She was dipping her hand into her purse and touching things."

"Touching things?"

"Door handles, handrails, keys on an ATM machine. I followed her into a store. She was picking things up or running her fingers along them. Then she touched my cheek." Zach raised his hand to his face; he could still recall the warm stroke of her fingers. "The next day, I began coughing."

"Do you think she was spreading something? The Millennium Bug?"

"Dunno. But that's what I saw."

Elliott stared at Zach for a long moment, before turning to the control panel and checking the instrument readings. Zach gazed out of the window at the endless expanse of ocean. The sun had appeared and turned the water the deep blue of unwashed denim.

"Another thing that interests me," said Elliott, turning back to face Zach, "is the voice itself. Or its source."

"Like a radio signal, only our brains acted like the receiver."

Again, Elliott regarded him with appreciation. "That's a good analogy. You realise what you just described, don't you?"

"Telepathy."

"Nan, Sarah and Frank are more persuaded by the idea it was God's voice they heard. I've not tried to argue otherwise. If that's what helps them deal with it. Besides, who am I to gainsay them? It might have been God for all I know."

It was Zach's turn to look closely at Elliott. "But you don't really think that."

"Nope."

"Me, neither."

"So here's the rub. Whose voice was it, then?"

"Aliens?" Zach wasn't being entirely serious, but the smile he had ready died on his lips when Elliott nodded gravely.

"Thank goodness I'm not the only one who's going crazy."

Chapter Seven

The first few gulps of coffee hit Tom's stomach and spread caffeine outwards, startling his nerve-endings into tingling awareness.

He blinked. "Bloody hell! This stuff could strip paint."

Diane came as close as she ever did to grinning. "I did warn you. I like it strong."

Tom glanced at Ceri. She *was* grinning, enjoying watching him suffer.

"How do you do it?" he asked. "We must have put away three bottles of red between us last night, yet you're sitting here, bright-eyed and bushy-tailed, tucking into tinned tomatoes and—what are they? Frankfurters?—like someone who didn't touch a drop the night before." He groaned. "I like red wine, but it doesn't like me."

Ceri bit into a bright pink sausage. "You should get some food inside you. Make you feel better."

"I'll stick to coffee, thanks."

Tom felt something bump the outside of his thigh and glanced down. Dusty was nuzzling his leg, politely reminding him that he'd finished his breakfast and needed to step outside to attend to doggy business.

"Okay, boy. In a minute." He ruffled the dog's ears.

"I'll take him out," said Bri. "I could do with some fresh air. I'll catch up with Colleen and help her find Will."

"Thanks," said Tom. He looked at Howard. "But I don't think Colleen is too keen on Dusty."

"Dogs in general." Howard nodded at Dusty. "She's a lot better around that soft thing now, but probably best not to push it."

"You go on," said Tom to Bri. "I'll bring Dusty out shortly."

"Okay," said Bri.

Tom watched her go. She still looked washed-out, like an over-thinned watercolour, but her stride was firm as her strength started to return.

"So, Tom," said Peter. "The meeting's going ahead tomorrow?"

Tom waved his hand to indicate the restaurant area. It was filled with people eating and chatting.

"They keep asking about what's happened. About the Millennium Bug and the voice that brought them here. If we don't tell them what we know soon, there'll be a riot."

"Hmm," said Peter. "When you tell them what you know, there may be a riot."

"Well, they have the right to know. Then they can make an informed decision what to do next."

Howard cleared his throat. "Will you lead them, Tom, no matter what they decide?"

Tom laughed. "Me? Lead them? Absolutely not. I'm only agreeing to lead this meeting because Ceri won't."

Ceri smiled. "You're the teacher, Tom. Used to projecting your voice."

"You may not need to," said Peter. "There's a Belgian guy who arrived a few weeks ago. His English is poor, but I have enough French to get by. Turns out he's an electrician. He's been playing with the hotel's PA system. Rigged it up to work off the same circuit the generators are feeding."

"We can hold the meeting in the foyer, then." Tom took another gulp of coffee and shuddered. "I was anticipating having to pack as many as we could into that conference room downstairs. It's huge, but would probably only hold two thousand, two and a half tops." He glanced from the restaurant area out to the main foyer. "Here, people can use the bar, restaurants, reception and shopping areas. They can go up to the higher floors and fill the corridors in front of the balconies overlooking reception. Everyone who wants to come should fit in somewhere and be able to hear what I'm saying, even if not all of them will understand it."

Ceri grunted. "I think every group has at least one person who understands English. You'll need to allow frequent pauses for them to translate to their friends."

"Peter, maybe you can stand up with me and say some of it in French or Spanish or whatever."

Tom didn't miss Peter's glance away, but before he could say anything Bri appeared on the run.

"Hey, slow down," said Howard. "You're not strong enough to—"

"Come quick!" Bri barely retained enough breath to get the words out. "It's Colleen…"

Howard was already on his feet and running for the door. Tom followed him, Dusty by his side. People turned to stare when he brushed past them.

Tom made it outside and paused. He heard a cry from the hill in front of the hotel.

"Help!"

He couldn't tell if it was Colleen, but it was definitely a female voice.

He took off after Howard, who had already reached the narrow road leading up the hill. Dusty ran alongside him; he would not go off on his own without Tom's say-so and Tom wanted to see what was happening before letting him go.

Howard was fit, but Tom had almost thirty years on him and overtook him halfway up the hill. By the time he reached the top, Tom's thighs and calves were burning.

Colleen was standing on the road, but her bearing was tense as though ready to take to her heels at any moment. She turned to Tom when he ran up.

"Thank God…" she muttered.

A man slouched against a wooden fence, next to a closed gate. A big man with lank hair falling across his eyes. Thick lips curved up in a sardonic smile. The man's hands were thrust into the pockets of his leather jacket.

On the other side of the fence, behind the man, stood Will, an uncertain expression on his face. When he noticed Tom and Dusty, he started towards the gate.

"No, Will!" shouted Colleen. Her voice was shrill, filled with panic.

Will stopped in confusion. He looked small and utterly frail next to the slouching giant and with his left arm bandaged to his chest.

"What's going on, Col?" asked Tom.

At that moment, a wheezing Howard reached them.

"Aw, shit…" Tom heard him mutter.

"Col?" said Tom.

She pointed briefly, almost contemptuously, at the stranger.

"He tried to rape me in Dublin. Dermot Ward; also known as Clint."

The man straightened. A low growl began in Dusty's throat. Tom reached down and stroked him briefly on the head. Dusty stopped growling, but remained tense, ready to spring to Tom's defence if needed.

"Yes, my name's Dermot," said the man in a soft Irish accent. His smile grew wider. He possessed extraordinarily fleshy lips. "Yes, I do sometimes go by the nickname Clint." He shrugged. "A man can't help the nickname his friends give him. If the shoe fits…"

"And the rape?"

Dermot took his hands from his pockets and spread them disarmingly. They were big hands; club-like.

"Rape's a strong word. Easy to allege. Hard to disprove."

"I saw you," said Howard. He was regarding Dermot with undisguised distaste.

"What did you see, old man, while you were skulking away in the shadows? Me and the beaut there was just getting friendly."

Colleen snorted.

More heavy breathing sounded as Ceri arrived. She took one look at the scene and moved towards the fenced enclosure.

"Ceri, wait!"

Tom tried to grab her arm when she went past, but she brushed his hand away. Ignoring the hulking Irishman, she strode to the gate. Holding it open, she beckoned to Will, who hurried forward. She hooked her arm around Will's neck, avoiding his injured shoulder, and led him back to the others. She shot Tom a glance of reproach.

"Colleen," said Tom, "has he done anything to you now? Or to Will?"

She shook her head. "He was by the fence talking to Will when I arrived. He hasn't moved from there."

"Why were you calling for help?"

"Oh, I was shocked to see him. I panicked. He didn't do anything. Not yet."

"So we're all friends here?" Dermot took a step forward and the growl came again from Dusty's throat. He glanced at the dog and Tom saw the black look that momentarily clouded the big man's features. It was a look which told Tom Dusty had made an enemy.

"Stay back, please," he said. "From what I've heard about you from Colleen and Howard, friends is something we're never likely to be."

Dermot's fleshy features broke into an open scowl. He reached behind him. Tom felt his hands curl into fists and his stomach turned over; he could not remember the last time he had been involved in a fistfight—when he wore short trousers and had scabbed knees, most probably. Then Dermot seemed to change his mind, for he brought his hand back, empty, and thrust it into his jacket pocket. His gaze was directed at Tom.

"Trust me," Dermot said in his soft voice, "you'd prefer to be my friend than my enemy."

Tom stared back for a moment, not out of bravado but because the man possessed an intensity it was difficult to ignore. He felt like a rabbit encountering a snake.

Dermot's scowl disappeared. The faintly sardonic smile returned.

Tom's hands relaxed and his stomach settled. He held the man's gaze for a moment longer, trying (but, he suspected, hopelessly failing) to warn him off.

"Come on, guys," he said, turning away. "Let's get back. Bri will be worried about Will."

She was waiting at the foot of the hill with Peter and Diane, looking pale and anxious. When they approached the bottom, she darted forward.

"Is everything all right? Will, are you okay?"

Shrugging off Ceri's arm, Will trotted to meet her. "I'm fine, Bri. I was pretending to play crazy golf and talking to a giant."

Tom met Ceri's gaze. It looked as troubled as Tom felt.

The last of the spoiled bedding and mattresses had been lugged to the cliff edge by the remaining drones and tossed over, flapping to the sand and rocks below. From there, they were piled onto the pyre, kept smouldering with mounds of seaweed.

George Wallace roamed the hotel, checking every room for contaminated materials that might have been overlooked. He found none. Before leaving each room, he closed the open windows. All traces of the smell of stale decomposition had been scoured clean by the spring breezes. It would be good to be able to sit without draughts howling down the stairs and through cracks in the doors. He had hardly removed his thick winter coat since they arrived at this hotel; had barely been warm in all the time they had been on this goddamned island.

Time. Not a concept he and his kind viewed in the same way as humans. Drones, he corrected himself. Then hesitated.

When their frontal lobes hadn't been fried by volts of electrical current, humans were capable of producing stunning artistic works and other wonders. Wallace had often sat mesmerised in front of a movie or marvelled at the depth of imagination and skill portrayed in a gallery exhibition. His admiration of human art might yet lead him to travelling Europe—and, maybe, beyond— scouring the galleries of London, Paris, Florence, Rome, Milan, collecting his favourite pieces (he would need a truck, a *large* truck) with which to surround himself in his new home when he eventually found a place to settle.

There were other matters to deal with first. The Great Coming. Then the Commune. Every intellect, those already here on Earth Haven and those now travelling through the middle reaches of Sol's system, would join as one to eradicate the surviving humans.

An image intruded on his thoughts.

The boy stepping into his line of sight the moment his finger tightened on the trigger to the point of no return.

Wallace pushed the image away.

After the Commune had taken place, he would have to deal with the traitor, and that might prove no easy task. As Milandra had noted, Ronstadt had an entire planet in which to hide out.

The small, pale body crumpling to the ground.

He shook his head, fiercely, like someone trying to dislodge a swarm of bees from his face. The scene at the Beacon, where he'd inadvertently shot the human—a boy no bigger than a grizzly cub—kept popping unbidden into his mind with increasing frequency. Especially during the nights, while he sat alone in long contemplation.

Before becoming one of the Keeper's Deputies, George Wallace had been an adventurer, travelling the world in search of excitement and objects of beauty, to participate in the former and appreciate the latter. It was this more aesthetic pleasure that he kept hidden. The other Deputies would never have suspected that behind the rough-and-ready exterior lay a connoisseur of art.

Of *human* art.

The Chosen, in particular, would scoff at him. Wallace considered for a moment and found he no longer much cared what the Chosen, or anyone else for that matter, thought about him. If he was displaying remarkably human qualities of individuality, he no longer cared about that, either.

He completed his tour of the hotel and closed the window in the last guest room. The drones' work was done. Simone and Lavinia could do what they wanted with them now.

Since the remaining dozen or so drones were no longer capable of experiencing free will or acting upon it, Wallace felt not a twinge of regret at the untimely end to which they would now undoubtedly come.

He wished he still felt the same way about humanity as a whole, but was not yet willing to confront the possibility his feelings on that score might be turning in a different direction. An unexpected and dangerous direction.

"I have to leave," said Colleen. "I have no choice."

She looked around at the faces assembled in the family suite: Howard, Tom, Ceri, Bri and Will. Dusty was also there, lying with head resting on paws like a canine sphinx. Colleen was growing used to his presence, though would never feel truly comfortable around him. It wasn't that she had a phobia of dogs—not quite a phobia. More a deep-seated fear driven by witnessing a childhood friend bitten, accidentally, on the arm when trying to separate two fighting dogs. After a few stitches and a tetanus shot, her friend had been fine, barely a mark to show for the incident months later, but it had left a deeper psychological scar on Colleen.

Howard nodded. "I'm going with you."

"There's always a choice," said Ceri. "Accuse him. Let him answer for what he did."

"To what end?" asked Colleen. "Believe me, Ceri, I've thought about what would happen if Dermot showed up here. I *could* accuse him of attempted rape, to be sure, but it comes down to his word against mine." She glanced at Howard and laid a hand on his arm. "He was right what he said earlier. You didn't see anything. At least, not enough. And he's sly. He'll come up with some feasible excuse for grabbing me in the dark." She sighed. "Even if people did believe me, what then? We have no police, no courts, no punishments or deterrents. We can't lock him up. What are we going to do…" she glanced at Will before turning her face away from him and mouthing the next words "… kill him?" She shook her head firmly. "I'm sure there are people here who would be willing to lynch him on my word, even if only to guard against any potential threat he poses. But, for all that he's a nasty piece of work, I don't want that on my conscience."

"Okay," said Tom. "Stay and we'll protect you."

Colleen gave him a sad smile. "That's sweet of you to offer, but it won't work. Didn't I say he was sly? He'll bide his time. You can't watch me every minute. Nor would I want you to. You've that meeting to think about and I've a feeling there'll be a lot going on after that. And aren't we heading for..." again she hesitated and mouthed the word so Will couldn't see "... oblivion? Who's going to give a damn about an attempted rape accusation in this climate? Or care whether he succeeds next time? And there will be a next time." She glanced again at Howard. "We were only with him a short while, but we are both agreed: he's the type to hold a grudge and not rest until he's repaid it."

Howard nodded. "He's a fantasist and, I suspect, a sociopath who was adept at hiding his true nature in the pre-viral world. Now—" Howard shrugged "—now he doesn't feel any need to remain in disguise."

Ceri cleared her throat. "I don't want you to go; I understand why you feel you must. But where will you go?"

"Well," said Howard, "I had family outside Lincoln. I'd like to go there to confirm... you know."

Ceri nodded. "And then?"

Howard shrugged.

"I've never been to Britain," said Colleen. "I'd like, maybe, to see a little of it before... before whatever is going to happen happens."

For a moment there was silence. Then Tom asked, "Has anyone seen Peter?"

"Not seen him or Diane since breakfast," said Ceri.

Tom frowned. "He's been a little quiet these past few days."

"He's sad," said Bri. "So's Diane."

Tom turned to her. "How do you know?"

"I can sort of sense it," said Bri.

"They think the spacemen will kill us," added Will. He said it matter-of-factly and Colleen, not for the first time, felt a surge of affection for the boy.

She nudged Howard with her elbow. He cleared his throat.

"There is one question to decide," he said. Colleen followed his gaze. So, too, did Tom and Ceri. Bri and Will looked back at them, Bri's eyes widening slightly. "Who is coming with us?"

"Hold on," said Bri. "There might be another way."

When they approached the long driveway that led to the hotel, Levente stopped the car and insisted they swap places. Aletta did not demur—it made sense. The Hungarian's driving skills were perfectly adequate, but with her rallying experience, she would be better at extracting them from a tight corner quickly.

She adjusted the driver's seat to accommodate her longer legs and gunned the engine. It sounded nothing like the roar of a souped-up rally car engine, but it would have to do.

Levente took the passenger seat, grimly clutching one of the assault rifles. He lowered the window and rested his arms on the sill with the rifle barrel poking outside. That was another thing: if it came to having to shoot someone, Aletta thought Levente less likely to hesitate than she.

"Okay?" she said.

"Okay."

Aletta pulled the car forward and proceeded cautiously up the drive. Before the hotel came into sight, she stopped. A man was walking down the hill towards them. Levente gripped the gun tighter. He spoke to her in a low, urgent voice from the side of his mouth.

"If feel anything…" He broke off to tap at his forehead. "Up here. Anything. Get us away."

Aletta didn't need to be told. She placed the gear shift in reverse and held the car on the footbrake, clutch depressed, ready to spring backwards at the first sign of anything untoward.

The man—rough-shaven, somewhere in his forties—continued down the driveway. He drew closer to Levente's open window and slowed his pace when he noticed the rifle. Before drawing level, he held out his hands palms down to show them he wasn't carrying anything. He stopped a few feet from the car and leaned forward to bring his face lower.

"Er, hello," he said.

Levente nodded. He did not raise the barrel to point the rifle directly at the man, but his state of readiness to use the weapon was obvious to all.

Without releasing her grip on the steering wheel, Aletta leaned to her left a little so she could see the man's face. He looked back at her warily.

"Hello," she said. "My name is Aletta. This is Levente."

The man nodded. "I am Pascal. Excuse, please. My English is not perfect."

"Francais?"

The man nodded again.

"I am from Sweden. Levente is from Hungary."

"Please," said Pascal. "The gun. Not necessary."

Aletta glanced at Levente. He continued to grip the rifle as though to release it would be to let go of his sanity. "I feel nothing," she said to him in a low tone. He shook his head, the briefest motion. She looked back at the Frenchman. "You must excuse us. We were in London. We met people, bad people. Our travelling companions… they killed one. Captured the others."

Pascal's eyes grew rounder at the mention of London. "*Mon Dieu*. Did you not see the signs?"

Aletta shook her head. "Not until it was too late. The bad people—who are they?"

"I do not know. Big meeting. Soon. To explain."

"Are there bad people here?"

"*Non*. Normal people here. Sad people. They come from Francais, Belgique, all over. America, too."

Levente addressed the Frenchman for the first time. "America?"

"*Oui*." He pointed up the hill in the direction from which he'd come. "Hotel there. Lots of people. Food. Drink. No rooms, all full." He waved one arm more vaguely. "But lots of empty houses." He looked again at the rifle. "No gun in hotel."

Aletta felt herself relax, just a little. She smiled at the Frenchman. He returned it, a touch uncertainly.

"*Merci, monsieur,*" she said.

Pascal straightened and continued on his way down the hill. Only then did Levente relax his grip on the rifle. He turned to her and let out his breath in a sour sigh.

"It seems okay," said Aletta.

The Hungarian nodded. "But still we be careful."

She shifted the car into first and got it moving up the hill. For the first time since they had fled London, she felt things really might be okay. For now, at least.

Chapter Eight

Streams ran through the grounds of the Celtic Manor, providing a ready supply of water, and rain was collected in tubs and butts. Although nobody had attempted to lay down formal rules saying people must use water for flushing toilets and personal hygiene, it was understood those staying at the hotel would avail themselves of these basic amenities to make life more pleasant for everyone.

Bri wrinkled her nose. Judging from the odours drifting from some of the rooms and from some people she passed on the stairs, not everyone was bothering to fetch water or utilise the deodorants and other toiletries freely obtainable in the hotel shops and storerooms.

She trod the corridor with a heavy heart. She sensed the period of calm they had enjoyed since arriving here, of feeling if not safe then at least civilised, was drawing to an abrupt end. Uncertainty and fear were striving to re-establish themselves as the norm.

The last thing Bri wanted was for their small group to split apart. For this reason, she had come up with an idea she believed might work.

"We could ask Peter and Diane to implant a compulsion into Dermot's mind that he needs to leave here and go far away, never to return," she suggested.

"Even better, to go and jump off a cliff," said Ceri.

"That probably won't work," said Tom. "I don't think only two of them acting together would be strong enough to get him to do something that's completely contrary to his best interests. Making him leave, however, that has to be worth a try."

Everyone had agreed that it was, indeed, worth trying if Peter and Diane were willing. If not, or if it was attempted and didn't work, they were also all in accord that Bri and Will should accompany Colleen and Howard to Lincoln.

Ceri had at first railed, but backed down when it was pointed out it would be better that the patients stick with their doctor, and that the hotel might not be the calmest place for rest and recuperation in the coming days.

To their credit, and so avoiding Bri demonstrating her stubborn streak—it had begun to resurface as her strength returned—the adults did not try to *insist* she and Will go, but left the final decision to them. Bri had taken Will into the adjoining room. In answer to her question, the boy shrugged.

"I want to go wherever you go, Bri," he said.

"Oh, great. In other words, I have to decide on my own." She thought for a few moments. "Okay. I can see the sense in us going with Howard. He *is* a doctor and saved both of our lives. We're a lot better, but we're still weak and our wounds haven't yet healed. Especially yours, Will. It would be a good idea to be with him when our bandages come off. And there's still the risk of infection. Howard knows what we need to take to guard against it and what antibiotics we'd need if we did get infected." She blew out heavily between pursed lips. "Oh, shit, I think we'll have to go, but I'm really not sure."

She paused in case Will had anything useful to add. He said nothing; only gazed at her trustingly. He would go along, she knew, with whatever she decided. Sometimes, she hated that he held such faith in her. So far, all this had got him was shot.

In the end, she had agreed that if Colleen and Howard needed to leave, they would accompany them upon one condition: that she and Will be either returned to the Celtic Manor or not obstructed from making their own way back at any time they wished.

Colleen didn't hesitate in agreeing; Howard a little more reluctantly and only after Bri assured him they would heed any medical advice he gave them.

She was now seeking out Peter and Diane to ask them to accompany her to where the others awaited so her idea could be put to them. It was Diane's room she came to first. After receiving no response to her knock, she tried the door. It was unlocked and she went in.

The bed was neatly made and there was no sign of any personal belongings. That did not strike Bri as strange; she hadn't noticed Diane had any personal belongings.

She went back into the corridor and walked on to Peter's room. She hoped she would find him alone since there was something else she wanted to mention to him.

Back in Salisbury, when Howard had eventually been persuaded by Peter and Diane to operate on Bri, the question of anaesthesia had arisen. It was vital that Bri lie absolutely still during the procedure, yet neither Howard nor Diane had sufficient knowledge of anaesthetics to risk placing her under. Peter had come up with the solution, one that had worked perfectly.

Bri lay on her back on the operating table, her forehead shaved and doused in iodine that made her skin tingle. Peter sat next to her and gripped her hand.

"You must reach out," he said, staring into her eyes, "and enter my mind. I'll let you in and you must submit to my will so that when what's happening to your body makes you want to return to it, I should be able to hang onto you. It's essential you submit your will to mine. I sense you're otherwise too strong for me to hold, even with that blood clot pressing against your brain. Now, come to me…"

As she had done when helping Will's and Joe's minds repair themselves, Bri let her intellect slip free and flow into Peter's head. If she'd retained use of her mouth, she would have gasped at the vast canvas of colour she met, from a swirling kaleidoscope of primary colours to swathes of vibrant greens and pulsing purples. She allowed herself to sink deeper, to let the colours wash over her. When the tug came, trying to yank her mind back to where it belonged, Peter's psyche held hers tightly. Whilst in its clutches, Bri had been helpless not to see things Peter might have preferred to keep private.

Later, when she had returned to her own body, the blood clot removed from beneath her forehead, she had fallen into a deep, sedative-induced sleep. Since then, she had never been alone with Peter to ask him about what she'd seen deep within his innermost thoughts.

Now. I'll ask him now.

She knocked and tried the door in the same motion. It opened and she walked into a room in similar condition to Diane's: bed made, no mess, no sign of personal belongings. Frowning, Bri stepped to the other side of the bed. On the bedside table she noticed the envelope.

Sealed, three words neatly printed on the front: *Tom and Ceri.*

Minutes later in the family suite, she handed the envelope to Tom. He opened it, removed the single sheet of paper and read aloud the words printed on it.

My dear friends

By the time you read this, Diane and I will have left the Celtic Manor and South Wales. I am sorry to have departed without saying goodbye, but you'd have tried to persuade us to stay and, I confess, I would have been tempted. But there is much to risk by us staying; little to gain.

Over the past weeks, I have been chatting to people and listening to their speculation. Remember, I can speak many European languages. And I have heard similar attitudes prevailing among the Americans.

People are looking for answers. When they find them, they will want to strike back in any way they can to cover their hurt, avenge their dead loved ones, prolong their survival… or merely to do something but sit around waiting for more calamity to befall them.

Diane and I would present easy and obvious targets. Even those who don't believe the story Tom must tell them will not balk when the mob turns against us. And turn it shall. We will be seen to represent your enemy and will be torn apart.

Believe me when I say I don't blame people for the way they are feeling. I know that you, Tom and Ceri, have experienced the same emotions. Brianne and Will, Howard and Colleen, too. Pain, dread, loss, bewilderment, despair. Hardly surprising after what you have endured at the hands of my people.

'My people'—I sometimes feel I am more human than not. My loyalty to my kind has become overwhelmed by my love for humanity.

We have done all we can to help you directly. There may be other, indirect assistance and we are going to see what we can do to provide it.

I will not say much by way of advice. I fear any counsel I can offer will be crushed beneath the will of the majority. A raging majority, too blinded by its own agony to listen to reason above the need to smash and kill.

Mankind must make its own choices from here on in, for good or ill. I wish it well.

Megan had a favourite Welsh hymn: Calon Lan. *As you probably know, it means 'Pure Heart'. Be of pure heart, my friends. I suspect it may be necessary to demonstrate it before the end.*

Peter.

Tom finished reading and stared down at the sheet of paper. Bri felt tears prickling her eyes and blinked them away. She looked at Ceri, who had grown ashen. Will walked quietly to Bri's side and she placed an arm around his uninjured shoulder. Colleen and Howard grasped hands.

At last, Tom looked around at them, his expression grim.

"This changes nothing," he said. Bri had never heard him speak with such quiet determination. "You four must still leave for your own safety." He looked at Ceri. "You and I can handle the meeting."

Ceri took a deep breath and her features took on some of Tom's fortitude. She nodded. "Course we can."

Tears once more welled in Bri's eyes. This time she was powerless to hold them back.

Explosions blew trees to matchwood and buildings to tumbling blocks of stone. The jungles burned, driving winged creatures skywards in a valiant effort to flee the scorching updraughts. Most fell back in flames.

Under the percussive forces unleashed onto it, the ground

rippled, toppling towers and monoliths. Land-based creatures fled, their terrified calls adding to the mayhem, but there was no refuge. Increasingly powerful artillery met with ever-more-violent counter strikes in a desperate bid to gain supremacy.

Milandra flew above the carnage. A glimpse of burnished armour told her she was in the memory of the same person, the one she believed to be Sivatra. The flying machine the woman travelled in was different from the one she had flown in during an earlier memory. This craft flew like a dragonfly, darting from side to side through the air to avoid the storm of missiles. Sivatra was pressed deep into the body-moulding seat, held tightly in place by secured straps. Three others—another woman and two men— tight-lipped and clad in similar armour, were strapped into seats around her. Nobody spoke. Words would remain unheard beneath the din of detonations and screaming engines.

The craft arrowed down to land in a familiar clearing. The dome on the nearby structure had gone, leaving a jagged hole. The building itself bore a lopsided look as though part of its foundations had been blown away.

Sivatra and her companions unstrapped themselves and leapt from the craft, which took to the air again before their feet had touched the shaking ground. They landed, rolled and came upright in one fluid motion. Without pausing or breaking stride, they ran for the building. The alloyed flexibility of their armour, and easy familiarity with it, allowed full freedom to sprint and dodge. They ran in zig-zag movements, mirroring those of the flying craft. Graceful athleticism, fleet-footedness and lightness of step allowed them to reach the building without injury from the explosions in the air and the pulses of plasma energy that flew at them from what remained of the jungle to either side of the clearing.

They raced inside the arched entryway and slowed to a walk once in the relative safety of the entrance hallway. A grim-faced man met them, his armour bearing the dents and scorch marks of heavy combat. He pointed to the end of the hallway, where two vast wooden doors barred entrance to the Great Hall that lay beyond.

At Sivatra's gesture, her three companions hurried to the doors and stooped at their base. They stood, nodded and all stepped to the side, pressing themselves to the cool stone of the walls. With a white flash and a deep *crump*, the doors folded as if made of flimsy cardboard, not tougher-than-teak *isuz*. Stepping over their smoking remains, Sivatra entered the vast space they had concealed.

The sound level increased as noises of battle intruded through the gap left by the shattered dome. Sivatra's feet crunched on broken glass while she strode to the centre of the hall where her enemy awaited.

Milandra recognised him as the man who had faced her across the great table in the earlier memory. He wore a white cloak, soiled by the dust falling with every explosion.

Sivatra stopped before him.

He did not open his mouth to speak—speech would be difficult amidst the racket of war—but Milandra sensed he was communicating with Sivatra, and she with him, through her mind.

Except at the end. Clearly, slowly enough that Milandra could gain the sense of what he said, the man uttered aloud his last words.

"*Să naparsudu'ndan ul săr nanturian.*"

We cannot escape our nature.

Sivatra stepped smartly backwards. Without taking his eyes from her, the man reached beneath his cloak and extracted a dark object. He twisted it and clutched it to his chest. A bitter grimace touched his lips before he vanished in a spray of blood, flesh and shattered bone when the device detonated.

Turning on her heel, Sivatra nodded at her companions, who had lined up behind her. While fresh explosions shook the building—the bombardment was growing nearer—they made their way from the Great Hall and down the hallway, where the man who had met them awaited them at the entrance.

Together, the five of them ran outside to join the battle...

The memory faded and Milandra opened her eyes. There was one memory remaining of the secluded batch she had found. The picture was almost complete. She already had a good idea what that picture would show; she wished with all her heart she was wrong, that at the last moment the image revealed would be not what she was now expecting.

She paused only long enough to eat some food to restore a little energy, before plunging back to the depths of the collective memory and into that last hidden one.

She was sitting in a high-backed chair in an underground chamber. Rocky walls glowed red in light reflected from outside by glass tubes and mirrors. A woman stood over her, clutching a needle-tipped vial filled with a light blue liquid.

The woman gazed intently at her. Although she could not catch glimpse in the mirrors of a reflection of the body she inhabited, Milandra by now could recognise Sivatra from the feel of her psyche.

Sivatra nodded and drew in a deep breath. Held it.

For all her courage and ferocity in battle, Milandra sensed Sivatra did not like injections. The needle attached to the vial drew closer and Sivatra closed her eyes.

The scene winked out…

To be replaced almost immediately by a new one.

This time, she stood on a raised dais in a much larger subterranean chamber that stretched into a shadowy distance. The chamber was packed with people. Thousand upon thousand stood before her. Watching her.

She took a step forward to the edge of the dais and raised her arms. The low hubbub of whispered conversation died.

In the silence, Sivatra spoke two words.

"N'acnipnara jan."

Accept me.

The crowd stood perfectly still and hushed. Each face was raised to gaze at Sivatra with expressions bordering on adoration.

Any remaining doubts were subsumed into their welcome.

Sivatra *reached…*

Milandra let out her breath in a deep sigh and opened her eyes. She nearly knew the whole story.

The final pieces of the jigsaw must be hidden elsewhere in the collective memory, ensuring that only a dedicated hunter would find them. Milandra mentally rolled up her sleeves and prepared to search deeper.

Zach watched the man tape the notice to the lamp-post. He stepped forward to read it over his shoulder.

> *General Meeting*
> *Celtic Manor Resort Hotel*
> *Tomorrow @ 12:00 noon*
> *All welcome*
> *(The meeting will be conducted in English. No weapons to be carried, open or concealed. Thank you.)*

"What's that about?" he asked.

The man shrugged. "No idea, mate. I'm only helping out by putting these up in Caerleon. Others are putting them up in Newport and the surrounding areas. I don't think they know what it's all about, either."

Zach looked closely at the man. He was around forty, thick of girth but thin of hair.

"You're a Brit?"

"Yeah. From Oxford, but lived in the Dordogne for the last four years. A cottage deep in the French countryside." A shadow passed across his face. "Didn't protect us from the fucking virus. I'm the only one who survived."

Zach wasn't any good with platitudes. He didn't offer any. Instead, he said, "You're the first Brit I've seen since coming to Britain. Plenty of Spanish, Danes, Germans, Americans, a few Canadians, but no Brits. You seen any others?"

The man's face creased in thought. "Now you mention it…

The couple who asked me to put up these notices are British. Welsh, I think. A couple of English kids, too. And there may be another Brit with them, an older bloke." He nodded at the notice. "They're at the hotel. Think they were the first ones here. But other than them, nope, I can't think of any other British people I've seen." He frowned. "Odd."

"Hmm. These Brits at the hotel, they're the ones calling this meeting?"

"I think so. Maybe they know what's been going on. The virus, the voices and what-have-you."

"Let's hope so."

"Well, I have more notices to put up. See you at the meeting."

"Sure."

Zach watched the man walk away. He remained standing, deep in thought, oblivious to the comings and goings around him of people walking up to read the notice.

"Hey, Zach!"

He turned. Amy, Sarah and Frank were walking towards him. The man had his arm around Sarah's waist, which had expanded while her bump grew. Sarah's outside arm was linked through Amy's. The pair had not started off well—girl stuff, Zach reckoned—but had become good friends during the latter stages of the transatlantic voyage while they shared the misery of frequent bouts of sickness.

Amy's eyes shone in the spring sunlight; her thick hair glowed chestnut. As well as shedding more than a few pounds, she had lost the short-treaded gait with which she used to carry her bulk around. To Zach's untrained eye, she looked like a confident, sexy young woman.

It wasn't only fat she had lost. Whatever emotional baggage she had been carrying, loaded onto her by a bitter and prejudiced mother, appeared to have been shed. In between her bouts of seasickness while they crossed the Atlantic, Zach had noticed the change in her, brought about he believed by the close confinement with their new companions. She had passed from awkward, hesitant introvert, through days of soul-searching self-awareness and from there to this new Amy. Not for the first time, he felt glad he hadn't left her behind in Maine.

Behind the youngsters, ambling at a more sedate pace befitting their advanced ages, came Elliott and Nan.

"What's that?" asked Sarah, squinting at the notice behind Zach.

"A meeting," said Zach. "Tomorrow at the Celtic Manor. The place we went when we first arrived."

"And where America regained the Ryder Cup," said Frank, a smile playing at the corners of his mouth.

"Huh?" said Zach. "Didn't Europe whup our asses last time the Cup was played? I'm sure I listened to it on the radio."

"No, sir, that was the *last but one* time it was played," said Frank, the smile breaking out fully.

"He's right, Zach," said Amy, her smile even broader than Frank's. "I caddied."

"Me, too," said Sarah with a giggle. "At least, I drove the golf buggy."

Frank nodded and leaned in to kiss her cheek. "Lucky we got that gennie working to charge the buggies up. Or you'd have been watching from the clubhouse. You have to take it easy, missy."

"Er, anyone care to tell me what the heck you're talking about?" Zach felt amused and bemused at how much he had grown to like these people.

"Well, sir," said Frank, "it was like this. Being so close to a Ryder Cup course and with so many Europeans here, I thought it was high time we got our revenge. So I found another American who was game—"

"You also discounted anyone who didn't play off at least a fourteen handicap," interrupted Elliott, with a grin.

"Why, sure. I didn't want to lose this time. I mean, it could be the last." His jollity faded briefly, but he quickly resumed his tale. "Then it was merely a case of finding a couple of willing Europeans and some clubs." He shrugged. "The fairways are like meadows, the greens like shag pile rugs, but I'm pleased to report that the good ole' U.S. of A. adapted better to the conditions and prevailed by more than six points."

"Of course," added Nan, a twinkle in her eye, "it helped that the European team consisted of an Italian and a Norwegian who barely knew one end of a club from the other."

Zach could not help but chuckle. He had not laughed much in more than forty years. It felt good.

Elliott stepped up to the notice. When he turned back to face them, the humour had gone from his eyes.

"This meeting," he said, looking at Zach, "what's it about?"

"I think," Zach replied, "that tomorrow we'll get the answers to our questions."

Chapter Nine

It rained heavily throughout the night, but by late morning the sun had dried the grass banking in front of the hotel sufficiently that people were able to sit on it and enjoy the warmth. The breeze still contained a nip, a reminder it was April and this was Wales, not the Algarve.

The open-plan bar and restaurant areas leading off the main foyer had standing room only, and not a great deal of that remained. The balconies overlooking reception on the first few floors were crowded. The foyer had been cleared of forlorn Christmas decorations and was now filled with people. The warm, dry weather had allowed them to open the plate glass windows on their hinges and swing them back like vast doors so that people could come and go easily, and stand outside and still be able to hear when the meeting was underway.

Ceri stepped out to smoke a last cigarette before it started. Most of the chatter she could hear from the groups of people who had settled in the sun was conducted in foreign languages. She guessed those whose English was good were inside and would report to their non-English-speaking friends later. It meant the crush they had feared might occur if everybody tried to crowd into the hotel all at once did not materialise.

The sun lifted Ceri's spirits. They needed it. The previous afternoon, she and Tom had helped Howard to push one of the hotel's minibuses out of the basement car park and bump start it on the hill outside. With the engine running, they pumped air into the sagging tyres with an electric pump running from the vehicle's cigarette lighter socket. Tom handed to Howard a syphoning kit consisting of a length of plastic tubing and a screwdriver.

"Rustled this up for you," he said. "Was going to give you mine, but I've a feeling I'm going to need it yet."

They joined Howard, Colleen, Bri and Will on the minibus as Howard drove it away from the hotel. A mile or so outside the hotel grounds, satisfied nobody had noticed them leaving or was attempting to follow, Howard brought the vehicle to a halt. After hugs all around and one or two tears, Tom and Ceri jumped out and stood waving until the bus was out of sight, heading east towards England. The walk back to the hotel had been with leaden steps and heavy hearts.

Ceri flicked the cigarette stub away and went inside. She weaved between knots of people to reach the concierge desk behind which a pale-looking Tom stood, peering uncertainly at the assembled crowd. Dusty lay on the floor, partly under the desk. He thumped his tail when she stepped behind the desk to join them.

Tom offered her a tentative smile.

"Ready?" she asked, squeezing his arm by way of encouragement.

"As I'll ever be." He craned his head as if looking for somebody.

"What's up?"

"Wondering where Joe is. He could tell them about what they get up to at Hillingdon Hospital."

Ceri shook her head. "Not seen him."

"Ah, well. It was a thought." He took a deep breath. "Here goes nothing."

Tom stepped up onto the wide wooden block that had been brought in from one of the conference rooms to act as an impromptu stage. Ceri handed him one of the cordless microphones; there were two others ready to be handed around for the inevitable questions.

Ceri stood before the PA system and switched it on. She raised her thumb to Tom.

"Um, hello," said Tom into the microphone. Ceri had spent a large part of the morning testing the volume and she was satisfied his voice would be audible without being deafening. "I hope you can all hear me."

The hotel fell silent apart from the shuffling of feet and occasional cough, while every head turned to face the concierge desk. Ceri immediately felt her face flush. She looked up at Tom and savoured the relief it was he who stood up there facing them and not she.

"Um, okay," said Tom and tried to smile. Too forced, more a grimace. "My name is Tom Evans." He gestured towards Ceri, who felt her face grow hotter. "This is my friend, Ceri Lewis. Both of us hail from just down the road. Apart from me and Ceri, there are only two other people we are aware of—two young people wearing bandages, who you might have seen with us until yesterday—living on mainland Britain, who survived the Millennium Bug and who haven't been turned into something resembling a shambling zombie from a third-rate horror film."

He paused and gestured to Ceri. She removed the top from a bottle of water and handed it to him. He sipped it greedily. A low hum of muttered conversation arose.

"That's better," said Tom, passing the bottle back to Ceri with a wink. He held up a hand, palm flat, and bounced it a little in the air; the muttering immediately died away. All signs of Tom's nerves had disappeared; he looked like someone used to addressing an unruly classroom. "I'm getting ahead of myself. I think the best thing to do is to tell you our tale from the beginning. There will be plenty of time for questions. All I ask is that you let me tell our story to the end before you ask anything. Is that okay with everyone?"

He received a low murmur in reply.

"Thank you. The first part of our story will be a familiar one and I can brush over this part. We fell ill with the Millennium Bug. We survived, whilst our family and friends didn't." Tom took the briefest pause that to Ceri indicated he wasn't in any way trying to make light of people's loss, but they were gathered here today for something else and he needed to press on with it. He was rather good at this, she thought.

"Where our tale might depart from yours," he continued, "begins when I met my first survivor. His name is Peter and, later, he and I found Ceri.

"Peter told me he came from a small village outside Cardiff and he was driving around looking for survivors. Though I didn't really notice at the time, he never said he had fallen ill with the virus and lost loved ones. He *did* mention the loss of his wife, but she had died many years before and not from the Millennium Bug.

"A couple of other things about Peter. He showed me something remarkable. I have a dog. Dusty. He's down there on the floor in front of me, half-asleep. Peter had never seen Dusty before, yet he made him lie down, chase his tail and stand up again by doing nothing more than point at him. He also said some things that made me suspect he knew more about the Millennium Bug than I did. Hell, than anyone did. He admitted as much to me, but would only reveal little bits at a time. It was frustrating."

"Where is this Peter?" asked an American voice from somewhere near the front of the audience.

"He's not here," said Tom. "He *was*, but left yesterday." He looked at the person who'd asked the question. "Please, let me get through the story—I've barely started—and then you can ask whatever you want once I've finished."

Tom told them everything. How the Millennium Bug had been systematically disseminated throughout the planet; about the images Peter had shown them of spacecraft and tidal waves; of the pursuit from the Sea King helicopter; how Diane had recovered fully from what had appeared to be mortal injuries; about the Beacon and their failed attempt at preventing its activation. And everything of relevance in between, including the likelihood that soon after arrival of the remainder of the other species another Commune would be held and this time, swollen with power, it would not be persuading people to remain where they were, or suggesting they come to the U.K., but compelling them to slit their writs or step off high buildings.

The only part Tom omitted was their encounter with the nuclear submarine, *Argute*, and the point-blank refusal of Acting Lieutenant Commander Irving to believe their tale of disease-spreading, mind-controlling alien invaders. Tom and Ceri had agreed their story was depressing enough without burdening everyone with the realisation that their only chance of gaining military assistance had been lost.

Tom's speech was punctuated by gasps from the audience. And dark mutterings. And half-choked cries of rage or anguish. When Ceri glanced about as the tale drew to an end, she noticed a few people quietly sobbing.

"So," Tom said, "we came here as soon as the children were well enough to travel. Peter and I spent a couple of weeks driving around the coastline, placing notices warning people not to go near London. Then you all began to arrive.

"And that is our story. You now know as much as we do." He licked his lips. "I'll give you a few minutes to absorb it; I know it's a lot to take in. Then I'll do my best to answer your questions."

Tom turned off the microphone, jumped down from the platform and grabbed the bottle of water. He sat back and took a long slug.

"Well done," said Ceri. "You couldn't have done any better."

"Hmm. I'm not sure they believed most of what I told them."

Ceri shrugged. "We can only tell them what we know. It's up to them what they make of it."

She looked out into the foyer. People had formed into small groups. A babble of debate arose, punctuated by the occasional raised voice.

Tom drained the bottle of water. "Still think we should argue that violence isn't the best way forward?"

"Yes." Ceri sighed. "I don't think it will work either, but we have to try."

"Let's get it over with. Then I think I'll join you in a bottle of vodka."

"We'll both need it."

Tom clambered back onto the wooden block and switched on the microphone.

"All right," he said. The noise quietened and heads turned to face him. "Does anyone have any questions?"

Immediately, a clamour of voices was raised.

Tom put out his hand again in the shushing motion.

"There are too many of us to call out. Perhaps, if you have a question, raise a hand?"

A forest of hands shot into the air.

"Ceri will pass around the spare microphones."

Ceri stepped out into the crowd.

"To your right, Cer," said Tom. "The tall gentleman there… no, over a bit… yes. I think his hand was up first."

There was enough space between people not to have to squeeze past and Ceri quickly found the man Tom had indicated. She handed one of the microphones to him.

"One moment, sir," said Tom. "To your left, Ceri. The lady in the blue jumper was next. Now, sir, what's your question?"

While Ceri made her way to the woman, she listened to the man speak.

"Hello. My name is Günther. I am from Dusseldorf. My question is, do you believe the plague was deliberately started by these, um, people?"

"Yes, Günther," replied Tom, "I do. Peter did not take part in the spread of the disease, but he showed us the container which held the powder. It looked like a stainless-steel vacuum flask. I saw him dispose of his powder in the North Sea."

"Powder?"

"Yes. They designed it to kill over ninety-nine percent of humanity. They spread it over handrails and banisters, that sort of thing. Anything we touch. We stood no chance."

Ceri made her way back to the German to retrieve the microphone and take it to the next person whose hand was raised. Tom turned to the woman she had given the other mike to.

"Hi. I'm Madeleine and I'm from South Carolina. Sailed into Liverpool a week ago." She gave a short laugh. "Went clear around Ireland when a southerly gale blew us off course and nearly came ashore on the Isle of Man. We were going to aim for London till we saw the notice telling us to head west instead." She cleared her throat. "To speak frankly, your tale seems like a steaming pile of doggy-do, except for one thing. I heard those voices in my head as clear as I can hear you, Tom, and I know y'all did too." A low murmur of agreement rippled through the audience. "Since we can't all be having the same hallucination, I have to conclude, much as it pains me, that you are telling the truth."

"Thank you," said Tom. "Do you have a question?"

"I was coming to it. The rest of these *people*… aw, to heck with it. Call a spade a spade. They're *aliens*, ain't that what you're saying? So the rest of these aliens are on their way and when they get here they're liable to make us commit suicide. My question ain't only directed at you, Tom, but to everyone here. What are we gonna do to stop that from happening?"

A deep hush followed the woman's question. Tom broke it.

"Thank you again, Madeleine. You have cut right to the purpose of this meeting. This is something we have discussed and have come to our own conclusions. I have no doubt many here will feel attack may be the best form of defence." A rumble of agreement greeted Tom's remark. "But Ceri and I have faced them with guns in our hands. In only small groups—four or five of them—they combine minds, or whatever they do, and can completely overpower us. There are almost five thousand of them in London. It won't be a fair fight. And they don't die easily. The woman—Diane Heidler—we saw her recover within weeks from injuries that should have killed her. But, listen, there may be other ways. We can talk to them. Persuade them we are worthy of sharing this planet with them—"

He could get no further. He was drowned out by an uproar of voices raised in anger.

While Tom waited for the noise to subside, Ceri handed one of the microphones to a giant of a man who had been standing patiently with his hand raised. With a start, she recognised him as the man who had caused the commotion by the crazy golf course the previous morning. The leather jacket gave him away; the thick lips confirmed it. He smirked when he took the mike from her.

When the outcry began to die away, he raised the microphone.

"My name is Clint. I'm from Dublin and I have a question for Tom." His accent was a strange one: undeniably Irish, but with a twang of something else. American, maybe. "The woman you mentioned. Diane, I think you called her. She took part in spreading the Millennium Bug?"

"Yes," Tom replied. "In the States. Around Los Angeles and Las Vegas, I believe."

A woman's voice cried out from the balconies, "I had family in L.A."

The Irishman's smirk grew wider. "Tell us, Tom, why you let this woman live? Not only that, if I've understood you correctly, you helped her to get better."

Another rising tide of voices threatened to drown out Tom's reply. He raised his voice. "Diane saved mine and Ceri's lives. She helped to save the lives of Brianne and Will. Without her surgical knowledge, Howard could not have saved them alone."

Clint made a dismissive noise in the back of his throat. "Sounds to me like you're an enemy sympathiser."

Tom's angry response cut across the fresh uproar. "Don't be ridiculous!" Ceri glanced at him. High spots of colour had appeared in both cheeks. "I lost people I loved to the virus. I had to bury my mother in her garden because there was no one left to come and take her corpse. My girlfriend died lying in other people's blood and shit and piss. I was going to propose to her on Christmas Eve. The children I taught..." His voice tailed off and he lowered his head.

Before the Irishman could say anything more, Ceri snatched the microphone out of his hand and moved smartly away, but she didn't miss the black scowl he directed at her. She handed the microphone to a tall, fair woman.

"Yes, hello. I am from Sweden. My name is Aletta. I don't really have a question, but I want to tell you all something. My friend here—" she indicated a thick-set man by her side "—and I landed near Dover. We had three companions. We did not go to the port or see any notices. We drove into London and came across some of these people. Aliens, if you like. They killed one of our companions and captured the others. What Tom said about their power, that they can take over our minds, it is true." The thick-set man nodded emphatically. "Oh. And I do not think sparing this woman, this Diane, means Tom is a—how did you say it?—a sympathiser with the enemy. I think it means he showed compassion. That he is human."

Whether her words would have made any difference to the mood of the gathering, Ceri never found out because the woman's head turned at the sound of approaching engines. Ceri followed her gaze to see people outside making way for three khaki lorries, which drew up in front of the hotel. Army lorries. A man climbed down from the passenger side of the lead vehicle.

Ceri recognised him when he strode into the hotel, took in the scene with a glance and leapt onto the concierge desk. Hands on hips, Joe Lowden gazed at the assembly.

"Is the meeting done?" He didn't have a microphone. He didn't need one. The hotel had fallen deathly still and his voice rang out clearly. "Have you all decided to fight the bastards?"

Ceri looked behind Joe to Tom, expecting him to say something. But he remained still, with his head hanging down. Dusty had emerged from beneath the desk and was nuzzling at Tom's shoes.

"Well?" demanded Joe. "Gonna let them get away with it? These *fuckers* who murdered our families without batting an eye. Who attached electrodes to the heads of survivors and fried their brains. Gonna stand to one side and say, 'Carry on, old chaps. Don't mind us. You take our planet while we lay down and die.' Or—" his wide-eyed stare became a dark glower and his voice dropped to a growl "—are we going to look them in the eye and say, 'Fuck you, E.T.! This is our home. You'll pay for what you've done.' I say, make them pay. Make them bleed and writhe and die. Like they did to our friends and families."

"Er, excuse me," said an American voice over the PA system. A grey-haired man had raised one of the microphones. "My name's Elliott. I'm a high school English teacher from Philadelphia. I'd like to ask, how are we supposed to fight these aliens? What with? We brought some weapons with us from the States, but only enough for our group."

Joe let out a low chuckle and waved an arm towards the lorries outside. "Glad you asked, Elliott, my man. See those lorries? Those *trucks* as you Yanks would say? Filled to bursting with assault rifles, submachine guns, grenades and mortars. Enough for every man and woman here to arm themselves to the teeth. Enough ammo to fight an army fifty thousand strong." He grinned. "Handy things, army bases. And there are a *lot* of army bases around here." The grin faded and his stare grew intent. "So what do you say, Elliott? What do you say, my good people? Do we fight?"

For a moment, there was silence. Then a voice from the balcony called out, "Yeah. Let's fight!"

"That's the spirit," said Joe. "What about the rest of you? Do we fight?"

More voices cried out in the affirmative.

"Not loud enough," shouted Joe. "What do you say? *Do we fight?*"

As though from a bursting dam, the wave of voices crashed over Ceri, making her wince. She glanced again at Tom, who raised his head at the din. He met her eye and shrugged.

We tried, he mouthed.

Yes, they had tried. Even without Joe's grand entrance, she doubted it would have been enough.

Mankind was once again going to war.

Part 2: Comrades in Arms

Chapter Ten

In Asia and Oceania, Africa and South America, central and western parts of the United States and Canada, the east and far north of Europe, survivors who had not been close enough to the U.K. to receive the summons were nevertheless on the move.

Within days of waking to find their loved ones and neighbours dead, those who overcame the dark despair had found themselves compelled by a strange and persuasive voice to remain where they were. Even the majority, who did not understand the literal words of the message, grasped their import and obeyed them.

For weeks, survivors did not venture far, concentrating on staying alive and clearing their immediate surroundings of the dead. Decaying corpses were tossed into seas or rivers, flung into ravines or set aflame without ceremony. It is difficult to feel compassion for inanimate flesh when you are weak, shocked and uncertain whether you will see out the day.

Indeed, staying alive proved beyond the ability of many, particularly in tropical climes or in the south where a sun-blessed summer helped along the process of decomposition and encouraged new perils. Vermin and scavengers proliferated. Pestilence spread. The scent of living man was supplanted by the stench of death, emboldening predators. In some parts of the world, man was displaced at the top of the food chain by the great cats or giant mammals, or even the humble rat if gathered in sufficient numbers.

Those who possessed the wit and means to arm or barricade themselves against disease and carnivores eked out those days of being shackled to their immediate locales. Long days of filthy labour and solitude. When the compulsion placed on them by the Commune loosened, they began to spread out in ever-widening orbits. More perished when they encountered deadly fauna that had not inhabited the area, or not in such great numbers, when last they had ventured out.

Others met their demise in the sub-zero temperatures of northerly lands like Alaska or Russia when the power failed and they exhausted their more primitive methods of staying warm, or when the need to hear the voice of another or feel another's touch drove them out of shelter into driving snow and winds that froze fingers and noses black.

Gradually and inevitably, the hardiest or luckiest survivors began finding each other. When initial mistrust was overcome, small pockets formed, became groups.

In cities like Beijing, Kolkata, Cairo and Mexico City, disease was the biggest post-Cleansing threat, but those who outlasted that, and the dangers and deprivations that followed, found each other more easily than those spread out across the steppes of Mongolia or pampas of Argentina.

New difficulties emerged. The virus had killed billions of people without distinction based on skin colour or religion or social standing or any one of the hundreds of reasons people treat others differently. It had behaved with equal lack of discrimination towards those it spared.

Young and old, brown and yellow, Catholic and Muslim, there were survivors of every colour, creed and bent. From Supreme Court judge to crippled beggar, all echelons of former society were represented in this strange new world.

As people banded together, so the good and bad in humankind began to jostle once again in the perpetual dance of civilisation.

More died, but not over food. In southern parts, crops were ready to harvest, fruit hung ripe on trees, water teemed with fish; many survivors trod in the footsteps of their ancient ancestors by foraging and hunting. In the north, there were plenty of canned, bottled and dried foodstuffs to last well into the summer and beyond. The world food shortage had been solved at a stroke.

No, it wasn't arguments over food or water that caused further fatalities. Any random gathering of humans will include those who yearn to be calling the shots, to be above the rest. In this strained new world, such quests for power, if opposed, were not decided by campaign and ballot, but by knife and bullet.

Acts that would once have constituted crimes continued to be committed. Murder, rape, wounding and assault, though not much theft: little point risking violent retribution by taking something from another when there is plenty of everything lying around waiting to be picked up. The late President of the United States had exhorted those who would survive to forget concepts like 'property' that were likely to become meaningless in a world containing only a million people. And so it proved.

Some took advantage of the absence of structure and authority to play out dark fantasies that would for ever have remained dirty, sweating secrets in a world with laws and those to enforce them. Sometimes, apparently motiveless acts of violence were driven by old prejudices the perpetrators felt they no longer needed to keep bottled away, eating at their insides like a malignant growth. Most went unpunished. Others were subjected to mob judgement and summary sentencing, which usually amounted to execution.

But such incidents were relatively rare. Men and women who hadn't laid eyes on other humans for a month or more were in the main gladdened to be amongst their own kind once again, relieved others yet lived.

Although none of the survivors heard the voice of Milandra calling them to the U.K., all had been touched by the Commune. In hushed whispers across flickering fires, they debated what supernatural forces were at work for each to have heard the same words without seeing the source of the voice that had spoken them.

They sensed something momentous was going on elsewhere in the world; something in which they would play no part, but that would determine their destinies.

While three thousand Europeans and Americans prepared for battle in a luxury hotel and nearby towns in South Wales, the rest of the world held its breath.

~ ~ ~

Will stared at his left shoulder in the mirror. A puckered dent showed where the slug had entered. Behind and around it, the flesh had sunk where it had wasted from the damage caused by the slug's path through his torso and his inactivity during the months of recovery.

Both entry and exit wounds were as fully healed as they were likely to be, and Howard had removed the bandages. With a week of April remaining, the doctor allowed Will to take off the sling for an hour each day and had given him a series of exercises to get the joint moving.

It wasn't much fun. The shoulder was stiff and painful, the arm skinny and weak. Every movement made it feel the flesh around the wound was tearing anew, cartilage and sinew parting, muscle separating. With Bri's encouragement, Will did his best, but it was going to be a long, painful process to regain even a quarter of his arm's former movement.

Bri's bandages had also come off. The indentation in her forehead was smaller than Will's entry wound and was already largely hidden beneath her regrowing hair.

Will brought his right hand across and touched the scar. The skin around it was as pale as a vampire's, with vivid weals and marks like the veins on a bloodshot cornea. He poked at it, fighting an urge to push through the flap of skin covering the hole and keep going, scratching the maddening itch as he went until his finger emerged from the exit hole. He pressed harder and the skin grew whiter. Harder again, until it felt his finger was on the verge of entering his chest. For a few seconds, Will maintained the pressure, wondering at the notion that it would feel good—painful, yes, and messy and risking infection, but overridingly *good*—to force his finger through his shoulder.

He lowered his hand and watched the angry red marks reappear with the pressure released.

Sighing, he turned away from the mirror and dressed, then

placed his left arm back in the sling. He stepped to the window and looked out.

A windswept, rain-drenched seafront, empty and forlorn. From his attic window, Will could glimpse a pier and funfair, bowling greens and gardens, amusement arcades filled with slot machines and video games. He was sick of the silence wherever they went and the sight of ragged Christmas decorations, a constant reminder of all that had been lost.

They had spent days in a village outside Lincoln. Almost a week doing nothing. Howard wouldn't let anyone help him to dig the grave. They sat and watched; there was little else to do, unless you were Colleen, in which case you drank.

In some weird get-up that reminded Will of an episode of *Dr Who*, Howard dragged the remains of his brother, sister-in-law and nephews in sheets from their bedrooms to the garden and lowered them into the grave. They watched him shovel mud—it had rained a lot since they'd left the Celtic Manor—into the hole until it formed a low mound. Glancing at the dogs slinking past the garden on an almost hourly basis, Howard found a wheelbarrow and used it to transport rocks from neighbouring gardens until he had enough to cover the mound.

Finally, he nailed two lengths of wood together to form a cross and planted it between the rocks.

Will, Bri and a rather unsteady Colleen joined Howard by the side of the cairn.

"I used to be a religious man," he said, "but lost my faith during a gap year as a relief worker in Thailand in 1980. They were being overrun by refugees flooding in from Laos, Vietnam and Cambodia. The condition in which they arrived, the numbers they lost along the way, the tales they told of the brutalities from which they were fleeing... how can a God that's supposed to be about love and compassion allow these things to happen to such defenceless people? The answers offered by organised religions to these questions have never satisfied me. I have never been able to square the cruelty and indifference and suffering that abounds in this world with a loving God." Howard paused and glanced about. "And hear that. No sounds but the wind and the crows. Even had I still been religious, the Millennium Bug would have put paid to it once and for all." He looked down at the grave. "My brother, Terry, was younger than me by six years. He was a good brother. His wife, Elaine, I wasn't so keen upon, but she bore him two fine sons who reminded me of their dad. Rest easy, brother. May I be wrong and we meet again in a better place than this."

He bowed his head and remained that way for a while. When he looked up, he glanced at Colleen. "I'm ready for that drink now."

The next day, Howard had driven them to Skegness. Here among the gulls and rodents, the dogs and cats, they had stayed. And the sheep. Will could see them now, in the gardens and bowling greens across the road. Around a dozen of them, heads down, munching, glancing at the humans if they came near but otherwise paying them no attention.

The cats and dogs had grown wilder. Will would no longer venture outside without Bri. The animals would approach within a few feet, spitting or snarling, jaws slavering, eyes filled with need, their centuries-long friendship with man forgotten. As soon as they detected the protective pall Bri erected around them, they slunk away, mewling or whining pitifully.

Bri and Will had watched one starving dog try to bring down a sheep. The victim had bleated, bringing its friends on the run. Forming a tight, woolly pack around the intended meal, the sheep had driven the dog away.

"It won't take the dogs long to realise they need to work together," commented Bri. "Then it'll be curtains for the sheep."

Will shuddered, remembering the dogs that had nearly made a meal of him in London.

He missed Dusty. And Tom and Ceri.

He liked Colleen well enough, but she never wanted to do anything except drink. She rarely went outside; when she did, even if in the company of Bri, she insisted on carrying a golf club she had broken into a sports shop to obtain. Whenever a bird or animal turned its head in her direction, she'd bring the club clattering down onto the ground. Will thought that if she ever stepped outside without Bri, she was going to need more than a golf club to protect herself.

As the weather continued to grow warmer, the corpses rotted away to reveal yellowing bones and grins that sometimes gave Will bad dreams. The supply of free meals was coming to an end and the dog population had started to turn on the cats and vermin, and each other. The sheep, as Bri had noted, would likely be next. Even with Bri's protection, Will wondered how long it would be before the dogs came for them.

Howard was spending more and more time with Colleen in the hotel bar. Now that Will's and Bri's dressings had come off and the risk of infection had passed, now that he had buried the remains of his family, he seemed without purpose. He was in the bar with Colleen, drinking whisky and smoking cigars, and it was barely midday.

Will sighed and wondered where Bri had got to. He had spent most of the morning looking for her, all over the hotel, but there was no sign of her. He glanced back down at the street, and there she was. She looked up and saw him watching her; she waved. Will waved back and grinned. He turned and hurried down the stairs to meet her.

"Bri! Where have you been?"

Bri closed the hotel's front door behind her. "Where are Colleen and Howard?"

Will nodded towards the door which led off the reception area into the bar.

"Already?" Bri grimaced and lowered her voice. "Do you want to leave? Get away from here?"

He nodded. "But where… how…?"

"I've sorted the 'how'. As for the 'where', we can talk about that once we're on the road. All I know is I can't waste any more time here."

"Okay." Will had no idea what Bri meant by having sorted how they would leave. Thanks to his stupid shoulder, he would only be able to grip a bicycle handlebar with one hand so long-distance cycling wasn't an option. But Bri was probably the most clever person he had ever met; if she said she'd found a way for them to leave, he didn't doubt it.

"Come on, then."

Bri started towards the bar. Will followed.

Howard and Colleen sat on stools in front of the polished wooden counter. A grey haze hung in the air above them and the atmosphere was thick with the smell of cigar smoke. They both glanced around. Howard smiled.

"All right, you two?" he said.

"Fancy a drink?" said Colleen, waving with her glass towards the array of upturned bottles and optics in front of the mirror lining the back wall.

"No," said Bri. "Will and I are leaving." When Howard opened his mouth to speak, Bri held up her hand. "Remember: we agreed to come with you on condition we wouldn't be obstructed if we wanted to return."

Colleen looked at Howard. "That's true," she said.

Howard glanced down at the glass in his hand. He placed it on the counter and slid it to one side. "If you want to go back," he said, "I'll take you."

Colleen nodded. "Yep. It's what we agreed."

"Thanks," said Bri, "but we can make our own way back."

"How?" asked Howard. "It's a long way."

Will watched Bri closely; he, too, wanted to know how she intended getting them to wherever they were going.

"I'm going to drive us back," said Bri.

"You can drive?" Will said.

Bri grinned at him. "I got Joe to show me how. He owed me a favour. Peter let us use the Range Rover. And since that's what I got used to driving, I've found another one in a garage on the edge of town." She held up a key fob. "It's not brand new, but it's only got four thousand miles on the clock. Plus, I picked up a jump starter from another garage so we can get it going. We'll take the starter with us and it can recharge through the cigarette lighter as we go along."

"Are you quite sure you're confident to drive, young lady?" asked Howard.

Bri nodded. "Peter said the biggest danger on the roads used to be other drivers. Since I don't have to worry about them, it shouldn't be a problem."

Colleen was looking at Bri with a widening smile. "What about petrol?" she asked. "As we've found out, not every car will allow you to syphon off fuel."

"It's a diesel model," said Bri. "And I've found some containers of diesel in the back of the garage. They must have been keeping them for emergencies. They're in the back of the Range Rover now, together with a supply of snacks and drinks from the machine in the customer waiting area."

"You seem to have thought of everything," said Howard. "Are you quite sure—both of you—that you want to go back?"

Bri glanced down at Will. He nodded firmly, not wanting to leave any room for doubt.

"I'm sure, too," said Bri. "We're grateful for everything you've done for us, but we're a lot better now and there's no need for us to stay with you any longer. We both miss Tom and Ceri."

"And Dusty," added Will.

Howard glanced at Colleen, who shrugged.

"Okay," he said. "We'll come and see you on your way. Make sure you can get the car started. What about the tyres?"

"I think they're okay," said Bri. "If not, the jump starter also has an air compressor. Maybe you'd help me…?"

"Of course."

Bri glanced at Will. "Is there anything upstairs you want to take?"

"My backpack from Harrods."

"Oh, yes. I want mine, too. Then we may as well get going. We could be back by this evening."

Will felt a rush of excitement. Only minutes before, he had been wondering what to do with himself for the rest of the day.

"Steady on, now," said Howard. "There might not be other drivers on the roads, but there are still plenty of hazards: dogs, sheep, cows, abandoned cars. And you've not fully recovered your strength yet. Nor Will. Better to go slow and steady and spend a night in a motorway services. Most of them have motels on their grounds. Remember: you promised to heed any medical advice. So that's my advice. Take your time; take frequent breaks; get plenty of rest. Okay?"

"Yeah, okay."

Colleen slung back the last of her drink. "I'm coming to see you off, too. First need to pee and grab my club."

An hour or two later, Will was sitting in the passenger seat of a white Range Rover. Bri sat behind the wheel, gunning the engine, which had started first time with the aid of the plastic box on wheels. Using the same box, Howard had inflated the tyres until he was satisfied and they had said their goodbyes.

Jerkily, forcing Will against his seat belt and making him wince at the pressure placed on his left shoulder, they pulled away from the garage. Bri turned onto the main road and began to head out of town. Will craned back and gave a last wave to Howard and Colleen before they disappeared from sight.

The gearbox crunched and the car jerked again while Bri struggled to find the next gear.

"Sorry. I will get the hang of it." She found the gear and the ride smoothed out. "Take a look in the glove compartment in front of you."

Will opened the drop-down compartment and gasped. He reached forward.

"Careful," said Bri. "I can't find a safety switch, lever, whatever it's called, and I'm not sure whether it's loaded. So keep it pointed away and don't touch the trigger."

Will laid his hand on the cold metal of the pistol. He closed his fingers around the grip and pulled it carefully out of the compartment, making sure not to let his index finger slide into the guard and over the trigger.

"Wow," he said. "Where did you find this?"

"Our police have armed units," said Bri. "I went hunting in the police station. Found the keys that opened the well-locked places. I think that's a Glock 17. Brought plenty of spare magazines for it, too."

"Our own gun," breathed Will.

"We're going to need it. The dogs are growing hungry and soon may not pay any attention to my aura. When we stop for the evening we'll have a go. Make sure we know how to use it."

"Me, too?"

"Of course. But best not let any adults know we've got it. They can be a little weird about stuff like this."

Will carefully—reverentially—replaced the pistol and closed the glove compartment. "Our own gun," he mused. "Bri?"

"Yeah?"

"Let's stop soon."

It had been more than a week since Jason Grant had seen Milandra. He knew from the depleting stores in the adjoining cottage she had been out to fetch more food. He had packed what remained in the back of the car he'd made ready for their drive down the coast.

There was nothing more he could do in this village. He was satisfied he had packed all available food and bottled water. All the petrol he could syphon was in containers in the car's trunk. Diesel, too.

He had been in contact with George Wallace, who informed Grant he had located a portable diesel generator in a council depot and had taken it to the hotel. It was waiting for Grant to arrive to hook the hotel up to it. He had offered to share the knowledge of how to connect the hotel to the generator, but Wallace had declined.

We can wait Wallace had sent. *The Chosen is bored out of her tiny mind now she's killed all the drones, and is hankering for watching movies or playing computer games. Won't hurt her none to wait a few more days…*

He had sounded almost gleeful.

Grant had also been in touch with Tess Granville. Activating the power grid had gone well. There had been no fires; having the drones switch off appliances had paid off. Rats had become less of a problem. Tess suspected London's vermin population was being driven into hiding by cats and dogs now the ready supply of corpses had dwindled with the onset of milder weather. Dog attacks on drones were increasing. Tess had diverted half of the teams from catching rats to dealing with feral dogs.

New teams had been set up to capture humans who had been coming to the U.K. from continental Europe and, to Tess's puzzlement, from the east coast of North America.

I've probed some of them she sent. *They heard a voice telling them to come. It said something about a final reckoning for mankind. It must have been Ronstadt, though I wouldn't have thought he'd be powerful enough, even with Heidler's help, to cross the Atlantic. There could be more outside London. Maybe we should send teams out to comb the rest of the country for them.*

Hmm. It's mysterious Grant sent back. *But don't waste time sending teams out of London. If humans are amassing outside the city, I suspect you'll know about it soon enough.*

You mean, they might attack us? Best make sure everyone's armed and alert.

Yep sent Grant. *They would be foolish to attack—it won't help their cause—but we know from their history they often choose the foolish path. If you are attacked, let me know immediately.*

The influx of humans to London had dried to a trickle a week ago, Tess reported, and they hadn't picked up any new ones for days. All told, around nine hundred new drones had been created in the past two months.

Wembley Stadium had been cleared of human remains and was ready to host a Commune, if required. With a seating capacity of ninety thousand, it would comfortably hold them all. Milandra could be seated on the football pitch to harness the minds of seventy-five thousand people and set them free to reach every surviving human throughout the world.

No. Not Milandra; more likely the incoming Keeper. Milandra would do what was required of her, but Grant knew she would prefer this task, if it fell to be performed, be carried out by another.

He arrived at the edge of the village and made for the bench where he had last seen her. It had rained for most of the past week and Grant had taken advantage of today's break in the weather to take a stroll along the coastal path. He had been admiring the clifftop views when Milandra summoned him.

The bench came into sight and Grant could see her sitting in the sunlight. She seemed different. A little more hunched, a touch less plump, flashes of grey at the sides of her head…

"You look older," he said, when he reached her.

Milandra turned to look up at him. Her face was lined; dark bags hung beneath her eyes. She offered him a wan smile.

"Come, Jason. Join me."

He sat. "You found everything you were looking for?"

"They *were* Sivatra's memories. And it was she who hid them away. The final memories I needed to complete the story were even better hidden. Took me a week to locate them."

"She didn't want them to be easily found. Why?"

The look that passed across Milandra's face was so dark Grant almost recoiled. "Sivatra made it difficult for her memories to be found with good reason." She sighed. "Jason, I can't tell you the entire story now. I will, but when we reach the hotel. The others need to hear this, too, and I'm too tired to tell it more than once."

"Are you ready to leave? The car's good to go."

She nodded. "You're a good man, Jason. Near everyone else I know would be pestering me to tell them what I learned. Not you. You simply shrug and accept I'll tell you later." She smiled, but it faded almost as soon as it appeared. "Know this: everything we've thought about our past is wrong. Not only wrong. It's *deliberately* wrong."

Grant felt the first stirring of unease. "A lie, then?"

"Yes. A lie. A great big whopping lie."

Peter reappeared from behind the outbuilding. "There's a hotel back there, overlooking the sea. We've definitely found them. They have a red double-decker London bus and I saw Lavinia Cram. Haven't seen her since Florida in the 1930s."

"She didn't see you?" asked Diane.

Peter shook his head. "I kept well hidden."

"Milandra calls them her 'Deputies'. I still can't sense her."

"Me neither. She's the Keeper. When she wants to be *incommunicado*, she can make her psyche invisible. And we daren't try to probe any of the others. The only one who might be receptive is Jason Grant, but I barely know him. Yes, he helped us that morning at Stonehenge, but he might have simply been doing Milandra a favour and considers me a traitor like the others do."

It was for this very reason Diane had questioned the wisdom of their approaching the Deputies, but Peter had been adamant.

"If we can get them on mankind's side," he'd argued, "then there might be some chance of persuading the newcomers that humanity's time isn't necessarily up."

Diane wasn't convinced, but did not revisit the argument. They had spent much of the past week debating what they should do once they had located Milandra and her small group of companions. Peter's arguments sounded weak to Diane. She suspected he was keeping something to himself, something that went to the crux of why he seemed prepared to risk his life over a cause that was already lost.

All Milandra had told them that morning in Wiltshire was they would be going to Cornwall, where they would remain to witness the Great Coming. Peter had driven the Range Rover to the most southerly point of mainland Britain, The Lizard peninsula. They had started exploring the coastline westwards, observing every coastal hotel along the way, looking for signs of inhabitation; a laborious process, since they did not want Milandra's Deputies to know they were coming. Every attempt she and Peter made to locate Milandra had been wholly unsuccessful. It was as if she had disappeared.

Peter glanced around at the deserted car park. "Might as well leave the car here," he said.

A movement caught Diane's eye. From the road down which they'd driven not half an hour ago, a man was walking towards them.

"Someone's coming," she said in a low voice and nodded at the man. Peter turned to face him.

As he drew nearer, Diane could see the man held a dark object in his right hand down by his thigh: a pistol.

Another movement, this time from the direction of the hotel. Two women. One dark, one blonde. The darker one also carried a weapon: a snub-nosed submachine gun. She nodded at the approaching man. "You were right, George. They were snooping around the hotel."

The man stopped in front of them. "I was taking a stroll along the lane to the farm when I heard your car engine. Noisy things, engines, these days."

Diane sensed the attempted probe and slammed the door firmly shut. The blonde was staring at her. The woman laughed and spoke in a high-pitched voice, like an excited teenager.

"Oh, my, we have two of our own here. I think we can all guess who…"

"Heidler and Ronstadt, I presume?" said the man.

"And you're George Wallace," said Peter. He nodded at the darker woman. "Lavinia." He turned to the blonde. "You must be the Chosen."

"I'm the Chosen. You're the Traitor. And you…" The blonde continued to stare at Diane, considering her. "What did you do to Bishop?"

"Bishop?" Diane didn't bother to conceal the sneer. "His

rashness almost got us both killed. The helicopter we were in crashed. He was trapped by the seat straps. I could have cut him free…" She let the rest of the sentence hang in the air.

"Why are you here?" asked Lavinia, looking at Peter.

"To speak with you." Peter made a show of glancing around. "Though I hoped to speak with Milandra and Jason Grant as well?"

"They are otherwise engaged," said the Chosen. She giggled, reminding Diane once more of a teenager. "Hey, Raccoon." She glanced at George Wallace. "Now's your chance to get the Traitor. Save you hunting him later."

Wallace blinked and looked down at the pistol in his hand as if he had forgotten he was holding it. Slowly, he raised it and pointed it at Peter's face.

Peter stiffened as the man's finger tightened on the trigger.

Dermot Ward had never experienced empathy. He couldn't imagine—didn't understand or care—how others felt. He had not done well at hiding this trait throughout his adult life. It usually materialised in him laughing or saying something others found cruel or offensive, resulting in verbal, occasionally physical, confrontations.

It became difficult to hold down jobs. Making friends he'd always found to be problematic; keeping them became impossible. The rare attempt at asking a girl out on a date ended in disaster when he made some comment about her hair or what she was wearing or her family to which the girl would take great exception, much to Dermot's mystification. He never saw these incidents coming; the only way to avoid them was to avoid passing comment at all. As such, he drifted into a reclusive existence.

Being accused of stalking by a former work colleague hadn't helped. True, he had followed her around, found out where she lived, cased out her flat on a few nights, but in an effort—so he told himself, and he believed it—to learn more about her to be better able to please her when he eventually asked her out, not for anything more sinister. The girl only agreed not to involve the police when Dermot offered his resignation and wrote, at his soon-to-be-former employer's prompting, an apology in which he assured her he would not bother her again.

He eventually discovered lone night working offered the best employment conditions for a man of his particular type of intellect. For that is what he truly believed: that what others perceived as oddness, even creepiness, their inability to mesh with him, was due to his superior intelligence. People's dislike of him he put down to envy. That he may be lacking in certain attractive personality traits did not occur to him. Accurate self-analysis is unlikely to be found in a narcissist.

A night security guard at a warehouse stocking electrical appliances suited Dermot. A few circuits of the building, flashing his torch to scare off any would-be intruders, every few hours wasn't taxing. The rest of the night he got to sit in the portacabin office, watching DVDs or surfing the internet.

He had always been a fantasist, making up exploits he would never come within touching distance of actually experiencing. The internet gave his imagination free rein. Under a number of pseudonyms, Clint (or Damien or Dirk or Samson) concocted an increasingly outlandish series of identities with which he roamed the web in anonymity, spinning his deceit to anyone who cared to listen. That the young, impressionable women he liked to target might themselves be middle-aged, overweight men with personal hygiene issues never crossed his mind.

Then he fell ill and the internet fell silent.

Later, when he thought he might be the last human left alive, he went hunting for apparel that supported his fantasies: cowboy boots, leather jacket, Stetson. The only Luger he could find in Dublin had been a replica; he still wanted to get his hands on the real thing. The military assault rifle strapped to his back would do a fine job for now. A more than fine job, yes, siree. And he still had the switchblade, tucked away into his back pocket. When he found the bitch, it was the blade he wanted to use. He had been keeping it clean and sharp especially for her.

Riding a scooter wasn't that difficult without other traffic on the roads. The worst part was the rain, slickening the road surfaces and causing the visor of his helmet to steam up. He took it easy, trying not to think about swerving to avoid a cat or sheep and ending up on the tarmac with a shin bone poking out of his jeans while hungry dogs drew nearer, attracted by the scent of blood and fear.

There was no rush. They had a few days' start, but he knew where they were headed. The old git of a doctor had mentioned more than once in his whiskey-induced haze that he was from a village outside Lincoln. He hadn't said the name of the village, but how many could there be?

It had taken days after the car park incident in Drury Street for the swelling to go down and to be able to walk without looking like he was trying to impersonate John Wayne; weeks for the bruising and discolouration to fade. He still experienced dull aches deep in the pit of his stomach and suspected he was pissing blood. With every cramp, every hissing breath while he waited for it to pass, every pink tinge he noticed to his urine, he vowed to slice her.

Dermot had noted that she and the old git weren't at the meeting. He had stayed afterwards long enough to be given an assault rifle and shown how to use it. Slipping away unnoticed had been a cinch.

He hadn't found them in Lincoln and followed the coast road out of the city. Most people, he figured, would end up by the sea when they had a deserted island on which to live.

He had pulled over for a break—his balls were aching after a prolonged spell on the scooter—when he heard the engine. Too late to take cover, he ducked behind the scooter and peered at the white Range Rover while it shot past.

Chapter Eleven

Given man's propensity for allocating to events names that lend them a sense of grandeur, of which they are not always worthy, it perhaps shouldn't be considered a surprise that the series of increasingly brutal skirmishes which began on a blustery morning in late April came to be known, if only fleetingly, as The Battle of London.

Not since The Peasants' Revolt of 1381 had a hostile, armed force marched against the city. Now another force, two thousand strong and bristling with modern weaponry, approached from the west.

Today's London consists of a mass of outlying towns and villages, each once (and, sometimes, still) imbued with their own style and character, which have become swallowed by the original town's expansion to form part of the urban sprawl. In some places, a sense of separation is maintained, either through deliberate planning or as a serendipitous consequence of other development. Take Slough: a buffer of green belt and the M25 separated it from Greater London proper. Just off the M4 at junction 6, it seemed as good a place as any in which to make an advance base.

Five days after the meeting in the Celtic Manor, a convoy of lorries, minibuses, cars and vans left South Wales and made its way along the M4. The young, elderly and infirm remained behind, along with many who did not fall into any of those categories but who did not wish to join in. Comments were passed, names called and scuffles broke out, but by and large those intending to fight were too busy learning how to use assault rifles, submachine guns, hand grenades and 60mm mortars to overly concern themselves with those who didn't want to fight.

Advance base camp was established in a hospital at the southerly edge of Slough, near the motorway and with plenty of hotels, houses and shops nearby. There were at least two nurses and a paramedic amongst the survivors who had made it to the Celtic Manor. They had been charged with manning the hospital and making ready to receive the injured. Even Joe, with his infectious energy and lofty aspirations for the forthcoming battle, did not deny there would be casualties.

At dawn the next day, the ragtag army assembled. If folk had changed their mind and slipped away during the night, their absence wasn't mentioned. Everyone, except for the half a dozen or so (including a young American lady two months' pregnant by the name of Sarah) who would remain at the hospital with the nurses and paramedics, clambered aboard the vehicles that had brought them to Slough and set off across heathland, through villages and over the M25 motorway, aiming for Hillingdon Hospital roughly seven miles away.

"Unless anybody has a better idea," Joe had told anyone willing to listen the previous evening, "I suggest we make for the hospital in Hillingdon. If they have it set up like before, there'll only be a handful of them to deal with. They'll be armed, but we'll outnumber them something like ten to one. And once we've taken the hospital, it will stop them carrying out any more mutilations."

Nobody within earshot made any other suggestions. Joe had taken that as acquiescence and directed the lead vehicle towards Hillingdon.

They took the hospital without having to fire a shot. That's not to say shots weren't fired. Many were. Some into the air in triumph; most after the rapidly disappearing BMW in which the few 'people' they discovered at the hospital fled in face of the numbers advancing upon them. It is doubtful any of the shots caused as much as a scratch in the car's paintwork.

While others checked the hospital buildings to make sure they were clear, there was only one place Joe wanted to visit. He strode along the corridor to A&E and entered the long room with the curtained cubicles along one wall. The last time he'd been in here, he had been made at gunpoint to stand in line awaiting his turn to enter the cubicle into which ordinary people were stepping and from which shambling automatons were emerging. When he'd tried to make a break for it, he had been forced through some form of mind control into the cubicle.

He made for the plastic curtain and yanked it back. The urine-stained trolley was still there; it smelled pungent, as though recently used. The machine with the things they attached to people's foreheads (what *were* they called?) was still there, too. When last Joe had been here, it had been wired up to a series of car batteries. Now the cable led to a socket in the wall; they must have got the mains electricity supply back in operation. Joe stared at the machine for a long moment, his lips compressing into a thin line. When he raised his rifle and blew the machine to smithereens, it brought people on the run.

"S'okay," he said, "just putting some ghosts to rest."

Buoyed by their unexpectedly painless victory, Joe wanted to press south, working through West London towards Heathrow Airport around which, he reasoned, *they* were most likely to be concentrated. And it was time to move on foot to be able to fan out and make it more difficult for *them* to avoid the advance.

He didn't seek out anybody with military experience to solicit their advice. He didn't ask for opinions or question whether his way might not be the best way.

Leaving their vehicles behind at the hospital and proceeding on foot wasn't the only mistake they made. When the rats caught them in the open, it seemed it could be their last.

The evening following the meeting, while they shared a bottle of vodka amidst the chatter of excited people, Ceri glanced around the bar before addressing Tom.

"Hark at them," she said. "They're all so animated."

"Easy to see why. They once more have a purpose. Some aim in life."

"One that's going to get them killed."

"Maybe. But look at them." He gestured at the crowded room. "Teenagers. Pensioners. Women. They might be going to their deaths, but can you imagine, in this world, a braver way to meet your end?"

"Foolhardy, more like."

"Courageous, too. Heartbreakingly so." Tom gave a deep sigh. "I'm not particularly brave. In fact, I suspect I'm a bit of a coward. But I don't want to spend the last weeks of my life sitting here confirming it while all these people go off to war for me."

"*For* you? How can it be for you when you don't even agree they should be fighting?"

Tom glanced down at his glass, picked it up and drained it. When he looked back at Ceri, her expression had changed from exasperated to resigned.

"I do think," he said, "that we—that's the broader 'we', not me and you—need to fight. As soon as Joe made his entrance and started winding people up, I knew he was right."

"Despite what happened at Stonehenge?"

"*Because* of what happened at Stonehenge. But not only Will's shooting. My mam and Lisa. The children in my class. Dusty's owner. Hell, even Ross the Boss, my old headmaster. I want people to fight for them. For everyone they killed."

Ceri lit a cigarette and regarded Tom through narrow eyes. She was silent for a long moment. Then, "You're right."

"You're agreeing with me?" Tom laughed. "Can I have that in writing?"

Ceri remained serious. "I lost my son, my husband, my parents, my friends. I think it's a suicide mission, but we're all going to die anyway when the rest of them get here. Die now, die in a few weeks." She shrugged. "You not tempted to join them?"

"Very much so," said Tom. "But we've gone up against them once and nearly got ourselves killed. And we've warned our people what the others are capable of with their mind-control shit. We've done our bit."

"You said you don't want to sit here while everyone else goes off to fight. So what *do* you want to do?"

"Well, I'd like to get a couple more weapons. No, don't look at me like that. I'm not trying to be Rambo again. These will be strictly for self-defence only."

"Okay." Ceri dragged deeply on her cigarette. "I'd quite like an assault rifle to complement the shotgun. Then what?"

"Perhaps find ourselves a fancy new set of wheels and then…" He tailed off deliberately to allow her to finish the sentence.

"Go find Bri and Will."

Dusty, lying beside Tom's chair, raised his head at the sound of the names. Tom grinned.

The following day, Tom nursing a thick head, Ceri, to his chagrin, looking as fresh as a daffodil, they joined the long queue of people waiting to be allocated weapons.

Over the succeeding couple of days, they practised with their weapons of choice out on the fairways and greens, in billowing rain and gusting wind. Ceri proved to be as proficient with an assault rifle as she was with a shotgun. Tom, on the other hand, found that firing a submachine gun scared him even more badly than a shotgun; at least with the latter he maintained some degree of control. With the submachine gun, he felt like a tom cat spraying in all directions to mark its territory. He vowed to use the weapon only in extreme need and, if he needed to fire a gun at all, to use the shotgun. As for hand grenades and mortars, they frightened him more than the machine gun.

Early in the morning of the third day, they found Joe on his way out to the golf course, laden not with golf clubs but with mortar shells and tubes.

"You're not coming with us," he said, after Tom had started to explain. He didn't sound surprised. "That's okay. You don't need to have a reason, but I think you have plenty. I saw what you went through thinking the boy had been killed."

"We're going to find him and Bri," said Ceri. "We encouraged them to leave before the meeting. Now that it's over…"

Tom shifted uncomfortably. He didn't want the lad to be so understanding.

"Look, Joe," he said, "we know we don't need to tell you about the power of their minds, particularly when a few of them band together."

"Nope. You don't."

"I think the message may have been lost the other day amidst the excitement caused by your arrival. Try to make the others understand they need to keep their distance. Fight them from afar if possible."

Joe smiled, but it didn't reach his eyes. It made Tom want to shiver. "Thanks for the warning." He gestured at the equipment in his arms. "We'll chuck bombs at them when we can, but I suspect much of the killing will have to be done up close and personal. Might be the only way to make sure the bastards are really dead."

"Be careful," said Ceri. She leaned forward and placed a kiss on the boy's cheek.

"Yeah," echoed Tom, "be careful." Since Joe didn't have a free hand to shake, Tom clapped him on the back.

"Ah, careful's my middle name," said Joe. "Hope you find the youngsters. Say hello to Bri for me. That's one special girl. Keep her out of harm's way."

"Right then," said Tom, once Joe had left. "Let's go swap the Nissan for something a bit more upmarket."

An hour later, in a showroom on the outskirts of Newport, the engine of the brand new Peugeot 508 GT Saloon roared to life and Tom disconnected the jump leads from the Nissan's battery. With an air pump already deployed on the tyres and the new car's tank brimming with petrol from the five-litre containers they had filled by syphoning on the way, they were ready to go. They would stop for food and water on the road to top-up what they had brought with them.

Tom switched off the Nissan's engine and tapped the car fondly on the bonnet. "You've done us well," he said. He smiled at Ceri, who was sitting behind the wheel of the Peugeot, looking as though she couldn't wait to get the car onto open road.

He walked over and slid into the passenger seat. A damp nose nuzzled his neck. He turned and stroked Dusty's head. The dog looked quite happy in his basket on the back seat.

"You ready?" said Ceri. "We'll need to keep going for a few hours to charge the battery up before we think about stopping."

"Aye," said Tom. "Let's go find those kids."

As the white Range Rover ate up the miles, Bri grew accustomed to the clutch and gearbox, and the journey became smoother. She didn't have a complete feel for the vehicle's dimensions and had come perilously close to scraping the passenger side when passing stationary vehicles.

"Sorry," she remarked, yanking the steering wheel sharply to the right when Will drew in a hissing breath as the latest potential obstruction loomed large. She let out a nervous giggle. "My dad always said women don't have good spatial awareness."

That got her thinking about her parents and brother, and the next few miles passed in silence. When Will gasped again, Bri jerked at the wheel, but the road was clear.

"What's up?" she demanded. "I wasn't in danger of hitting anything."

She glanced to her left. Will was craning around in his seat to look back the way they had come.

"Well?" Bri said. "What you looking at?"

"Nothing."

Will turned to face the front again. Next time Bri glanced at him, he was looking down at his lap where his fingers twined and untwined.

"Right, buster!" Bri stepped hard on the brake, forgot to dip the clutch and brought the car to a jerking, stalling stop. "Shit!" she muttered.

She pressed the button that started the vehicle, her heart in mouth in case the battery had not yet charged sufficiently to start. To her relief, the engine coughed back to life, but promptly stalled again. She had left the engine in gear and, once more, had not depressed the clutch.

"Shit! Shit! Shit!" Uttering a silent prayer to the god of naïve girl drivers, Bri made sure the gearbox was in neutral before pressing the starter. "Oh, thank you, thank you, thank you…" She turned to Will and grinned. "Phew! Thought I might not be able to get us started again. Anyway, matey, the reason why I stopped in the first bloody place: I know something's up. Tell me."

Will continued to stare at his lap.

"I'm waiting," said Bri, in what she hoped was her sternest school ma'am voice. She fancied she did a passable impression of Miss Jennings, her school I.T. teacher, who could freeze a class into silence merely by clearing her throat.

Will sighed. "The Giant," he said.

"Huh?"

"The Giant." He pointed over his shoulder with a thumb. "Back there. I saw the Giant."

"Giant? Giant? Like, seriously dude, what are you talking about?" Bri stared at the boy, wondering if he was losing his mind. It wouldn't be surprising if he was. Maybe they all were, a little.

Will sighed again. "The Giant who came and talked to me. At the crazy golf."

"Crazy golf? You mean, back in Wales?"

Will nodded.

Bri had heard of somebody's blood running cold, but had always imagined it to be writers' hyperbole. Now she knew differently. When she realised what—or, more accurately, *who*—Will was referring to, it felt as if the contents of her veins and arteries had been replaced with meltwater from a glacier. She shivered involuntarily and hugged herself.

"Okay," she said slowly; she felt if she didn't enunciate deliberately, she would start to gabble and spook Will, too. "You're talking about that big Irish guy. The one who Colleen said tried to rape her. Where did you see him? What was he doing?"

"Like I said, I saw him back there." Again, Will indicated the direction from which they'd come with his thumb.

Bri turned and craned her neck so she could peer out of the rear window. She half-expected to see a gigantic man come striding towards them, red in the face with exertion, or anger, and was relieved to see the road behind them empty.

She looked back at Will. He was gazing at her with no hint of artifice in his open features.

"What was he doing?" she asked.

Will shrugged. "Dunno. He was sort of crouching down behind one of those crappy motorbikes. Like he was hiding or something." The last word sounded like 'sumfing' as Will's cockney roots became apparent.

"Crappy motorbike? What, like a scooter?"

"Yeah. A scooter."

Bri thought for a moment. If it was the Irishman from whom Colleen had fled—and she had no reason to doubt Will—what was he doing out here if not…?

"He's going after Colleen and Howard," she murmured.

Will nodded.

"You didn't really want to say you saw him because you know we'll have to go back and warn them and you don't want to go back. Is that it?"

Again, the boy nodded.

"I don't want to go back either." Bri sighed. "But we have to."

Will nodded for a third time.

"You can still speak, yeah?"

This time the nod was accompanied by a grin that faded almost immediately.

Bri shifted the gearstick into first. The road was wide and empty, but it still took her several attempts to turn so that the car faced in the opposite direction. She picked up speed and they headed back to Skegness.

The message arrived while Tess Granville was ten miles to the east, and slightly north, of Hillingdon Hospital, inspecting the approaches to Wembley Stadium.

Tess? It's Baker. I was at the hospital in Hillingdon.

One moment… Tess motioned to the man guiding her around

the empty streets and walkways. "Something's happening. We may need to cut this short. Give me a few minutes." She stepped to one side. *Baker… you* were *at the hospital?*

Yeah. An armed force of humans came. Estimate at least fifteen hundred strong. Difficult to be more accurate since I didn't see them out of their vehicles.

You didn't engage them?

I was instructed not to. Besides, there were only four of us. We'd have stood no chance.

No. And, good. I don't want them to be challenged. Not yet.

Lull them into a false sense of security? I like it.

Where are you now?

West Drayton. We let them see we went south.

Excellent. Pass the word: no one is to go north; no one is to challenge or engage with them. I'm on my way back. D'you know the library in Drayton?

No, but I'll find it.

You and the rest of your team from the hospital meet me there. Root out some maps of the area while you're waiting for me. Oh, and some food. Think we'll need it.

Okay. What shall I tell them?

Tell them they are going to be part of the War Council.

This gets better. Anything else?

There should be teams nearby looking for rats or feral dogs. Contact them and give them these instructions…

A few minutes later, Tess was on the road, heading for West Drayton, making sure she gave Hillingdon a wide berth. Baker, a dour man with a South African accent, was waiting for her at the library. He wasted no time in small talk.

"We've made contact with seven teams. Each of them knows where there are large concentrations to be found. Most of them are underground out of harm's way so have been left alone."

Tess smiled. "Sounds perfect. Let's send these drones a welcoming party, shall we?"

A dog with matted fur and slavering jaws followed them back to the hotel. Colleen turned around frequently and brandished the golf club with both hands, as though it were a claymore. Each time, the dog slunk back a few yards, its sly gaze never meeting hers.

Apart from remarking he was glad it was only the one dog, Howard seemed unconcerned. No, more than a lack of concern: he was preoccupied, distracted.

"You okay?" Colleen asked, when they were once more settled on stools in the hotel bar. "They'll be all right, you know. That Bri's got her head screwed on straight. And Will worships her. He'll do whatever she says."

She poured a generous slug of scotch into her glass. Without much help from Howard, she had finished the only bottle of Irish whiskey the hotel stocked and had moved onto the Scottish stuff. Not quite peaty enough for her palette, it would serve until she could find a supply of Irish. She slid the bottle along the bar to Howard.

"Yeah, they'll be fine," said Howard. "I'm not worried about them, not any more." He glanced at the bottle of whisky, but did not pour from it. He slid off his stool and walked around the bar. When he came back to resume his seat, he clutched a bottle of lemonade.

Colleen sipped her whisky. Scottish or Irish, the numbing sensation when the warmth hit her stomach and spread like questing tendrils through her nervous system was the same, and most welcome. Before the Millennium Bug, she had been an occasional drinker, a social imbiber, happy to swill the hard stuff with the best of them at parties or work functions, content with a cup of tea or coffee or the occasional glass of wine when snuggled up with Sinead on the sofa in their flat.

Sweet Sinead. Sweet, cloying, sloughing Sinead, who had shambled through Colleen's nightmares with grasping talons and gaping maw, trying to call Colleen's name but only succeeding in uttering a high-pitched mewling due to the swollen, blackened tongue and crumbling teeth.

Whiskey had banished this nightmare version of her lover. Gradually Colleen's mind, almost torn from its moorings, had tightened, helped in no small part by Howard's calm assurance. While it did, so her need to drink to keep the dream Sinead at bay diminished.

There were plenty of other reasons to drink in this new world. Staying permanently sozzled prevented Colleen's waking thoughts from turning dark and introspective; stopped her pondering her limited prospects. Without Sinead by her side to anchor her to the moment, Colleen was apt to worry about the future. In the current climate, such musings may lead to a short step off a tall building.

In one sense, then, though Colleen had told Howard in Dublin she intended drinking herself to death, it was the fact she was all but pickled that was presently keeping her alive.

She tipped back her glass and finished her latest tot. Leaning across the bar, she pulled the scotch bottle towards her.

"Not partaking?" she asked Howard.

He shook his head. Sighing, he sat straighter, as though he had come to a decision, and looked at her.

"I need to go back," he said.

"Back where? Lincoln or Wales or Ireland?"

"Wales. At least, I'll need to begin there. To find out if they've decided to fight; if so, where the battle's taking place. London somewhere, I suppose, but it's a huge city."

"London? You want to fight?"

"Good lord, no. I'm a doctor. People are going to get hurt. I might be able to help."

Colleen poured herself another liberal shot of scotch. "I suppose, though you said it yourself on more than one occasion: you're no surgeon."

"No, I'm not. But, like Peter said when he persuaded me to operate on Brianne, I'm the nearest thing they have to one. Mind, I could do with Diane by my side. Her knowledge of surgical procedure is greater than mine."

"I can't come with you. You know that."

"You could come so far. I'll leave you somewhere safe then pick you up later once I've found out what's happening."

"If Dermot sees you, he might go for you. Or follow you."

"I'll exercise caution." He turned to face her and took hold of her hand in both of his. "Look, I know we came away to keep you from that nutcase, and I don't want to do anything that's going to place you in danger, but I can't sit here drinking away the rest of my life when there may be people risking their lives for us. I *have* to help them in the best way I can. Do you see that?"

Colleen breathed out heavily. "You're a good man, Howard. I—"

She broke off when the door into the bar creaked open. A head peered around.

"Phew!" said Bri. "I thought I could only hear your two voices, but I couldn't be sure."

"What are you doing back?" asked Howard, letting go of Colleen's hand and getting to his feet.

"I, er…" Bri blushed. "This is going to sound silly. He must have imagined it."

"Who did?" asked Colleen softly. "Imagined what?" A knot had started to twist deep inside her stomach.

"Well," said Bri, stepping fully into the room, "Will thought he saw that Irish guy. The big one who was talking to him by the crazy golf."

"Where did he see him?" asked Colleen. Her voice continued in its gentle pitch, belying the turmoil erupting behind the scenes.

"A few miles away. We came back to warn you."

Colleen darted a look at Howard.

"We have to get out of here."

All the colour had drained from Howard's face. He swallowed and nodded at Colleen.

She looked back at Bri. "Where's Will?"

"I left him in the car. I'll go and get him. Oh, and guess what—we have a gun."

"This one?" came an oily voice from the door.

As if she had bitten into a sloe berry, all the spit left Colleen's mouth. Standing in the doorway were two people. Foremost, looking pale and scared, stood Will. Looming over him, holding a pistol, stood Dermot Ward, also known as Clint.

Chapter Twelve

Wallace's finger tightened around the trigger and Peter's body tensed in anticipation. Not that tensed muscles would limit the damage from a pistol fired at his face at a range of fewer than six yards. No, his body couldn't help him now.

It wasn't considered polite to probe a peer without consent, but courtesy did not figure large in Peter's current priorities. He probed. And immediately sensed Wallace's reluctance to kill him.

I loved her Peter sent. *Look…* He opened his mind, allowing Wallace access to his innermost memories.

Wallace looked and, in so doing, opened a return path to his own memories. As was understood in such circumstances, Peter did not take advantage. Nevertheless, as was also understood, it was impossible for Peter not to catch a glimpse of Wallace's deepest thoughts and emotions.

Not a word Wallace sent. *Or I will pull this fucking trigger.*

Peter said nothing. He sensed the other intellect withdraw from his mind. Slowly, Wallace lowered the gun.

"What the fuck?" Lavinia regarded Wallace in disbelief. "Why don't you put a bullet in his head?"

"Something passed between them," trilled Simone Furlong. She clapped her hands gleefully. "Oh, you boys, keeping secrets from us girls."

Peter turned to Simone. "No secrets, Chosen."

"He fell in love with a human," said Wallace, addressing Simone and Lavinia. "I mean, *really* in love, the way only they can normally experience. Lived with her for sixty years. Held her in his arms while she died of old age. It changed him. Made it impossible to carry out his part in the Cleansing." He shrugged. "He didn't hold back from spreading the dust out of betrayal to us, but out of love for them. I can't kill him for that."

"No?" said Simone. "I can." She motioned to Lavinia, who handed over the submachine gun. Simone raised it and once more

Peter stared down a black barrel.

"No!" Diane Heidler stepped forward. Peter had almost forgotten she was there. "What are you doing, Simone? We're not about killing each other. That's what humans do, remember? They're supposed to be the mindless drones, not us. We are the higher beings, evolved beyond the state of savagery humans can never hope to surpass."

Peter thought about Bri and what he had witnessed when examining her mind. The girl was living proof that what Diane had said wasn't true, though now was hardly the time to raise it.

Simone swung the weapon around to point it at Diane, who blanched but stood her ground. Simone wore a grin that was slightly off centre, giving her a manic appearance. Peter wondered if she was playing with a full deck; it wouldn't be the first time the greatly extended lifespan enjoyed on Earth Haven had driven one of their number insane.

"Did *you* spread the dust?" Simone asked Diane. "The pixie dust? The tragic magic pixie dust?" She paused and her grin grew wider. "Of course you did. In a children's playground, on the slide and swings and merry-go-round." She tittered again. "Very good. Very inventive. Infect the children and the parents will soon be coughing."

Diane jutted out her chin. Peter had never seen her look so defiant. "Yes," she said in a flat tone, "I spread the powder in a playground. Watched a child come along and rub it into his eyes. Watched his mother snort it up her nostrils. I watched and walked away and continued to spread it. From Los Angeles to Las Vegas, I played my part. Do I get a gold star? Or should I regret it?" She shot Peter the briefest of glances. "Yes, I regret it. I won't kill another human, not with a virus, not with a gun, not with my mind. If that doesn't fit your philosophy, Simone, then you'd better kill me as well."

Peter took a deep breath, ready to spring to Diane's defence, although he knew there was little he could do. The silence was broken by an unexpected source.

"Maybe you'd better kill me while you're at it." George Wallace stepped forward, holding out his pistol butt-first to the Chosen. "'Cause I'm done with killing dro— humans, too."

"Fuck, man, you've lost it," muttered Lavinia.

Without lowering her gun from Diane, Simone looked at Wallace. She made no move to take the pistol from his grasp.

"Well, well, Raccoon-boy," she said, "here's one for the books. Angry old George becomes a drone lover. What next? Go seek out a human to make your wife? Plead for clemency for the survivors? Maybe—" Simone's voice dropped and a glint appeared in her eyes "—maybe try to sabotage the Great Coming?"

Wallace snorted. "I'm no traitor, as you well know. If the consensus is to kill off the survivors—and I still can't see any other outcome—I won't take part in the Commune, but neither will I try to obstruct it."

Simone stared at him for a moment, her lips twisting in contempt. Then she looked back at Diane.

"He may be right," she said, her voice low and menacing, stripped of all vestiges of schoolgirliness. "He's probably no traitor. A pussy, yep." A further snort of derision came from Wallace; Simone ignored him. "And you, Diane, you're a strange one. Difficult to read. Regret? Hmm, maybe, but you played your part in the Cleansing, of that I'm certain. And you've since helped drones, though not enough to make you a traitor. You won't let me in to take a peek, but I believe you killed Troy Bishop." She shrugged. "He was a pig of a man. A rogue. If anyone didn't have the good of the whole at heart, it was dear Troy. Probably better off without him. Which only leaves…" She swung the weapon away from Diane. For the third time in as many minutes, Peter faced the business end of a gun. He suspected this would be the final occasion.

"Shoot me, Simone, and be done with it," he said.

"You don't deny you're a traitor to your people?"

Peter shook his head. "We designed humans to be aggressive, to procreate, to colonise this planet, to evolve. We then decided to wipe them out because they proved to be too successful at the very things for which they were created. If refusing to take part in their annihilation because I had grown to love them makes me a traitor then, yes, that is what I must be."

"That's what I thought," said Simone. "Goodbye, Ronstadt."

Peter closed his eyes.

And opened them again at the sound of the engine. All heads turned towards the road. A car was heading towards them. When it pulled up, Peter recognised the man behind the steering wheel: Jason Grant. The passenger door opened and Milandra eased her bulk out of the vehicle. She looked around the small company, her eyes narrowing when her gaze passed over the gun in Simone's hands. The Chosen, as though with the greatest reluctance, lowered the weapon.

"Well," said Milandra with a beaming smile. "This *is* convenient. All the Deputies gathered in one place." She nodded at Peter and Diane. "Our errant members are here, too. I have something to tell you, something that concerns you all. Shall we go inside?"

It wasn't so much a menacing advance as a stroll in the spring sunshine with guns. South of Hillingdon Hospital lay a pleasant residential area, with tree-lined roads, middle-class suburban semis, schools, golf courses and parkland. Lulled by the ease with which the hospital had been taken, people sauntered along with their friends, chatting and joking. The line grew thinner and fractured when some took one road, some another, others a path across playing fields. So long as they headed south, no one seemed concerned whether they proceeded in any kind of order.

"I don't like this," muttered Zach. His gaze flickered this way and that, trying to cover all possible angles from which attack might come. He carried the assault rifle—one of those he had found in the army convoy on the road outside Augusta—casually, but ready to bring to bear at the first sign of trouble.

"Me neither," agreed Frank. He, too, appeared tense. Zach had provided him with one of the American assault rifles and he bore it with a familiar ease. "Surprise has gone. Any possible advantage we had has been surrendered by allowing the enemy at the hospital to escape. This advance is unstructured and slow. If they hit us now while we're spread out, disorganised, we, to coin an expression, is fucked."

"Yep, all ways to Hell."

Despite his grave misgivings about the lack of structure and leadership, Zach felt more alive than he had in years. He knew why. Carrying an assault rifle, a weapon designed to kill other men, completed him, but in a way he despised. The conflicting sensations added to his unease.

He glanced at their companions. Amy walked alongside Nan, bearing her firearm with an air of 'this is something new to me but, by golly, I'll use it if I have to'. She noticed his glance and smiled. Nan and Elliott walked together, the slow pace suiting them. The elderly woman carried her rifle with the assurance of someone long accustomed to handling guns. Not so Elliott; his rifle was slung over his shoulder and bumped his hip with every step. Judging by the expressions of irritation that passed over his face, Elliott would as soon be rid of the weapon as have to carry it. Zach held no confidence the man would be able to use the rifle with any degree of competence.

"Frank," Zach said. "What say you and me ride point? Look out for our little group."

Frank nodded and stepped away to take up position on the far side of Elliott. Zach maintained his place near Amy, but a few yards away so his view was not obstructed. The line had grown so strung out the nearest people were more than twenty yards ahead. Others were further behind or to the sides, thinning out more as people chose different routes, nobody providing guidance or coherence.

Since he happened to be looking ahead when it started, Zach was the first to see the commotion. Amy and Frank, with the keener hearing of youth, were the first to hear it.

A small knot of people in front of them suddenly broke apart and scattered. Zach stopped and threw out his arm to indicate to the others they should halt, too. On the other side of Elliott, Frank had already done the same. Then Zach heard what Frank must have already heard: screams and shouts. Moments later, gunfire.

"Everyone, down!" he hissed.

Zach dropped into a crouch and glanced left to make sure they had all followed suit to present themselves as smaller targets. He peered forward, unwilling to commit to any course of action until he knew what they were up against.

The road ahead widened at a four-way intersection. A circular concrete bump separated the roads from each other. Zach had heard of these; 'mini roundabouts' the Brits called them.

People were running back and taking one of the roads to either side or towards them, seemingly at random, driven by panic. Some turned and discharged their weapons, although Zach could not see at whom or what they were aiming. In the meantime, people coming up behind had reached the point where Zach and his small party crouched in the road. Unwilling to pass them, yet curious as to what was happening ahead, the newcomers milled about. It was becoming a little congested.

A young man, wide-eyed, ran by them, ignoring the questions people called to him. A woman staggered past, skirt torn, blood running freely down her legs from several gashes.

If she answered questions, Zach didn't hear. He was watching what else was approaching.

The roads and sidewalks had come alive in the form of a brown, undulating carpet. Moving fast. It took Zach a few moments to believe the evidence of his own eyes. There were too many of them, thousands, acting in concert like fish in a shoal.

People behind him had also seen.

"Rats!" screamed a woman.

"Run!" shouted a man.

"Stand and fire!" shouted another.

There was no time to look for cover, no time to prepare.

"No shooting," shouted Zach to his companions. "Too many people about."

The rats broke over them in a wave. For the next few minutes, the world became a furry, biting, clawing nightmare.

Gunshots, yelps of pain and cries of revulsion vied for supremacy against a background of squeaking and claws clicking on asphalt. Amidst it all, Zach swung his rifle from side to side, crushing dozens of rats, only for scores more to take their places. Amy, Nan and Elliott followed his lead, wielding their rifles like clubs, kicking out at the creatures that made it past to bite and claw at their legs.

Beyond the melee, at a row of houses set back from the road, Zach glimpsed Frank. The young man was beckoning frantically to him from an open doorway to one of the houses.

"Amy! Run to Frank," Zach hollered, struggling to make himself heard. "Nan! Elliott! And you." He took one hand off the butt of his rifle long enough to point to where Frank waited for them.

The swarm of vermin was not lessening. Neither were the screams and gunfire reports, all underpinned by a frantic squealing. Faster than they could be shot or battered, more rats appeared. People who had made a run for it were overtaken and forced to fight or fall beneath the relentless weight of numbers.

Zach swung his rifle faster, ignoring the burning complaints of the muscles in his arms and back. Crushed rats fell away under the fury of his onslaught and a clear space formed around him.

"Now!" Zach yelled to Amy.

She stopped swinging her weapon and darted towards the houses. Moving a little slower, Elliott followed. Nan had started after him when she let out a strangled shriek, let her weapon fall to the ground and stumbled to her knees. Immediately, twenty or more rats were upon her.

Zach dropped his rifle, bounded forward and began yanking the creatures off her with his bare hands. They felt warm and frail beneath his grip; he could crush their ribcages with one squeeze if he had the time or inclination.

"Nan! You have to get up," he hissed in her ear. He lacked the energy to yell any more.

He tried to get a hand under her arm and haul her to her feet, but she was a dead weight, her head slumped to her chest.

"Nan, come on. You have to help."

Her hands hung down by her sides. Rats were chewing on her fingers; she made no move to dislodge them. More rats were scrabbling up her back. One had made it to her head and was biting at her hair. With a low grunt of disgust, Zach grabbed it and tore it free. A lock of grey hair came away with it.

Zach's jeans and jacket grew heavy under the weight of rats clambering over them. His legs became leaden; he wanted to kneel next to Nan.

Then strong hands were gripping his arms, pulling him away. He felt the same hands brushing at his back, removing vermin. He resisted, trying to reach back to Nan, who looked as though she was wearing a coat made of live, wriggling creatures.

"No, Zach! Leave her." It was Frank's voice.

"Huh? Can't leave her…"

"She's dead. A stray bullet hit her. Most of her face is missing."

Feeling as if he had entered some crazy dream world where he was once more eighteen and watching his friends get blown away, except this was taking place in a concrete jungle where his friends had grey hair and cardigans, Zach allowed Frank to lead him to the house from which Amy and Elliott peered anxiously. When he passed the kneeling figure of Nan, Zach glanced back and saw that Frank had spoken the truth.

Rats tore greedily at the little that remained of the old lady's face.

Simone handed the submachine gun back to Lavinia while they walked towards the hotel. She had been tempted to shoot Ronstadt despite the Keeper's arrival, but reluctance to take that final step towards disobedience (and, necessarily, affirmation of ambition and individuality) had won out once more, although it was becoming a close-run thing.

Soon, she kept telling herself, and 'soon' was approaching fast. Perhaps as close as a week away. When the Great Coming took place, Simone would challenge Milandra for her position as Keeper even as the rest of their people descended from the sky. Then, after the old bitch had stepped, or been forced, aside—she rather hoped it would be the latter; boredom was making her antsy and spoiling for a fight—Simone would stand every chance of becoming Keeper for her entire people. Nobody seemed to know how it would be decided which Keeper, the incumbent on Earth Haven or the incoming, would take precedence over the other, but she intended being at the forefront of such deliberations. Whatever the outcome, she ought to be well placed to venture out into the empty planet in a position of power, ready to establish a base somewhere in the Caribbean or the Tropics and surround herself by sycophants who could help her plot to acquire more power. For what would be the point of ambition and individuality if not to try to advance her station in the new world? And having already spent almost four millennia on Earth Haven, what else could she do that she hadn't already done many times and in many ages? Pursuing personal glory had thus far been denied her by her people's need for anonymity. That consideration no longer applied.

They reached the hotel. As they were about to walk in, Jason Grant stepped aside, nodding to himself. All present knew what that signified.

He glanced at Milandra. "It's Tess Granville," he said. "They've come under attack. I need to speak with her."

Milandra nodded. While Grant turned away, she looked at Simone.

"I might as well take this opportunity to eat," she said. "I'm exhausted."

Simone could not resist. "Yes, you look it," she trilled in her best schoolgirl voice. Her 'flibbedy gibbet' voice as she thought of it. She wasn't sure if anyone, least of all the Deputies, were taken in by it, but she didn't care; it was too much fun to do. "You really should be taking it a little easier at your age." She noted the faint tightening at the corners of Milandra's mouth and chalked up another tiny victory. "Lavinia, the Keeper's old and hungry. See to her." She flapped her hand as though dismissing a slave.

A broad grin on her face, Simone turned and entered the hotel.

From the journal of Elliott King:

So much for being the next Faulkner or Fitzgerald. Looks like the task appointed to me in my twilight years is not to compose a great work of fiction that will accord me honor and respect throughout the literary world, dare I say putting me in the running for a Pulitzer.

I am to be a chronicler. Instead of the Hemingway or James of my generation, I'm fated to be the Pliny of today's Vesuvius, recording the death throes of a fading species. For so it appeared to the people of Pompeii and Herculaneum, that it was the end of days.

And so it seems to us. It is doubtful whether those ancients in the first century A.D. appreciated the calamity they faced—the hail of pumice and ash, the poisoned air—was localized. In one sense, the peril we, this small band of 'we', face is narrow since there are people in the wider world who will go on living even though we perish.

But for how long? The inevitability they, too, will meet their end before the summer is through makes our feeble efforts seem less futile, of some value greater than worthless. Perhaps even noble.

I can embrace being a chronicler, maybe the last chronicler of mankind. What I cannot embrace is the pretence of being a fighter. I am no soldier, guerrilla, freedom fighter. I have never hunted, never discharged a firearm, never killed a living creature. My parents brought me up to value books, not guns. The only battle I ever fought was with my sexuality. I won, repressing my true nature to avoid bringing shame to my family in times when shame would indeed have been the outcome had my true leanings become known.

Caught up in the fervor of the moment, embarrassed at Nan's ready willingness to fight (she is—*was*, though it breaks my heart to write it—my senior by four years), and Amy's (she, too, has never held a gun before), and Sarah's (she's two months' pregnant, for Chrissakes), I agreed to go to war. Who was I kidding? Nan could tell in New Jersey I was unfamiliar and uncomfortable with handling firearms. Frank and Zach shared a look when I said I'd go into battle with them. They were kind enough not to say anything, but I understood its meaning: *why is* he *going? What help can* he *offer?*

They were right to question. At the first sign of trouble, my bowels liquefied, my arms became saplings quivering in fall gales. I only overcame the impulse to flee from fear my legs would fail to carry me in their abruptly leaden state.

After surviving that first attack, I gave my gun and grenades away. I am armed now only with this pen and notebook. The pen is mightier than the sword, right? Not so sure it beats a 9mm round to the head, but metaphors aren't supposed to be taken literally. It's why they're called metaphors.

Not that I've had to dodge any bullets. Not yet. We haven't so much as caught a glimpse of our adversaries. If they are near, they hide within office buildings or churches or schools or houses. This is a large, sprawling city. It offers many places of concealment. They are watching us. Sending beasts against us. They don't *need* to show themselves.

I have Frank and Zach to protect me, and—I'm not ashamed to say it—Amy, too. What that girl lacks in natural ability she makes up in enthusiasm.

"Ain't never been 'thusiastic 'bout nothin'," she said (making my inner English teacher cringe), when I commented on her apparent keenness to shoot somebody. "'Cept now I guess I'm anxious to bag me some alien on account of 'em murd'rin' muvvafucks killin' my momma."

Okay, okay, I'm exaggerating Amy's patois, but I never got the chance to write fiction, so indulge me.

Sarah's not with us now. That makes it sound as though she died, which she didn't. That was Nan. Frank let Sarah accompany us as far as Slough; they pronounce it to rhyme with thou, not tough. Short of hogtying her to a tree, I don't think he could have made her stay behind in Wales, but he was adamant she would advance no further. He's not one to stamp his foot or raise his voice, but stubborn as that young lady can be, she saw something in Frank's eyes that made her give in with barely a whimper. She agreed to help at the hospital; they're setting up some type of triage system to assess casualties as they arrive and sort into seriously and not-so-seriously injured. Quite an essential aspect of battlefield medicine that, when operating teams are inundated, will ensure those who need treatment the most receive it earliest.

Of course, there's a major problem. Nobody else has said it, but I'm not afraid to mention the pachyderm in the room, a twenty-foot monster with blazing red eyes and tusks that could plow fields.

We have no doctors.

Not sure if I'm straight on this, but I understand there to be a doctor, who helped some kids survive a brain injury and a gunshot wound, and a nurse with battlefield surgical experience—supposedly in World War II, though some things I still find hard to believe—but the doctor has disappeared to no one knows where or why, and the nurse is one of *them* and has also disappeared to, again, no one knows where, but perhaps the why is a little more obvious.

A doctor would not have done Nan any good. We don't know who fired the bullet—in that chaos it could have been almost anyone. The slug entered her skull below her left cheekbone, shattered her top jaw, expanded and exited stage right, taking her nose and most of her forehead with it. Her startled cry was a reflex; she was dead before her knees hit the asphalt. Thank goodness for small mercies.

The rats dispersed eventually. We cowered in a house and watched them chew on Nan's corpse for what felt like hours, but was probably twenty minutes. Whatever demon drove them (something *must* have been driving them; rats don't act like that ordinarily) left them and they drifted back to whatever hole they'd emerged from.

We buried her wrapped in a rug in a school athletic field. Frank and I both spoke a few words over the grave; Frank because he believes in Jesus; me because I believed in Nan. Then we followed everyone else back to Hillingdon Hospital.

Zach raged. He found the boy, Joe, and vented at him about the lack of discipline and leadership, but he soon ran out of steam. He knew he was shouting at a boy who had no clue how to lead or even pretended he did. Joe let him rant, watching him carefully, curiously, waiting for an opening so he could ask a question.

"How do we kill them? Show me how to kill them."

Zach stared at the boy for a long moment.

"You don't kill 'em unless you can see 'em. You don't see 'em unless you draw 'em out of cover. Do you know where the enemy is hiding?"

The boy didn't hesitate. "No. I don't even know whether they are hiding."

"Well, taking a Sunday afternoon stroll ain't gonna flush 'em out. We go in the vehicles we came in. South. Tomorrow."

Chapter Thirteen

Nobody moved. Howard stood in front of his stool. Colleen sat on hers. Brianne had turned to look at the doorway through which she had entered only moments before.

Dermot's left hand gripped Will by his good shoulder. In his other hand, he held a pistol. A brown leather strap, standing out from the black leather of his jacket, ran across his chest and the barrel of a rifle poked from behind his back.

"Doubt if this is loaded," said Dermot, holding up the pistol.

He pointed it at the ceiling and pulled the trigger. The gun jerked violently in his hand and he nearly dropped it. The report was shockingly loud and Howard's bladder almost let go. Bri uttered a small shriek. Will jumped and scrunched up his eyes, while a shower of plaster fell on him.

"Oops. My mistake." Dermot chuckled like a kindly uncle telling a joke. He moved the pistol to his left hand so he could shake his right. "Quite a kick. Thought for a moment I'd broken my wrist." He moved the gun back to his right hand. This time, he gripped it with both hands while he pointed it up. "But I'm still not sure it's loaded. Maybe it was a round left in the chamber…"

He pulled the trigger and another report almost deafened Howard. A chunk of plaster fell from the ceiling, narrowly missing Will. An acrid, boiled egg smell reached Howard's nostrils.

He stole a glance at Colleen. She had gone as white as Will's plaster-covered hair. She noticed his look and shot him a grimace, before addressing the Irishman.

"What do you want?"

"Now, is that any way to greet an old friend?" Through the ringing in Howard's ears, Dermot's voice sounded even softer than normal.

"Seriously, Dermot," said Colleen, "we're not friends."

A smile stole over the man's fleshy lips. "Oh, my beaut, we are *so* going to be friends." He uttered a barking laugh. "Well, let's say we'll become close. *Very* close."

In the silence that followed, a small voice spoke. "Please, sir? Can I stand by Bri?" Will was craning his neck to look up, and up, at the man.

Without taking his eyes from Colleen, Dermot gave Will a light shove that sent him stumbling forward. Bri held out her hands and Will grabbed one with his good hand.

"I'm sorry, Bri. I didn't see him. He opened the door and took the gun from me." Will looked back at Dermot, his voice full of reproach. "That's *our* gun."

The Irishman ignored him. He hadn't taken his eyes off Colleen.

Bri hugged Will to her and led him to the seating area. They sat side by side on a settee in the corner.

Howard breathed a silent sigh of relief. With the children as out of the way as they could be, he could concentrate on the man with the guns. He held out his hands in a placatory gesture.

"Dermot… or would you prefer Clint? Why don't you put the pistol down, there's a good chap."

Dermot's glance darted his way. "Why don't you shut the fuck up, there's a good chap." He looked back at Colleen. "That was quite a kick you dealt my manhood, beaut. I've not had opportunity to test it out, see if it's still working. I think you and me will go upstairs to a bedroom and find out." His tongue came out to lick his thick lips.

Howard saw, from the corner of his eye, that Colleen had to work hard to suppress a shudder. He needed to put an end to this now.

Again holding his hands out, palms down, he took a step towards the Irishman. "Come now, Dermot, I'm sure we can sort this out. Man to man." He took another step.

Howard heard Bri's cry as though from a great distance.

"No, Howard! He's going to—"

Dermot's gaze once more flickered his way. He raised the pistol with both hands and pointed it at Howard's chest. A flash came from the muzzle and Howard's hearing abandoned him.

No pain.

He stared at the ceiling. It was stippled and cracked. In need of a coat of paint.

The faces of Colleen and Bri appeared. They looked shocked. Distraught. They distorted, running like melting wax. Becoming his wife and daughter.

Howard went to them.

While Grant communicated with Tess Granville in London, Lavinia and Milandra went to the hotel kitchens to arrange sustenance for the Keeper. The Chosen flounced off somewhere, leaving Peter and Diane in the company of George Wallace.

"This is cosy," Wallace muttered. He led them through the building to the conservatory running the length of the hotel's rear, overlooking the ocean.

Wallace slumped into an armchair. Glancing down, he appeared to notice—as though he'd forgotten—he still held the pistol. With a *clunk*, he dropped it onto the occasional table next to his chair.

He glanced at Diane and Peter. "This was set up as a restaurant. We cleared out the tables and chairs and brought in this comfortable stuff." He waved a hand to vaguely indicate the array of mismatched armchairs and sofas arranged to take advantage of the view. Then he stared off into space, seemingly forgetting they were there.

Diane pointedly cleared her throat.

"Huh?" said Wallace.

"Is it okay if we sit down?" she asked.

Wallace shrugged. "Sure. Ain't no one pointing a gun at you now."

"And it makes a nice change," said Peter, with a tight smile. He sat in an armchair near Wallace.

Diane took a sofa next to Peter. It stood at an angle so that she could look at the two men or at the ocean merely by turning her head.

For a few minutes, nobody spoke. Diane gazed out at the Atlantic, watching it turn from denim blue to gunmetal grey when clouds scudded across the sun. She listened to the men start a hesitant conversation.

"So, George," said Peter, "I saw that you were in Italy during the Renaissance."

"Not a word in front of anyone, remember?"

"Afraid of gaining a reputation as a drone lover? Don't worry. Diane's not going to say anything. I doubt she's even listening. If she is, I doubt she cares. So. The Renaissance?"

Wallace did not reply for a long moment. At last, he gave a deep sigh. "Okay. Sure, I spent the fifteenth and sixteenth centuries in Italy. Rome, Milan, Venice, Bologna… And, as I know you saw, I was also in Florence." His tone became wistful. "They were the best days. I've forgotten most of the lingo, but I'll never forget the masters. Or their art."

"Who did you know?"

"I met most of them. Donatello, Bellini, Botticelli. Later, Michelangelo, Raphael, Titian. And, of course, Verrocchio in Florence and, through him, his most famous pupil."

"Da Vinci."

Wallace fell silent again for a few moments. When he resumed speaking, his voice contained a note of respect. "He possessed the greatest intellect of any human I've ever met."

"They are capable of so much." Peter's tone sounded musing. "But, intelligent as Da Vinci undoubtedly was, I've long been sceptical he came to imagine flying contraptions and submarines in the fifteenth century without some help. Perhaps someone whispering in his ear who comes from a place where such machines are commonplace."

Diane stole a glance at Wallace. He did not speak, but shifted in his chair as though finding it lumpy.

"Ah, keep your secret, George," said Peter. "It's not encouraged for our sort to have secrets, but then what exactly does 'our sort' even mean any more?"

Wallace grunted. "I guess you'll be the last person to know the answer to that. How could you fall in love with a human?"

"Don't know." He shrugged. "I was powerless to prevent it."

"Yet despite not taking part in the Cleansing, you wanted the Beacon to be activated. You want the Great Coming to succeed, at least to the point the craft enters Earth Haven's atmosphere. But you are not motivated for the greater good. Your reasons are entirely selfish."

"Completely."

Diane glanced at Peter. He was staring straight ahead, fiddling with something around his neck.

"It's not likely to work, you know." Wallace's tone sounded tender. Diane did not know what they were talking about, but found the changes she was detecting in both men fascinating.

"Nevertheless…" said Peter.

A door opened and the Chosen came in.

"Are you boys building bridges?" she trilled, as though she had not herself been pointing a gun at Peter's head less than an hour ago. "I hope so. We all need to get along for, you know, the greater good an' all." Simone gave a schoolgirl giggle and flounced over to an armchair the other side of Wallace. She sat in it sideways, jean-clad legs draped over one arm.

The door opened again and in came Grant, followed closely by Milandra. A stout, florid-faced man, whom Diane had not seen before, came in next. He smiled at her and Peter in a friendly fashion.

"Wotcher," he said in an accent which reminded Diane of Will's. "I'm Rodney Wilson, but plain old Rod will do."

Lavinia brought up the rear, closing the door behind her. They all took places near the others so anyone could address everyone else without having to raise their voices.

Milandra smiled around at them.

"That's better," she said. "A good feed banishes weariness. When I'm done talking to y'all, I intend finding a sunny spot and soaking up some rays to finish the job. But before I begin to tell you a story you all need to hear, Jason can update us on the situation in London."

Diane sat forward. It had been a few months since she had left London sitting next to Troy Bishop in the cabin of a Sea King helicopter and she was curious to hear what progress had been made in the capital city.

"Thanks, Milandra," said Jason Grant. He rubbed his hand down one cheek. "Think I might join you to soak up those rays. That discussion with Tess has left me feeling a little drained myself." He looked at Peter and Diane. "I'd like to formally welcome you. The, er, misunderstanding from earlier is done and dusted, I hope. Simone?"

"Huh? Oh, yeah, whatever."

"George? Lavinia?"

"We're cool," said Wallace.

"If Simone and George are cool, then I guess I am, too," said Lavinia.

"Good. Okay, then London. Tess had two matters to report. The first concerns the Great Coming. I'm pleased to say the craft carrying our people from Earth Home is within telescope range of Earth Haven."

"Are there telescopes that powerful in London?" asked Peter. "I thought with all the light pollution, they had been located elsewhere."

"That's true in most cases," said Grant. "But London University has an array of telescopes to the north of the city at Mill Hill. Since the Grid came back online, we've had a team of observers up there watching the night sky. We've got all streetlamps and other illuminations switched off around there to give them the best chance of spotting the craft."

"I didn't know it would be visible until it was within Earth Haven's atmosphere," said Wallace. "What with its anti-matter coating an' all."

"It's not visible in the usual sense," agreed Grant. "More an absence of light. A little like an approaching black hole."

"Okay, all I'm hearing now is blah blah blah," said Simone. "Have they seen the ship from Earth Home or not?"

"They have. And they calculate it will arrive here ten days from now, which I make to be May fourth."

"Ha!" said Peter.

Grant nodded at him, before continuing. "The craft is directly on course for Earth Haven. All our efforts with the Beacon are bearing fruit."

"The Great Coming is nearly done," said Lavinia. "Cool. What's the second thing?"

"The second thing," said Grant, "is that a force of armed humans is attacking the city."

"How can that be?" asked Wallace. "I thought there weren't any humans left in the U.K. Only the drones in London."

Diane glanced sharply at Grant, then at Milandra. Neither of them caught her eye. It seemed they hadn't shared their early morning escapade near Stonehenge with the other Deputies.

"Humans have been arriving in Britain from the continent and from the east coast of the United States and Canada," said Grant. "Many of them have blundered into London, where they have been captured and, er, *treated* by our people."

Wallace gave a low whistle. "Wonder what made them come here. Some sort of group instinct?"

"I guess," said Grant. "Whatever, they're here and a force greatly in excess of a thousand strong is in London. A well-armed force."

"Why?" asked Rodney Wilson. Diane thought he looked quite forlorn. "What can they hope to achieve?"

"Well, Rod," said Milandra, "consider it from their point of view. Their families and friends have been killed. Everything they know has come to an end. They're frightened, bewildered, alone. For many, striking back in one last act of defiance is all that's left to them."

"I s'pose, Miss Milandra, when you put it like that. We spread a deadly virus without so much as a by your leave. Can't really blame 'em for being a little pissed off. Oops, beggin' your pardon."

"When you say, 'attacking the city'," said Wallace, "what exactly do you mean? It's a mighty big city and an army of less than two thousand will hardly overrun it."

"They've taken Hillingdon Hospital where the treatment centre was set up. There was only a handful of our people there and they escaped without harm. The humans marched south towards Heathrow, but were beaten back without much difficulty. Well-armed they might be, but they're also disorganised, leaderless, inexperienced. There are many elderly and young of both sexes among them, and seemingly few with military experience."

"They were beaten back, you said." That was Lavinia. "So there's been an engagement. How many casualties?"

"Estimates place human casualties at seventeen dead, upwards of thirty injured. Our casualties: zero."

"Zero?" Lavinia looked incredulous.

"None of our people has sustained as much as a scratch," said Grant. "There are certain, ah, *strategies* we can employ that should demoralise the humans while keeping our people safely out of harm's way. I anticipate this uprising, rebellion, whatever you want to call it, will be over before the Great Coming in ten days' time."

"What sort of strategies?" asked Wallace.

"Well, we sent packs of rats against them. Tess's idea."

The Chosen clapped her hands in delight. "Rats! Yay!"

"And the humans lost seventeen in an attack by rats?" Now Wallace looked and sounded incredulous.

"Rats in sufficient number can overwhelm people on their own. Don't forget, they can't control them like we can. I understand they broke up when attacked and fled piecemeal so the rats were able to pick some off individually. And many of the casualties were shot by their own side in the confusion."

Simone laughed. "Stupid drones."

"Tess isn't expecting the humans to give up just yet. She has a few more tricks up her sleeve."

Milandra sat forward. "Unless anyone has any further questions of Jason? No? Then it's my turn. Make yourselves comfortable while I tell you a story…"

From the journal of Elliott King:

We stayed in the hospital for the rest of that day and overnight, licking our wounds. I doubt anyone had escaped being bitten or scratched, although most injuries were superficial. The medical base was summarily transferred from Slough to Hillingdon. Sarah and the nurses had gathered supplies of antiseptics and antibiotics, which they brought with them, and were kept busy all afternoon. It wasn't until early evening that Frank was able to take Sarah to one side to explain about Nan. She and Nan had hit it off from the outset; that was one conversation I was glad not to witness.

The following morning, we set out south again, but this time in a convoy of vehicles. It wasn't glaringly obvious, maybe because we were still a disorganized bunch, little more than a rabble, but I think maybe our numbers had shrunk overnight. Who can blame anyone for slipping away under cover of darkness? I'd have probably done the same if I wasn't among the only friends I have left.

They sent dogs after us that day. Wild-eyed, panting, salivating, they came at us in wave after wave. Vehicles sustained deep dents and cracked windows from the ferocity of the assaults—the animals showed scant concern for their own safety—but held firm. We grew accustomed to the snarling thuds while we drove through the residential district we had strolled through yesterday. One or two people threw open high windows and took ineffective pot shots, until word came around to conserve ammo for when we might really need it.

We only lost one person that morning. When her minibus slowed at an intersection, she threw open the door and stepped off unarmed. She stumbled and almost fell, but regained her balance. In her early thirties, at a guess, she wore an expression of exaltation while she glanced around, looking for dogs. She didn't have to look far. They were approaching her, fast. I watched in horrified fascination when she held out her arms toward the frenzied creatures as though imparting blessings. Only at the last, when they fell upon her, did her expression change. It stayed with me, that alteration in her eyes like a switch had been thrown, as whatever fever possessed her fled in the face of chomping, slavering reality.

I had intended to ask someone who was on the bus with her what she had been like in the moments before deciding to step out, whether she had given any clues to what had prompted her to surrender her life to blind, bestial hunger, but I never did. The chaos that came later drove all such thoughts from my mind.

Other than that incident and the cosmetic damage to our vehicles, we advanced without hindrance beyond the residential area to a district of light industry. There they awaited us.

That is where we learned they were capable of more than setting vermin and feral beasts on us.

So much more.

Chapter Fourteen

Tom relaxed and enjoyed the journey across the centre of England. He gazed out at the passing countryside, seeing it in a detail that wasn't possible from behind the steering wheel. Everywhere looked greener, bushier, more verdant, even the roads and pavements, as nature began to undo man's works.

They were content to travel in silence; a companionable rather than an awkward silence. They broke it only to remark upon how flat and featureless the scenery had become. Accustomed as they both were to the hills and valleys of their homeland, the Fens seemed an alien landscape, stretching flat and unbroken for miles in every direction as far as their gazes could reach.

They reached Lincoln late morning. Ceri parked by the cathedral, reputed to have been in ancient times the tallest structure in the world. They snacked in its grounds, while Dusty attended to canine business and investigated interesting scents.

"Where now?" asked Ceri, when they were ready to go.

"Coastal road," said Tom. "Howard told me that when he'd checked on his family and dealt with any remains—he's not a stupid man; he's expecting to find corpses—they'll probably make for the coast. Skegness is the nearest seaside resort."

An hour or so later, Ceri drove along the seafront in Skegness. She proceeded cautiously, swerving to avoid the occasional dog and, more disconcertingly, sheep that wandered into the road.

"How on earth are we going to find them?" she said. "We don't even know they're here."

"You concentrate on the road and I'll keep watch for the hotel minibus they came in. I won't be able to miss that." *Assuming they haven't ditched it for something else* Tom thought.

He was beginning to wonder where else Howard and Colleen might have gone, and how they would even begin to go about locating them, when he saw it.

"There! Up ahead on the left. The minibus." He let out a long sigh of relief. "See it? Next to that white Range Rover."

As they drew closer, they approached a scooter standing by the kerbside. Tom stared at it, turning his head while they passed. A sense of foreboding seeped into him like treacle, dark and insistent. Why the sight of a scooter should spark such a sensation he had no idea, but did not dismiss it out of hand as fanciful. The level-headed Tom was slowly being replaced by a more credulous version.

Ceri brought the Peugeot to a halt next to the minibus and killed the engine. She craned her neck to see what buildings were nearby and pointed to the closest one.

"That looks like a hotel," she said.

Tom climbed out of the car, letting Dusty out behind him, and walked over to the minibus. He peered through the windows, but there was nothing of note to see. More interesting was the Range Rover; it was parked at an angle as though left there in a rush or by an inexperienced driver. The passenger door stood open.

There was nothing Tom could point to and say it was the source of his sense of dread, but still the feeling grew. He could taste it, a metallic flavour, a little like blood.

Dusty ran to the Range Rover and began sniffing around it, tail wagging. He jumped through the open door onto the passenger seat and looked back at Tom.

Wuff?

"What can you smell, boy?"

Tom walked over. Ceri joined him.

"Isn't that…? Yes. Tom, their Harrods bags are on the back seat." She looked at him, a quizzical expression on her face that turned to alarm. "What's wrong?"

"I'm not sure," said Tom. "Something. I feel I'm in a dream that's about to turn into a nightmare. I just don't know how yet."

Ceri looked up at the hotel. "They must be in there. Let's go find them."

"Bring a weapon."

"You're scaring me. What do you think we're going to find in there?"

He shrugged. "I'm probably being stupid, but humour me, okay?"

Ceri ducked into the Peugeot, re-emerging with her assault rifle. Tom watched her raise the weapon, sight down the scope and ensure the cross-bolt safety mechanism was disengaged. She removed the magazine and checked it had a full complement of thirty rounds before slotting it back into place. Keeping her fingers outside the trigger guard and the barrel pointing to the ground, she stepped to his side and nodded.

"Ready. I hope this isn't necessary."

"So do I. Dusty? Here, boy."

The dog trotted obediently over. Tom lowered his hand to pet the dog's head and to let him know he was to stay by Tom's side.

He walked up the short flight of steps and tried the hotel door. It opened easily. He swung it wide and stepped inside, holding it open for Ceri to follow. He began to address her in a low voice. "Where do you think—"

The gunshot came from down a short corridor that led off the reception area. It was followed by a scream.

Tom froze, wanting to run towards the noise, afraid to. Not for the first time, his legs refused to co-operate and his knees locked like an elephant's, rooting him to the spot.

Like she had at Stonehenge when noticing Will inside the circle of bluestones, Ceri took the initiative. She pushed past Tom, bringing the rifle to bear as she ran down the corridor. Dusty growled, straining to take off after her.

After what seemed like minutes, but could only have been seconds, Tom made his traitorous legs move. Ceri had already reached a door at the end of the corridor and was pushing it open.

Dusty reached the doorway before him and bounded through it.

"Wait, boy!" Tom called, afraid of what danger might lie on the other side of the door.

He raced through and skidded to a halt, almost colliding with

Dusty who had stopped at his command. It took Tom a few moments to comprehend what he was seeing.

The room consisted of stools arrayed before a wooden counter and a small seating area. On the floor in front of the stools lay a motionless figure, over which two female forms huddled. One was a girl with tear-streaked cheeks: Bri. Opposite the bar, Will cowered in a sofa, his gaze transfixed by the gigantic figure standing at the end of the bar. Over the figure's shoulder protruded the barrel of a rifle; in both hands it clutched a pistol, aiming to Tom's left, where Ceri stood.

The stock of the assault rifle was jammed tight into Ceri's right shoulder, the scope to her eye. Her right index finger curled around the trigger. The short barrel pointed unwaveringly at the head of the giant.

Tom recognised the figure as the Irishman he had met in the Celtic Manor a few days back; the one from whom Colleen and Howard had fled. Dermot something. *What was he doing here?*

"Tom!" Bri called to him in a voice shrill with disbelief and grief. "He shot Howard."

Tom's mind whirled, trying to make sense of the information bombarding it. So far, it wasn't doing a good job; he was little more than an observer to this drama.

The other female looked up. Colleen's face was as pale as chalk dust, her expression as dark as soot. She began to rise to her feet.

"Not only shot him," she said in a toneless voice. "Killed him."

She gained her feet and stepped towards Dermot. She must have been within his field of vision, but he didn't move his gaze from Ceri. While Colleen approached him, her hands twisted into claws. Before she could sink her fingernails like talons into the man's face, his left hand released his grip on the pistol and his right hand darted out as fast as a striking snake. Then he was gripping the pistol two-handed again, still pointing it at Ceri. It had happened so quickly Tom would have missed it had he blinked.

Colleen gave a startled cry and stumbled, blood spurting from her mouth. Her hindmost foot hit the body lying on the floor, her other tangled with Bri, and she fell backwards with a thump.

The steady growl coming from Dusty changed pitch, growing higher and more strained, like an engine dropping gear to take a tight bend.

Without shifting his attention from Ceri, Dermot muttered, "Keep that fucking dog away from me or it'll end up like the doc."

Tom lowered his hand to Dusty's scruff and gripped it tightly; the dog was quivering as though standing belly-deep in snow.

"Drop the pistol." Ceri spoke for the first time since entering the bar. Her voice was without inflection, yet conveyed a deadly intent. "Drop it now or I'll put a bullet between your eyes."

Dermot's thick lips twisted in a sneer. "Pull that trigger and the boy gets it." He swung the pistol away from Ceri and pointed it at Will.

Later, Tom would wonder how things might have played out differently if the Irishman hadn't threatened Will. He could imagine at least one scenario in which it would have been possible for Dermot to walk away with his life. But turning his gun on Will was a mistake. A fatal one.

"Nooooo!" Bri sprang from the floor and flew at Dermot. He had already demonstrated his deadly speed when striking Colleen, but on this occasion Bri was quicker. Head lowered, she ducked under the pistol and his outstretched arms, and hit him in the solar plexus.

The air left Dermot's lungs in a *whoosh!*, he grimaced in pain and staggered back against the wall. His hands flailed, his finger tugging involuntarily on the trigger of the gun.

Tom felt something zing past his face and a cold puff of air on his cheek. Two loud reports sounded almost simultaneously before his world fell silent. But these things he only noticed on the periphery. His main focus was on Dermot.

The man's left eye exploded like an overripe grape. A trickle of blood appeared on what remained of his lower eyelid and began to run down his cheek. The expression in his remaining eye was one of deep puzzlement. In slow motion, he slid down the wall until he was sitting, legs splayed out like felled saplings. A hole had been blown into the wall behind where he'd been standing; a hole surrounded by ivory, grey and black globules. A scarlet trail, like a giant slug's, led down the wall to where his head had come to rest.

Tom glanced at Ceri. A wisp of smoke curled from the barrel of her rifle. She still held it to her shoulder, lips compressed into a thin, white line. Beyond her, Will looked paler and smaller than ever. Colleen lay with her legs across the body—Howard's body, Tom now understood—over which she'd tripped, hands clutched to her mouth. Bri crouched on the floor in front of the bar where she'd ended up after her headlong rush at Dermot. She shook herself as though to clear her head, stood and ran to Will. They clutched at each other like drowning men.

A ringing started in Tom's ears when his hearing began to return. Realising he was still half-stooped, clutching Dusty's scruff, he dropped into a full crouch and threw his arms around the dog's neck; Dusty planted a wet snuffle on Tom's cheek to show him he was all right. Faint sounds began to make themselves heard above the ringing: Colleen's moans, Bri's sobbing, Will's murmurs.

Tom turned to Ceri. He placed his hands on the rifle and tugged. For a moment or two, she clung on grimly, before letting go. Tom placed the rifle on the floor, standing it against the wall, and took Ceri in his arms.

It was like hugging a tree. Tom held her at arms' length and stared into her eyes. She stared back, unseeing. He glanced at the bar. An open bottle of whisky stood on the wooden surface. In three short strides, Tom crossed to the bar and grabbed the bottle; he also picked up the bottle top before returning to Ceri. He poured a measure of whisky into the top and brought it to Ceri's lips. Using the edge of the top to force down her lower lip, he tipped the whisky into her mouth and took half a step back.

With a splutter and a grimace, life returned to Ceri's features. She gasped and her gaze darted around the room, coming to rest on the slumped figure of Dermot. She gasped again, louder; Tom could hear it clearly—the ringing had faded to background noise.

"Cer? Are you okay?"

With what seemed like a massive effort of will, Ceri tore her gaze away from Dermot.

"I killed him."

Her face crumpled and Tom stepped forward to take her once more in his arms. This time, she hugged him fiercely back and he held her while she sobbed hot tears against his shoulder.

Milandra settled into the armchair, making it groan. She cleared her throat and all eyes turned to her.

"Before you emerged from the placenta," she said, looking from one to another of her audience in turn, "the Keeper of that time imparted to you certain knowledge: of our language, our culture, our history. It is about the last I need to speak to you. Our history.

"We all know the official tale. Our arrival at Earth Home to find a deserted planet we made our own. After many, many millennia, our sun, expanding towards dwarf state, devastated the surface, forcing us to dwell below ground. The fruitless search for the secret of faster-than-light travel to be able to escape our solar system to find a new planet to colonise. How we discovered artefacts left behind by an ancient species that inhabited Earth Home before us. The millennia that passed while we struggled to break the ancients' code; the joy when it was cracked at last and revealed the secret we had long been seeking. Even better, blueprints for a faster-than-light craft and directions to a planet many light years distant that would support our life forms."

She took a deep breath and a sip of water. Nobody spoke. They all, even the Chosen, watched her with varying degrees of curiosity.

"Worryingly," she continued, "the decoded black tablets of the ancients spoke of another species, a savage, warlike species that hunted them. This explained another mystery: why the ancients felt the need to travel to the other side of the galaxy sixty-six million years ago, with the great use of resources and all the risks that entailed, at a time when Earth Home's sun would not have been a threat to the planet's surface. In fact, Earth Home then would have been a lush, verdant planet, much like Earth Haven is today. So the ancients left Earth Home, not in a premature attempt at escaping a dying sun, but to flee a violent enemy. This raises another question, one we have never been able to satisfactorily answer."

Milandra glanced around, eyebrows raised.

"What happened to the warlike species?" supplied Jason Grant.

"Precisely. In all our long years on Earth Home, we saw neither sight nor sound of that other species. And, believe me, we kept careful watch, and more. There are whole sections of memories in the collective banks devoted to the search for them: where they come from, where are they now, what is their level of technology, what threat do they pose to us? But we have uncovered not one scrap of evidence, other than the ancients' tablets, that lead us to believe the other species actually exists."

Milandra took another sip of water. "Okay. That summarises what we learned before tearing off the birth shroud. Are we all agreed?"

She waited until she had received seven nods.

"Good." Another deep breath. "What I need to tell you today is that a great deal of that history is fabrication. Invention. To put it another way, it's complete and utter bullshit."

In the ensuing silence, a mix of expressions passed over the faces of her audience: puzzlement, disbelief, dismay. Some exchanged glances as if wondering whether their Keeper was losing her mind. *Fair enough* thought Milandra. *I'd probably wonder the same thing in their shoes.*

She held up her hands to stem the inevitable questions. "Let me explain. You can throw all the questions you want at me later.

"I have spent the last couple of months shut away in a cottage in a village north of here. I have been searching the archives of our communal memory for answers.

"Answers to what? you want to ask. Good question. A vague

sense of unease has been growing in me over the last century. Nothing concrete, nothing serious, more a sense of something being amiss. Since the end of the last world war, during the slack periods while putting the plans for the Cleansing in place, my thoughts turned to questioning all I had once accepted.

"Why, for instance, did our collective memory only commence a century or two—we're not even certain when—after arriving at Earth Home? Where did we live *before* Earth Home? Before our collective memory began, did we record our history in some other way? And the real puzzle: why could we find no trace at all of the ancients' enemy?

"Those were the directions in which my musings strayed. And that might have been as far as they took me if it wasn't for something Jason said."

"I did?" said Grant.

Milandra smiled at his expression of bemusement. "It was when we were walking to meet Rod at the parking lot where the red buses were parked. You said you were concerned our people arriving from Earth Home may not consider us to be part of the whole since we had been away from them for so long. It sparked a notion, a nagging one that grew stronger the more I tried to forget it. I felt I had to delve into the collective memory banks and that within I would find the answers to the questions I had asked myself, and more." Her smile faded. "So it proved."

"What did you find?" asked Wallace.

"I'm coming to it." Milandra glanced out at the ocean. The sun was out, making the tips of the waves glint. She could feel her cells tingling with anticipation to be outside, soaking up Sol's life-giving rays. "What I sought was well hidden. Deliberately concealed. Sifting through the mass of memories was energy consuming, as Jason can confirm."

Grant nodded. "Must have eaten your way through an entire Walmart's worth of food."

"Yep. Used damn near as much energy as *reaching* or *sending* or even conducting a Commune. But it was worth it to find the truth, hard though it might seem to some of you." She sighed. "So what of that truth…

"The first memory I found was of a vast, black ship speeding through the outer reaches of a solar system. It was the interstellar ship of the ancients, fleeing Earth Home. Eight smaller craft appeared from the edge of the system, an advance scouting party of a larger space fleet.

"The scouts opened fire upon the black ship, but it was travelling at close to light speed, too fast for their missiles. Except for one. The missile intercepted the ship's path and pierced its outer hull, sheering off part of the propulsion mechanism designed to provide upthrust within a planet's gravity. That same mechanism whose absence may have caused the ship to crash into the surface of the planet to which it was headed."

A gasp came from Peter Ronstadt. "Earth Haven. *That's* why the ancients' ship fell and caused the tidal wave that wiped out the dominant indigenous life forms."

"You begin to understand," said Milandra softly. "Indeed, I am once more indebted to Jason for helping *me* to understand."

Again, Grant's face crinkled in puzzlement.

"You asked from whose viewpoint I was watching the ship being attacked," explained Milandra. "This memory was of an incident happening at the edge of deep space. There is only one place the viewer could have been. There weren't eight scout craft attacking the ancients' ship; there were nine. I—rather, the person to whom the memory belonged—was on board the ninth ship."

She paused to allow this information to sink in, although she didn't anticipate the full import would hit home yet.

"I found other memories," she continued. "I learned through whose eyes I was seeing. Someone you've all heard of, though she died many, many millennia before the oldest of us was born. Her name was Sivatra. The first Keeper."

Only Jason Grant, who already knew the identity of Milandra's memory companion, did not make an expression of surprise or shock or disbelief.

Without pause to allow room for questions—the day was wearing on and she yearned to be in sunlight—Milandra went on to relate the memories she had experienced: the jungle landscape, the failed negotiations, the fierce fighting and the vanquished leader's self-destruction.

"Civil war?" said Grant. "What does it mean?"

"Well, for one thing," said Milandra, "it was our forefathers who damaged Earth Home's surface. I saw waves of concussion knock flat jungles, raze mountains, create scorched wastelands. Sure, solar flares and winds probably came along later and completed the job, but it was our people who were responsible for setting the planet along the road to becoming the barren wilderness we knew."

"But what were they fighting over?"

Milandra gave the slightest shrug. "I could only understand the occasional word I heard, but can extrapolate meaning from context and body language. My guess, but an educated one, would be the two sides disagreed over something that went to the very being of our species."

"It was us." Peter sat forward in his chair and stared at Milandra with shocked understanding. "Wasn't it? It was us."

Milandra slowly nodded.

"What does he mean?" asked Simone, no trace now of little girl shrillness. "What was us?"

"The ancients fled Earth Home," said Milandra, "in fear of being attacked by a deadly enemy. An enemy we have found no trace of. There's a very good reason for that.

"There *was* a warlike, violent species that hunted the ancients. In fact, it found its quarry while the ancients were trying to make good their escape."

Milandra nodded again as comprehension began to dawn in the faces of every member of her audience.

"Yes," she said. "The nine scout ships which attacked the ancients' craft were ours. The warlike, violent species was us."

~ ~ ~

The tension inside the transit van increased the further south they advanced. Aletta and Levente sat opposite each other on bench seats in the back of the van. To the side of them, the benches were fully occupied, stretching into darkness towards the windowless rear doors. A musky, sour odour pervaded the air: the scent of fear.

Aletta peered forward, over the driver's shoulder. Brake lights were showing on the vehicles ahead. The convoy had passed an industrial park and joined a main road leading due south. They had not been troubled by attacks from dogs since at least a mile back, and 'troubled' was probably too strong a word for what had been more a minor irritation.

Although many years had gone by since she had been accustomed to handling firearms while hunting with her father in the forested hills near their home, Aletta had volunteered to fight without hesitation. Levente hadn't been so keen on returning to London. When she asked him whether he would go back with her, a look of such anguish filled his face she did not ask again. It was only while the convoy was preparing to leave South Wales that the rear door to the minibus in which Aletta sat was thrown open and the heavily-laden Levente clambered in.

"Not go without me," he said, squashing into the seat next to her.

He leaned an assault rifle against the back of the seat, laid a submachine gun across his lap and lowered to the floor a canvas bag that clanked with the dull sound of magazines and grenades knocking together. He half-turned to face her and banged his clenched fist to his chest.

"Me from Hungary," he proclaimed. "Me man, you woman. Man look after woman."

He looked so serious Aletta was afraid of hurting his feelings if she allowed the giggle to escape. After a brief internal struggle, she managed to suppress it. She inclined her head.

"Not necessary," she said, "but thank you." She glanced at the hardware surrounding him and smiled. "Do you have enough weapons?"

Levente shook his head and his expression, if anything, grew more serious. Darker. "Not enough to fight bad people."

Now the Hungarian sat straighter as he, too, peered through the windscreen of the transit van. The driver had reduced speed to a crawl and was pulling to a halt behind the vehicle immediately ahead, a twenty-six-seater coach. Aletta could not see anything to suggest a reason for stopping.

The musky odour inside the van grew stronger as the nervous tension cranked up a notch. It was in complete contrast to the atmosphere of the previous day, when people had strolled from Hillingdon Hospital. She and Levente had been lucky, coming through the vermin attack unscathed. They had been passing a detached house with ivy climbing the front wall when they became aware of a commotion ahead. Without waiting to identify the cause, Levente tugged at Aletta's sleeve, motioning towards the house. The front door opened at their touch and they entered, closing the door behind them. Levente headed upstairs, Aletta close behind. They had watched open-mouthed from a first-floor window while a torrent of frenzied brown creatures swept down the street like a flash flood.

The transit van came to a stop. Over the rumble of idling engine, Aletta heard voices. The driver turned around in his seat.

"Everyone out," he said loudly. "Arms at the ready."

The darkness resounded with the clinking and clacking of magazines being checked, rounds chambered and grenades stowed in jacket pockets. The rear doors were thrown open and grey daylight illuminated scared faces.

Aletta's stomach churned; she lowered her head and belched quietly into her hand. She followed the people to her left, shuffling along the bench seat and climbing out of the van into late morning drizzle.

The drivers remained aboard the three vehicles that had been in front of their transit van, engines still running. Passengers from these and Aletta's van had disembarked and stood around in the rain, stamping their feet nervously, clutching weapons to chests like shields. The vehicles behind pulled up in a long line, but nobody got out. People peered through windows curiously, some pointing, making Aletta feel like a zoo exhibit.

She looked ahead, beyond the lead vehicle, scrunching her eyes against the steady drizzle, which acted like a mist. A couple of hundred yards away stood the reason for them stopping.

The road climbed a gentle gradient to a point where the trees either side fell away; it must, Aletta thought, be bridging a river or railway line. A row of people stood shoulder to shoulder across the road at the bridge's apex. Behind them, four black vehicles sat side by side, blocking the road.

She nudged Levente and nodded towards the row of people. He looked where she had indicated, squinting. When he looked back at her, the colour had drained from his face.

"Bad people?"

Aletta shrugged. "Too far to see in this rain. I think that maybe we will find out."

"If bad people, we cannot go near." Levente took a hand off his rifle—the submachine gun was dangling by his hip; the bag of grenades and magazines dangled by the other hip—to tap his forehead. "Not in here. Not again."

Aletta didn't respond. A man was working his way towards them, bringing the people from the front vehicles with him. When he drew closer, Aletta could see it was the man who had made such a dramatic entrance during the meeting back in Wales; the man who had brought all the weaponry. Except, she corrected herself, he wasn't a man at all, but a boy, not much older than her son Alger, taken from her by the virus in his seventeenth year. She pushed the thought to one side; now was not a time for grief.

The boy reached them and the people from the front vehicles gathered around so that he formed the centre of a rough circle.

"Is everyone armed and ready?" he said. Not waiting for an

answer, he gestured roughly to the hill. "I count twenty-five people lined up across the road. I don't think they are *them*; as far as I can tell at this distance, they are human. But they aren't like us any more. Their brains have been damaged until they're more like vegetables than people. If *they* have put them here to block our progress, we must make them move. Even if it means harming them. We must be ruthless."

"Are they armed?" asked a man.

"I cannot see any weapons," answered the boy, "and we outnumber them at least two to one, but we must proceed cautiously." He motioned towards the many waiting vehicles. "We shouldn't need to risk anyone else for such a pathetic welcoming committee."

"What about those SUVs?" asked someone else.

The boy opened his mouth to reply, but Levente was quicker.

"*Them*," he said. "In the black cars."

"Maybe," said the boy.

"Not maybe," said Levente. "We saw. Before. It is *them*."

"Good," said the boy. "Let's kill them."

"No," insisted Levente. "Not good."

But the boy—wasn't his name Joe?—had already turned away. The crowd parted to let him pass and closed up behind, following him tightly.

"Wait…" said Levente.

Nobody was listening.

Aletta placed a hand on his arm. "Stay here," she said. "It is okay."

The Hungarian turned haunted eyes towards her. "You go, I go. *Igen*." He shook his head. "Not good."

Side by side, they fell into line and walked up the gentle slope. Their company spread out, occupying the entire width of the road.

Aletta could now see more clearly the people who awaited them. Men and women, young and old, standing with hands behind backs, heads bowed, rain dripping from sodden hair. The clothes they wore were filthy, little more than rags. Not one person raised his or her head to watch their approach.

She looked beyond them to the black SUVs. The glass in the windows was tinted, allowing nothing to be glimpsed of the interiors. The engines were turned on, thrumming quietly in the way of well-tuned, powerful cars. A sense of the dread that Levente was clearly experiencing made itself felt inside Aletta at the sight of the vehicles. Her stomach bubbled, threatening to erupt at any moment.

Their pace slowed as they drew nearer. When within ten yards of the waiting people, the company came to a stop.

Still there was no movement, no raised heads, no signs of awareness from the people in front of them.

Aletta glanced at her fellows. Some held their guns to their shoulders, fingers on triggers, ready to begin firing in an instant. One or two looked terrified. Most appeared unnerved by this display of indifference.

Levente glanced at her and grimaced.

"Not good," he whispered.

"No," agreed Aletta. "Not good."

She meant it, too. Something here was bad. Out of true, like bruises on a baby.

The boy, Joe, strode forward. He stood in the no man's land between the two lines and raised the submachine gun he carried to his shoulder. Aletta was directly in line with him and could see at what he was aiming: not the people, but the black vehicles beyond them.

"Come on, then!" Joe yelled.

A few things happened at once.

The people standing in line before them, as one, raised their heads. The black vehicles began to reverse; since they had been parked a little beyond the apex of the hill, they needed to drive back mere yards for only their roofs to remain visible. Levente uttered an exclamation and strode forward to stand beside Joe. He glanced back at Aletta, his eyes shining.

"Look," he called to her, raising an arm to point at a man in the line, a grin lighting his face. "Jerzy!"

Aletta looked at the man to whom he was pointing and gave a start of recognition. It was the Pole who had travelled from Ostend with them. So Jerzy was his name. And next to him, if Aletta wasn't mistaken, stood the young, dark-haired Croatian. But something was still very wrong.

Their faces. Both men, and those standing next to them, wore expressions of such vapidity they might be tailors' mannequins. Strings of spittle drooled from limp lips and vacant eyes stared ahead, unseeing.

"No, Levente," called Aletta, but the Hungarian was already striding towards their former companions, rifle clutched uselessly in his left hand, his right arm held out to greet the Pole…

… whose hands came out from behind his back. Not empty.

She darted forward, the warning forming on her lips, but Jerzy—or whatever he had become—raised the pistol and pointed it at Levente's head. The vacuous expression did not falter when he pulled the trigger.

The rain had made the skin of Aletta's face icy cold, almost to the point of numbness. As a consequence, the spray of blood and brain matter that engulfed her felt as warm as mulled wine. She didn't even notice the tiny cuts to her cheeks caused by fragments of Levente's skull.

The Hungarian slumped to the road. There was no time for Aletta to rush to his side, feel in vain for a pulse, cover what remained of his cooling face with a jacket.

For the young Croatian, and each of his slack-jawed companions, had brought pistols from behind their backs. And Jerzy's pistol was now pointed at her.

Part 3: Calon Lan
(Pure Heart)

Chapter Fifteen

The craft passed the moons and rings of Jupiter, resisting the effects of the gas giant's gravity and magnetic fields with ease. Having travelled across more than four hundred and seventy light years of the galaxy, negotiating perils in deep space humanity has not even imagined, nothing within Sol's system would hinder the craft's voyage to Earth Haven.

Its coating gave the craft the appearance of being sleek and black. The distilled essence of nothingness, condensed to a veneer not much thicker than a fingernail.

"How much farther?" is how the words the woman spoke would have translated into English. They had not yet encountered that language.

The man glanced at the displays on the bank in front of him. "Allowing for the greater rate of deceleration as we approach, we shall enter Earth Haven's atmosphere in the time it takes for 9.26 of the planet's revolutions about its axis."

The craft's velocity had already slowed to less than one percent of light speed and would continue to decrease while it neared its destination. They were confident the power of their surface thrusters would allow them to put down safely on the ocean very near to where the signal had originated. The craft had been designed with storage areas to hold the large number of buoyancy aids with propellant systems to carry them to land where the remnants of the advance party should be waiting.

"And what shall we find upon our arrival?"

The man shrugged. "Who can truly say? It has been five millennia since the ten thousand left Earth Home. That is but a blink to us, but on a young, vibrant planet such as Earth Haven it may represent a significant period during which certain species might have evolved dramatically."

"Certain species… you mean the drones."

"They were given impulses that drive them to procreation,

instincts to protect and nurture their young. It's quite possible they now number in the millions."

The woman breathed out heavily. "*Millions?*"

"All we can say with certainty is our people survive on Earth Haven. The signal proves that."

"But how do a mere ten thousand control millions of drones?"

"I do not know. Yet the way is clear or the signal would not have been sent."

"And our people? You harbour no doubt that what we intend is the correct course?"

The man glanced at her sharply. "You already know the answer to that. They still labour under attitudes instilled in them by the wisdom that prevailed when they left Earth Home. The false wisdom, created by that bitch Sivatra and propagated by generation upon generation of Keeper. You took part in the decision that the office of Keeper shall end when we have secured Earth Haven. You agreed to the proposed solution to the problem posed by the ten thousand." His voice dripped menace. "Do not question the decision to eradicate them."

The woman bowed her head in acquiescence. "I will not, Keeper."

"Are you sure you won't come with us?"

Colleen nodded. Impulsively, she threw her arms around Ceri's neck and hugged her tightly.

"Thank you," she said in a low voice that only Ceri would hear. "You freed me."

She stepped back. Ceri offered her a smile, a sad one that Colleen did her best to return.

"Where will you go?" asked Tom.

Colleen shrugged. "Never been to Britain before. Might work my way up the coastline to Scotland. Perhaps find a castle to live out the last of my days. Or maybe south. I've been wanting to visit Brighton since I was a teenager and saw *Quadrophenia*." Despite her loose front teeth, cut gums and thick lips from where Dermot had struck her with the pistol, her resulting lisp did not distort her speech to such an extent that no one could understand her.

"Steer clear of London."

"I will."

"And you'll be okay with that scooter?"

"Yes." She glanced at Bri. "Thanks again for the offer of the car, but I don't know how to drive one and I can't be arsed to learn now." She patted the seat of the scooter; they'd found the keys in Dermot's jacket pocket. Tom had filled the petrol tank from a plastic container he kept in the boot of his swanky car. "This baby's a doddle to drive."

Will nudged Bri. "Oh, yes," she said. "Please, Colleen, me and Will, we want you to take our gun. You'll need one if you're going to be on your own. The dogs are growing hungry and your golf club might not be enough to keep them away."

"That's a good idea," said Tom. "I don't want to leave you on your own, but at least if you have a gun..." He tailed off as though unsure what else to say.

Colleen had been mulling over the possibility of acquiring pepper spray as a means of defending herself against feral animals. It would, she imagined, be easier to use and more effective against a pack than a gun. She didn't think pepper spray was legally obtainable in Britain so she wouldn't find it in shops, but she had an idea British police sometimes carried it; it may be worthwhile investigating any police premises she passed. She had no wish to carry a gun, least of all the one that had been used to kill Howard, but it made sense for her to have it in the meantime, until she could locate some spray.

"Okay. Will, Bri, I'd be most grateful to take your gun. It's very kind of you."

The ghost of a smile touched Will's face. It was the nearest he'd come to smiling since the events of the previous afternoon.

Once the initial shock had worn off, Tom had taken charge, ushering everyone out of the bar. When Colleen passed him, he handed her the bottle of scotch. Tom had insisted they all, except for him, take a walk and not return until dusk. So she, Ceri, Bri and Will had stepped out into spring drizzle and walked numbly along the deserted seafront. Dogs and rats and gulls gave them a wide berth, almost as though they could sense their shock and grief. Colleen dabbed at her bleeding mouth with a handkerchief and sipped gingerly from the whisky bottle.

When they returned to the hotel hours later, Tom looked exhausted. Colleen stepped past him and poked her head around the door to the bar. The corpses of Howard Newton and Dermot Ward, a.k.a. Clint, had gone. So, too, had the globules of flesh from the wall next to the bar, although the blood stains there and on the carpet where both men had fallen were still visible, like red wine spillages, and a metallic smell tainted the air. Colleen withdrew, closing the door firmly behind her.

The slug from the stray pistol shot had punched a neat hole in the wall of the corridor opposite the door to the bar. Colleen inserted her index finger into it. *Could have been Tom's head* she thought. Judging from his expression while he watched her, Tom had been struck by the same thought.

Later, before darkness had fallen completely, Colleen went out of the hotel's back door from the kitchen. She walked around the corner of an outbuilding, noting the padlock had been broken off, and stood staring at the small lawned area. It was marked by two fresh mounds of earth. A shovel lay discarded to one side.

"Goodbye, Howard," Colleen murmured, although she did not know beneath which mound the doctor lay.

Before retiring to her room with what remained of the bottle of scotch, she looked out Tom and embraced him.

"Thank you," she said, drawing away, "for not burying him in the same hole as Dermot."

This following morning, as they all gathered in the roadway outside the hotel, Bri *did* manage a smile, although it looked forced and weak. She displayed no physical after-effects of her headlong charge at Dermot. First Tom, then Ceri, had looked closely at the healing injury to her temple and declared themselves satisfied she had not reopened the wound.

Her mental scars might take longer to heal, thought Colleen. The same could be said of them all. Ceri, in particular, was still weepy and shaky, struggling to come to terms with having taken another's life.

Bri stepped forward and handed to Colleen the pistol they'd had to prise from Dermot's fingers.

"Be careful," said Bri, "it's still loaded. I'll fetch you the spare bullets."

Colleen hefted the weapon in her hand. It felt surprisingly heavy and cold, and not as abhorrent to the touch as she'd imagined. On the contrary, its solidity soothed her, anchoring her to the here and now when the more fanciful side of her nature wanted to fly free to the stars so she would never again have to think about loss and grief and death. With Howard gone, her mind might soon begin once more to unravel.

Bri returned with a clinking carrier bag. Colleen glanced inside when Bri handed it to her; it contained half a dozen or more magazines packed full with brass cartridges.

"Thank you," she said. "I hope I never need to use your pistol, but it will be a comfort to have it by my side." She found that she meant it, too, and not only because she had a defence against any wildlife that might take a notion to attack her. If she ever needed to go to Sinead, now she had a quick, certain and painless method at her fingertips.

"Okay," said Tom, rubbing his hands together. "Shall we get going?"

Will nodded, but both Ceri and Bri hesitated, regarding Colleen with anguished expressions. Fresh tears brimmed in Ceri's eyes.

Colleen smiled and found that, despite the pain of cut lips and bruised gums, it felt natural. "Really," she said, "it's okay. I want to be alone. I *need* to be alone."

"If you change your mind," said Ceri through a stifled sob, "we'll be in Cornwall. Land's End."

"I know. Tom's given me directions. Now, go."

Colleen watched Tom and Ceri climb into the Peugeot, where Dusty patiently awaited them, and Bri and Will clamber into a white Range Rover. She waved when the vehicles pulled away and stood watching them until they had vanished around a bend in the road.

She did not expect to see any of them again.

It was as well the roads were empty and all she had to do was follow the Peugeot. In addition to her inexpertise and inexperience, Bri's driving was somewhat hampered by the blurring effect of the tears that insisted on running down her cheeks on a regular basis.

She wiped them away with a handkerchief growing soggy through use. Will didn't even notice. Head resting against the door pillar, his eyes were closed and he breathed deeply. She let him doze. If his method of dealing with shock was to succumb to slumber, she was fine with that. It prevented him seeing her blub and she was fine with that, too.

Bri barely gave a thought to where they were heading and what had prompted it. The message had come to her the previous afternoon, while they had been out walking along a rainswept seafront. Dogs and cats, scavenging for vermin, turned wild eyes towards them. Bri maintained the protective aura without it any longer causing her head to ache and, for now at least, it continued to keep the animals away.

They had stopped to watch the grey waves roll in. Colleen stood a little apart, sipping scotch and sobbing quietly. Ceri stood with her arm around Will's shoulder; on this occasion, he didn't seem to mind. Bri stood on Will's other side. She gave a gasp when the voice spoke inside her head.

Hello, Bri. Don't be afraid. My name is Milandra. Your friends Peter and Diane are with me.

Bri had begun, instinctively, to try to expel the invading intelligence, but she recognised the voice as the one that had spoken to her inside the cycle shop in Lambeth, and the mention of Peter's and Diane's names made curiosity overcome caution.

We are in a place called Land's End in Cornwall said the voice. *Ah, I see that you know it. There is plenty of room in the hotel for you and your companions.*

It is only fair to tell you the man who shot the boy is also here. He wants you to know you have nothing to fear from him. Anything else he wants to say, he can tell you himself if you decide to come.

Please consider coming here. As quickly as you can. While we speak, almost two thousand humans are attacking my people in London. I am afraid it will not go well for them and their actions may seal mankind's eventual fate.

The remainder of my people are travelling here from a place many light years distant from Earth. They will arrive ten days from now. When they come ashore, I want the first human they encounter to be you, Bri. You do not yet realise it, but you may represent the next stage of mankind's evolution. You may represent mankind's best—only—chance of saving itself from complete annihilation.

The voice paused.

That is a huge responsibility to lay on the shoulders of a teenage girl, but I make no apology. Besides, I can see my words make little impression on you. Your emotions run to sorrow and regret. You have endured a tragedy, one that is too close, too raw, for you to take in the full import of my words.

Nevertheless remember this: come to Cornwall. Come today or tomorrow or the next day. But come.

The voice fell silent. Both Ceri and Will were gazing at her with concern. She was about to say something when the voice spoke again. Quieter; the mental equivalent of a whisper.

Bri, I am still here, but now I am alone and I must be brief.

The others do not know we have spoken before when I helped you to escape from London. It is better they continue not to know.

I must tell you that your coming here is not without risk. I believe you are safe from the man who shot your friend, but I am unsure about her. *Still, I will protect you as much as I can, and Peter and Diane would lay down their lives for you, although you won't get Diane to admit to that.*

Come to Cornwall. Bring your friends.

This time, Bri was sure the voice had gone. While it was still fresh in her mind, she relayed to Ceri and Will everything it had said about going to Cornwall, omitting only the part about her being mankind's best hope of salvation. That was something she didn't understand or want to consider. Some things were too big, too damned scary, to think about.

"Are you sure?" Ceri sounded as scared as Bri felt. "This Milandra wants us to go to Cornwall?"

Bri nodded. She glanced down at Will. "He's there," she said. "The man who shot you."

Will reached out his good hand and gripped hers tightly. "But so is Peter?"

"And Diane. I won't go if you don't want to, Will."

"I don't mind, Bri. He won't try to shoot me again, will he?"

"Milandra said he won't, but I don't know."

"You can't go," said Ceri. "It's way too risky."

"More risky than being amongst humans?" Bri nodded back towards the town. "There are two men shot dead back there. Not an alien within a hundred miles."

Ceri opened her mouth, paused with it still open, then closed it again. She fumbled in her jacket pocket for her cigarettes.

Bri looked back down at Will.

"What do you say, buster? I swore I'd never leave you again and I mean to keep my promise. If you don't want to go to Cornwall, we ain't going."

Will stared at her for a long moment, bottom lip tucked between his teeth. She could sense indecision washing off him as clearly as she could smell salt from the ocean.

"If you want to go," he said, "I'm coming with you."

Being mindful of his injured shoulder, Bri reached out and hugged him as tightly as she dared. Ceri watched them, a look of deep sorrow on her face, but she said nothing more.

That night, Tom and Ceri came to see her. Tom wanted to hear about the voice and listened closely while she repeated what she'd told Ceri and Will earlier.

"What have you decided to do?" he asked, when she had

finished her tale.

"Will and I are going to Cornwall." She felt her chin jut out, but defiance it transpired wasn't necessary.

Tom regarded her intently for a long moment. Then he nodded. "Ceri and I are coming with you."

Without quite knowing why, Bri burst into fresh tears.

That had been yesterday. Today, after saying goodbye to Colleen, the four of them were driving in convoy to Cornwall and, so far, Bri had leaked most of the way.

She had never been what she thought of as a girly girl; not one for fancy frocks or Parisian perfumes or shoes with heels like stilts. Her interests were more surfing and cycling than boy bands and *Twilight*. Uncontrollable weeping didn't fit her character profile.

He had saved her life; she had tried to save his.

While Howard lay on his back on the floor of the hotel bar, a dark red stain spreading across his shirt, Bri had looked down at him and reached into his mind. Not knowing if there was anything she could do, she found his psyche. Immediately, she knew. This wasn't like trying to heal an old hurt as she had done with Will and Joe; attempting the same here would be like trying to staunch a breached river bank with a bucket of sand. All she could do was watch Howard slip away. She could not even offer comfort; his mind had become as insubstantial as foam. With nothing to which to anchor herself, she had returned to her own head, but not before seeing Howard's last thoughts had been of his family. That gave her some measure of solace. Ironic, really: she had gone to offer comfort, but had found some herself.

Bri's right hand came off the steering wheel. She raised it to her temple and touched the indentation where the man had struck her with the paperweight. Her hair had grown back and the egg-like lump had disappeared, but she could feel the hole beneath her skin where her skull had not yet completely fused. It would only close at all because she was young enough that her bones were still growing; a few years older and she would have been left with a hole in her skull for the remainder of her days.

Howard had created that hole with a bone drill in Salisbury Hospital under the careful watch of that strange woman Diane. Bri's psyche was held tightly by Peter so that her head could not so much as twitch and she avoided the acrid odour of scorched bone. Later, she asked Peter about the smell. "Take a fingernail clipping," he said, "and burn it with a match. That is what it smelled like when Howard drilled into your head."

Peter had persuaded the doctor to perform the procedure with the help, Bri suspected, of a little of his 'special' persuasive powers. Even so, Howard had not agreed without first speaking to her. Gripping both her hands in his, he looked intently into her eyes.

"Brianne," he said, "you have to understand I am a *general* medical practitioner. I deal with the treatment and relief of conditions like influenza and mild psoriasis and ear infections. If a patient presented to me with a subdural haematoma, I'd be referring them straight to the A&E Department of St James's Hospital, not attempting to operate on it myself. For very good reason. Surgeons undertake years of specialised training, acquiring knowledge of anatomy and dextrous skills that I do not possess. Diane will assist me and she has experience of these procedures, but she isn't a surgeon, either." Howard took a deep breath and his gaze became even more intense. "If you allow me to attempt this procedure, there's a chance you will die because of my ignorance and ineptitude."

"And if you don't attempt the procedure?"

Howard's gaze did not falter. "There's a chance the condition will kill you anyway. It's likely, in light of the fact your symptoms haven't worsened, the subdural bleeding has stopped by now and the pooled blood is coagulating into jelly. But if it isn't removed and continues to press against your brain..." He shrugged. "Like I said, I'm no surgeon, but I don't need to be to know an untreated subdural haematoma is often fatal. And there's more."

"Go on."

"The main diagnostic machinery, like X-ray machines and MRI

scanners, don't work from the emergency electrical systems running off the generator. Too heavy on the juice, I suppose, so they'll only work off the main grid. Diane has found a portable X-ray machine that will run off the emergency circuits so we won't be going in completely blind. We have a working bone drill with a guide we will set to the minimum depth so it will be virtually impossible for me to drill too deep and cause more damage. No, the main risk comes when I attempt to remove the blood clot. Since we don't have a theatre team or post-op care, the best way to remove the blood quickly is, we think, to aspirate with percutaneous needle and syringe.

"If I can remove the blood without causing damage—that's a mighty big 'if'—but if by some miracle I can do it, there are other possible complications. If the bleeding hasn't stopped, there's nothing I can do about it. To attempt to repair damaged blood vessels will require us to remove a section of your skull. Quite simply, that's not a procedure I have the ability to carry out. Not under any circumstances."

Bri nodded. "Okay."

"There will still be the risk of infection. We have the means to sterilise the instruments we'll be using and there's an abundance of sterile dressings. Antibiotics are in plentiful supply. I think if we get to that point, the risk of infection will be no greater than if we were in a fully-operational hospital. It might even be a reduced risk due to the absence of other patients and staff. How often did we used to hear of people going into hospital with one complaint and, while there, coming down with some sort of nasty bug they wouldn't have caught if they hadn't been in hospital?"

Bri opened her mouth to speak, but Howard silenced her by increasing his grip on her hands to such an extent she almost cried out.

"There's one last thing. I've been saving the worst until last." He took another deep breath. "We cannot risk anaesthetising you. We don't possess the knowledge and it's simply not an option. So, I will have to drill a hole in your head and insert a needle into your skull while you are awake. You will need to keep perfectly still the whole time. The slightest movement at the wrong moment could cause irreparable brain damage or worse."

Bri gazed back into Howard's kindly eyes. She could read a mixture of emotions there, and sense them flowing off him: fear that she would agree so he would have to perform the procedure; terror that he would mess it up and damage or kill her; hope that she would refuse his offer so he wouldn't have to go through with it; anguish that she would refuse his offer and so condemn herself to an early grave. She could also read a calm assurance behind that compassionate gaze, a quiet confidence arising not from cockiness or arrogance, but from long years of acquired knowledge and experience of dealing with infirm people. She made her decision.

"If anyone can pull this off," she said, "it's you. Do it."

And he did. She didn't even have to lie still as it turned out, thanks to Peter's brainwave and his mental strength to hold tightly to her psyche when it yearned to fly back to her own head.

Yes, she was grateful to Peter. And to Diane for assisting with the procedure and for helping to nurse her back to full health. But her undying gratitude belonged to Howard for his courage in saving her life.

Now *his* life had been snuffed out. Just like that, with one twitch of a madman's finger.

And for that she wept.

Chapter Sixteen

The coastline in and around Land's End, rugged and unspoiled, bounded to one side by the restless ocean, to the other by windswept heath and farmland running to meadow, provoked in Peter Ronstadt memories of the tales he had loved in the days when personal entertainment mainly came in the form of books. Images of wreckers and smugglers and pirates swirled through his mind while he wandered the desolate clifftops and beaches, feeling his cells open like spring buds in the sunlight.

Milandra had invited him and Diane to stay to witness the Great Coming. Jason Grant and Rodney Wilson seemed happy enough for them to remain. George Wallace could not be described as happy, but he appeared more at ease with their presence than he did at the prospect of Bri and, in particular, Will being there. Lavinia Cram's disinterest bordered on indifference. Only Simone Furlong was openly hostile, although Peter noticed she was often truculent with the other Deputies and, especially, towards Milandra.

"The Chosen doesn't want us around, but at least no one's about to fire a bullet through my brain," Peter told Diane with a chuckle, a heartfelt one. It is easier to be magnanimous when not staring into the dark depths of a gun barrel.

Since the Keeper's revelations about their history, a peculiar atmosphere pervaded the hotel as they tried to come to terms with learning their beliefs were founded not on reinforced concrete twenty feet thick, but on shifting sandbanks that the raging torrent of Milandra's words had washed away.

As far as Milandra said she could tell, and Peter saw no reason to disagree with her, the ancient civil war that had devastated the surface of Earth Home had been fought over a major philosophical difference of opinion. Sivatra and her followers had wanted to put an end to antagonism to other species and begin an era of enlightenment in which learning, arts and cultural enrichment became the ideals, where introspection and not violent aggression became the norm. The other side had wanted to carry on as before.

"We were parasites," Milandra said to a hushed room. "Traversing the galaxy, landing on habitable planets, destroying native species and ruthlessly exploiting resources until the planets became uninhabitable." She gave a deep sigh, filled with regret. "We wrought nothing but destruction wherever we went. An infestation, like locusts. A plague every bit as devastating to its victims as the Millennium Bug."

There was a pause.

"Where did we come from originally?" asked Lavinia quickly, as though breaking the silence mattered more than the answer.

"Not even Sivatra knew. That knowledge is lost in the mists of time immemorial. She wanted to do the same with our true nature: consign it to the darkest depths where it might remain hidden while a new history, one in which we could take pride, was invented."

"And they fought a war over that?" The Chosen sounded incredulous.

"Yes, Simone. Wars have been fought over less. Sivatra's side won, but at great cost to the environment. She subsequently did all she could to make sure it was not incurred in vain."

"Sounds like you admire her," said Grant.

"She risked everything to do what she thought was best for our people. How could I not admire her? When the war was over, she oversaw the sealing away deep underground of the tablets left behind by the ancients. She underwent a process that altered her DNA to allow her psyche to become the depository for our group consciousness. She linked to every person who had survived the war—from both sides. From that moment, the memories and experiences of every one of our kind who died would pass to the Keeper."

Milandra glanced repeatedly at Simone while she told them how Sivatra had forged the systems and processes they all took for granted. It was, thought Peter, as though she were trying to make Simone aware of what had been sacrificed to change their people's destiny; to make the Chosen more serious about the responsibilities that would fall to her. Judging from the way Simone's gaze wandered and her attention zoned in and out like a human child's, Milandra was facing an uphill task.

"Each Keeper," Milandra continued, "would forge the link anew with every new-born. Sivatra introduced the role of Chosen, passing on her DNA to enable the Chosen to become Keeper in turn. She did not make it a cast-iron rule that each Keeper and Chosen should be exclusively female, but the practice was implicitly encouraged. And why?" Milandra sighed. "I had to go deep to find the memories that confirm it—she hid them away from the rest to make the job of reconstructing the whole story even harder, I guess—but I eventually located and viewed them. Whether she was correct, I don't know, but Sivatra took the view, supported by many of those closest to her, that a woman discovering the truth about our past would be more likely than a man to keep that knowledge to herself."

"What, like you are now?" said Simone. Peter was reminded again of how deceptive her appearance of childlike inattentiveness could be.

"If to disclose the truth meant causing unnecessary pain and suffering, then I would perpetuate the lie." Milandra's smile seemed tinged with sadness. "But I think the time has come when we need to know the truth about ourselves. If we are to stand in judgement of another species, one in which we instilled our own characteristics and instincts, should we not fully recognise ourselves in order to judge the other fairly?"

"I don't doubt you, Keeper," said Lavinia, "but what if you have misinterpreted the memories?"

"That's a fair question. If you like—and this offer holds for every person in this room—I can show you. See Sivatra's memories for yourself. But not today. I need the last of my strength for one last task, one I need you all to help me perform."

When Simone Furlong discovered that Milandra proposed to invite to the hotel the human girl who had led them such a merry dance in London, and her young friend, and the two adults who Ronstadt had saved from the effects of the Commune, she took incredulity to a new level. Wallace's face fell but, surprisingly, he raised no verbal objection. Even laid-back Lavinia was more vociferous in her disapproval than he.

"Let me explain," said Milandra, "then we can vote whether to invite them.

"In my view, we have done mankind a grave disservice. Long have we poured scorn on them, belittled them, levelled allegations of shallowness and stupidity against them. We called them 'drones'. We said that violence runs at the core of their being. Thinking that we were the peaceful, altruistic species, we put ourselves on a pedestal, smugly congratulating ourselves for being the enlightened, sophisticated ones, while looking down our long noses at selfish, aggressive humanity.

"The clues were there all along as to how mistaken we were, right under those long noses, yet we failed to see them for what they were." She paused to look at each of them, lingering on Simone and Wallace.

"Haven't we always said mankind was made in our image?" she continued. "At the same time as we scoffed at them for being so warlike. How could we not see the dichotomy, the delicious irony?" Milandra uttered a rich chuckle. "Of course man is aggressive; selfish, yes, impetuous, self-serving, cruel. *He was made in our image.* Whether through some species memory or genetic imprint that couldn't be erased, man is only obeying his base instincts by behaving like he does. It is not his fault—we made him that way. For his base instincts are ours."

Peter grunted. He had been listening with mounting dismay and could keep quiet no longer. "So we wiped out mankind for obeying instincts that we, however unwittingly, instilled in them?"

Milandra nodded. "That's about the size of it." She shrugged. "There's nothing we can say or do now that will make up for the

Cleansing. And nor do I think that we should. Even had we known the truth about our past, it was clear that humankind had grown too big, too powerful, to allow the Great Coming to take place. A cull was necessary."

"Yes, it was," said Simone with feeling. "So why all this bleeding heart bullshit?" She shot Peter a dark glance.

Milandra held up a hand to forestall Peter's retort.

"We cannot change the past," she said, "but we can influence the future. Maybe, once the Great Coming has taken place, we can advocate for the preservation of what remains of mankind, rather than its total eradication. I think we owe them that much at least.

"And we can begin by inviting this small group to stay here. Get to know them; allow them to know us. Let them be the first humans our people meet when they arrive from their long journey. What do y'all think?"

Milandra gazed around the room, meeting each person's eyes in turn and not moving on until they had spoken.

Peter was first and he didn't hesitate. "I think I have already made my feelings pretty clear by not taking part in the Cleansing. You have my vote."

Jason Grant nodded. "And mine."

Rodney Wilson coloured to have so many gazes turn his way, but his voice was clear and strong. "London's not the same without its people so I vote to try to save 'em."

Diane next. She returned Milandra's gaze steadily. "If you'd asked me three or four months ago, I don't know how I'd have answered." Peter didn't miss the slight hesitation before she spoke again. "I held no particular affection for humans; I went about my part in the Cleansing willingly enough, although I felt I was doing so out of some misplaced but unavoidable loyalty to my own kind."

"Obeisance," murmured Milandra.

"Yes," said Diane. "That's how I acknowledged your message instructing me to start spreading the virus." She shrugged in the way that seemed so familiar to Peter now and *so* Diane. "I hold no particular affection for our people, either. My decision is clear; it was made the moment I obstructed Bishop in his pursuit of Peter and the two humans. When I allowed him to die in the helicopter, there was no going back for me. I vote to save them."

Milandra nodded and turned to Wallace. He stared down at his feet. "George?"

He kept his head down for a long moment. When he looked up, his cheeks burned, though not as brightly as the defiance in his eyes. "I said I hated humans. I said I hated the girl. That part was true. I *did* hate her, but only because she was showing us what humans could be. How smart, how compassionate, how fucking pure. It was like a mockery of everything I stood for and I hated her for reminding me I had once loved them." His cheeks glowed brighter while he glared around at the group. Then his shoulders sagged. "She's like the template of how I thought they would turn out. I'm glad I didn't shoot her. I'll regret to the end of my days I shot the boy, although I feel mightily relieved, if I understand you correctly, Milandra, that he lived?"

Milandra nodded.

"It was a close call," said Peter, unable to resist twisting the knife a little.

"I'm glad he's alive," said Wallace. "If he comes here, I will say sorry to him, face to face. I vote 'yes'."

Lavinia Cram returned Milandra's steady gaze with an unwavering stare of her own. "Not feeling the love for drones. Seems like I'm in the minority. Sorry, can't vote for 'em, but I won't vote against 'em neither. I abstain."

Milandra turned last to face the Chosen, raising her eyebrows in mute enquiry.

"Really?" said Simone. "You're gonna ask me how I'm voting? I ain't gone soft in the head like some of the pussies around here." She shot a venomous glance at Wallace. "Drone lover," she hissed. Wallace ignored her.

"Do I take that as a 'no'?" asked Milandra.

"Fucking right it's a 'no'."

"But you'll assist me in contacting her. And, if they come, you won't harm them." They were statements, not questions.

Simone glared at Milandra; the Keeper gazed steadily back. Peter could almost see the power of the clashing wills like two cords of electricity, Simone's an enraged scarlet, Milandra's a calm yellow, meeting in a storm of orange lightning.

The Chosen dropped her gaze first. Her lips pursed as though she'd sucked the sourest slice of lime and her voice dripped resentment. "I'll help. I won't hurt one hair on her pretty head; nor the others." The sullen expression faded and she clapped her hands together, once more the joyous teenager. "It'll be fun to have someone new to play with. They can help me find more rats to burn."

"Hmm. Let's be sure it's only the rats that get burned, shall we?"

Simone returned Milandra's sweet smile, but Peter could not help feeling it was the sort of smile that would be given by a cobra in the instant before it struck.

No sooner had the sound of gunfire reached their minibus, than Zach was out of his seat, rifle in hand, making for the door. Without hesitation, Amy followed. She glanced back when she hit the rain-slickened road; Frank and, more reluctantly judging from his expression, Elliott were also coming.

The shooting sounded much louder to Amy now she was outside, but it was already beginning to tail off. What had started off resembling an explosion in a firework factory had become intermittent. Staccato. It was coming from the direction in which the vehicles had been heading.

Their minibus had been towards the rear of the lengthy convoy. Amy hurried to keep up with Zach as he strode along the line of idling vehicles. Near the front of the convoy, they reached a transit van with its rear doors standing open—it, and the four or five vehicles ahead, appeared to be empty apart from their drivers.

By the time they passed the lead vehicle, the sound of gunfire had stopped. Zach continued on the main road, heading up the incline towards the figures milling around near the brow of the hill. Amy followed, her legs complaining at the pace she was making them maintain to keep up with him. She could hear the low murmur of Elliott and Frank talking as they came along behind.

Amy wrinkled her nose when the first coppery tang hit her nostrils. She glanced down; the asphalt beneath her boots was running with more than rainwater.

Zach came to a halt ten yards or so before the hill's summit. Amy stopped by him, resisting the urge to pinch her nostrils against the earthy stench of ordure that combined with the smell of blood in a heady mixture. After clearing the tenement building in Portland of corpses and attempting to set them alight, she had smelled worse, a lot worse. And she had seen worse, or at least as bad, in the form of poor Nan.

Nevertheless, her stomach lurched at the sight of so many bodies. Thirty, forty, maybe more. Unlike the blackening, bloated corpses back home, these people had died in violence, only moments earlier. The steady drizzle was not heavy enough to wash the blood away entirely, so thick did it lie on the ground, but was discouraging it from congealing, meaning wounds still dribbled or glistened.

White-faced survivors, some injured, stood or sat amidst the bodies and blood and excrement and lumps of unidentifiable flesh. A woman writhed on her back, clutching at her stomach, whimpering in pain.

Zach turned and shouted back to Frank, gesticulating down the hill.

"Go back and get those empty vehicles up here. P'raps forty-five corpses; twelve injured. At least one severely."

Frank, coming up at Elliott's pace and still yards away, blanched, nodded and turned back. Elliott continued on until he stood by Amy's side.

"Oh my god," he muttered.

Zach stepped forward. Amy, her stomach still in turmoil, wanted to turn and run down the hill, but the compulsion not to stray far from Zach's side was stronger. She might have made new friends in the form of Sarah and Elliott, developed and overcome a crush on Frank, but it was still to Zach she looked for guidance and protection when the serious shit went down.

Stepping gingerly, as though that might prevent her getting blood on her boots, Amy followed Zach through the carnage.

The woman who had been whimpering had fallen quiet. Her hands had dropped to her sides. Pink and purple rolls of intestine spilled from the gaping hole in her stomach.

"Forty-six corpses," Zach muttered as he passed her.

Further on, a woman sat on the road, staring at the body of a thickset man missing the back half of his head. Zach stopped and lowered himself to his heels with a grunt.

"Miss?" he said.

The woman, fair-haired with flecks of grey showing at her temples, turned to look at Zach. Her face resembled a gory mask, the rain struggling to rinse away the blood covering it, but her eyes were strikingly blue and clear, giving lie to her generally dazed appearance.

"He was my friend," she said. Her voice was thickly accented, though she enunciated clearly and Amy had no difficulty understanding her; her tone was matter-of-fact, as if remarking on the drizzle. "The only friend I had left in the world."

"What happened here?" asked Zach.

"They were people. Like us. Jerzy and the Croatian. I never did remember his name." She shuddered. "They shot at us. Jerzy killed Levente. He tried to kill me."

"Did you see any others? Er, anyone who wasn't a person?" Zach glanced at Amy and grimaced as if to say, 'What a ridiculous question.'

"You mean *them*." The woman shook her head slowly.

"They were in black four-by-fours," said a voice.

Amy and Zach both glanced at the speaker. It was Joe, a drawn, pale Joe with splashes of blood on his jacket and hands that shook.

With a grimace and a popping sound from his knees, Zach stood.

"How many?" he asked.

Joe shrugged. "Tinted windows. They reversed out of sight as soon as I pointed my gun at them." His voice was toneless. "I tried to go after them, but that's when the shooting started. I killed three people."

"Your first?"

"Yes."

"That's why you're in shock." Zach glanced at the fair-haired woman. "Don't think you're the only one. It doesn't get any easier, though you'll reach a level of numbness."

"I don't want to kill any more humans. I want to kill *them* fuckers." Joe's eyes grew brighter and he seemed to mentally shake himself, sloughing off some of his lethargy. His eyebrows drew together in thought. "They have to be nearby."

"Huh?"

"*Them.* They control us by combining their minds. To make us burn bodies and rats and mattresses, they told us what to do and let us get on with it. At least, once we'd been treated at... um, hospital, can't remember the name..."

"Hillingdon?" suggested Amy, surprising herself by remembering.

Joe shot her a smile. "That's it." He raised a hand, which had stopped shaking, and ran it through his hair, dislodging rainwater as though squeezing a sponge. "Do you know, they refer to us as 'drones'. Once we've been treated at the hospital, that's what we become. Mindless, drooling drones." He gestured at the corpses. "That's what these people were." He bit his lip pensively. "The point is, they only had to combine their minds and tell us the once. Then we'd do it and keep on doing it until someone told us to stop. But that was for the menial stuff. I don't think that'll work when they want us to kill other humans."

"Why not?" asked Zach. "If the humans have become mindless drones, as you put it, why won't they obey *all* orders?"

Joe frowned. "I can't explain…"

"Because," said a new voice, "killing goes against the grain." It was Elliott; he had come and stood next to Amy. "If I understand correctly, young man, these people have been subjected to some sort of electrical treatment that has damaged their brains, but not destroyed them entirely."

Joe nodded. "I'm proof of that. I had help to get better, but I'd started to recover without it."

Elliott nodded at the bodies lying in the road. "Even those poor souls must have retained basic thought processes as otherwise they would not have the capacity to obey the simplest instruction. They cannot, therefore, be accurately described as 'mindless'. At the very least, their basic humanity must be preserved, their instincts as to what is right or wrong. Being made to burn dead bodies would be unpleasant, but not fundamentally wrong. On the other hand, killing people in cold blood without reason is, to every right-minded person, morally repugnant."

"Yes," said Joe. "I could never have said it like you, but that's what I mean. *They* are trying to get us to do something that's so wrong they can't simply tell us to do it then bugger off. They have to be nearby so they can *keep* telling us to do it. Otherwise, we'd stop doing it."

"Okay," said Zach. "They have to stay close to retain control. How close?"

Joe shrugged. "Twenty, thirty yards?"

"Do they have to be able to see the people they're controlling?"

"I don't think so. When they reversed the four-by-fours, they dropped out of line of sight of the humans. Yet the humans hadn't started firing then so they must have still been able to control them even though they could no longer see them."

Zach's brow furrowed in thought.

Amy looked around. The assortment of empty vehicles had

arrived and Frank was helping to load the injured onto the bus for transport back to Hillingdon for treatment.

"We'd better give Frank a hand," she said.

Zach nodded distractedly.

"Mortars," said Joe. "You're thinking about mortars."

"I don't know how you knew, but that's precisely what I was thinking about." Zach's eyes narrowed while he regarded the boy. "We'll need two lines. One to lay down covering fire to keep the humans they're controlling at bay. The second armed with mortars to fire beyond the humans at *them*. If they have to be nearby to exert control, there lies their weakness. Let's take advantage of it."

Joe's eyes shone. "Yes!" He clenched one hand into a fist and punched the air. "Let's send these fuckers back to whatever hell they came from."

The featureless countryside slipped by. Ceri longed to see hills and valleys again. All this flatness looked weird to a Welsh girl. Alien.

Never mind. They would soon be out of the Fens and then the landscape would become more familiar. She was happy to sit and watch it; let Tom do the driving.

"I went on honeymoon to Cornwall," she mused. "A week in a little fisherman's cottage overlooking the harbour in Polperro. That's the cottage that was little, not the fisherman, though he might have been."

She knew her tone was wistful, but couldn't help it. Tom didn't seem to mind; he grunted and smiled.

That honeymoon seemed a lifetime away. Paul trim and tanned, before his hairline began to recede like an outgoing tide. She had been wrinkle- and stretchmark-free, with no sign of the pot belly she hadn't been able to shift since giving birth to Rhys. Long, sun-filled days of eating freshly-caught crab and mussels; longer, sultry nights of little sleep.

"Polperro," said Tom. "Think I've been. Narrow streets with tiny smugglers' cottages?"

"Aye. That's the place. Bri comes from Looe, the next town up the coast."

"If she wants, we can pay a visit."

"I doubt she'll want to. Her parents and brother are still there, in their house."

"Ah."

They lapsed into silence. Ceri doggedly kept her thoughts turned to happier times. Anything not to think about the events of the previous day.

Not being in any particular hurry, they stopped often. Sometimes they'd snack. Usually, one or more of them would pop behind a hedge or wall to attend to business. Ceri would smoke a cigarette and Dusty would go off exploring, though Tom would never let him go out of sight.

"Too many feral strays about now," he said. For that reason, they kept a loaded firearm within easy reach whenever they left the safety of the vehicles. So far, they had not had cause to use it. The only animal they encountered had been, of all things, a pig. It had come snuffling along the side of the road, but stopped in its tracks when it heard their voices. Snout twitching, it stared at them in silence, but bolted with a startled squeal into the adjoining woodland when Dusty trotted towards it. Bri had to talk Will out of chasing after it to capture it for a pet.

"Do you think she'll be all right?" Tom asked, when they were once more underway after a comfort break.

"Who, Bri?"

"Sorry, you're not a mind-reader. I was thinking of Colleen."

"I don't think she intends to drive the scooter off a cliff, if that's what you're asking. But, no, I don't think she'll be all right. She was close to Howard."

"He was a lovely bloke."

"Not to mention the only doctor we had." Ceri shifted in her seat. "I'm trying not to dwell on yesterday. Never having killed anyone before and all that."

"Sorry."

"It's okay." She let out a long, shuddering sigh. "What have we come to, Tom? It's not like we don't have enough problems without going around killing each other. I expect there's killing going on in London, too."

"No doubt. Not that it's any consolation, but at least they haven't gone there looking to kill other human beings."

"You're right. It's no consolation."

"Well, let's hope their actions don't jeopardise our chances of surviving beyond the summer."

"Jesus, Tom, you're a barrel of laughs. And, no, don't say sorry again."

"Um…"

Ceri quickly cast about for a topic with which to change the subject. She remembered something she had meant to ask Tom earlier. "Bri."

"What about her?"

"Have you noticed anything, er, unusual about her?"

"How d'you mean?"

"Unusual. Strange. Out of the ordinary."

"Give me a for instance."

"Okay. She seems to be able to tell when someone wants something without them having to say it. When we stopped just now, I was thinking I'd quite like a chocolate biscuit. Bri reached into the snack bag and passed me the packet."

"Huh. You mean, she read your mind?"

"Not sure. I think she picked up the thought, but without even realising it. She acted as if I'd asked for the biscuits, but I'd only had the thought a moment before. I hadn't *said* a word. And Will made a move towards the biscuits a moment after Bri. As if he, too, had picked up on my thought. When Bri handed them to me, he sat back as if what had happened was perfectly natural, as though he also believed I'd actually asked for the biscuits."

"Maybe he wanted a biscuit himself."

"Maybe. So you haven't noticed anything unusual?"

"Can't say that I have."

"Forget it, then. Perhaps I'm imagining things."

Yes, that must be it, she thought. Imagining things. How could a sixteen-year-old girl suddenly start reading other people's thoughts? This was real life, not a Ray Bradbury novel. And yet Peter said Bri's brain, as a result of her injury, had changed, become more like his and Diane's. Something about fresh neural pathways and activated synapses. Perhaps one consequence of the alterations was the ability to pick up on electrical impulses given out by others' brains. If that were true, it didn't explain how Will appeared to have acquired the same ability, even to a lesser degree.

"Are we doing the right thing?" said Tom.

"How do you mean? Going into the lions' den?"

"Ha! That's one way of putting it."

"All I know is that Bri was determined to go and I don't want to let them out of our sight again."

"And we have little to lose."

"True. I can't see why this Milandra would want us there, but it will give us the chance to ask her why they murdered our families."

"Do you think she's going to tell us anything different from what Peter and Diane have already said?"

"Nope. But I want to look her in the eye when she replies. At least we might get the satisfaction of seeing her squirm."

"Satisfaction? You reckon? I think we're far more likely to feel hugely frustrated and angry when the smug bastards try to justify their actions."

Ceri glanced at Tom. There was an unusual edge to his voice. He stared at the road, his knuckles white on the steering wheel. "You okay?"

"Not really. I feel—and I make no apology for saying it—that we're probably heading to our doom."

She looked out at the passing countryside. They had left the flatness of the Fens behind and the uniformity of the landscape was at last broken by rolling hills and tree-clad dales. Crops of rapeseed flowered in a profusion of dazzling yellows; hedgerows and avenues bloomed white and pink blossom; varied shades of green of field and hillsides, meadows and forests, provided a verdant backdrop. The world could be a beautiful place.

Struggling to keep her voice steady, she said, "No need to apologise. I think you may well be right."

Chapter Seventeen

To her surprise, Simone Furlong found that activities which used to keep her amused for hours had lost their attraction. Not even her favourite video game, *Grand Theft Auto*, or her favourite movie, *Clueless* (Simone was convinced Alicia Silverstone's character had been modelled on her; she didn't allow the fact that the time she'd spent in Hollywood had been during its infancy in the 1920s spoil a good fantasy), could maintain her interest for long.

Maybe it was the chance to find more rats to kill but, come rain or shine, she preferred being outside to sitting in front of a flickering screen. This caused her to spend time in contemplation, a very un-Simone-like activity. Beyond essential sunlight regeneration, she had never been an outdoor sort of girl, especially now she was living in a place with such a crummy climate.

If introspection resulted in any firm conclusion, it was that the sudden liking of fresh air could not be down to rats alone. True, she had spent a lot of time outside in London, when her eyes had been opened to the fun that could be had with small, furry rodents, but she didn't believe she was so shallow as to have her entire outlook dictated by such fleeting pleasure.

The real clue lay in the way her glance kept creeping skywards, peering between clouds in daylight or between stars at night, looking for a sign of the imminent arrival. She had one sunny morning wandered along with her face turned up, imagining a tiny black spot appearing in the sky and growing larger and larger, only to abruptly find herself lying on her back, a sharp pain in her ankle where she had sprained it in walking off the mini-cliff that had appeared unnoticed in her path. She'd lain there for hours, channelling the sun's healing rays to tighten her stretched ligaments sufficiently that she could hobble back to the hotel, where she ate like a bear preparing for hibernation until her ankle was as good as new. This was an incident she kept to herself; she could imagine the hilarity with which Wallace would greet the tale if it were to reach his ears.

Had Simone been the type to self-analyse, she might have considered the fact she was born on Earth Haven to have something to do with her increasing sense of excitement and renewed purpose. Unlike the other Deputies, she had never set foot on Earth Home and had therefore always harboured a feeling of being different, set apart from them, not a sensation that rested easily with her people's mantra of strength in togetherness, that the whole is infinitely greater than the sum of its parts. Perhaps, then, the arrival of the remainder of her people would remove that sense of separation. Her promotion to Keeper would close the loop, make her feel at last an integral link in the chain; more than a link: the concrete-set ring to which the chain was secured.

She did not pursue such a line of reasoning; at least, not with conscious thought. All she knew was the impending arrival of her people from Earth Home filled her with anticipation. Ambition, too, one she could prepare to achieve by jockeying herself into a better position by being the Keeper here on Earth Haven when the Great Coming took place.

With April fast disappearing, Simone sought out Wallace and Lavinia, waiting to catch them with no one else within earshot. Her opportunity came one afternoon, when the two of them were heading out to surrounding settlements in search of more diesel for the generator.

"I'm coming with you," she said in a firm tone she hoped would brook no debate. Wallace opened his mouth to object. "Shut it, Raccoon-eyes. I'm coming with you. Get over it."

Wallace shrugged. "I was going to say it'll be nice to have you along, but whatever."

Lavinia rolled her eyes. "Jeez, you two. This is going to be a fun ride."

Simone sat perched on the edge of the seat in the back of the car, her arms around the front seats the better to speak to the others.

"Here we are," she said, once Lavinia had pulled the car out of the car park and set off down the road leading inland, "just the three of us. The Three Amigos. The Three Stooges. The Marx Brothers."

"There were five of them," said Wallace.

"I can only ever remember three. Groucho, Harpo and the other one." Simone tittered. "What do you guys think of the drones?"

"Do you mean the 'people'?" said Wallace.

"Oh, is it still Love the Drones Week?" She clapped Wallace on the shoulder. "Not to worry, George, you're still feeling guilty about shooting the boy. You'll get over it. It's not like you killed him or anything."

"He'll never recover full use of his left arm."

"Pardon me for being a realist an' all, but he's going to lose the use of pretty much everything before long."

"Not if we can persuade the others to spare them."

"Come on, Georgie-boy, we all know that's not going to happen."

"It might. When they see the girl and what she's capable of. Glad I didn't shoot her. And don't call me Georgie-boy."

"Okay, okay. Don't get your knickers in a twist." She laughed. "D'you like that? Don't get your knickers in a twist? I heard the boy say it. The Brits can be quaint."

"Milandra says the girl can do pretty much everything we can," said Lavinia. "But she doesn't know how to control it."

"Maybe we can spare her, then. For further study. One day she'll fall down dead, though. Like they all do." Simone thought hard; she was coming to the crux of the matter and must choose her words carefully. "Hmm. Perhaps Milandra can train her. She can be like her pet. It'll give Milandra something to distract her. She looks weary to me. Tired of bearing the weight of all our worries on her shoulders."

Lavinia glanced at Simone in the rearview mirror. "D'ya think?"

"I do. It's not surprising. She's been Keeper for a mighty long time. For much longer than she would have back on Earth Home."

"That's true," said Wallace, "but then we prob'ly would all be dead by now if we were still there."

"Not me, seeing as I ain't ever been there." Simone felt a flush of the familiar resentment and tamped it down. "Maybe Milandra should have the freedom to enjoy the last years of her existence. Kick back. Take up a hobby. Like dro— er, humans do."

"What," said Wallace, "like *retire?*"

"Why not? Even though we're infinitely superior to them, doesn't mean we can't learn something from them."

"Ha!" exclaimed Lavinia. "Like to see you suggest that to Milandra."

"Yeah." Wallace chuckled. "She'll tear you a new one."

"Not if we *all* suggest it to her. The three of us. Together." *Careful, now, we're coming to it…*

"Like she'd listen," said Lavinia.

"We could—" Simone paused for effect "—*persuade* her." *There. It was out.*

"Huh?" Wallace half-turned so he could look at her. "You mean, force her?"

"I think *force* might be too strong a word. Encourage. Cajole. Make her see it would be for the best if she stepped aside."

Wallace's eyes narrowed. "The best for *who?*"

"Don't you mean 'whom'?"

"Don't deflect. If Milandra agreed to step down as Keeper, always assuming such a thing is possible, then you're hoping to take over?"

"Of course. I *am* the Chosen."

"And you think you're ready to take on the responsibility, do you?"

"Yes. Why wouldn't I be?" Simone could hear the hint of sullenness in her tone; she didn't like the line Wallace's questions were taking. "I'm ready, right, Lavinia?"

Lavinia glanced at her in the mirror and immediately looked

away, but not before Simone had read the doubt in her eyes.

"Come on, guys," she said, though she knew she'd lost them; had never had them. "Milandra's old and tired and past it. We all know it."

Wallace faced the front, shaking his head. "You're an ambitious bitch, Simone, I'll give you that. But now is not the time to make a play against Milandra. The Great Coming is only days away. She'll never be persuaded to step aside now, of all times. And, quite honestly, I don't think she should. A change like that should happen later, when the others are here and assimilated. It might happen anyway, what with there being another Keeper on her way. A choice will have to be made between them."

"There'll be a second Chosen, too." Now Simone could not mask the churlishness in her voice. "What if they choose the other one over me?"

Wallace shrugged. "Then you'll have to join the ranks of mere mortals with us."

"Yeah, baby," said Lavinia, "be one of us."

"Yeah," said Simone. She forced herself to put on the little girl voice. "We'll have fun and shit, right?"

"Right!" agreed Lavinia.

Simone sat back and sidled across behind Wallace so she'd no longer be visible in the mirror. She didn't want them to see her true expression.

From the journal of Elliott King:

The German writer and former soldier Ernst Jünger is generally considered to have glorified war in his writings. I have a confession: despite recommending his work to students as a counterpoint study to *All Quiet On the Western Front*, I have never read it. Nor shall I, for I have learned over these endless days there is no glory to be found in war.

Courage, yes. Camaraderie, loyalty, fortitude. Yes, yes and yes. Armed conflict can bring out our nobler side. To see a man, eyes wide and hands trembling, grit his teeth and stride forward, thumbing his nose at fear, is to see him at his most imperious. Godlike, almost.

By 'man', of course, I include woman, for there are many women fighting—and dying—with us. If they feel war is male folly, that if only women were in charge there would be no armed conflicts, they are too kind to say so. Or perhaps they feel that, for once, it is not our fault.

Our small group has gained a new member. She is Swedish, by the name of Aletta. She was left on her own after our first direct encounter with the enemy. Her only friend, a Hungarian, was shot by a drone—they have such little humanity left in them I cannot think of them as people any longer—a Pole who had been their traveling companion. Aletta says none of the essence of the man remained in the figure who pulled the trigger and blew the Hungarian's brains out. Or maybe she tells herself that to be able to reconcile the fact she in turn shot him dead.

Our numbers grow fewer by the day. Each night, some slip away in the darkness. Nobody comments; nobody blames. In each encounter, we suffer fatalities and serious injuries. The beds in Hillingdon Hospital must be filling rapidly. And the morgue. I try not to think about those poor people who require surgery or other specialist care. Assuredly, Sarah and her colleagues are doing what they can, but I suspect it will not amount to more than providing pain relief.

Estimates vary, and nobody has the inclination to conduct a head count—it would only confirm we are dwindling. My estimate? Maybe seven hundred of us remain, around a third of what set out from Hillingdon that sunny afternoon what seems a lifetime ago.

We do not leave the dead behind on the streets, but pile them into vans and send them back the way we came, unloading them at an industrial area we passed through days ago. There's an empty warehouse there with steel roller doors that should keep out the most determined scavenger. The plan is to dig a mass grave when this is all over and lay our fallen to rest together for eternity. There is a rather gaping flaw in that plan, but I guess if none of us survives then we can all rot above ground together. Happy thoughts.

Happiness. What a tricky concept amidst death and carnage. I guess I could describe myself as happy at this moment, sitting in some sort of safety inside an office building somewhere in West London, with locked and barricaded doors and food in my belly. It's all relative.

Food has been more of a problem than anyone anticipated. As Zach keeps muttering darkly about, there is no supply chain. We brought all the ammunition, grenades and mortar shells with us, enough to service an army ten times our size, so that's not an issue. But we didn't bother to bring food, expecting to merely pick it up as we went along. It hasn't proved to be quite that simple.

We have passed through many residential zones; come across grocery and convenience stores. There must be Walmart-sized supermarkets, though we haven't encountered them. We enter these smaller stores looking for canned and dried goods, anything long-life that should still be edible. Apart from the occasional snack of dubious nutritional value, we are met by empty shelves. It's the same with the residences we enter in the hope (expectation has long gone) of finding food. The occasional can of beans, if we're lucky, or packet of chips, though they call them 'crisps' here, strange people. And there's something else odd about the houses. Zach drew it to my attention; I doubt I would otherwise have noticed.

"No corpses," he remarked, while we made another fruitless search of a house.

Amy wrinkled her nose; she possesses the keenest sense of smell of us all. Ironic, Zach reckons, since when he met her she smelled like a bobcat's lair.

"A faint odor," she said. "There *were* corpses here."

"The bedding's all gone," said Zach. "Mattresses, too."

I needed it spelling out. "What does that mean?"

"These houses have been cleared. Corpses, contaminated

sheets, usable food. Same thing's happened with the stores."

"But… huh." I still didn't get it. Sometimes I can be slow on the uptake; I'd never have made a detective.

"Don't know why they've got rid of the corpses, but I can guess why they've taken the food."

Then I got it, too. "Soon they'll have seventy thousand extra mouths to feed."

"Yep."

"And that's why they've been clearing corpses—seventy thousand extra people to accommodate."

Zach nodded. "Could be."

Seeing all those empty store shelves and kitchen closets brought it home: there really is a shitstorm due to arrive in the form of seventy thousand extra-terrestrials to supplement the five thousand already here. That significantly smaller number has brought the human race to its knees; with their comrades on board, they'll be able to do anything they want. Anything.

In that moment, I felt weighed down by desolation and futility. Something must have shown in my face because Amy asked me if I was okay. I waved her away and found somewhere to sit. If I didn't take a moment, I'd most likely expire there and then through sheer panic.

While I sat there trying not to hyperventilate, I questioned our sanity in going after these 'people'. They held all the aces: outnumbering us, able to manipulate a small army of 'expendables' and familiar with the city. It also now appeared they controlled the food supply. Oh, and they had seventy thousand reinforcements on the way.

What did we have to set against them? Seething rage; a desire to take some sort of vengeance, no matter how puny; a desperation born of the knowledge we would all soon be dead.

Maybe those things were enough. Better to go down fists flailing in a last gesture of defiance, however futile, than to perish on bended knee with an unheard plea on our lips. At least, that's what I told myself and, so doing, got my terror under control.

When we walked out of the house, I did so with shoulders back and the confident step of the righteous.

That newfound assurance did not last. After each new skirmish, it becomes more difficult to find a way to ferry out our dead without drawing gunfire. I heard snippets of a whispered conversation between Zach and Frank. 'Hemming in'; 'encircling'; 'funneling'. I don't quite follow how this is achieved or why we are ineffective in countering it, although I assume it has to do with simple math: a lot can easily ensnare a few.

I have not heard anyone suggest we cut our losses and flee the noose before it draws tight. That gives me a warm sensation I struggled at first to recognise as pride in my fellow man and woman. If it is one of the last emotions I feel before I die, I shall count it a blessing.

There is little enough else for which to be thankful. Our new fighting tactic—laying down rifle and machine gun fire to keep at arm's length the drones, while mortar rockets are aimed at the line of black cars behind them—bore immediate fruit. A direct hit on one of the vehicles made it jump four feet into the air, blowing out its tires and windows, stunning its four occupants. The other vehicles fled, without pause to offer assistance to their stricken comrades. Our enemy is ruthless both in defence and flight.

When the drones had been dispatched, Joe sprinted to the damaged vehicle, whooping with unrestrained joy.

"Got the fuckers! Got the fuckers!" he yelled, over and over.

Unburdened by heavy hardware, I was among the first to reach him while he stood staring into the vehicle. The stench of scorched rubber and smoke hung heavy in the air. Four figures reclined in the interior: three men and a woman. Groans and gashes and blood. Those not groaning lolled in their seats, unconscious, held in place by seat belts.

"They're dying," I murmured.

"No," said Joe. "They'll survive." He looked up, eyes blazing with grim determination. "Get back. Everyone, get back." He fiddled with his jacket pocket and withdrew a grenade. He yanked out the safety clip. People around me began to move away in a hurry.

"No!" I yelled.

He looked at me for a moment as if one of us had lost his mind and it wasn't him.

"It's barbaric!" I insisted.

"It's justice," Joe said. The calmness of his voice made him, somehow, seem even more insane. "Now get back."

For the briefest moment, I considered trying to take the grenade from him, had even taken half a step toward him, when he yanked the main pin and tossed the grenade through the space where the windshield had been.

I turned and broke into a shambling run. Two seconds... three... four. The blast nearly knocked me onto my face, but my flight had taken me far enough and the chassis of the black car contained the worst of it. I looked back.

Joe was returning to the vehicle. Thick, gray smoke poured from it. Cupping a hand over his nose and mouth, Joe reached the car and peered in.

Eyes streaming, face blackened, he reeled away. He coughed and looked at me, raising a thumb.

"Got the fuckers."

He grinned, abruptly turned his head to one side and vomited onto the asphalt.

To the best of my knowledge, the four mangled bodies lying in that wreckage represent the sum total of the fatalities we have inflicted upon our enemy throughout this entire campaign. The rats alone have killed more of us.

Some are calling this conflict The Battle of London. Massacre or Rout of London would be nearer the mark.

Yet, I must not despair. The sky outside has grown dark, but I can continue with my scribblings. Wonder of wonders: this office building has power. The windows are tightly shuttered with blinds, but we are taking no chances in announcing our position to anyone looking for us out there. We do not turn on the overhead fluorescent strips; we use small reading lamps taken off desks and shaded in the leg spaces beneath them.

Faces appear haggard in the shadowy light; eyes large and black-ringed. It is not advisable to lie down in close proximity to another person, unless you enjoy the sour odour of sweat-damp, unwashed bodies. The other smells are impossible to avoid.

I blame the pickled eggs. Tonight we shall go to sleep not to the accompaniment of empty stomachs rumbling like distant thunder, but to the trumpeting of excess wind. We passed a bar— a pub?—whose kitchens had been ransacked, but there was also a kitchen in the living area upstairs that had been overlooked. Used as an overspill storage area for the bar and restaurant, it contained catering-sized jars and cans of meats, vegetables and fruit. A *lot* of them; the bar's owners must have stocked up for the festive season at the same time as the Millennium Bug hit and ruined everyone's Christmas.

Not forgetting the eggs. I had never tried an egg marinated in vinegar before, but I must confess to taking an instant liking to them. We also found boxes of chips (yeah, yeah, I keep forgetting, *crisps*) and salted nuts. Not enough that we could eat like kings, but sufficient for everyone to take a big chunk off their hunger.

We should sleep well, if rather musically and fragrantly, tonight. I've a feeling we shall need our strength for the coming days. The going will be tougher, the stakes higher.

If we look like employing a tactic that might be successful— like the mortar strike that claimed four of their lives—they change tack. They have stopped using the SUVs. They wait until we are approaching an area congested with buildings—no more open-space encounters for them and, trust me, they control precisely where we engage. We tried enticing them into a wide, tree-lined avenue by sending forward a small patrol, but they were having none of it. For hours the patrol waited like a tethered goat, but the tiger didn't show.

They send drones out, while they stay hidden in nearby buildings, close enough to control the drones, but making it near-impossible for us to reach them. Our mortar shells rock the buildings, make holes in the outside walls, but can do nothing more than bring dust and the occasional chunk of plaster down on them in their hiding places. They have plenty of time to move to a safer place if we attempt the sustained mortar attack required to cause severe damage.

They stay ahead of us, just far enough that we follow. They lead us to the east, towards the old city, dragging us farther and deeper into the concrete mire. And the spots they choose for confrontation lend themselves to close-quarter fighting, not distance tactics. Narrow streets, enclosed courtyards, rabbit-warren alleyways. London is the ideal city to wage guerrilla-type warfare. Our enemy knows the city; to most of us, it's a confusing mishmash of the ancient and the modern. To them, it is a chessboard; they are grandmaster to our novice.

Soon, they will instigate the move that will result in checkmate.

The breeze whipping off the ocean dropped in intensity and the clouds took on the wispiness of summer. The last week of April and the first week of May in Cornwall was a period of sunny, balmy days and starlit, chilly nights.

It was also a period of inactivity. Of waiting. Apart from routine tasks, like topping up the generator and food preparation, at which everybody took their turn, only Jason Grant was busy. He received regular updates from Tess Granville about the situation in London; his War Reports, as he half-jokingly referred to them. The levity ended when they suffered their first fatalities.

Milandra had taken to spending mornings going for long walks along the coastal path. The spectacular scenery, the wildlife—the same seal would pop its head above the water at one rocky stretch and bark a hello most days—and, above all, the sunshine conspired to instil in Milandra a sense of contentment. Not even the tensions caused by the arrival of the humans and the imminent excitement of the Great Coming could upset her equilibrium.

It was while she headed back to the hotel after a lengthy stroll, her body feeling as trim as it had in centuries, that the strength ran out of her legs and she sank onto a grassy hummock. She lowered her head and breathed deeply, knowing what was coming.

When it was over, she remained where she was, letting the sunlight revive her spirits. Later, back at the hotel, she sought out Grant. He took one glance at her and his face clouded.

"Go on," he said.

"We lost people in London. Four of them. At the same time."

"Oh shit. Four? No wonder you look ashen. Who was it?"

Milandra reeled off the names: three men, one woman.

"Jensen Frayn?" Grant gave a deep sigh. "I fought alongside him in Persia in the early days."

Milandra put out a hand and squeezed his forearm. "So I saw from his memories."

"It's where I ended up when we dispersed after activating the first Beacon. Jensen came along a decade or two later. We both went by different names back then."

"As did many. Will you speak with Tess?"

Grant nodded. "A change of tactics is clearly called for. I suspect Tess will already be on it."

Afternoons Milandra spent with Brianne. Will, too, who would barely leave the girl's side. Milandra didn't mind. She had taken an instant shine to the boy, with his serious façade masking a ready wit and cheeky smile.

She had waited outside with Peter Ronstadt and Diane Heidler for the humans to arrive. Two cars pulled up and discharged two adults and two younger humans. A black dog also jumped out of the adults' car. It wagged its tail on seeing the children and licked at their hands, but made no attempt to approach her, Peter or Diane.

The man climbed out of his car rather awkwardly, cradling a shotgun. When he saw Peter and Diane, he turned and left it in the vehicle. The woman bounded forward and threw her arms around Peter's neck. He didn't seem to know how to react, whether to look embarrassed or pleased. His face settled into an expression that conveyed both at once.

When she pulled away, the man stepped up and pumped Peter's hand.

Unable to get near to Peter, the girl approached Diane and enveloped her in a great hug. Milandra grinned. The look of discomfort on Diane's face was comical. It was underlain by something else, a hint that said she could get used to someone showing her affection.

Milandra waited until acquaintance had been renewed before stepping forward.

"Welcome," she said. "I am Milandra." She turned to the girl and smiled. "Bri. Like the cheese but without the e."

Bri offered a hesitant smile, but her glance flickered to the man and woman. Whatever rush of gladness had infused them on seeing Peter had dissipated. They stood glaring at Milandra, negative emotions radiating from them like fever: anger, sorrow, desire for revenge, fear. Milandra could sense them like the taste of a pungent dish. So, too, could the girl.

Spreading her arms, Milandra addressed the adults. "Please, come in peace, if not in friendship. Naturally, I understand how high your feelings are running, but know this: here, now is not the time or place for recriminations."

Milandra pushed a little—enough to have some effect but not so much they would notice—soothing sensation their way. She didn't yet know, but would learn, that Bri saw her balm as a yellow blanket; Milandra saw hers as a soft wave of foam, breaking gently over the inflamed psyche, dampening and calming.

Their stony expressions loosened a little.

"I see you have weapons," said Milandra. "I won't insist you surrender them during your stay, but I ask that you do not carry them around the hotel. Please lock them in your car. That way, you can still access them if you're exploring further afield and need them for protection."

The man and woman exchanged a glance. The woman nodded.

"Okay," said the man. "I suppose we ought to introduce

ourselves. My name is Tom. And this is Ceri. Bri you seem to already know. The young man is Will."

Milandra nodded to each in turn. "I shall allow Peter and Diane to show you to the rooms we have made ready for you. There is an abundance of food in the kitchens. I shall see you later when you have eaten and settled in. Then you can meet my Deputies."

Ceri spoke for the first time. "We've already met some of them. One of them put a hole in Will." She watched Milandra closely, as though hoping she would blush or look away. Milandra did neither.

"I warned Peter you should keep away from the Beacon. Only danger awaited you there. To bring a young boy was foolhardy in the extreme."

It was Ceri who coloured. "We didn't. He—"

Drop the antagonism sent Milandra, making the woman's eyes open wide in surprise. *It won't benefit you in the long run.*

Milandra turned and walked away. She hadn't planned on *sending* Ceri a message; it had been an impulse, but one she was glad she had indulged. It didn't hurt to remind humans who was in charge.

They spent those warm late-April and early-May afternoons in the hotel gardens, lounging in the sun with cold drinks (Jason Grant had wired up a refrigerator to the circuit operating off the generator), exploring the extent of Bri's abilities. Bri had allowed Milandra into her mind after only the slightest hesitation. Milandra could see instantly what Peter had meant: the girl's psyche was illuminated like Cape Canaveral on launch night, with blazing neural pathways and flaring synapses Milandra had not seen before in a human. She found to her astonishment that the girl was already accomplished at *reaching*, having performed this action at least three times on Will and someone called Joe, who Milandra recognised from Bri's memories as the young man she had seen sneaking away into the darkness outside the Beacon. Since this was a far more difficult skill to perfect than *probing* or *sending*, which didn't involve the entire psyche leaving the host body, Bri mastered these lesser skills with only the most perfunctory guidance.

"Well," said Milandra, sitting back in the wicker chair, which creaked ominously. She ignored it; she was used to her weight making furniture complain. "There's not a great deal I can teach you. For the skills to become second nature, you merely need to practise them."

Bri nodded.

"Now," continued Milandra, "you can by all means use me as a training partner and Peter will also help. Maybe Diane. Jason's a little busy, although Rodney would, I'm sure, be happy to assist. If you can drag him away from fishing."

What about me?

Milandra glanced sharply at Will. The boy was regarding her with wide eyes. She leaned forward, drawing another groan from the chair.

"When did you learn how to send?"

"Just now."

"That was the first time?"

The boy nodded.

Bri was watching them, wearing a perplexed frown. "What's going on? Will knows how to send?"

"Apparently so," said Milandra. "Will, would you allow me to take a peek inside your mind? It won't hurt and will take less than a minute."

It took less than thirty seconds. The boy's psyche also displayed new pathways; not as many or as vivid as Bri's, but present and active.

"I can see where you repaired the damage caused by the electric current," said Milandra to Bri. "There are only faint scars remaining. Good job." Milandra turned to Will. "Bri went into your mind and made you better. At the same time, certain improvements were made to your brain. That's why you can send."

Will's eyes grew wider with wonder.

"Do you mean... I'm like a spaceman?"

Milandra smiled. "A little like one, yes."

"But how?" said Bri. "You said my brain changed because of the blow to the head from the paperweight. Will wasn't hit; he was electrocuted."

"I don't think it was electricity that altered Will's brain. I think it was whatever you did to repair the damage." Milandra regarded the girl with a keen gaze. "That's not something I possess the power to do."

"But I don't know what I did." Her brow furrowed again. "What does it mean?"

"I think, young lady, that you, and to a lesser extent Will, represent the next stage of human evolution. And humanity's best chance of persuading those who are coming that it deserves to continue."

Bri snorted. "No pressure, then."

"You and Will possess something none of the adults have. When I probe you, I sense no artifice, merely an innocence only the young possess before age and cynicism drive it away."

"A pure heart," murmured Bri.

"What's that?"

"Oh, something Peter wrote."

"A pure heart," mused Milandra. "Yes, I like that. It's a good way to describe you both. That, combined with your new brain patterns, may be enough for my people to come around to thinking that saving what remains of humankind may not be such a bad idea."

"You don't believe that, though. I can sense it."

Milandra considered for a moment telling a lie, but opted for the truth. "No, I don't believe it will be enough to save you."

Chapter Eighteen

From the journal of Elliott King:
This shall be my final entry in this journal. There is one further incident I must relate; one I have been skirting around, afraid to confront. It will cause me pain, but I owe it to Sarah to continue. If nothing of me survives, perhaps these pages will somehow make it into her hands and she can know the truth.

Sarah, if you ever read these words, believe me when I say, *you must not blame Amy.* Though it was her hand which held the weapon, her finger that pulled the trigger, she was no more in control of her actions than a puppet.

They changed tack again. Three drones stood ahead of our slowly advancing column of vehicles. Only three. The column moved forward two abreast; we were in an older part of the city where the streets were narrower. The drones stood at the end of an alley that was narrower still. With a line of parked cars already filling one side of it, there would be room for our vehicles to enter the alleyway in single file only. If we were ambushed, which seemed highly likely, there would be no room to turn. We'd be toast.

In fairness to Joe, he wasn't so blinded by his hatred of all things alien he couldn't see what a bad idea it was to drive into the alley. He brought the convoy to a halt and came over to our minibus to confer with Zach and Frank. Moments later, they were stepping down to the sidewalk with him. Amy and I glanced at one another, she nodded to Aletta, and the three of us followed. Our vehicles continued, leading the convoy on, following the road around to the right and avoiding the alleyway.

Frank and Joe took the lead, pausing to peer down the alley. High buildings loomed either side, blocking out much of the sunlight and the clear (remarkably so, thanks to no air pollution and airplane contrails) sky. The three drones hadn't moved; they stood at the end of the alley in front of another tall, gray building.

The men raised their rifles, sighted and fired. Two of the drones dropped to the ground, twitched once or twice and lay still. The third turned and disappeared.

We continued forward. Amy and Zach went next, with me and Aletta bringing up the rear. We went single file, with Frank, Amy and me hugging the left-hand wall next to the line of parked cars; Joe, Zach and Aletta took the right-hand side, staying close to the buildings abutting the road and sidewalk.

As we moved down the alley, the grumble of engines behind us grew fainter.

They targeted me, presumably because I was at the rear. The intention must have been to force me to fire on the others; I would probably have been able to get most of them before they could react.

I felt them as an itching sensation at my temple. The sensation intensified, making me stop and gasp, and sank *into* my head as though a swarm of hornets had flown in there. My hands came up of their own accord and that is when they must have realized I wasn't carrying a firearm.

The itching invasion of my skull departed as quickly as it had come, but I knew something was seriously amiss. I shouted a warning which Zach must have heard since he looked over at me, a puzzled expression on his gnarled features.

My gaze moved from him. The buildings behind Zach held no windows at ground level, but wide, sash windows on the higher floors. A man stood behind the glass in the lowest window above Zach's head. It was difficult to make out with the height and angle, but I could see at least two other people standing beside and slightly behind him, with the impression of more. No drones these; the man stared down with an intensity a drone would not be capable of exhibiting.

I followed the direction of his stare, distantly aware that Zach was already on the move, crossing the narrow street toward us. My gaze halted on Amy.

She was raising her rifle, pointing it at the back of the person in front of her; pointing it at Frank.

Even as I knew it was too late, I yelled. It was drowned out by the sharp report. Frank crumpled facedown to the sidewalk. If there is comfort to be had from this account: he could not have suffered. The shot passed directly through his heart. He would not even have known he had been shot.

Amy swung the rifle away before Frank's body had completed its tumble to the ground. Aimed it at Joe. But Zach had arrived on our side of the alley. He reached out to the barrel of Amy's rifle, grabbed it and forced it up, wincing when the heat seared the skin off his fingers. Amy's second shot *zinged* off a building and harmlessly away.

I caught a glimpse of her face. All sign of the real Amy had gone, replaced by a featureless mannequin. Eyes like stagnant puddles, lower lip dangling with the first line of drool already falling, facial muscles slack and undefined.

My gaze darted back to the window. The man continued to stare at Amy. I saw Aletta and called to her.

"Up there! That window!" I pointed at it.

Aletta looked where I was indicating, stepping off the sidewalk to gain an angle to make the window visible. She must have been able to see the man because she threw her rifle to her shoulder and fired.

She was quite a shot. Hurriedly though she'd performed the action of bringing up the rifle, aiming and firing, all in one rapid motion, the glass in the window starred and a hole appeared in front of the man's face. A bead of blood showed on his forehead before he stepped back from sight.

Amy stopped struggling and allowed Zach to take the rifle from her limp hands. She stumbled as though about to faint. Then she noticed Frank's still body in front of her.

If I'd been in any doubt that Amy had not been in control of her actions—and I was in none whatsoever—it would have been completely removed by the sheer misery in her wail of anguish.

Zach, Joe and I watched her turn Frank over. It was obvious he was dead.

Aletta kept her rifle trained on the building opposite, but the man and his companions did not reappear.

Not yet. I suspect we have witnessed the next escalation, the cranking-up by the enemy. What better way to demoralize an opponent than by forcing people to turn on comrades, on themselves? How can we counter such measures?

My writing hand grows weary, my eyelids heavy. Almost everyone is asleep. Some cry out; it has become normal. Most twitch.

Thus ends this journal. I no longer have the stomach to record the last days of humanity. For I am certain that is what we are witnessing. Our enemy is too resourceful, too cunning, too cruel, even for a foe as violent as man. We shall succumb. I can see no other outcome.

This isn't the non-fiction equivalent of *The Scarlet Letter* or *The Great Gatsby*. Even were my writing skills up to the standard of a Harper Lee, which I hoped they might one day be, my subject matter is too grim, too graphic, too fucking sordid, to be considered among the great American writings. Even were there anyone left to make such a judgement.

I may not be able to write like him, but I can leave the final words to Hemingway:

The world is a fine place and worth the fighting for and I hate very much to leave it.

Go on then. Say something.

Will blushed. *I don't know what to say.*

Bri laughed, reached out and ruffled his hair. "Yay. You did it."

"I did?"

"In my mind I heard you say you didn't know what to say."

"Oh, wow, Bri. We can talk with our minds. We're, um, psychopathic?"

"Something like that." Bri yawned. "We'd better not overdo it. Milandra said even holding a short conversation with our minds can be tiring, and I don't want to wear you out. Not if you're going to do more physio on your shoulder later."

"Er, Bri?"

"Yep?"

"George wants to help me do my exercises." He looked at her anxiously.

Bri smiled to herself. The man named George Wallace had almost broken down in tears on meeting Will, and he did not look the sort of man given readily to weeping. Bri's stomach had been doing somersaults while they sat in the conservatory waiting for Milandra's Deputies to join them. The last time she had seen Wallace he had been pointing a gun at her, his face contorted with hatred.

Tom and Ceri both looked pale and tense. Even Peter and Diane appeared uncomfortable. They sat a little away from everyone else in hard, upright chairs, not speaking. Only Will seemed at ease, slouching in an armchair and munching a bar of chocolate. Bri remembered when she had first met the boy. He had been stinking and bleeding, wearing little more than rags and a vacant expression. She'd handed him a bar of chocolate and almost had to show him how to eat it.

Milandra walked in, smiling at them. Behind her came a tall, muscular black man with a kind face to whom Bri took an instant liking.

"Hi, folks," he said in a deep voice. "I'm Jason. It's good to see you all here."

They took seats nearby. Behind them came an attractive, dark-haired woman, who Bri could not recall seeing at Stonehenge, but who had a noticeable effect on Tom. He started violently in his seat, almost dropping the bottle of beer he was clutching. By his side, Dusty rose to his feet, hackles rising, a low growl sounding in his throat.

"Easy, boy," said Tom, placing a hand on the dog's head. The growl tailed off, but Dusty remained alert.

The dark-haired woman stopped by Tom and looked down at

him.

"I'm Lavinia Cram," she said. Her accent was American, her voice as dusky as her looks. "You must be Tom. I won't try to offer excuses for what happened at the Beacon. And I won't apologise—I *was* trying to kill you." She uttered a short laugh. "But I won't try to kill you again."

Tom glanced up at her. "Big of you," he muttered.

The woman shrugged as if Tom's opinion mattered not to her. Her gaze moved from Tom to Dusty. The dog made no noise, but his teeth remained bared in a silent snarl, his eyes all pupil while he stared at Cram.

"Hello, dog," she said. "Did you enjoy chewing on my wrist?"

She stared back at Dusty. His ears laid flat and his lips closed to hide his teeth. He uttered a faint whine.

Tom half-rose to his feet. "What are you doing? Leave him alone."

Dusty lowered his muzzle to the floor. The front part of his body followed, then his hind legs, until he was lying prone before the woman in submission.

Cram gave Tom a contemptuous glance. "Just showing him who's boss," she said, walking away to take a seat next to Jason Grant, ignoring the dark glare Milandra shot her way.

While this had been going on, a blonde, young-looking woman had entered and gone directly to sit down. She waved vaguely in their direction.

"Hi, drones," she said. "I, too, have agreed not to try to kill you again. At least, for now. I make no promise about what happens after the Great Coming."

Jason cleared his throat. "Okay, Simone. Let's not bring that up now. In the spirit of friendliness, yeah?"

The woman was already looking away as though bored. Bri, too, had turned her head, but not through tedium. She was taking deep breaths to try to keep her stomach under control, while looking up at the man who had walked in and stood before her and Will.

Tall, slim, russet-haired, he resembled a ranch hand from a cowboy film, the one who didn't quite have the screen presence to take the lead role, but who would be a dependable man to have by his side.

"My name is George Wallace," he said quietly. He glanced at Tom and Ceri. "I *do* apologise for what happened at the Beacon." He turned back to Bri. "I wanted to kill you. Had I succeeded, I'd have regretted it to the end of my days."

Bri didn't know what to say. She returned the man's gaze and nodded, briefly. Not forgiving him exactly, but suggesting they could be cool. It seemed to be enough for Wallace. His eyes widened in gratitude. Then he turned to Will.

The sling holding the boy's left arm to his chest had become grubby, but stood out against his dark tee-shirt like an accusation.

"Didn't mean to shoot you," said Wallace. He blinked hard. "Can you forgive me?"

Silence fell over the room. Even the two women, Lavinia and Simone, were watching closely, a hint of a smirk on the latter's face.

Will regarded the man solemnly. "Do you promise not to try to hurt Bri again?"

Wallace nodded.

"Cross your heart and hope to die?"

"Er, yeah. Sure."

Will raised his eyebrows. Waited.

"Uh…" Wallace raised his right hand, extended his index finger, licked it and made the shape of a cross on the left side of his chest.

Will smiled. "Do you have any video games?"

Bri's gaze cleared as she shook herself free of the memory. Will was watching her anxiously.

"Sorry," she said, "I was miles away. You want to do your exercises with George?"

"Yes. And then he said he'll let me teach him how to play *Football Manager*. I told him he can't manage Millwall 'cause they're my team, but he didn't really get it. I don't think football means the same thing to him. Is it because he's from America?"

"Dunno. Probably. Do you want to teach him how to play?"

Will nodded. "But only if you don't mind, Bri."

She reached out and grabbed his good hand. "Course I don't mind, silly. It gives me chance to do something I've been meaning to do since we got here."

Later, Bri watched Will walk away by the side of George Wallace, looking frail and tiny next to the tall, easy-ranging Deputy. It was strange, she thought, that this man had tried to kill her, had almost killed Will, yet they were perfectly happy for Will to go off alone with him. Bri could not sense any hint of deceit or ill intention coming from Wallace, merely contrition for what he had done at Stonehenge. Nevertheless, she thought she might mention it to Ceri and Tom in case they wanted to keep an eye on Will.

She found them sharing a bottle of wine on a wooden bench overlooking the sea, discussing the recent turn of events that had brought them to Cornwall.

"… surreal," Tom was saying, "that we're here sharing food and drink with the very people who caused the Millennium Bug and waiting for more of them to arrive. Oh, hi, Bri."

Ceri smiled at her. "Where's Will?"

"With George. They've gone to the beach to do exercises for his shoulder."

Ceri's smile faded a little. "I still don't feel comfortable with *him* being around Will. Especially only the two of them on their own."

Tom drained his wine glass. "I was thinking of taking Dusty for a stroll. Perhaps we'll go down to the beach."

"I'll come with you," said Ceri.

"Actually, Ceri," said Bri, "I was hoping you'd come with me to find Peter. I need to talk to him and maybe you can help."

Ceri's eyes narrowed. "Explain."

Bri did. When she'd finished, Tom gave a low whistle. "*That's* what he was going on about."

Bri and Ceri both looked at him.

"In Scotland," said Tom. "It was the morning after you and Will left in the middle of the night, Bri, before we'd realised you'd gone. I found Peter rinsing out a metal canister, like a vacuum flask, in the sea. He was acting weirdly, talking about how he'd have used the powder to kill the sailors on the submarine if Irving had agreed to fire missiles at Stonehenge. You see, the powder was how they spread the virus. The powder *was* the virus, I think. Anyway, Peter was crying and babbling on about selfishness and desire. I didn't really have a clue what he was going on about, but now I have some idea." He stood and whistled. Dusty came bounding out from a stand of trees beyond the hotel. "I'll go for that stroll and check on Will. You two go and speak to Peter. Try to make him see sense. You'll be much better at that sort of thing than me."

The sun had passed its peak by the time they found Peter. He was in the car park, stripping the rear door of his Range Rover, trying to beat out the dent caused by an encounter with a drystone wall in Herefordshire.

"I must be mad," he observed dryly when Bri and Ceri approached him. "There are plenty of brand new vehicles sitting around in showrooms waiting for someone to come along and drive them away. But I'm kind of attached to this one."

"Do you have time for a break?" asked Ceri.

"Time?" Peter grinned. "That's something I'm never short of." The grin faded. "Sorry. That was in bad taste." He pointed to a low wall running around one side of the car park. "Shall we take the weight off our feet?"

Where the wall formed a corner, Peter sat one side, Bri and Ceri the other so they could look at him while they talked.

"Okay," said Peter, "what's this about?"

Bri began. "Remember when Howard—" She stopped when her words caught in her throat; simply mentioning his name brought back the image of him lying on that grubby carpet, his life slipping away. Still too near, too raw. With an effort, she pushed the image away. "Sorry. When I was having the operation to fix the blood clot in my head and you let my psyche in, held onto it so my body would lie still on the operating table?"

"Of course I remember," said Peter.

"Well, when I was inside your head…" She paused again, almost afraid to continue; she felt like she was confessing to spying. She took a deep breath and the words came in a rush. "I didn't mean to see but it was right there and I couldn't help but look at it though I tried not to and I tried to pretend I hadn't seen it and not say anything to you but I can't stop thinking about how sad it's made you and I don't want you to be sad and I think if you go through with what you're planning it will make you even sadder and—" Bri stopped to draw in a stuttering breath. To her surprise, tears were coursing down her cheeks. She wiped at them with the back of her hand.

Peter's expression during Bri's outburst had ranged from puzzlement to bemusement. He glanced at Ceri and raised his eyebrows.

"Er, Bri's the one who saw; I think she should be the one to say it." Ceri reached out and rubbed Bri's upper arm. "Come on, love. Spit it out."

"Okay." Bri composed herself and looked at Peter. "You're planning on bringing back your wife. Cloning her."

"Ah." Peter's hand moved to his open shirt collar; his fingers crept inside his shirt.

"Her locket," said Bri. "You wear it around your neck. It contains a lock of her hair. Her DNA."

Peter brought his other arm up, fiddled with something and held up a heart-shaped locket dangling from a fine silver chain. He opened the locket and gazed down at it for a moment. Then he placed it in the palm of his hand and brought it forward to show them. On one side of the locket was an old photograph of a woman; on the other, beneath a tiny glass cover, a curled lock of fair hair.

"The times I've longed to stroke that hair," breathed Peter. He drew his hand back and closed the locket.

"This has something to do with why you want your people to get here," said Ceri.

"The detailed knowledge of cloning remained on Earth Home," said Peter. "If something were to happen to the rest of our people in transit, the knowledge would be lost for ever. So, yes, I want the Great Coming to succeed. I *need* it to succeed, at least up to a point. Once our people are within Earth Haven's atmosphere, their knowledge and experiences will pass to the Keeper if something happens."

"And if they arrive safely?"

"Then I shall simply ask the new arrivals to share the knowledge. Any of us can request the sharing of knowledge."

"And with this knowledge you will create a copy of your wife. Megan, wasn't it?"

Peter nodded.

Ceri's voice softened. "Bri's right, you know. If you go ahead with this, it will only make you sadder."

"Having Megan returned to me will make me sadder?"

"Well, apart from anything else, she's bound to die again."

"Not necessarily. With the cloning knowledge will come details of how to manipulate DNA. I shall give her the same ability to regenerate that I possess."

"Okay," said Bri. "But you'll still be sadder."

Ceri was regarding Peter closely, eyes narrowing. "And I think you know it," she said softly. "You realise as well as we do that any clone of Megan won't *be* Megan. It might look like her, smell like her, sound like her, but it won't *be* her."

"You're referring to her soul," Peter said in barely more than a whisper.

"If that's what you want to call it," said Ceri, "although any religious beliefs I had went out of the window when the Millennium Bug came in. Doesn't really matter how you label it, but we're talking about the personality, the experiences, the memories that made Megan who she was. Her very *essence*, if you like. You can produce a copy of her—a whole bunch of copies;

you could have a harem of Megans—but not one of them will truly be her. I'm sorry to say this, Peter, but the Megan you loved disappeared the day she died. She's gone. For good."

Such a wretched look came over Peter's face that Bri felt compelled to scoot over next to him and put her arm around him.

"You're right," he whispered. "I know it. I've always known it." He bowed his head.

Ceri placed her hand on his knee and squeezed. After a minute or two, Peter looked up.

"How do you live with it?" he asked. "The pain of loss. I can't bear it."

Ceri grunted. "Such is the human condition. Time helps us to bear the pain, grow accustomed to its weight."

Peter let out a deep sigh and straightened. "I would like to thank you ladies for your concern. I'm really rather touched."

Bri withdrew her arm and Peter stood, taking a pace forward before turning to look at them. He placed the chain of the locket around his neck and reached up to close the clasp.

"Everything you say I believe to be true," he said. "Nevertheless, I intend to proceed with my plan. I may only be able to replicate Megan's looks and sound and scent, and not her soul, but I'd rather live with an imperfect copy than with the agony of losing her entirely."

Bri felt her jaw drop. "But, but, Peter, you'll be playing God." She didn't know where the words came from—she didn't believe in fire and brimstone and all that—but blurted them out anyway. "You'll be damned."

Peter shrugged. "Then damned I'll be."

There had been many opportunities to leave. Simply slip out while everyone slept and melt away into the darkness. Sentries had been posted for the past couple of nights while the net drew tighter, but to keep the enemy out, not comrades in. She could have walked away unchallenged, but something made her stay.

Or someone. Aletta had never before met an American. It now

looked like she would live out her life surrounded by them. Amy, with her social awkwardness; Elliott, with his pen and notebook, and cheerful pessimism; Zach, with his abrupt manner and consummate skills as a rifleman.

Hmm, Zach. The rugged, reticent mountain man, perhaps fifteen years her senior. Gruff, grizzled, uncomfortable around people. Evidently fond and protective of Amy, yet not possessive. Respectful of Elliott's intellect, but not cowed. And towards her, Aletta? He was courteous, she supposed, when he had cause to notice her at all. It puzzled her that she should wonder whether he thought of her.

She was forgetting Frank. Only dead a few days and passed from her thoughts already. That is what comes of fighting for your lives, she mused; it drives out most other considerations, including mourning for lives already expended.

Even Amy had put it behind her. The girl knew it was her rifle that had killed Frank; had watched it happen, she said, like viewing it on a TV screen. Yet she claimed not to feel any guilt.

"How can I feel guilty?" she asked. "It was my finger that pulled the trigger, but it wasn't *me* working the finger."

That night, the night of Frank's death, was the last time Aletta could have walked away.

The trap closed the following evening. When the van containing the half-dozen or so bodies of people who had lost their lives in that day's fighting tried to leave under cover of darkness, gunshots rang out and the driver slumped against the steering wheel. The van careered across the road and embedded itself in the wall of a concrete office block.

By dawn, the remainder of their vehicles had had their tyres slashed or fuel tanks punctured. None was spared.

The young man called Joe, who seemed to be the leader in as much as he was the one who drove people on, exhorting them, encouraging them, inspiring them with his enthusiasm for the fight, shrugged.

"We advance on foot," he said.

Voices had been raised, protesting they would be wide open to attacks by vermin and dogs.

Joe looked too tired to argue and, besides, he probably knew they were right. He pointed in the direction from which they'd come.

"That's the way back," he said, "but I don't think the way remains open."

Of the dozen or so people who tried to leave, three were killed and two were wounded. The uninjured carried and dragged the wounded back with them. A Canadian woman, skin grey with shock, had taken a bullet in her side. Without surgery, she would be dead by noon of blood loss or shock or both before septicaemia had time to kill her. A middle-aged Frenchman, shot in the chest, died within minutes.

They left the Canadian woman behind. When they tried to move her and the pain made her scream and tears spurt from her eyes, she had insisted on staying with a bottle of water and her submachine gun. An hour on, and they all heard the brief burst of gunfire and the single, answering shot.

Days followed of frenzied scampering from building to building, battling packs of wild dogs and carpets of rats that harried their every step. If they remained in one place for too long, concentrated strafing from heavier weaponry forced them into moving or else be buried beneath tumbling masonry.

Any attempt to retrace footsteps was met with impenetrable, concentrated gunfire. If they tried to break out to either side, take alleyways or roads that were not the obvious ones to choose, they came under what they had come to think of as 'psychic attacks': the eyes of one or more of their number would glaze over and they would begin taking pot-shots at comrades or turning their guns on themselves. When a man started yanking pins from grenades, killing seven and wounding five more, they stopped trying to deviate from the route laid out for them. Gradually and surely, they were funnelled precisely where the enemy wanted them to go.

The fight was with a faceless foe, one that knew the layout of the battleground and dictated where the conflict took place. Since Aletta had fired at the group of people who had been 'controlling' Amy, she had only twice more caught glimpses of similar groups, which had vanished before she could level her weapon.

Hunger and tiredness became major problems. The 'banquet' of a few nights ago seemed a distant memory. All remnants of food had been removed from the buildings past which they hurried. The harassment continued after dark, never relenting, never allowing them to snatch more than minutes at a time of restless sleep.

Until now.

Aletta's eyes flickered open. Light entered through the high windows of the building. Morning had found them still alive. Nearby, others stirred from slumber. The floor was cold and hard, but everyone had slept for hours. All who survived: fewer than three hundred.

They were at the end of the line. Terminus. Manipulated to end up here, in what would likely become a killing ground, their tomb. She looked around. An empty industrial building with bare, concrete floors, brick walls and corrugated steel roof. A warehouse.

The air smelled dank. A river or canal was near. At least the floor was dry.

It must have been past midnight when they had stumbled, beyond weary, into this building. An army of rats and dogs had followed them all day, snapping at their heels and at each other, maintaining a steady pace but not attempting to overtake them. People—*their* people, the ones with blank stares and drooling lips—kept pace with them in the streets running parallel to the one they were hurrying down. When darkness fell, the others carried torches, the old-fashioned sort with flames and black smoke, to make them and their weight of numbers visible, dispelling any notions there might be escape in those directions.

At first, some had taken shots at the slack-jaws, but others stepped up to take the places of those who fell and fire was returned, forcing them to seek cover and bringing the pursuing vermin and dogs nearer.

On and on they had trudged, tiredness and hunger making every step an effort. Past houses and shops, offices and factories. They stopped wasting valuable energy breaking into buildings looking for food. It had all been stripped away. Some attempted escape—or maybe they were simply exhausted and looking for somewhere to sleep—sneaking into houses when they thought the eyes of the enemy could not be upon them. Shots would ring out minutes later.

When they were forced down the final alleyway, a dead end with a high brick wall barring their way, the only place they could go was into this warehouse. Once inside, the door barred with a sturdy length of wood that looked as though it had been left there for that purpose, they had been left alone. The cruellest irony, maybe, to allow them a last night of sleep so they would be more alert for their final day. She felt sure this is what she had opened her eyes to: her final day.

Aletta glanced at her companions. Elliott, pale and haggard, twitched in his sleep like a dog, looking every inch a man in the twilight of life. Amy issued tiny moans, as though reliving the past week in her dreams, and turned frequently like a roasting hog. Only Zach gave the appearance of sleeping soundly, curled onto his side, using his arms as a pillow. Except his eyes were open, watching her.

She felt herself blush and hurriedly cast her gaze elsewhere. When she dared glance back, he was still watching her.

"Good morning," he said.

"Good morning. Um, what do you think will happen today?" She didn't really want to know, but felt she needed to ask him something.

"I expect they'll finish it. We have nowhere to go. Almost out of ammo." He sat up and shrugged.

"We can take some of the fuckers with us," said a voice. It was the young man, the 'leader', who had lain down near them. Joe.

Zach looked at him.

"Nope. They won't need to show themselves. Only one door out of here. They can take us out when we leave." He nodded at the high windows. "Or break the glass and lob grenades in. It's a turkey shoot and we're the turkeys."

"It has all been for nothing," said Aletta.

"Maybe not nothing," said a new voice. Elliott sat up, wincing. "Oh, these old bones aren't suited to lying on cold concrete."

Amy, too, opened her eyes.

"What did you mean by 'not nothing'?" asked Joe.

"Human history is littered with instances of defiance in the face of overwhelming odds." Elliott snorted. "We can be ornery critters when we put our minds to it. Maybe our refusal to roll over and die will stand as a fitting tribute to all who have gone before."

"Nobody will know," said Amy. She looked close to tears, bottom lip tucked between teeth. To prevent it quivering, Aletta guessed.

"That's possible," agreed Elliott. "It may come to pass there will be no one left to know or care what happens to us. But I'm an optimistic old fool. I believe mankind will endure in some form or another. And I'm going to leave them this." He reached inside his jacket and extracted his notebook. He placed it on the floor beside him. "My account of what we've done, up until a few days ago. Maybe someone will come through here and find it."

"This is it," said Aletta. "This is the last day of my life. Of all our lives."

They looked at each other. Nobody contradicted her.

Milandra called them together: her Deputies, Rodney Wilson, Peter Ronstadt and Diane Heidler, and the four humans. Plus one dog, which kept very close to Tom. They met in the conservatory with the morning sun pouring through the glass. It promised to be another fine day. Milandra had thrown the doors wide to allow fresh air in and heat out.

"Well, friends," she said, when everyone was seated, "today is May fourth. Today is the day we have awaited for nearly five millennia. Today is the day of the Great Coming."

Nearly everyone present glanced to the windows, eyes raised.

Milandra laughed. "There is nothing to see yet, although I sense they will be entering Earth Haven's atmosphere at any moment. *Then* there will be a spectacle."

"Will we see a spaceship?" asked Will.

Milandra nodded and the boy's face lit up with wonder.

Simone Furlong rose to her feet.

Here it comes thought Milandra.

"A momentous day calls for momentous decisions," said Simone, no trace of the little girl in her voice.

"Now, Simone?" said Milandra. "In front of everyone?"

"This affects everyone." She glanced at the four humans. "Except the drones."

"Let it go, Simone," said George Wallace.

The Chosen sneered at him. "Shut up, drone lover. We all know it's time she stood aside."

"No!" exclaimed Jason Grant.

"It's okay, Jason," said Milandra. "I've been expecting something like this. Before we go on..." She looked at Tom and Ceri. "Take Bri and Will outside, if you don't mind. Simone's correct about one thing: this doesn't concern you." *And I need Bri out of harm's way.* She didn't know how far the Chosen was prepared to go, but she didn't want to be worrying about the girl while she dealt with it.

She waited until the humans had filed out, the dog trotting along beside them.

"Okay, Simone, so what exactly is it you want from me?"

"You know. Stand aside. Make me Keeper." *Get out of my way, old woman* Simone sent.

"You think you're ready to accept the responsibility?"

"Yes. I'm ready."

"No. You're not." *I doubt you'll ever be* Milandra sent.

Simone smiled. "I thought you might be resistant to change." She turned and bent over the chair in which she'd been sitting. When she straightened, she was holding a pistol. "So I placed this down the side of the chair earlier." She pointed it at Milandra.

Grant bounded to his feet and stepped in front of the Keeper. "Put that gun down, Simone," he said in a low voice.

"Get out of the way, Jason," said Simone. "She's old and tired. Killing her will be a kindness."

Milandra chuckled. "You're right about me being old and tired. You're wrong about everything else."

"I'm going to be Keeper," insisted Simone. "And now, before the Great Coming."

"Not like this, Simone," said Lavinia. She took a step towards her.

The Chosen swung the pistol to point it at Lavinia.

"You've got to be fucking kidding me," said Lavinia. "What you gonna do—shoot us all?"

"If I have to."

A howl rent the air; it came from outside.

"That's Dusty," said Grant.

"Indeed it is," said Milandra. "He can sense them as well." She glanced at the Chosen. "It's too late, Simone." She heaved herself to her feet. "They're here."

Chapter Nineteen

Throughout the northern hemisphere, people stopped what they were doing and looked up.

In a patch of sky that until moments before had been clear, a curiously spiralling bank of clouds gathered, like candy floss forming on a stick.

Beyond the clouds, a dark spot appeared as though a hole had been torn in the atmosphere to let the absolute blackness of space show through, but only those with the keenest gaze noticed it. The clouds, forming as rapidly as they were, would soon obscure it.

Although nobody knew what they were looking at, everyone experienced the same sensation: an inexplicable feeling of deep, primeval dread.

On stepping outside the hotel, Will and Bri made off towards the observation point overlooking the ocean, while Tom and Ceri sat on a bench outside the conservatory.

"Wonder what all that was about," said Tom. "Can't say I'm not glad to get out of there. You could cut the atmosphere with a knife. I get the feeling Simone would shoot us as soon— What's wrong?"

Ceri's head had turned to the sky. All the colour had drained from her face. Tom followed her gaze.

"Oh," was all he could manage.

He tore his attention away from the spiralling cloud formation. Ceri looked at him with an expression of utter wretchedness.

"It's happening, isn't it?"

He nodded. His mouth had gone completely dry.

Dusty, sitting at Tom's feet, stood and gave a *wuff?* Nose twitching, his tail came out stiffly like a lurcher's. He raised his snout and let out a howl. Tom hadn't heard him make such a wolf-like noise since the day they found Ceri and were almost brainwashed by the Commune.

Heart racing, he leaned forward and stretched his arms around the dog, trying to quieten him. Dusty uttered a pitiful-sounding whine, then lowered himself to his haunches and did not utter another sound, though he trembled like a leaf in a breeze.

Both Tom and Ceri turned their heads towards the patter of hurrying feet. Will appeared around the corner of the hotel.

"Come quickly," he said breathlessly. "The submarine's back."

Tom exchanged a glance with Ceri before they both hurried after the boy.

Beyond the rocks protruding from the sea along this part of the coast like frostbitten fingertips—responsible for the doom of many a ship on stormy nights in centuries past—riding the swell with an easy grace, floated a craft they had seen before: HM Submarine *Argute*. Men stood on the exposed decks, many of them gazing skyward.

Excitement lanced through Tom as if he'd been intravenously injected; not merely excitement. A sensation he hadn't felt in so long he'd forgotten what it felt like: hope.

A bright yellow dinghy was being carried over the rocks at the water's edge by three men. A fourth person, a woman, was looking up at them, waving.

"Isn't that...?" began Tom. He wanted to rub his eyes; they were seeing things he was struggling to take in.

"Yes," called Bri, who was standing at the top of the wooden steps leading down to the narrow strand of shingle. "It's Colleen."

"Be careful," called Ceri, but Bri had already started down the steps.

Tom turned at sounds behind him. The eight non-humans had emerged from the hotel. Most of them stood looking at the sky, but Peter and Diane were hurrying over to him. He peered past them.

"Why is Simone holding a gun?"

"To shoot Milandra," replied Diane. Tom's confusion must have shown on his face because she added, "Best not to ask."

Tom returned his attention to the beach. He didn't like putting his back to Simone when she was carrying a pistol, but he needed to make sense of what was happening below him.

"Two of those men have rifles," said Peter. "We need to move the children away in case there's shooting." He glanced around. "Where's Bri?"

"Down there," said Tom.

He glanced around, looking for Will. Ceri had stepped to the boy's side and held her arm protectively around his good shoulder.

The dinghy had been pulled beyond the water's edge and the three men were making their way to the cliff. Colleen had disappeared. Seconds later, she and Bri came into view at the top of the steps.

"Cer?" said Tom. "Dusty too?"

Ceri nodded.

Bri and Colleen approached them, an uncertain smile on Colleen's face. Ceri reached out her free hand and briefly squeezed Colleen's arm.

"Glad to see you're safe," Ceri said, "and I'll give you a proper hug later, but for now I need to get Will and Bri out of the way." Bri opened her mouth to say something, but Ceri silenced her with a curt shake of her head. "No arguments. There might be shooting."

Bri glanced around fearfully and, judging from how the colour drained from her cheeks, noticed the gun in Simone's hands. She stepped to Ceri's side without another word. Ceri said something to Will, who called to Dusty.

"Go on, boy," said Tom and the dog trotted over to Will. Dusty had stopped looking at the sky as though he knew there was nothing he could do about what was happening up there; he didn't like it, didn't understand it, but accepted it.

Ceri led Bri, Will and Dusty to the side of the main hotel building and out of sight behind the thick stone walls. Her face reappeared, peering around the wall so she could watch what transpired.

Colleen stepped up to Tom and gave him a hug. She smiled at

Peter and Diane, before her smile faltered.

"Who are they?" She nodded towards Milandra's party.

"The head honcho and her crew," said Tom. "But how did you get on the sub?"

"They picked me up in Kent and I brought them here. I came ashore with someone who knows you."

"Irving?"

"Yes."

Tom's attention was distracted by two things. Milandra and the others had approached the cliff edge and were gazing at the submarine. Three men appeared at the top of the steps, two of them clutching rifles and looking ready to use them if necessary.

The third man, tall with a Desperate Dan jaw, nodded at Tom and stepped forward.

"Mr Evans, I seem to recall?"

"Irving? I didn't recognise you without your bio suit. Not afraid of catching the virus now?"

"We know it's no longer active." His tone and expression betrayed no emotion. "What is the situation here?"

"Um. Where to begin." Tom nodded towards Milandra's group, who had begun to take an interest in the new arrivals. "They are the ones who started the Millennium Bug. You probably still don't believe it, but they are not from this planet. There are another five thousand of them in London. A small army of people—normal people, like us—has gone to London to attack them. The plump lady is their leader. Her name's Milandra. I think she may not be all bad." He turned to Peter and Diane. "These are our friends. Ha! Never thought I'd say that about you, Diane. Also not of this planet, but they have helped us." He looked up to the sky. The clouds had multiplied, thick and grey with orange-tinted edges. "And up there, somewhere behind that weird cloud, seventy thousand more of their lot are arriving. When they do, it is highly probable they shall finish what the Millennium Bug started."

Before Irving could respond, the ratcheting of two rifles being readied to fire sounded and he whirled around. His men had raised their weapons to their shoulders and pointed them at Simone. She was regarding them with an expression of amused contempt.

"Drop the pistol!" one of the men barked. "Now!"

"Uh, bad idea," muttered Tom.

Each member of Simone's small group was staring at the men, Milandra's gaze particularly intense. Simone tittered and stepped to one side. The men continued to point their rifles at the empty space where she had been standing.

"What's going on?" demanded Irving. He took a step forwards. Simone raised the pistol and pointed it at him.

"No you don't," she said.

In fairness to Irving, thought Tom, he had some bottle. He returned Simone's gaze, straightening his shoulders and bringing himself up to his full six foot plus height.

"Excuse me, madam," he said, "but you sound American. Perhaps you didn't know that we don't carry guns in the U.K.?"

"Sure I know. But maybe you should forget about nationalities and shit. None of that stuff matters any more."

Simone lowered the pistol and began to walk towards the two men with the rifles. They remained frozen into position; only their eyes moved, watching her helplessly while she approached.

"You see," she said, "the Keeper's psyche has been boosted by five others, but that's only sufficient to hold you in place, there being two of you an' all. It's not enough to make you step off this cliff. Not that the Keeper would do that." She lowered her voice to a conspiratorial whisper. "Too much of a drone lover."

She reached the men and pried their unresisting fingers from the weapons. When Irving lifted a foot to move towards her, she waved the pistol lazily in his direction. "Uh-huh," she said. Irving remained where he was.

Simone freed the first rifle and dropped it over the edge of the cliff. Tom heard it clatter to the rocks below. The second rifle soon followed. Simone patted down the men, then turned to Irving.

"What about you, Mr boss man? You packing?"

"I must protest," said Irving. "We are members of Her

Majesty's Royal Navy—"

"That's sweet, but just tell me if you're packing. You know, carrying a weapon?"

Irving's jaw, already prominent, jutted out further. "No. I don't have a weapon about my person."

"Thanks, but I'll make sure."

Irving stiffened, but didn't try to prevent her patting him down. Simone gave him a smile before flouncing back to the others. Only when she reached them did the intensity leave Milandra's gaze.

The two sailors sagged, breathing out heavily. They glanced uncertainly at Irving.

"Sir?"

Irving shrugged.

"Do you believe now?" asked Tom in a low voice. And—" he raised his eyes skywards "—there are more on the way. Might not be a bad idea to blow them from the sky before they land?"

Irving whispered back, "Don't blame me for not believing you before. It's a crazy story." He straightened and made a shushing gesture with his lips.

Milandra had moved forward and addressed him.

"Would you mind telling me precisely what your intentions are, Mr…?"

"It's Irving. Acting Lieutenant Commander James Irving of Her Majesty's Submarine *Argute*."

"And my name is Milandra. Despite what you might think, I am not your enemy. The woman with the pistol? She probably *is* your enemy, but she's not in charge. Not yet at any rate." She called over to Simone. "And put that pistol away before you hurt someone."

Simone scowled, but flounced back to the hotel. When she reappeared, she was no longer holding the weapon.

As she returned to Milandra's group, Ceri, Bri, Will and Dusty emerged from hiding and came back to Tom's side. Ceri nodded at Irving. He nodded grimly back.

Ceri turned to Colleen and gave her a big hug.

"Where's the spaceship?" asked Will.

"Coming," said Tom. He glanced at Ceri and grimaced.

Irving had point-blank refused to answer any of Milandra's questions. His men stood by, stony-faced, ignoring everyone.

"I can probe you, you know," said Milandra. "Although you can usually keep us out, I am the Keeper and as such know ways to evade your defences. Still, that would be extremely rude of me and would not help you to see we aren't necessarily on opposing sides. However, I shall assume your submarine is equipped with surface-to-air missiles and shall take the appropriate precautions when the time comes." She glanced up. "Which won't be too long."

Before Irving could say anything in response, a beeping tone sounded from his jacket.

"That's my commanding officer," he said. "I need to make a report." He reached into his jacket and extracted a walkie-talkie. He moved away and began to speak into it in a low voice.

Milandra watched him for a few moments before stepping to his side and tapping him on the shoulder. He jumped.

"Sorry to startle you," she said, "but I'd like a word with your commanding officer, please."

"Er…"

She held out her hand. With obvious reluctance, Irving handed the walkie-talkie to her.

"His name?"

"Commander Napier."

"Okay. What do I do, press this button?"

Irving nodded. "And release it again to receive."

Milandra raised the set to her mouth.

"Hello? Is this Commander Napier?"

Tom was not standing close enough to hear the reply; all he could hear was a crackle.

"My name is Milandra. If you're currently standing on the open deck of your craft, please identify yourself by waving your left arm above your head. Like I'm doing."

Tom looked at the submarine. One of the figures on the deck raised an arm and waved it in the air.

"Thank you, Commander Napier. I expect you have noticed some unusual atmospheric activity going on as we speak. Strange cloud formations, that sort of thing. I don't fully understand all that scientific stuff myself, but I am led to believe it has to do with the large amount of concentrated anti-matter that is approaching. Has a strange effect on the water vapour in the air. Makes it coalesce into a rather fetching spiral pattern. But that's neither here nor there. The real reason I need to speak with you is to tell you it is pointless arming your missiles in readiness for firing them at what will soon emerge from the clouds."

The faint embers of hope that had ignited inside Tom upon seeing the *Argute* extinguished themselves as though Milandra's words were a bucket of water.

The walkie-talkie crackled and Milandra listened.

"Of course you deny you are carrying missiles," she said. "And I realise I cannot prevent you from arming them, but you will be wasting your time. We cannot let you interfere with the Great Coming. We have waited almost five millennia for it to take place. So we will take preventative action when the rest of our people are within range to lend me their intellects. Be assured it will not harm you, but I doubt from my observations it is an enjoyable experience. I shall now bid you farewell, Commander Napier."

Crackle.

Milandra handed the set back to Irving. "He wants to speak to you again."

Irving walked away, muttering into the walkie-talkie.

Tom uttered a deep sigh. Judging from her drooping shoulders and despondent expression, Ceri had also harboured hopes they might have a way to strike back. They should have known better; Milandra and her people had been so thorough up to this point it was inconceivable, now Tom thought about it, that they would not have a plan or the means to counter any interference the remaining puny humans could come up with.

"They *are* arming the missiles," said Colleen in a low voice only Tom and Ceri would be able to hear. A waft of stale whisky hit Tom's face; Colleen had evidently not turned teetotal. "What was that Belinda woman on about? How can they stop them from being fired?"

Ceri kept her voice low in response. "It's Milandra, not that I suppose it matters. They will combine mental forces with the seventy thousand newbies. Together, that will be enough to make every survivor on the planet slit their throats. Controlling a submarine crew won't present a problem."

"Unless," said Tom, "the submarine dives into deep water. It's what stopped them hearing the Commune."

Ceri looked doubtful. "Will they still be able to fire the missiles from deep water?"

Tom shrugged and looked at Colleen.

"Search me," she said. "Better shush. She's coming."

"What now?" said Tom in a loud voice.

"Now?" said Milandra. "I suggest you watch the show. It should be quite spectacular."

Though Zach and his companions did not know it, and would not have cared if they did, the building in which they found their last night of refuge had once been a bonded warehouse near the banks of the Thames in West London. Whilst structurally sound, the building had fallen into disuse and had been sold to a property developer in October with a view to converting it into high class apartments in hope that this rundown, largely industrial area would become the new trendy district for those unable to afford the sky-high rents of Chelsea and Kensington.

There was time for the developer to clear the last of the rusting machinery and rotting tea chests before the world of development, commerce and more or less everything man-made or -driven came to an abrupt halt.

The only way to leave the warehouse was through the barred door by which they had entered; the only escape from the alley was to retrace their steps. The high brick wall in the other direction dropped away to the dark waters of the river.

A steadily increasing hum of conversation, punctuated by the occasional gasp, made Zach interrupt cleaning his rifle to look around. Most heads were turned to the high windows.

The air outside had dimmed, although the sky through one side of the building looked clear and blue. Not so the other side. A swirling mass of cloud obstructed the sun. Zach had never seen a formation like it.

"Wow," he murmured.

Amy looked at him with wide, dark eyes. "It's like the end of days."

The Swedish woman, Aletta, sat with her long legs bent in front of her, hugging her jean-clad knees. "It is true," she said flatly. "They are coming."

Elliott dropped his gaze from the windows. "If they are coming, maybe we should be going." He shrugged. "Perhaps they'll be a little distracted."

Zach looked from one to the other; they were all waiting for his reaction. Joe, too, had stopped staring at the sky to listen and watch. Zach met his eye and the boy gave an almost imperceptible nod.

"Think Elliott could be right," said Zach. "Don't see what we have to lose. I'd as soon die with the breeze on my cheeks as trapped in here like some slaughterhouse calf."

Joe slapped a fist into his palm. "Yes," he hissed. Louder: "Yes!"

Heads turned to look their way.

Joe jumped to his feet.

"Most of you know Zach by now," he said, addressing the vast room. "You've seen how well he can use that American rifle he carries. But he's a quiet chap. Not given to rabble rousing or displays of emotion. He thinks we should make a break for it while the enemy is distracted by what's happening up there. I think he's right. So here's the choice you face. Stay and be exterminated like the vermin and mad dogs who have been chasing us. Or go out there and fight."

"That'll mean certain death," came a voice.

Joe nodded. "But so will staying in here." He threw out his hands. "Look at this place. Concrete floor, brick walls, high windows. It's like a prison. Ask yourself: if this is going to be my last day on Earth, do I want to spend it in a cell?"

Zach rose slowly to his feet, wincing at the stiffness in his bones. Aware that every head had turned to watch him, he kept his gaze down, but his voice remained steady.

"Of my own making, it's true, but I've spent most of my adult life in a prison of sorts. I ain't going to die in one."

Joe reached down and gripped Amy by the hand, pulling her to her feet. As though on impulse, he leaned in and kissed her full on the lips. Zach could not help but smile when he noticed the blush spread across her face, visible even in this dim light. Amy stared at Joe. He grinned at her. Perhaps to hide her confusion, Amy turned and addressed the room in a faltering voice.

"Prison. I guess I was in one, too. My momma… well, that don't matter no more." She took a stuttering breath. "I'm going with Zach and Joe. If I got to die, I want to do it out there by their side."

Amy glanced at Zach and smiled; in that instant, she looked as beautiful as any woman had ever appeared to him. Her gaze went to Joe. She brought her hands up to his cheeks, leaned in and kissed him in return. A soft sigh came from the watching people.

Elliott stood with a grunt.

"Well," he said, letting his gaze pass around the room, "I have to confess I've never been near a prison. Literally or metaphorically. Unless you count my sexuality, but frankly that's no one's damn business but my own. Then there's this building. Since we seem to be according it a status on a par with Folsom, then, no thanks, I don't want to stay." He held up his hands to show they were empty. "Only problem is, I don't have a weapon. My role in this venture has been one of chronicler. That won't be of much use to you when we walk out that door. So perhaps someone better provide me with a gun."

"I'm sure that can be arranged," said Joe. He looked down at Aletta. She held out her hand and he yanked her up.

She looked around at her companions and smiled.

"The people I travelled to Britain with have all gone," she said. "You are all I have left in the world. It would be an honour to spend my last minutes in your company." She turned to the room. "I go, too. With my friends."

For a moment, there was silence. People glanced at each other. Then slowly came the rustling sound of a crowd rising to its feet. A minute or so later and every person in the building was standing.

"Okay," said Joe. He glanced at Zach; the dancing enthusiasm had been replaced by a grim tautness. "It looks like we all go."

The clouds turned the colour of flaming coals, swirling and boiling like a witch's cauldron being stirred. Almost two miles off the Cornish coast, a deluge of rain fell onto the Atlantic Ocean in an area approximating a circle hundreds of yards across. A hot, rushing wind sprang from nowhere, whipping the surface of the water into a frothing frenzy.

When it seemed the clouds must combust in a conflagration that would evaporate the sea and sear the ground, they parted and whipped away, scattering like foam in a gale.

Rays of revealed sunlight slanted down as though heralding a divine visitation. The golden light bent around the black shape that emerged from the dispersing vapours.

Black. Total, unbroken. A blackness so complete, it wasn't even a presence of something; more an absence of everything. Judging from the way the drones scrunched up their faces, they were finding it difficult to focus properly on the descending craft.

They weren't the only ones to be thrown a little out of kilter by its appearance. Milandra had been busy organising the Deputies and Rodney Wilson, preparing them to assist her in harnessing the incoming intellects to paralyse the sub, but she had paused, staring at the craft with a puzzled frown.

Perhaps Simone, had she been paying closer attention herself to the descending ship, might have acted differently, but she was watching the door of opportunity swing wide. She gleefully stepped through and slammed it shut behind her.

On board the craft, the incoming Keeper concentrated on slowing its descent, mindful of past disasters. Not that he cared for the fate of this planet—there were other planets to exploit; the galaxy was almost endless and merely one of an endless number of galaxies—but the ship held the last remnants of his species and was built for speed, not to withstand collisions with firm surfaces.

Once safely down, they would get to work clearing up the mess they were bound to find. The drones would have multiplied, evolved, might exist in large numbers, perhaps in the millions, difficult though such a magnitude was to imagine. They would need to act quickly, combining intellects and commanding all drones to self-destruct.

He wasn't overly concerned at any threat posed by the drones. They had received the signal sent from Earth Haven. As well as pinpointing the planet's location, the signal was only to be transmitted if the way was clear.

The resistance he anticipated would come from those of his former people who survived. From reports received while its spacecraft still functioned from the advance party of fifty millennia ago, they knew Sol gave extraordinarily long life, even by their standards, and it was perfectly possible a large contingent from the ten thousand settlers of five millennia past yet lived. That they had existed alongside and among drones for such a period and not been contaminated by their selfish individuality was inconceivable. That, coupled with their ingrained beliefs in lies and half-truths—not their fault, but the reach of that scheming bitch Sivatra was long indeed—meant assimilation back into the ethos and doctrines of the new-improved species would be so difficult as to not make it worth the effort.

They would need to act decisively, peremptorily, eradicating their surviving people without mercy or regret. Then and only then could they regroup and begin to rebuild their depleted resources, take what this planet had to offer and move on to pastures greener.

But his concentration was breaking. A distraction. A nagging, insistent demand for assistance to counter an immediate and deadly threat. The Keeper recognised the invading intelligence as one of their own, one whose knowledge of Earth Home was second-hand, confirming their suspicion of survival, perhaps even expansion, here was correct. There was no time for further examination or investigation into why the pulse had been sent if the way was not, in fact, clear. The threat to the craft was, so the intelligence made clear, real and imminent.

All others aboard held their breath, ready to follow his lead. The intelligence demanded it be obeyed or refused to the peril of all. A snap decision was required.

Not knowing from where the threat came, or what form it took, he could not assess its severity. The craft was designed for interstellar travel and contained no weaponry systems; if defence ever became necessary, it would consist of fleeing faster than an opponent. The craft did contain a combat probe, which operated better in the vacuum of space than within the confines of a planetary atmosphere, but that they nevertheless would have deployed ahead of their approach had they not received the signal.

As it was, the craft possessed a soft underbelly it was offering to any potential assailant who might be waiting below. There was little choice other than to trust the demanding intelligence.

The Keeper resisted the call only for the moments it took for him to check the hull thrusters were operating at full capacity and would continue to reduce the rate of their descent sufficiently to allow a safe landing on the ocean surface.

The intelligence raged. The Keeper submitted. His people followed.

~ ~ ~

Irving spoke urgently into the walkie-talkie.

"You should have visual now. It's within range. Take it down."

He released the button and waited for a response. The set remained silent.

Irving had walked away from the knots of people so as not to be overheard and his route had taken him out of sight of the *Argute*. He hurried back towards the cliff edge, casting worried glances at the black object descending from the sky. It was difficult to get a handle on precisely what shape the craft was; it denied examination, growing fuzzy and indistinct the more it was stared at.

Some sort of commotion was going on amongst the people milling about the cliff top, but Irving paid no attention. He needed to see the *Argute*. It was still there, floating easily in the swell, which had increased since the appearance of the black craft. Men stood on the exposed decks, but even from this distance they looked unnatural. They were still, statue-like. While he peered uncertainly, a figure toppled over in a particularly heavy upswell of the ocean.

"Stevens! Manning!" Irving hissed to his two men; they had not moved from the spot where they had been unceremoniously disarmed. They were glancing from the sky to the nearby commotion, expressions of deep unhappiness and disbelief on their faces. Irving snapped his fingers. "Pay attention! Binoculars. Field glasses. Do either of you have a pair?"

Stevens paid him not the slightest notice, but Manning's eyes cleared. He fumbled in his jacket pocket and extracted a set of binoculars.

"Sir?" he said, handing them to Irving. "What's going on?"

Irving shook his head. He raised the binoculars and focused them. A face came into view, frozen into a rictus of fear. More faces, all immobile. Men had fallen to the decks and lay in danger of being washed away if the waves grew higher.

He could not see Commander Napier, but hadn't expected to. He should be in the control room, ready to give the order to fire. The missiles were primed and armed. Orientation and targeting would be a doddle; the subject was descending almost directly towards them, growing larger by the moment.

He handed the glasses back to Manning.

"Something's wrong," he said. "I can't raise the *Argute*, though I was talking to Commander Napier not two minutes ago. Everyone I can see on the decks and around the conning tower seems to be, er, frozen."

"Frozen, sir?"

"Not moving. Immobile. See for yourself." He waited until the rating had raised the binoculars and issued a low whistle. "We need to find out what's causing that immobility and do something about it. Fast." He turned to the other man. "Stevens? Stevens! Snap out of it, man!"

Stevens looked his way, but his gaze was vacant. The lights were on, but there was no one home.

"Okay, Manning," said Irving, "it's up to me and you."

When the ship burst from the clouds, Bri's bladder almost let go.

"Oh, wow! Bri, look!" Will tugged on her arm, his expression rapturous.

She didn't like it; it made her feel queasy, like looking at one of those weird three-dimensional pictures you had to stare at until your eyes went funny to see the full effect.

"It's got booster rockets," said Will in a tone of awe. "They're slowing it down so it doesn't crash."

"Yeah."

Bri glanced to either side. Both Ceri's and Colleen's expressions mirrored how she felt. Tom kept shooting worried glances out to the submarine and around the patio area as though looking for someone.

Further away stood Milandra, most of her companions clustered behind her in a loose group. Except for Simone. She stood apart, a look of intense concentration on her face.

Bri pulled away from Will's side—he didn't even notice—and approached Milandra.

"Excuse me…"

"There's something wrong," said Milandra. "There's a great deal wrong." She looked at Bri and Bri felt it.

She turned away and hurried back to her friends.

"Tom. Ceri. Colleen. Listen. Milandra's really worried. She saw something. I'm not sure what, but it's about the spaceship."

All three faces looked pale in the new brightness of the day. The ship would come down too far out to sea to cast a shadow on the land.

"What's the matter?" said Tom; he seemed a little distracted. "Hurry, Bri. I need to speak to Irving."

The man from the submarine had appeared, still clutching his walkie-talkie, striding with a look of grim purpose towards his men.

Bri took a deep breath. Behind her, some sort of scuffle had started and there came a raised voice, but she pushed on.

"The beings on that ship. Aliens, or whatever they are. They don't come in peace. They're not only going to kill us. They're going to kill Milandra and her people, too."

Chapter Twenty

The moment Milandra set eyes on the descending spacecraft, she knew it was too small to hold seventy thousand people. Not merely a little undersized; she had been expecting a craft twice as large as this one.

She could sense the new arrivals' intellects buzzing like a swarm of hornets at the edge of her consciousness. Combining thousands of minds to control the crew of one submarine would be a little like using a flamethrower to light a cigarette, but she needed to call on the new minds to boost those she already had at her disposal. Otherwise, the best she could do would be persuade someone on board the *Argute* to sabotage the missiles or the sub itself. She did not want to be the cause of any more human death, at least not until a fully ratified Commune. Even that she would perform with a heavy heart.

Milandra probed, trying to find out how many were aboard the incoming craft. But someone had beaten her to it. Another intellect, almost as powerful as her own.

She glanced around. The Chosen had moved to where she had an uninterrupted view of the submarine, staring at it with a fierce look of concentration. Milandra probed again… and jerked back as though burned.

Simone had taken control of the thirty thousand minds aboard the craft. Only thirty thousand, still sufficient for most purposes, but less than half of the number they had expected.

During the millisecond she had been inside Simone's head, images had flashed through Milandra's mind with the speed of a turbocharged projector. Fighting, dying, stone torn asunder, revolution and revelation.

"What's she doing?" asked Grant by her elbow.

"Still trying to become Keeper. Every mind on the craft has joined with hers. She's preventing the crew on the sub from shooting its missiles." She turned to look at Grant. "Jason, there are only thirty thousand of our people aboard. And they are *our* people no longer."

Grant's eyes grew wide. "Only thirty thousand? What's happened?"

"Another civil war. The truth about our past must have been unearthed by the Keeper on Earth Home, but she didn't keep it quiet. It sparked disagreement, unrest, war. This time, the traditionalists won, but at what huge cost. More than half of our civilisation wiped out. The survivors intent on resurrecting the old ways. The way of the cuckoo, the parasite, the apex predator." Milandra sighed deeply. "We are the only ones who remain of all our people who do not believe in the old ways, who want to continue to strive to be peaceful, cultural, altruistic, despite knowing the truth."

"And their intentions towards us? You glimpsed them, didn't you?"

Milandra nodded. "After all we have done to prepare the way for their safe arrival, I am afraid gratitude will not be forthcoming. They not only intend to kill the remaining humans. They intend to kill us. Every last one of us."

Grant sagged. "Huh."

"Oh, fuck," said George Wallace. He, Lavinia and a bewildered-looking Rodney Wilson had drawn close enough to hear. Peter Ronstadt and Diane Heidler were approaching, concerned looks on their faces. Wallace took a step towards the Chosen. "Simone!" he roared. "Let them go!"

"No!" Milandra glanced at Grant and nodded.

He put out a muscular arm and grabbed George Wallace by his collar. Wallace immediately started to struggle.

"Listen, George, you stubborn ass," hissed Milandra. "While the Chosen has control of them, they can't do much else. They can't deploy their combat unit, they can't steer their craft, they can't take evasive action."

Wallace stopped struggling and the anger melted from his features. "You mean...?"

Milandra nodded. "But you will all need to help. When they learn what we mean to do, they will try to overcome the Chosen. As you know, once one of us takes control of others' psyches with their consent, the only way they can be released is with the controller's acquiescence. Whether thirty thousand acting in concert can alter that cardinal rule, I don't know, but I'm certain they will try. You Deputies and Rod must bolster her, do what you can to keep the thirty thousand under Simone's control." She looked at Ronstadt and Heidler. "Peter? Diane? Will you help?"

"My aim has already been achieved," said Ronstadt. "The knowledge I seek is here within Earth Haven. It will be of no use to me if they overcome and kill us. Yes, of course I'll help."

"I'm batting for humanity," said Heidler. "And for us, I suppose. So, yeah, I'm in."

"Okay, gather near Simone and be ready to lend your mental support. She's going to need it and it might not be enough. Do not do anything yet. I shall let you know when." Milandra glanced away when movement caught her eye. "What now?"

Three men were marching towards Simone. Milandra, with her deceptive turn of speed, stepped into their path.

"Tom? Mr Irving? Sorry, but I don't know your name."

"Er, it's Manning, ma'am."

"We have a bit of a situation going on, gentlemen. Would you mind telling me what you're doing?" Milandra glanced at the sky. The craft was appreciably lower, almost filling the horizon. "And quickly, please. We don't have much time."

"Milandra," said Tom, "we have to bring down that ship. But we can't while Simone is doing whatever she's doing."

Irving held up his walkie-talkie. "I can't raise my commander or crew. There are men on the open decks who cannot move. The sea is growing rougher. They are in danger of being swept overboard."

"Mr Irving, how long will your commander need to be able to fire his missiles?"

Irving hesitated.

"Oh, come *on*, Mr Irving. We both know there are missiles on that sub. How long will he need?"

"A minute. Maybe two."

"Then stand where you can see me and be ready with your radio. Tom, keep everyone else out of the way. Let us do what needs doing."

She didn't wait to see if they would obey her instructions, but turned on her heels. The Deputies, Rod, Peter and Diane had gathered around the Chosen, who continued to stare fiercely at the submarine. More fiercely than required merely to hold its crew in stasis until the craft made its landing.

Milandra reached, and saw.

Simone, stop! I know you're about to force a member of the crew to open the ballast tanks and send the sub to the bottom of the ocean with its hatches open. Big mistake.

Fuck off, drone lover.

Look into their hearts, Simone. Really look. They aren't going to make you Keeper. They're going to kill you. And not only you, not only the humans. All of us. Look and tell me it ain't so.

Silence, but Milandra could sense the Chosen had stopped the crewman from opening the valves that would flood the ballast tanks with water.

Simone?

Oh, shit, Milandra. What have I done?

Nothing that can't be undone. Release the crew.

More silence.

Simone?

I can't. They suspect I'm up to something, tricking them. They can sense it.

Well, it's a two-way street. Always two ways. I'm going to send help. The Deputies, Rod, Heidler and the one you call 'Traitor'. Let them all in.

Hurry.

Simone's face had turned bright red with the effort she was making to maintain her grip on the newcomers' intellects. Milandra sensed them struggling to break free like a sail in a typhoon.

The gazes of Jason Grant and the others were fixed on her. She nodded.

Now she sent. *Help her.*

Milandra looked out across the ocean. The black craft was nearing the end of its journey. The boosters that had sprung from hidden compartments along the edge of the wide hull were performing their appointed task of slowing the craft's descent to allow a safe landing on the water's surface. Her people—if that's what she should still call them—had done an admirable job of gauging the required strength to cope with Earth Haven's slightly stronger gravity. The ocean beneath the thrusters must be frothing into a white frenzy; waves were being thrown towards them at increasing height and velocity.

Without anyone capable of adjusting the *Argute*'s trim and lie, the submarine pitched and yawed in the heavier conditions. While Milandra watched, a supine figure rolled off the open deck and splashed into the sea.

Her gaze was snagged by fresh movement. A yellow dinghy cut through the water, its outboard motor almost inaudible above the rising wind and waves. It was being piloted by one of Irving's men—hadn't he said his name was Manning?—and two figures sat in the bow, reaching forward to pluck the sailor from the sea.

Milandra looked at the small clutch of humans. Both Tom and Ceri were missing. Colleen, Bri and Will had moved to a bench near the cliff edge and huddled there with the dog.

She turned her attention back to Simone. In the nick of time.

A steady stream of blood ran from each of the Chosen's nostrils. Her eyes were squeezed tightly shut, her hands clenched into fists at her chest. The other three Deputies, together with Rod, Peter and Diane, clustered around Simone, staring intently at her. Jason Grant's gaze flickered her way, briefly, but she read the message clearly in his eyes.

Help us.

Milandra reached and found a maelstrom.

~ ~ ~

Before leaving the warehouse, Zach took a quick inventory of their ammunition.

"Not enough for everyone to have all they'll need," was his blunt verdict.

He divided the ammo amongst those who knew how to handle their rifles and submachine guns; to them also went the remainder of the grenades. There were no mortar shells left.

Those without ammo kept hold of their weapons—a rifle in Amy's case—and a spare rifle was found for Elliott.

"You're the beaters," Zach told them. "You'll form the front line. Your job will be to beat the holy crap out of anything with four legs that comes at us. Rat, dog, whatever. We can't afford to waste bullets shooting 'em."

"Won't we be a little, er, exposed?" asked a woman, who looked too dead beat to carry her rifle, let alone swing it like a club.

Amy was glad she'd asked. The same thought had occurred to her, but she didn't voice it for fear of sounding disloyal to Zach. And Joe. A warm tingling deep in her stomach appeared whenever she thought of Joe and the way he had kissed her in front of everyone. Her momma would turn in her grave, thought Amy, if she were in one.

"The rest of us will be immediately behind you," said Zach. "When we see drones, we'll shoot or grenade 'em."

"And any of those alien fuckers we see," added Joe.

"Aye," agreed Zach, "though I don't expect to see any. Not many high buildings on the approach here so nowhere for them to hide. Beaters, stay close together. Everyone else, stick to the beaters' asses."

They proceeded in tightknit formation. When they encountered the first wave of vermin and dogs, Zach called a halt and the rear lines flung grenades to wreak havoc among the creatures. Those that got through were met by swinging steel and plastic.

When drones appeared behind the waves of creatures, the shooters used bullets and the remaining grenades to destroy them.

But there were many drones. Too many. For every one they killed, it seemed another two stepped forward to take their place.

Slowly but surely their ammunition and explosives became depleted. Their lines grew thinner when people fell to bullets fired by humans who once would not have dreamed of killing another human, but who now had no concept of what they did.

Amy's arms ached and bled from multiple rat bites; if she didn't bleed to death, she reckoned she'd die of some horrible rat disease. Elliott was bleeding, too, and looked shattered, at the end of his tether. Aletta's fair hair had turned red with blood from a wound high on her scalp. She seemed about ready to drop. Zach fought next to Aletta with Joe alongside him, both of them flanking Amy; she would die between her two favourite people. Her main regret would be never finding out what it was like to lie with a man.

They had made good ground, put the warehouse out of sight behind them, when they came to the end of an alley lined with industrial units. The land opened up into a wide area of scrubland bordered by the river to one side, a high chain-link fence to the other.

The scrubland was covered with line after line of drones, maybe fifty deep and thirty across. Most of them armed. Behind the drones, and so shielded from frontal assault, in front of twenty or more gleaming vehicles, *they* stood. In excess of a hundred, standing silently, come to watch the last act of this tragedy. They cast frequent glances at a sky once more bright with sunshine.

Amy guessed their spaceship was coming in to land. She hadn't had time to turn her head up to look. Now she didn't have the energy.

Zach issued his last order. Amy couldn't remember when he'd assumed the mantle of unofficial general from Joe. It didn't matter.

"Beaters, to the rear. When we run out of ammo, we'll become beaters, too. Use that time to regain your strength. Then beat out as many of their soft brains as you can. It's been an honour and a privilege to fight alongside you people. Now it is time to die alongside you. Farewell, friends."

Amy's vision blurred. She didn't, therefore, see the drones advance.

Bri's gaze was torn between watching the final descent of the black ship, peering anxiously at the heaving ocean for glimpses of Tom and Ceri in the yellow dinghy, and looking askance at what she was becoming increasingly certain was the death of Simone.

Will huddled close, but for comfort, not warmth. Even he had become infected by the spreading sense of despair. A restless Dusty paced in front of them, running to the cliff edge to send puzzled barks out towards Tom, before running back to lick her or Will's hand. On the other side of Will sat Colleen, sobbing quietly, giving out an air of utter defeat.

The man from the submarine, Irving, stood nearby. He, too, seemed torn between gazing at the stricken submarine and the knot of people surrounding Simone. Now and then he'd bring an object to his mouth, speak into it and then pause, before his shoulders drooped in dejection.

Her glance stole again to Simone and her mind reeled in horror at the sight. Milandra, Jason and the others, including Peter and Diane, had linked hands and tightened their circle to form a sort of cradle for Simone. Without their linked arms to hold her up, it looked to Bri that she'd have fallen.

Blood soaked the front of Simone's blouse and had started to stain her jeans. It was running freely not only from her nose but from her eyes and ears, too. Bri couldn't remember from biology classes how much blood the human body contained, but there couldn't be a great deal remaining in Simone's. Yes, she knew Simone wasn't technically human, but she was indistinguishable in appearance from a young human woman so Bri didn't feel it unreasonable to assume her body would hold a similar amount of blood.

While she tore her gaze away again, from one terrifying sight to another, Milandra's voice spoke inside her head.

Brianne. I hoped we might do this without you. I was wrong. Please come.

She stood, but Will grabbed her hand to drag her back down.

"Let me go. I have to help."

"No, you don't. They're not even human. They killed our mums."

"But now they're trying to save us."

Will stared at her.

I love you, Bri.

Love you, too. Now let me go, buster!

He released her hand. Bri strode towards the circle of people.

She tapped Milandra on the shoulder. Milandra unhooked her left hand from Jason's, allowing Bri to slide in between them. She grasped Jason and Milandra by their arms, recompleting the circle. A hot, coppery smell wafted from Simone.

Bri took a deep breath and *reached*.

Simone's psyche was a swirling mass of pain and effort. Her grip on the intellects of the new arrivals had grown tenuous but, with the bolstering effects of the six combined minds who surrounded and supported her, she was holding on.

If Simone's grip was weakening, the incoming Keeper's and his people's corresponding hold over her will was like the grasp of a titanium vice. The more she struggled to free the sailors from the paralysis under which the combined weight of intellects held them, the tighter the interlopers' grip became.

Milandra's mind flitted like a dragonfly.

She encouraged Simone to hold on, although the Chosen had little option: endure or perish. She mentally patted Jason Grant, George Wallace and Lavinia Cram on the backs, silently exhorting them to stay strong, though she could sense their determination: Jason because he was made that way; Lavinia because, despite their differences, Simone was the nearest thing she had to a best friend; and George because of his repressed admiration of humans and their art. It was a secret passion of which Milandra had long been aware; some things could not remain hidden indefinitely from a Keeper.

She gave a virtual squeeze to the arms of Peter Ronstadt and Diane Heidler. They were at their limit, were supporting Simone to the extent of their abilities, but seemed to appreciate the gesture.

The former London Transport man, Rodney Wilson, was struggling. Unaccustomed to having to make extensive use of his mental powers, he was already spent.

Hold on for as long as you can, Rod. I'm going to find a way to end this.

He no longer possessed the strength to reply.

Since they were under the control of Simone, Milandra could not directly probe the minds of the new Keeper and his people. She could, however, delve into Simone's psyche and gain a glimpse of her captives (and captors).

The Chosen's past was riddled with incidents of cruelty towards humans; she had never moved beyond seeing them purely as drones, simple creatures not much further along the evolutionary scale from amoeba, created for one purpose alone— to serve the will of Simone and her kind. Milandra caught snippets of torture and killings, from ancient times in Alexandria and Rome, when Simone must have been very young, to more recently, like the torture and killing of a young woman in the check-in area of JFK Airport.

Drawing the equivalent of a deep mental breath, Milandra peeked into the trapped psyches of the newcomers from Earth Home.

It was akin to peering into a pit leading directly to Hell: swirling flames and sooty smoke of rage and hatred, guile and cunning, cruelty and artifice. These were the dominant passions, succoured by their Keeper's mighty intellect. They were growing more powerful, feeding off Simone's darker memories and characteristics. And not only hers. Each of the people providing a buttress to the Chosen possessed a darker side, like Lavinia's lack of empathy towards suffering or Rod's homophobia. That last was a strange one for an asexual being to possess, fuelled by spending too much time in the company of boors and bigots in the opium and drinking dens of old London; a superficial emotion to be sure, yet nonetheless a negative one upon which the newcomers fed.

The swirling flames danced faster and redder and brighter and hotter; Simone must prevail, and soon, or fail utterly.

Milandra knew she must risk that which she would only endanger at the end of all need. There was no other card left to play.

She withdrew from the vortex, reached, found and sent. Moments later, she was making room for Bri to join the circle.

Then she re-entered the maelstrom and watched.

At first, Bri was hesitant, her psyche showing as little more than a grey shade against the blacks and reds. Then, like the noon sun glinting off a polished surface, the girl's purity shone out as a dazzling ray of golden whiteness, dimming the flames and blinding eyes greedy with lust for scum and dross and all things foul.

Milandra probed and sensed their grip on Simone loosen. She knew it would not last long; they would soon recover. Even sixteen-year-old girls as sweet and innocent as Bri had *some* experience of lewd thoughts and dishonourable intentions; it had not been too long ago she had held a knife to a man's throat and nearly, very nearly, sliced it open. Only momentarily confounded, they would soon sense those darker aspects lurking beneath the bright beacon of her mind and would latch on to them, returning more powerful than before. Irresistibly so.

Simone sensed the loosening, too, and did not hesitate. Summoning the last of her will and courage and strength, she pushed with all her might, shoving against the grip that enveloped her, and freed herself. Her last act, before her brain seized and her heart exploded, was to release the sailors from their immobility.

Milandra withdrew and whirled around, yelling to Irving, "Now! Do it now!"

Irving brought the walkie-talkie up to his mouth so quickly he was in danger of losing some teeth. He barked something into it and released the button. The set crackled in response and Irving shot her a wondering look.

Milandra was already turning away, reaching in to where the Chosen's consciousness had been.

Everyone out! Full protective mode. I don't want to give them any easy targets if they try to return.

Simone slumped to her knees, head drooping to chest. A chest black with arterial blood. White, shocked faces of her Deputies, of Rod and Peter and Diane, of pure-hearted Brianne, gazed at each other and at Milandra and, most of all, at the fallen Chosen.

These things were peripheral to the Keeper. Her focus had moved inwards. The knowledge of what was coming could not prevent her drawing a sharp, gasping breath while Simone's memories and experiences flowed into her. Tears squeezed from her eyes, hot and stinging.

Mere moments or long minutes later, she could not tell, but it happened as the influx of the Chosen's memories began to lessen.

This time the air left her body in an *Oomph!* and she sank to her knees in inadvertent mimicry of Simone. As though from a great distance, she was aware of the concerned face of Jason Grant swimming before her vision. In the microseconds that remained, she managed to send: *Call it off.* She could only trust he would know what she meant; there was no more time.

The essences of nearly thirty thousand people washed over and through her, and her vision dimmed.

The day might have been sunny and warm, but Ceri was chilled to her very core. The dinghy tossed and lurched in the ever-angrier waves, treating her to a fresh soaking with every swell. Her stomach rose and fell like the sea; Tom had lost his breakfast.

It was he who noticed the paralysed sailor roll off into the surf; she who suggested they take the dinghy and try to save him. Irving's man—the alert one, Manning; the other looked as if he was a dozen slices short of a loaf, as her dad used to say—readily agreed to help.

Ceri was fed up of sitting around waiting for others to make things happen; had started to feel like an extra on a film set, there to make up the numbers. Now, as miserable and cold and nauseated as it was making her, at least she was doing something useful, no matter how ultimately futile it proved to be.

They were too late to save the submariner who Tom had seen fall in, but so far had rescued three others. Those three lay on their backs in sloshing water in the bottom of the dinghy; fortunately for them, Tom's breakfast had gone over the side. Not that they were in any condition to notice what they were lying in, even less to complain.

Each of the three men could move his eyes, but nothing else. Their chests rose and fell while they breathed, but this was evidently an instinctive action. They expressed their gratitude at being pulled from the perishing, foaming sea with their stares. Otherwise, they lay in the boat like dead fish.

Ceri's hands were numb from cold. Her arms and back ached with the exertion of hauling the sailors' dead-weights aboard. Her sodden clothes hung heavy, trying to drag her down to join the sailors in the footwell. A hot pain in her right buttock suggested a pulled muscle that would give her grief later, if there was a later.

While the dinghy rode each swell, and when there was no overboard sailor to rescue, or when their relative position to the *Argute*—a surprisingly large and sleek craft viewed at this close range—meant the sub wasn't obstructing their view, Ceri watched, mesmerised, the descent of the black object.

Being a fan of science fiction did not make her gullible and she had struggled to believe the evidence of her eyes as much as Tom, but there could now be no mistaking what had come from the skies. The *Argute* was black, but it was as bleached driftwood to ebony when compared to the descending object. A suggestion of sublime grace and beauty and unimaginable power, masked by intense darkness the senses could not compute; it appeared as a shifting, undulating, pulsing blob, a crazily inappropriate but accurate word to describe what Ceri's brain told her she was seeing. A blob, yet also a magnificent spacecraft.

The path of its descent was bringing it in to land, or rather, to splashdown, two or three miles out to sea from where the dinghy bobbed. The thrusters ranged along the edge of the ship had slowed its rate of descent to what Ceri judged with her inexperienced eye to be the perfect velocity to allow it to settle onto the ocean's surface without causing more than minimal damage, no matter how flimsy its outer hull.

And it was almost down. Even when viewed from the top of an upswell, the lower edge of the craft appeared more elusive and shadowy, as though it had slipped below the horizon.

Judging from his pinched expression, Tom also realised the ship had almost landed. Pale as a winter's afternoon, it was how he'd looked while he prepared to rush into the circle at Stonehenge, when terror had made him almost incapable of rational thought or deed.

They both heard the groans and looked down together.

All three sailors were moving, bringing hands to forehead, struggling to get up out of the sloshing water.

Ceri glanced at the *Argute*. The men who had stood stationary or lain where they had fallen on its decks for the last thirty minutes or so had sprung into motion, jumping to their feet, scurrying for the open hatch.

"Tom? What does it mean?"

Tom tore his gaze away from the sub and turned bright eyes towards her.

"They've released them," he said, speaking so quickly she could barely understand him. All traces of his fear of only moments before had been replaced by unrestrained excitement and the bright gleam of hope. "They've released the sailors. Whatever was holding them has gone. They're free to—"

He broke off and swung his head back towards the *Argute*. With a *hiss* and a *whump!* two lights, like extraordinarily bright and rapid flares, streaked from the submarine. Blinking at the glare, Ceri held her breath as the lights flew away, almost skimming the surface of the sea, in a direct line towards the spacecraft.

"Yes, my boys! Yes!" Manning shouted behind them.

Tom joined in. "More!" he yelled. "Chuck everything you've got at 'em!"

Not one normally given to overt displays of passion, Ceri found herself caught up in the moment. "Go, go, go!" she hollered, as though supporting the Welsh rugby team. "Hit them again!"

The sailors in the footwell, struggling to sit up in the bucking dinghy, sent up weak cheers.

As if in answer to their pleas, there came another dull concussion and two more bright lights took off towards the spaceship.

A horrible thought struck Ceri. "Oh, Tom, what if they're ineffective? What if it's protected by some sort of force field? A magnetic shield or—"

The sky to the west exploded in a gout of flame when the first two missiles struck home in the base of the spaceship. The sound of the explosion followed, bringing the dinghy to silence. All held their breath, bathed in orange glow, waiting for the next two missiles to arrive.

The second pair of Tomahawks flew true and found their target. More flame and explosions, and the black craft completed its descent to the surface of the Atlantic more rapidly than planned. Within a minute, it had slipped completely from sight.

Ceri leaned across and allowed her sense of relief to lend strength to her embrace. Tom hugged her back, eyes shining, but when he pulled away he frowned.

"What's the matter?" he asked, looking at Manning, who was yanking at the starter cord of the outboard motor. It sputtered to life.

The men in the boat's bottom had started scooping water with their hands and flinging it over the sides.

Without replying, Manning brought the nose of the dinghy around and pointed it at the submarine.

Ceri looked at the hatch. A man stood next to it, glancing over his shoulder and beckoning at them to hurry.

Then she understood. At the same time, comprehension must have dawned on Tom because his face once more drained of colour.

"Tidal wave," he managed to get out.

Ceri clung to the side of the dinghy while Manning opened the throttle fully and they smashed headlong through waves in their desperate rush for the sub. It was closer, much closer, than shore. Maybe they would make it in time.

She gave an involuntary cry when the man on deck disappeared into the vessel, bringing the hatch down behind him.

Then she saw the wave rising in the background. Maybe 'tidal', suggesting a wave of apocalyptic proportions, would be a slight exaggeration, but she wasn't about to argue. From the perspective of an overcrowded, inflatable dinghy, the wave looked enormous, dwarfing the *Argute* as it rushed silently towards them. Ceri had time to reach out and grab Tom before the submarine disappeared into a green wall.

She wondered about screaming—maybe better not with all that rushing water—then it didn't matter.

Ceri's world became a crashing, tumbling confusion of churning, slanting greens and blues and browns.

Then just black.

Chapter Twenty-One

Bri staggered and would have fallen if Jason Grant hadn't maintained a strong grip on her forearm. In front of her, a blood-soaked Simone Furlong knelt on the ground. Bri *reached*, but there was nothing to reach for. Simone had ceased to exist.

The sound of distant explosions came, but she didn't look up. The sight of Simone's still form transfixed her. It was only at the noise of two more explosions, so close together they nearly sounded as one, she was able to tear her gaze away.

Bri gasped when she noticed Milandra. The woman's skin had turned the colour of putty. Grant had obviously noticed, too. He let go of Bri's arm and rushed to Milandra's side.

He arrived as she slumped heavily to her knees. Her dazed look seemed to focus on him momentarily, before passing on to some unseen horizon.

Grant crouched by her side, checking she had settled back fully onto her calves and heels.

"Don't want her toppling over," he said to Bri. "She might be vacant for a while."

"What's wrong with her?"

"She's receiving into the group consciousness the memories and experiences of the people on that ship."

"Are they all dead?"

"I guess so." He stood and glanced around. "George! Lavinia! I need you."

He strode away.

Bri glanced out to sea. In the distance, a plume of smoke rose into the air, shredding in swirling winds. Of the black ship there was no sign, but her attention was diverted by an unusual sight. A dark line seemed to stretch across the ocean, closer than halfway to the horizon and drawing nearer. Her gaze not leaving the line, she walked to where Will sat with Colleen. They, too, looked out to sea.

"What is it…?" she began, but then she knew. "Oh, shit."

The dark line was a wave, travelling fast, almost on the submarine. Its hatches were closed so it should be fine, she thought, but the dinghy was another matter. A wall of water rose to meet the yellow boat and enveloped it.

"No!" moaned Colleen.

"Tom! Ceri!" shouted Will.

Dusty barked and disappeared. For an awful moment, Bri thought he'd jumped over the edge of the cliff, but then she remembered the steps that led down to the narrow beach.

The wave came on, but it had already lost much of its ferocity. Bri caught glimpse of a flash of yellow amidst the green and the dinghy popped out of the back of the wave. Empty.

"Oh, no," she murmured.

Colleen and Will had risen to their feet and were hurrying for the steps. Someone else had already reached them and started to descend. The man from the submarine, Irving.

As Bri made for the steps, the crash of the wave hitting the base of the cliff sounded from below. She increased her stride.

A short line of people made their way down the wooden steps in front of her. The wave had dashed itself against the cliff and dissipated, leaving behind a seaweed-strewn strip of sand. A black shape was streaking across it.

Dusty. He was heading for the figures that had been scattered along the sand, left behind in the wave's wake.

Five figures. Human figures.

Zach opened his mouth to give the order to open fire on the advancing lines of drones, when they came to an abrupt halt and lowered their weapons.

"What's going on?" Elliott hissed from behind him.

Zach didn't answer because he didn't have a clue.

The lines of drones parted. Striding down the path between the lines came three of *them*: an attractive, sandy-haired woman flanked by two men. When they had cleared the drones, they came to a stop. The woman unhooked the strap of the submachine gun from her shoulder and handed it to one of the men. She took a few paces forward alone.

"Please may I speak to whoever's in charge?" she said in an Australian accent.

Joe took a step forward and paused. He looked back at Zach.

"Come on."

Zach handed his rifle to Aletta. He nodded at Joe's weapon. Joe shrugged and passed it to Amy. Together, they walked to meet the woman.

"G'day," she said, when they stopped in front of her. "My name's Tess Granville." Her eyes widened as she took in the boy's features. "*You* again." She sighed and nodded to her right, to the west. Far in the distance, a dark column was climbing towards the sun. "The Great Coming. Something has gone fatally wrong. I have been contacted by Jason Grant. You may not know the name, but he is one of the Keeper's Deputies."

"I've come across him," said Joe shortly.

Zach had no idea who they were talking about; his expression must have said as much.

"No matter," said the woman. "He is in the west with the Keeper and the other Deputies. They were to welcome our people home. I do not understand how or why, but the people who arrived from Earth Home are dead."

There followed a moment's silence.

"Let me get this straight," said Joe. "All that corpse burning, the food collecting, the slitting of throats at Stonehenge, all that was for nothing?"

"Fuck," Zach breathed. Both of them looked at him. "I'm probably the one person on this godforsaken planet who benefitted from the Millennium Bug."

"We call it the Cleansing," said Tess. She frowned. "But how would any human have benefitted from it?"

Zach shook his head. "That's not important. What *is* important is the Millennium Bug, the Cleansing, was also for nothing."

Joe's eyes widened. "You're right." He threw back his head and uttered a loud, braying laugh. "It was all for nothing. You idiots!"

Tess Granville had the grace to look uncomfortable.

"So where does that leave us?" asked Zach. He suddenly felt weary to the bone; he wanted to lie down and close his eyes. Perhaps when he woke up the world would seem less crazy.

Tess looked him in the eye. "I have been instructed to call off hostilities."

"Huh." Zach exhaled heavily. "You mean, you're letting us go?"

"So long as you stop attacking us, we'll let you pass unmolested. All we ask is that you make your way back to Hillingdon Hospital. We'll send food and medical supplies."

"Why?" asked Joe, his voice dripping with suspicion. "Why are you letting us go and why do we have to go back to that fucking place?"

"As to your first question, the answer clearly has something to do with the failure of the Great Coming." She shrugged. "I do not yet fully understand the implications myself. As to your second question, we are asking you to go back to the hospital because you already have people there and we need a base to which to deliver supplies."

Zach returned the woman's gaze. "This is no trick?"

Her expression didn't flicker and she didn't hesitate. "No trick."

"She's telling the truth," said Joe, as though he could sense it.

The woman turned to Joe. "That's where we met before. I can appreciate why you don't like the place."

Joe snorted. "I remember you now. Must have forgotten for a moment, probably 'cause you're not my type." He turned and began to walk back to their weary line of anxiously waiting people.

Tess grinned, the tension draining from her bearing. She called after him, "Not your type? You had your hands all over me, mate."

Joe waved over his shoulder, but didn't look back. "'Fraid I'm taken now, love." He reached Amy, who threw her arms around his neck.

"That's it then?" said Zach.

Tess nodded and held out her hand. Zach paused for a moment. His thoughts jumped back to December, to his local hardware store in Maine, when he had seen a woman touching objects for no apparent reason; when she stroked his cheek, a scratching sensation had begun inside his skull.

Zach reached out and firmly grasped Tess's hand. No unusual sensations, in his head or elsewhere.

Then Zach turned and followed Joe back to the line of people.

Not merely people. *His* people.

Jason Grant released the minds of George Wallace and Lavinia Cram.

"Thanks, guys. Couldn't have done that without your help."

Supporting Simone had left Grant drained, without the energy to contact Tess Granville alone. With the Deputies' assistance, he had managed—barely—to *send* to Tess and remain connected long enough to convey his, or more accurately Milandra's, message.

He peered closely at them. George Wallace looked haggard; Lavinia Cram haggard and distraught.

"Go eat, you two," he said.

Wallace's glance darted to the slumped figure of the Keeper.

"Don't worry about Milandra," Grant said. "She'll be fine when she pulls out of it. Shattered and in more need of food than you two, but just dandy. I'll keep an eye on her in the meantime."

He watched them trudge away.

Rodney Wilson sat on the ground nearby, arms clutched around knees, staring into space. Grant stepped over to him.

"You okay, man?"

Wilson turned a forlorn gaze to Grant. The man's eyes looked empty.

"That was horrible," he breathed. "Poor Miss Simone."

"Well, it's over now. Eat, Rod. Then soak up some sunlight. Rebuild your strength. You'll need it to drive us back to London. I suspect we'll be leaving tomorrow."

"P'raps I'll go fishing."

"Good idea. Eat. Then sit in the sun and catch some fresh fish for our supper."

Grant helped him to his feet and watched him walk slowly away. He needed to eat himself, but wanted to make sure Milandra had pulled out of it first. And he couldn't leave Simone kneeling in full view of everyone.

Once he had taken her body inside—her blood now stained his tee-shirt—and covered it with a blanket, he returned to the sunshine.

He stepped back to Milandra's side and lowered himself to the ground. There was some sort of activity going on behind him near the cliff's edge, but he ignored it. He stretched out his legs, leaned back on his elbows and let his head fall back to allow the full glare of the sun onto his face.

The hubbub behind him died away and he relaxed. The events of the last hour were surprising and perplexing, and had gone full circle—from excitement that the Great Coming was at last happening, to shock that their people intended to kill them, to relief that the Coming had failed—but he was too drained to ponder them. For now, it was enough to be alive with warmth on his cheeks, knowing a danger he hadn't even been aware of that morning had been averted. As to how this changed things, and change them fundamentally it undoubtedly did, that could wait until he had recovered and could think straight.

Grant was falling into a restful stupor when movement from Milandra roused him. He raised his head to look at her.

The Keeper was blinking in the sun, her eyes hooded and heavy as though she had been drugged. She turned her head towards him and squinted to focus.

"Jason...?"

Grant sat up and held out his hand to take hers. He squeezed reassuringly.

"All done?"

She nodded. He'd expected her to look exhausted, and she did, but her overriding expression could only be described as troubled.

"What's wrong?" he asked softly.

Milandra shook her head slowly. "Not all," she said.

Although Grant did not understand what she meant, he felt the first stirrings of unease.

"Not all what?"

"Not all of them died."

"The craft from Earth Home? Not all of *them* died?"

Milandra nodded.

The unease turned to alarm. Milandra grimaced and Grant realised he was squeezing her hand harder than he'd intended. He let it go.

"How many?"

"Thirty, I think. Difficult to be sure yet."

"They'll run. Hole up in Ireland."

Milandra again shook her head slowly.

"The reason I'm not sure how many survived," she said, "is that they're a little too far away. But soon I'll be able to sense exactly how many of them there are. You see, they're heading this way."

Tom came around to a familiar sensation: a damp tongue licking his cheek.

"Gerroff, you daft mutt." His words came from habit, not sentiment.

He groaned. His head felt like someone had mistaken it for a vat of grapes; his side like a heated knitting needle was being inserted slowly but deliberately.

Sand. He appeared to be lying on sand. And he was soaked through.

Gingerly, he opened his eyes and sat up.

"Oww!" he hissed through gritted teeth when the pain in his side intensified.

Dusty licked his face again.

"Good boy. Where am I?"

Then he remembered. He clenched his teeth in anticipation of fresh pain, but it was already subsiding to the point where he could look around without scrunching up his eyes.

A man lay on his back about three feet away. Blood ran from a cut above his eye and he groaned softly.

"Manning?"

The man's head turned towards him.

"I'm all right," said the submariner. "Whacked my head on the outboard motor. Gashed my forehead on the propeller."

Tom looked further. A woman was sitting up away to his right.

"Ceri!"

She looked at him without seeming to recognise him. Then her face cleared and she smiled. Unsteadily, she stood and tottered towards him. Dusty ran to meet her and licked her hand furiously.

While she approached, Tom clambered to his feet. The world lurched and he thought he might faint, but then it steadied.

"Tom, are you okay?"

"Yeah. Banged my head and think I might have cracked a rib, but seem to be in one piece. You?"

"A little woozy. Think I might have passed out for a few seconds. Otherwise, I'm fine."

Tom indicated Manning, and the two men sitting up beyond him.

"There should be six of us. I can only see five."

Ceri grimaced. "We're lucky any of us survived. The wave must have been losing strength or we'd have been dashed against the cliff."

Tim glanced back. The craggy face of the cliff was less than twenty feet away. Ceri was right: they had been lucky. The wave had deposited them beyond the jagged rocks crowding the water's edge and onto the narrow stretch of sand before the pebbles and rocks began that led to the base of the cliff.

A small party of people had descended from the cliff top and was picking its way towards them. Acting Lieutenant Commander James Irving led the way, followed by Colleen and Will, with Bri bringing up the rear.

Irving approached Tom and Ceri first.

"I wanted to express my gratitude for saving my men."

"We pulled three from the water," said Tom, "but it looks like only two made it."

"Well, um, thanks," said Irving.

"We accept your apology," said Ceri.

"Apology? What apology?"

"For not believing us in Scotland."

Irving had the good grace to blush. Before he could say anything more, his pocket beeped. He pulled out the walkie-talkie.

"Irving here. Over."

The set crackled into life. "Irving, it's Napier," said a clipped voice. "There are two objects heading this way from where that black craft went down. From what we can tell on the radar, they are some sort of boats, each big enough to hold at least ten people. The current would take them south, but they're coming directly at us. Over."

Tom felt a ball of dread curl tight in his stomach. He glanced at Ceri. The colour that had been returning to her cheeks was draining away.

"Deep water," Tom said to Irving. "Tell them to dive to deep water and stay there until this is over. I don't think the aliens will be able to take over their minds if the sub is submerged."

Irving frowned. "But if there are only twenty of them coming…"

"That might be enough," said Ceri. "They could make the *Argute* fire at us. Or make the men turn on each other. Or make Napier scuttle it."

"Okay," said Irving. He pressed the button on the handset. "Commander. Advise immediate submersion and removal from vicinity. Incoming hostiles likely to be sufficient in number to, er, influence crew. Running deep should avoid risk. How long until they get here? Over."

There was a pause before the walkie-talkie once more crackled.

"ETA at current speed and course, twenty-seven minutes. Is there any assistance we can offer? Over."

Irving looked at Tom. He shrugged. "They need to make themselves scarce."

Irving nodded and pressed the button.

"Negative, sir. Advise commence manoeuvres to vacate vicinity immediately. Over."

Another pause. When the voice came back on the walkie-talkie, it began with a sigh.

"Affirmative. Good luck, Irving. Over."

"And you, sir. Over and out."

Irving returned the handset to the pocket of his jacket.

"Are you two fit enough to make it back to the clifftop?" he asked.

"Yes," said Tom. "My ribs and head hurt, but I think I can walk."

"I'm fine," said Ceri. "I was feeling sick, but it's passed. Now I'm only terrified again."

"Okay. I'm going to assist my men. See you up top."

"I'll help," said Colleen. She, Bri and Will had joined them as Irving's conversation with the *Argute* commenced and had stood quietly listening.

Irving walked towards Manning and Colleen fell into step alongside him.

"Tom," said Will. "Are the spacemen coming?"

"Yes, Will. I'm very much afraid that they are."

The clouds presaging the arrival of the spacecraft had completely dispersed and the sun shone warmly. Peter found Milandra on a wooden bench at the side of the hotel, in full glare of the sunlight, a large platter of food balanced on her knees. Her hair showed more grey than black; deep lines spread from the corners of her eyes like crevasses in ice. She looked too exhausted to do anything, but was managing to fork food into her mouth, chew and swallow.

"Jason said you wanted to see me?" he said.

"Give me a few moments."

Peter took a seat on the other end of the bench and sat back with his eyes closed. He, too, was exhausted and could do with finding something to eat to help rebuild his strength. For now, the sun felt good on his face. He could feel his cells open to soak up the solar energy. He had fallen into a semi-dose when Milandra spoke.

"You know they are coming?"

He sat straighter. "I heard. Do you know how many?"

"I sense thirty of them."

"Is that sufficient to overcome us?"

"I fear so. There are only seven of us, plus the humans. While our support of Simone greatly weakened us, they drew strength from the encounter. I saw many things when I probed them during Simone's last minutes, but it is, as always, a two-way street. They in turn saw we are few and our mental reserves are sorely depleted. They come, rather than running away to lick their wounds, because they are confident they will endure."

"We have weapons."

"Yes and, as far as I can tell, they do not. That is our only hope, but I fear it is a forlorn one." Milandra forked more food into her mouth and spoke around it. "Their number includes their Keeper. His name is Stark."

"*His?*"

"Much has changed in our absence from Earth Home. He will be the last Keeper. He has severed the psychic link with the rest of his people. When he dies, the group memory dies with him."

"You have plans to make use of that knowledge?"

Milandra glanced at him. "I have a plan. One I hope not to have to use." She looked away. "One which I need your help to carry out successfully."

"I can't imagine what I can do to help."

"It is a task you will find distasteful. That anyone would find distasteful, except perhaps for Simone." She uttered a short, humourless laugh.

Peter's eyes narrowed. "Then why would I agree to perform it?"

"To save us. And in return for the knowledge you crave."

Peter drew in a sharp breath. "You saw my need… and you now possess the knowledge?"

"It passed to me from those who perished. Though it troubles me greatly the use to which you will put the knowledge, I will share it with you provided you agree to help me carry out the plan if required."

Peter's hand came up and touched the locket around his neck.

"Tell me," he said, "what I'd have to do."

"You can't stay. It's too dangerous." Ceri could hear the shrillness in her voice and feel her colour rising.

Bri shook her head and Ceri's frustration cranked up another notch.

"Tom!" she exclaimed. "Will you speak to her?"

They were standing in the hotel car park, next to the Peugeot. Tom had the car doors open and was taking out their firearms. He looked odd in the clothes he'd borrowed from Grant to replace his sodden ones; no odder than she looked, Ceri supposed, in the clothes she now wore that had belonged to Simone. The Chosen had been of slighter build than Ceri, but drawstring sweat pants and baggy tee-shirt fitted her well enough.

Tom straightened, wincing, and clutched at his side. "Bugger! That hurts." In his other hand, he gingerly held a submachine gun. He noticed her looking at him expectantly. "Aw, Cer," he said. "Look what happened last time we tried to make them do what we wanted. It didn't work out so well."

"But, he's only a child!"

"I'm not," said Will indignantly. "Besides, I want to see the spacemen."

"And I can help," said Bri. She glanced at the small array of weapons Tom had taken from the car and grimaced. "Maybe not with the guns, but I may be able to protect you. From their minds." She folded her arms across her chest. "Whatever. We're staying."

Ceri stared at her; Bri stared defiantly back. Ceri sighed as she felt the fight leave her. She was too tired.

"Oh, have it your own way. But you both stay close to me. And if I say we take cover, you bloody well listen."

"Okay," said Bri.

"Okay," echoed Will. "Thanks for caring about us, Ceri."

Despite herself, Ceri smiled. Then she looked at Tom.

"Pass me that assault rifle."

Diane sat in the hotel kitchen, stuffing food into her face. It had been quite a thoroughfare. Lavinia Cram, George Wallace and Rodney Wilson had all come in, piled plates with food and disappeared, not speaking to her or to each other, although Wilson had muttered something about being better at fishing than fighting. Jason Grant had also been in, loading a platter with food.

"For Milandra," he said.

He'd taken it outside and returned to load a plate for himself. Then he, too, left.

Of their kind, Peter was the only one who hadn't come in to make a dent in their food supplies. As soon as Diane thought that he walked in, looking pale and drawn.

"You okay?" she asked.

Peter shrugged and busied himself opening cans.

"We have about ten minutes," he said.

"Well, I'm done. I'm going outside to catch some sunlight. Where are Tom and the others? They lighting out?"

Peter shrugged again. She had never seen him so distracted. He began ramming food into his mouth, not looking at her. She left him to it.

Outside, the sun shone brightly and she sighed when she felt the warm light begin to suffuse her with energy. She could see that Tom and the other humans, far from lighting out, looked as though they were prepared to fight it out. Tom clutched a shotgun,

Ceri a rifle and Colleen a pistol. Will stood among them, unarmed. Nearby stood the clutch of sailors. Irving had a submachine gun dangling from his shoulder. The one with a wide gash to his forehead held a shotgun identical to Tom's. The remaining three sailors held no weapons.

Bri was standing next to a sailor, one of the two who had come ashore with Irving and Colleen in the yellow inflatable. He wore a blank expression. While Diane watched, the man's face changed, became alive. His eyes opened wider and he gazed wonderingly at the girl. Bri smiled and turned away to rejoin Tom's group.

Jason Grant emerged from the hotel, clutching a leather bag. He strode over to Irving's group and handed pistols to the three unarmed men, including the newly animated one. Grant walked back to where Milandra stood facing the steps that led up from the beach. Lavinia Cram, George Wallace and Rodney Wilson came and stood alongside her.

Grant rummaged in the bag and produced three submachine guns—Uzis, Diane thought, like the one she had disabled that belonged to Bishop. Keeping one for himself, Grant handed the other two to Lavinia and Wallace; they accepted them grim-faced. Finally, he took out two more pistols and offered them to Milandra and Wilson. They both shook their heads. Grant noticed Diane watching him and held out a pistol in her direction. She, too, shook her head, but offered a thin smile of thanks.

The last person to emerge walked stiffly from the hotel. Peter approached Grant and, to Diane's surprise, accepted a pistol from him. He checked it was loaded then came towards her, tucking the weapon into the waistband of his jeans in the small of his back.

"Why—" she began, but was silenced by a curt shake of Peter's head. Despite the food he had consumed, he still looked pale, as though he might throw up at any moment.

He turned and looked out to sea. Diane followed his gaze. The *Argute* had gone. Two dark shapes were approaching, making light work of the Atlantic swell. They were close enough for Diane to see why: constructed of some thin material, roughly circular in shape, the objects skimmed the surface of the water, propelled by unknown and almost silent means. The faintest high-pitched buzzing, like a distant swarm of hornets, indicated that a form of technology powered the discs, rather than something more arcane.

On their flat surfaces, held in place by unseen forces, knelt people, fifteen on each disc. The wind of their motion whipped their hair and rippled their clothes. The craft approached the rocks of the foreshore and passed over them, coming to rest on the sandy strip.

There came the metal ratcheting sound of weapons being readied to fire as the remaining Deputies stepped forward to the cliff edge. Following their lead, Irving and his four men also strode to the clifftop.

Diane sucked in a deep breath. The final battle for Earth Haven was about to commence.

Chapter Twenty-Two

George Wallace wanted to kick ass. Despite stuffing down his throat enough food in the last thirty minutes to feed a pony, despite the sunshine infusing his cells like water plumping raisins, he still felt tired and grouchy. He and Simone had never been exactly affectionate towards each other, had mostly been downright antagonistic, but she was one of their own and it was because of these bastards she was now gone. Moreover, the bastards had let Wallace *et al* blunder along on Earth Haven for five thousand years, while humans multiplied to the point that the integrity of the planet as a new home had been compromised. And then the bastards, having finally decided to make the journey to Earth Haven, arrived with the intention of killing not only the surviving humans, but the remaining Earth Homians to boot.

It was payback time.

Wallace raised the Uzi to his shoulder. When the people clambered off the discs at the water's edge, they did not spread out, but clustered together behind the figure of a blonde-haired man. It would be like shooting fish in a barrel.

"No mercy," said Wallace. "Remember, these fuckers came here to kill us. Let's make them wish they'd stayed on Earth Home."

"Amen," said Lavinia.

Wallace's finger tightened on the trigger.

The burst of bullets flew harmlessly into the air when Grant's bulk barrelled into him. He was thrown sideways, bundling into Lavinia, who went down in a tangle beneath him without having discharged her weapon. It all happened so quickly that Wallace might have imagined the puff of air that wafted into his face an instant after Grant hit him, but he had experienced something similar in World War I when a Turkish bullet flew past his cheek so close he felt its passage, and he didn't imagine the sharp report that came from his right where the humans stood.

"What the fuck!" exclaimed Lavinia, struggling to extract herself from Wallace's unintended embrace.

"Listen to me," hissed Grant's voice from above Wallace's ear. "Lend me your minds *now*. We have to be quick."

As Wallace *reached* and felt his, and Lavinia's, psyche join with Grant's, he glanced at the group of five sailors. They had turned towards the Deputies. Each face was twisted into a grimace; each weapon was pointing at them. Wallace recognised what was happening—he had caused it often enough himself. Each sailor was under the control of another, probably thirty others, and one of them had taken a shot at him.

A protective pall, buttressed by the added minds of Wallace and Lavinia, bloomed from Grant and settled over the sailors. Being in such close proximity to them, the three combined minds of the Deputies trumped the controlling intellects. The sailors lowered their weapons, looks of relief replacing the twisted expressions of moments before.

Wallace retained sufficient control over his own motor and neuron functions that he managed to extract himself from Lavinia and scramble to his feet. A glance down at the beach confirmed what he already suspected.

The survivors from Earth Home had lined up in a loose triangular formation behind the blonde man. He had been staring up at the sailors, his bearing a study in concentration, but his hold over the sailors now broken, he began to advance towards the cliff, the people behind following without breaking formation.

Grant also climbed to his feet.

"Back!" he ordered Irving and his men. "Go stand with Tom and the others."

Looking pale, the five men did as ordered and Grant released Wallace's and Lavinia's minds.

"I should have seen that coming," said Grant with a sigh. "We employed the same tactic in London."

Lavinia was peering over the cliff edge. "They're climbing the steps," she remarked, as though commenting on the weather.

"Back to Milandra," said Grant. "We've missed this chance. Let's hope we get another."

When she saw Irving and his men turn their guns on her Deputies, Milandra knew she would need to put her plan into action. The new Keeper Stark might only have twenty-nine people remaining to back him up, but he was nevertheless too strong for Milandra and her currently pitiful resources to withstand.

She spared a moment examining her feelings. For many months, she had missed the life-enhancing sunlight of Florida; the effort of helping Simone resist the power of the newcomers from Earth Home had drained her further. But in truth she had already grown tired to her core. Tired of being guardian to the millions of years of memories of her people. Tired of planning to eradicate almost an entire species for acting in ways it had been designed to behave. Tired of hoping the signal from Earth Home would come before a solution like the Cleansing became necessary. Tired of disappointment and frustration and dejection. Most of all, tired of living.

Not that she was ready to die; not quite yet. Even allowing herself to age—and Jason had not imagined it; since the Cleansing has been accomplished, she *had* been letting her cells degenerate— she reckoned on another century or two to grow old and slip away gracefully beneath the blue Floridian sky. As the passage of time was perceived by her kind, especially here on Earth Haven, a century or two was little more than the blink of an eye, but a blink she would prefer not to forego.

The moment of introspection passed. It was time for action.

Looking mightily relieved to step away from the cliff edge, the five sailors were making their way to the group of humans, with whom stood Peter and Diane.

Milandra strode over to them, utilising that well-hidden ability to move with deceptive speed when it suited her. Her glance took in Tom, Ceri and Colleen.

"You need to lose those weapons," she said loudly. "Possessing them makes you a target. And a threat."

Tom opened his mouth, but Irving cut across him.

"She's right. Those people…" He sighed as though about to commit himself to craziness. "Those *aliens*, the ones down there, who will shortly be up here, took over our minds. I was still myself, but I had no control over my body. They made me shoot at her friends."

"The same thing happened to us at Stonehenge," said Tom.

Milandra nodded towards the hotel. "Drop them back there. Then form up behind us." She looked at Bri. "You know how to protect against mind control—I've seen you do it. Without the guns, I suspect they'll leave y'all alone, but you must cast protection in any case." Her glance darted to Diane. "You'll have to help her."

Diane nodded. "And Peter."

Milandra grunted.

Peter shuffled his feet and did not look at her.

"Hurry," said Milandra and turned away.

She took a few paces forward and beckoned to Jason and her Deputies. *You, too, Rod* she sent.

Milandra faced the top of the steps leading up from the beach. Jason Grant took his place to her right, half a pace behind her. Lavinia Cram stood to her left. George Wallace and Rodney Wilson stood on the ends so that the five of them formed a tight V with Milandra at the point. Grant, Lavinia and Wallace held Uzis.

A shuffling of feet and low murmur of voices told her that Peter, Diane and the humans were taking their places behind them. She felt warm breath on her ear and Peter's voice whispered, "I'm right here if you need me. I pray that you don't."

Milandra nodded. When the blonde-haired figure of Stark appeared at the top of the steps, she sent to her Deputies: *Whatever happens, do not, I repeat, do not attempt any form of mind control against them. When they try to control us, let them in, only a little, just enough that I can lay down a return path to their minds. It's always a two-way street and my plan depends on it.*

You have a plan? sent Grant.

No time to explain. They're here.

Stark stepped forward far enough for the remaining twenty-nine of his people to file in behind him, retaining the triangular formation. He stopped maybe five yards from Milandra. Judging from the intense, single-minded expressions on his followers' faces, he still controlled their intellects.

"Milandra," said Stark. "This was not the welcome I'd imagined." His tone was stiff, probably due to working his tongue around a language he'd never before spoken.

"The welcome was proportionate to the gift you brought with you. We paved the way for you to arrive with the intention of killing us?"

A slow grin spread over Stark's face, but his eyes remained cold and dark, like chips of flint.

"A lot can change in five millennia," he said. "*We* changed."

"Sivatra. You discovered her memories."

"I see that you, too, have been curious as to what that bitch did. Tell me, what did you find?"

"I found…" Milandra paused. She felt as if she was sparring with this man, but he was merely jabbing and hadn't even begun to throw the punches of which he was capable. "I found it was our people who devastated the surface of Earth Home and forced us to live underground. I found that Sivatra attempted to hide our true nature."

"That being?"

"There was no warlike species from which the ancients fled. Or there was, but it was us."

Stark nodded appreciatively. "Very good. So it can't come as a surprise, then, to know the 'gift', as you so quaintly put it, we bring is that of oblivion."

"You see us as weak?"

"Of course. Tainted by the animals amongst whom you have lived for so long."

"You call them animals? Yet they are pure of heart and strong of mind as demonstrated when a mere girl loosened your grip on the intellect of the Chosen in which you were entangled."

Stark frowned and peered behind Milandra as though trying to pick out the one responsible for freeing Simone's mind from their grasp. "Yes," he said, "I did notice the new mind contained neural pathways foreign to us. Alien." He gave a smile that might have looked wry if it had reached his eyes. "It took us aback and allowed the one you call the Chosen to escape."

"We are not weak," said Milandra, keen to draw his attention away from Bri. "But I see little point in arguing. Although there is more than ample room on this world for all who survive to live and thrive, you do not seek conciliation, only conquest."

Stark spread his hands. "You see truly."

"You have no weapons. You are few. You cannot win this fight. And even if you do, more than four thousand of our people yet survive. How can thirty hope to overcome so many?"

"As for the immediate fight, you might be armed, but you are weakened. When we have dispatched you, we shall leave this land and travel south to where the sun—such a wonderful star—shines more powerfully. There we shall bide our time while we multiply. When we are sufficient in number, we shall finish what we start today."

From the corner of her eye, Milandra was aware of a movement to her left as Lavinia brought up her gun.

"I've heard enough of this shit," Lavinia muttered.

"Me, too," said Wallace and raised his Uzi.

Milandra made no move to stop them; they must provoke Stark into taking the action she anticipated and needed.

Then she felt it. An energy scrabbling at her mind, powerful and grasping, that, if allowed a firm hold, would squeeze the essence from her like a fist crushing a lemon.

She did not fully resist; allowed it access sufficiently that a return pathway opened, but not so much that her plan would be revealed.

Lavinia and Wallace both gasped. A burst of fire came from Lavinia's gun, but the shots spattered the gravel wide of Stark's group.

Milandra worked quickly, laying a trail to Stark's mind and, by extension, his people's, whose intellects he still controlled.

Continue to resist she sent to her Deputies. *Make him work to prevent you from shooting them. When the time comes, blow them to hell.*

My friends, do not blame Peter for what is about to happen. I made him do it because it is the only way. Live good lives. Farewell.

She paused and took a deep breath. A single tear trickled from her eye. She was aware of Grant turning towards her. He was too late.

"Now, Peter," she whispered.

Much as Tom disliked firearms, he felt exposed without the shotgun. He stood with his arm around the shoulders of Will and those of Bri, who stood next to the boy, his fingertips brushing the arm of Ceri, who stood the other side of Bri. He had shut Dusty inside the conservatory so that the newcomers would not attempt to use the dog for their own purposes.

He was vaguely aware of the protective blanket Bri and Diane were casting over them, like a warm, unfocused sense of security a child feels with his parents.

Milandra and the man from the spaceship were talking, but Tom barely listened. He was engaged in a whispered conversation with Will, who was disappointed the spacemen did not look less like ordinary people.

When the dusky Lavinia discharged her gun, Tom jumped and his fingers dug into Ceri's arm.

What happened next took everyone completely by surprise.

Peter stepped forward, holding a pistol. He stooped a little to pass his left arm around Milandra's waist—she leaned into his embrace as though expecting and welcoming it—and placed the barrel of the pistol to the back of Milandra's head.

"N—" There wasn't time for Tom to form the full word.

The front of Milandra's head exploded in a spray of blood. Peter moved the pistol down to between her shoulderblades and leaned back to take the weight of her slumping form. He fired again and lowered her body to the ground. The pistol dropped from his hand.

This took place in a matter of seconds, too quickly for anyone to react.

Jason Grant stared at Peter in mute horror. He raised his Uzi and pointed it at Peter's face.

Peter turned aside and vomited.

George Wallace stepped around Grant and took hold of the end of Grant's gun, forcing it to point at the sky.

"Hey, man," he said in the softest tone Tom had heard him use. "She said not to blame him, right? This is what she wanted."

"But, *why?*" Grant's face had turned chalky with shock.

Wallace nodded at the people from the spaceship. "That's why."

Tom looked beyond the Deputies.

The blonde man at the front of the group had dropped to his knees, face slack and eyes glazed over as if all his attention was focused inwards. The twenty-nine people standing behind him remained on their feet, but their intense expressions had been replaced by looks mirroring the vacuity of the man. Some of them swayed as if they might topple.

Lavinia looked from them to Wallace. "What the fuck?"

"Stark's receiving Milandra's memories. Not only hers, but the entire collection. And because he's controlling the others' intellects, they're getting them, too."

Lavinia grinned and glanced at the humans. "Grab your guns, people. Time to make hay."

She stepped forward, bringing her gun to a firing position at her hip. Wallace joined her. After a last dark glance at Peter, Grant stepped alongside them. Around Tom, people began to move back to where they'd left their weapons.

He glanced at Ceri and she nodded. Together they led Will and

Bri back into the hotel so they wouldn't see the slaughter.

Chapter Twenty-Three

The early days of May continued bright and warm. In meadows and hedgerows, abandoned gardens and parks, flowers bloomed. Insects proliferated and the balmy nights filled with their chirp and zither. The somnolent hum of bees and the scents of sap and pollen held promise of a long, hot summer.

Mounds of freshly-dug earth scarred the field adjoining the hotel. The scars would scab over with grass and gorse, the mounds would melt into rolls and hummocks, which seemed to be the default state into which all the arable land, the previously ploughed and seeded and orderly, was returning.

Two of the sailors Tom and Ceri hauled from the sea had survived their ordeal. The third had not been so fortunate. His body, together with the bodies of two more who had been washed from the deck of the *Argute*, were left ashore when the next high tide receded. The bodies of three more missing sailors were never recovered.

"I'll be on my way, then," said Acting Lieutenant Commander Irving.

"Glad to see you've dropped all the 'classified this' and 'classified that' bullshit," said Ceri.

"Yes, well, old habits die hard."

"What made you drop the bio suit and come back?" asked Tom.

"A number of things. We were cruising on the surface and heard the voice talking about coming to the U.K. to witness mankind's final reckoning. That's when we realised that, crazy as you sounded, you might have been telling the truth. We tested corpses at the U.S. Navy hospital for any trace of contagious diseases and found none. We found no evidence the United States Navy still exists in South Georgia, but we did find a survivor. He, too, tested negative for infection. He didn't babble on about aliens and suchlike, but he did confirm what you said about the speed with which the virus had spread and he told us about the previous voice, the one we didn't hear. He'd been about to attempt to cross the Atlantic single-handedly in a six-foot yacht. We offered him a lift."

"You came back still not convinced about the alien stuff?"

"We returned to Scotland to see if you were still there. On finding no sign of you, we followed the coastline south and came across Colleen in Kent. She had built a campfire on the beach and was roasting chicken. She knew where you'd be and came with us." He shrugged. "I still wasn't convinced about the alien mumbo-jumbo. I only fully believed you at the end when that craft dropped from the sky."

"Better late than never."

Irving held out his hand. "No hard feelings?"

"No hard feelings." They shook. "You know, you don't have to return to sea. You're welcome to come with us."

"Thanks," said Irving, "but it's where I belong." He glanced sideways at Ceri. "Even without all that classified bullshit."

Ceri and Tom waved while the *Argute* slipped away. Standing on the open deck, Irving waved back until he was gone from sight.

Peter sat at the water's edge, tossing pebbles into the waves. He heard the footsteps scrunching through the shingle behind him.

"They've gone," said Diane.

"Who?"

"The Deputies. The cockney drove them away in his red bus."

Peter let out a bitter sigh. "No fond farewells, then."

"I don't think Lavinia and Wallace hold any grudge against you. But I'd steer clear of Jason Grant in future."

Diane sat next to him, sighing as she tilted her head back to enjoy the sun. Peter waited, but the silence stretched on. He cleared his throat.

"If you're not going to raise it, I'll begin."

Diane glanced at him sharply. "What do you mean?"

"You know very well what I mean. When our minds were

melded, helping Simone, you know that I probed. Only a little, but enough to see."

Diane's lips drew into a thin line. "You *probed*? Without my consent?"

"Bollocks to that. Besides, I know you probed me back."

"I—" Her shoulders slumped. "Oh, what's the use. But you started it."

"I make no apology. It's curious…"

"What is?"

"That we went through similar experiences. Except where I embraced it, you rejected it."

Diane stiffened again. "I did. And I do."

"You sure about that?"

"Absolutely. What you're thinking is madness."

"I disagree. Madness would be having the means and not employing them."

"But you don't have the means."

Peter was silent. He sensed her words were masking her true feelings, as she was so long accustomed to doing. Her lover had been a doctor, a field surgeon with whom she had worked in France. She had spent the rest of her life after he died denying to herself she had been in love. Peter had seen the truth dwelling deep inside her where she could pretend it didn't exist.

It took a few minutes, but then Diane spoke again. "You *do* have the means?"

Peter paused before replying. It was still too raw to talk about comfortably; would probably always be so.

"Milandra knew if she established a path to Stark's psyche and she died, our group memories would, in the absence of the Chosen, flow to him. Even with the support of his people who he was controlling, he would not be able to cope with such an influx of memories without slipping temporarily into a trance during which he and his people would be completely defenceless." He coughed. "In return for me agreeing to assist her carry out her plan, she shared with me all the relevant knowledge that passed to her when the craft went down to the ocean bed."

"Well, good luck to you," said Diane. "If that's what you truly want—"

"Of course it's what I want. Look what I agreed to do in return for the knowledge!"

"You possess her hair. I do not have anything. Of *his*."

"You know where he's buried."

Diane gasped. Peter looked out at the sparkling waves, but could feel her stare burning him hotter than the sun.

It came from her in little more than a whisper. "Okay. Oh, god, yes. Okay."

At Hillingdon Hospital in West London, the gung-ho attitude, anger and sense of doom had dissipated. Exhaustion and sorrow dominated.

People recuperated in the hospital grounds and nearby parkland. They had been provided with ample food. Their dwindling medical supplies had been restocked so that the wounded could be treated, the fatally wounded made comfortable.

They had been promised their dead—those lying in the shuttered warehouse in the industrial park, and those that lay where they'd fallen in the streets and alleyways—would be disposed of. The plume of dark smoke that, for a day, darkened the sky to the east attested to the method of disposal.

"They're burning them," Elliott said.

Zach nodded. "Easiest way. Thorough."

Sarah stared to the east, fingers parted over the increasing spread of her stomach, her expression hard. Tears slipped unchecked down her cheeks. To her credit, she did not look at Amy to give lie to her assertion she did not blame her for Frank's death. Nevertheless, Zach thought it might be as well for Amy to move on. He would be doing the same.

A feeling of restlessness was growing inside him. It wasn't the old demons trying to return; their stridency had diminished to little more than white background noise many years ago. It was more a longing to be on the move. In the past few months, he had driven a substantial portion of the east coast of the United States and had cruised across the Atlantic Ocean, but this had only whetted his appetite to see more. Aside from the jungles of Vietnam, of which he'd seen his fill, there was a wide, empty planet to discover.

He knew he would never return to his cabin in the foothills of the White Mountains. The certainty did not fill him, as he might have anticipated, with regret. The cabin had served its purpose, had given him a sanctuary from the claustrophobic press of a planet inhabited by seven billion people. He no longer needed it.

Zach glanced at the woman.

"I'm coming with you," she had murmured in the night. "It won't be safe to travel alone. I'm as good a shot as you. I'm a better driver." She'd snorted. "You might be a better sailor."

Now she returned his gaze, jaw firm, resolute. Zach knew he'd met his match and the knowledge made him feel more alive than he had in decades.

"Yes," he said. "Come with me. Please."

Aletta smiled.

Tess Granville met them just off the motorway in West Drayton. She hopped onto the bus and Rodney Wilson drove on towards Wembley Stadium.

"Everything is ready," she said.

Jason Grant held out his hand and took Tess's firmly in his. "When she suggested you for the task of overseeing operations in London, Milandra chose well," he said. "Thank you for all you have done."

Tess smiled. "It was a blast."

"Where will you go, Tess? Back to Australia?"

She shrugged. "Maybe." Her smile faded. "It might take me some time to get used to the idea of being an individual, rather than a small cog in a large machine."

Grant squeezed her hand and released it. "Time is one thing that's not in short supply. When this is done, I'm heading back to

Florida. You're welcome to accompany me." He glanced at Lavinia and George Wallace. "You're all welcome."

"This is the last ever Commune, right?" said Wallace.

"Yes," said Grant.

"How come?" asked Lavinia.

"There won't be any call for another."

"So no more Keeper or Chosen?" asked Wallace.

"Nope," said Grant. "The position of Keeper was artificially created to perpetuate a lie. Milandra was the last."

"And the accumulated memories?" said Wallace. "What about them? We can't lose all that knowledge, can we?"

"It's gone," said Grant. "Stark had terminated the link to his people. When Milandra's memories flowed into him, there was nowhere for them to go when he died."

Lavinia gave a low whistle. "That's a shitload of stuff to lose."

"All that knowledge wasn't doing us much good. Milandra knew what she was doing."

"So when we die, our individual experiences and wisdom will simply… disappear?" asked Wallace.

"Well, there are other ways of saving useful knowledge," said Grant. "Libraries. Computers."

"Hmm. Books and hard-drives. Might take a while to set up a viable network of computers again, but there's plenty of paper and ink lying about."

"Yep. That's what I intend doing in Florida: writing books and growing old." Grant sighed wistfully. "I miss that sunshine."

"We're here," said Rodney Wilson, pulling to a stop in front of an imposing structure with a huge arch extending over it.

"Okay." Jason Grant took a deep breath. "Let's get this show on the road."

An hour later, he allowed his psyche to fly free and felt it swell as it was joined by almost five thousand other minds. Outwards the combined force soared, seeking the minds of human survivors throughout the world.

People of Earth Haven sent Grant. *This is the last time we shall address you. Most of you do not know who we are. It no longer matters.*

You have survived two threats, though many of you are not aware of the second. Some of you may also not be aware there are other survivors throughout the world. Maybe as many as a million. That is precious few to restart a species. There is a very real possibility mankind will slip into extinction.

Each day you will face danger: from wildlife, from the elements of nature, from starvation, from loneliness.

I urge you: put aside your despair. Arm yourselves; find and comfort each other; shelter and barricade yourselves; recreate families and communities.

The final reckoning of mankind has taken place. Man has been judged and his creator has been found wanting.

Make the most of your reprieve. Rebuild this world. Better still, construct a new one that you can be proud to leave to the generations that follow.

We have long referred to this world as Earth Haven. It is time to drop the Haven. Let it be Earth to us all. Let it be home to us all.

"I'm going to stay here with Sarah and the nurses," said Elliott. "Play grandpa to her little one when it comes along." He glanced at Zach. "If the little one survives." He shrugged. "Maybe I'll do some writing. Perhaps there *will* be someone around to read the next great American novel."

Amy stepped forward and hugged him.

She turned to Zach. And began to cry like a baby.

"Oh, golly," she said. "I didn't want to get all emotional."

Zach stepped forward and placed his hands on her shoulders. "Watch yourself. Stay close to Joe. You're still hopeless with a gun."

Amy snorted. "I know. That's why I'm glad I'll have Joe to protect me."

"He'd better," said Zach, favouring the boy with a measured stare.

For once, Joe didn't try to brush it off. He returned Zach's stare levelly.

"I'll look after her," he said.

"Make sure you do. And keep that hatred for those we've been fighting under wraps."

"Put it this way," said Joe, "I won't go looking for them. If, however, I come across any, I make no promises."

"Besides," said Amy, "they murdered billions. They don't deserve any mercy from us."

Zach looked at her. "You're right," he said, "but don't let the desire for vengeance control you." He held her gaze. "You helped me remember who I am. I won't ever forget you."

Amy threw her arms about his neck and squeezed him tight.

"You saved my life," she whispered. "And my honour, for what that's worth."

Zach pulled back so he could look into her face.

"Your honour," he said, "is worth the world. Don't you ever forget it."

In Cornwall, Tom gave a great sigh and looked at Ceri.

"You ready for goodbyes?"

She grimaced. "As ready as I'll ever be, I suppose. Actually, wait. There's one thing I have to tell you. Been putting it off."

"Okay." He shifted uncomfortably on the balls of his feet. "If this is about relationship stuff, I'm not very good at it."

"Oh, Tom, hisht and listen." Ceri took a deep breath. "Look, there's a reason I only had the one child. During Rhys's birth, there were complications. The following year, I underwent a hysterectomy. I can't have any more children."

Tom looked at her, wondering if there was anything more. "And?" he said.

"And nothing. That's it."

"Um… I'm sorry?"

"Huh?"

"I'm sorry you can't have any more children. Are you okay?"

Ceri blinked. "This was years ago. Of course I'm okay. The question is, are you okay with it?"

It was Tom's turn to blink. "Why wouldn't I be?"

Ceri thumped him in the arm. "You bloody useless man! Think for a moment. We're about to head out into a largely empty world. Humankind is on the verge of extinction. Producing new babies is going to be vital to avoid that. And you're talking about setting off into the unknown with a female companion who doesn't have a womb. And, no, this isn't Monty Python and we can't keep the foetus in a box."

Tom rubbed his arm. "You punch well," he muttered. "Now I know what this is about. You think I ought to see you as some sort of child-producing machine. Well, I'm sorry, but I don't see you like that at all. I think you're sweet, you make me laugh, you're a *much* better shot than I am, and there's absolutely no one else in the entire world I'd rather spend my future with."

Ceri stared at him for a long moment. Then she punched him again.

"Ow! What was that one for?"

"For being better at this relationship stuff than you make out."

"Can we go find the others now?"

They found them in the hotel car park. Tom had packed the Peugeot and white Range Rover with food and other essentials. They would travel east in convoy, Bri and Will following, until they had to ditch the cars for another mode of transport.

Bri and Will were saying their goodbyes. And, wonder of wonders, Dusty was being fussed over by Colleen.

"Going to miss you, you soft thing," she said.

As though to continue the let's-surprise-everyone motif, Dusty ran up to Diane and licked her hand, before bounding to Peter and rubbing against his leg. With a bark, he trotted to the Peugeot and stood next to it, waiting to be let in.

Colleen stood tall and clear-eyed; she hadn't taken a drink in days. Ceri threw her arms around her and held her tight.

"You can come with us."

The Irish girl shook her head. "I miss Sinead. And Howard. And whiskey. I need to stay put for a while. Get my shit together. Here's as good a place as any."

Ceri nodded and turned to Diane. She politely shook her by the hand.

"Thanks for missing when you shot at me," Ceri said.

"No problem," said Diane with a smile that, for once, didn't seem forced. "Maybe, if you ever shoot at me, you can return the favour."

Ceri returned the smile. "You're not so bad, you know. Almost human at times."

She turned to Peter and hugged him.

"You and Tom saved my life by turning up at my house that day. The offer stands." She glanced back at Diane. "For both of you. You're welcome to come with us."

Peter shook his head. "Thanks, but we'll go our own way. We have things to do that won't interest you."

"Hmm. Please, Peter, be careful. That's all I have to say on the matter. Where will you go?"

"South. Somewhere warm."

"That's kind of the general direction we're going, too. Well, so long."

"Goodbye, Ceri."

Lastly, it was Tom's turn. Colleen surprised him by kissing him full on the lips.

"That's for burying Howard. And for coming to our rescue."

"But, it was Ceri who shot him."

"And thank God she did. But you were there, Tom. I've seen you handling a gun. I think what you did took more courage than anyone."

"That may be a backhanded compliment, but I'll take it."

When he stepped in front of Diane meaning to shake her hand like Ceri had, Tom impulsively leaned forward and hugged her. When he pulled away, she looked shocked, but in a reluctantly pleased way.

"Thank you for everything, Diane," he said. "Please, keep an eye on Peter for me."

She nodded. "And keep those children safe. I've grown quite

fond of them. You mustn't tell them, though. It'd be bad for my street cred."

Tom laughed out loud, drawing startled glances from Bri and Will.

He turned to Peter, but was beaten to the draw. He was enveloped in a mighty hug.

"I'll miss you, old friend," said Peter.

"Ceri was right. You can still come with us."

Peter again shook his head. "Look, if things don't work out with our plans, we can always come and find you."

"It's a bloody big world out there and you won't be able to text me to find out where we are."

"Not text, no. Something better. As long as Bri's with you, and you're within a reasonable range, I'll be able to locate you."

"Ah. All that alien shit again."

"You need to look after that girl. She represents the next stage of mankind's development. If she ever has children, they may share her abilities."

"I will look after her. As though she was my daughter. Ceri and Will, too."

"And take care of yourself, Tom."

Tom walked to the car. He looked from Ceri to Bri to Will and patted Dusty on the head. He hadn't been exaggerating in what he'd said to Peter; they felt like his family.

"All ready?" he said. "For a great adventure?"

Six months later at Hillingdon Hospital, a boy was born to a young woman from Harrisonburg, Virginia. The grandfather figure who looked on heaved a sigh when the babe filled it lungs and let out a powerful cry.

Elliott stepped forward.

"What will you call him?" he asked.

"That's an easy one," said Sarah. "Say hello to Frank."

In a sunny courtyard of a large, fortified chateau near Marseilles in southern France, two papery cocoons tore apart.

A dark, tousled head appeared from one, followed by the long body and limbs of a handsome man. He looked uncertainly at the slight woman who stood, sobbing, before him.

From the second cocoon emerged the fair hair and fairer features of a young woman. She blinked at the man who stepped forward to greet her.

"Hello, Megan," said Peter.

About the Author

Sam Kates lives in South Wales, UK, with a family, a computer and *way* too many books. To connect on social media:

Website: samkates.co.uk
Facebook: www.facebook.com/writersamkates
Twitter: @_Sam_Kates_
E-mail: samkates@samkates.co.uk

Note

Please consider leaving a review—reviews can be of immeasurable help to authors in gaining visibility and running promotions.

Thank you for purchasing and reading this book.

To sign up for news of releases and special offers, most of which are only available to subscribers (no spam, promise):

www.samkates.co.uk/stay-in-touch/

– Sam Kates
December 2015